STONE

Also by Adam Roberts in Gollancz

Salt
On

STONE

ADAM ROBERTS

GOLLANCZ

LONDON

The right of Adam Roberts to be identified as the
author of this work has been asserted by him in accordance
with the Copyright, Designs and Patents Act 1988.

First published in Great Britain in 2002 by
Gollancz
An imprint of the Orion Publishing Group
Orion House, 5 Upper St Martin's Lane, London WC2H 9EA

Second impression reprinted in 2002

A CIP catalogue record for this book
is available from the British Library

ISBN 0 575 07063 3 (cased)
0 575 07064 1 (trade paperback)

Typeset at The Spartan Press Ltd,
Lymington, Hants

Printed in Great Britain by
Clays Ltd, St Ives plc

If a man does not feel dizzy when he first learns about the quantum, he has not understood a word. *Niels Böhr*

I remember discussions with Böhr that went through many hours till very late at night and ended almost in despair. And when at the end of the discussion I went alone for a walk in the neighbouring park, I repeated to myself again and again the question: Can nature possibly be so absurd as it seemed to us in these atomic experiments?

Werner Heisenberg

My heart is turned to stone
I strike it and it hurts my hand. *Shakespeare*

Understanding the nature of the quantum universe involves a profound reappraisal of the way we perceive our surroundings. If we see a natural object – an apple perhaps, or a stone – we know from experience that it will follow certain laws, the laws described by Newton. Imagine a stone lying on a table; we can measure it, apprehend it. We know that if we push it off the edge of the table it *will* fall to the floor; and if we are quick enough we can reach out and catch it as it falls. This means that we can see it falling, we can gauge where it is and how quickly it is travelling, and move our hand to intercept it.

But at the level of the atom, the *quantum* level, things are completely unlike this. We can measure the world of atoms, but our ability to measure is compromised – not by our measuring instruments but by the nature of things themselves. We can measure where an atom *is*; or we can measure *how fast it is travelling*, but we simply cannot measure where an atom is *and* how fast it is going. This is impossible.

The reasons for this are profoundly unsettling. Perhaps you think 'If only our instrumentation were accurate enough, we would be able to apprehend the nature of the quantum, to measure where it is and how fast it goes at the same time.' But if you think this you are wrong, and this is why: at the level of the quantum things *are not* in the way that we can confidently say that they *are* at the level of apples and stones. We cannot say an atom 'is' in the same way we can say that the stone 'is on the table.' From the atom's point of view, as it were, there are only 'probabilities'.

You have heard of the famous thought-experiment of Schrödinger's Cat. The cat lives in an opaque box. It so happens that opening the box will kill the cat, because of the way the box is constructed. We cannot see into the box, or X-ray the box, or anything like that. But we want to know whether the cat is alive or dead inside the box. If we open the box to look, then it is certainly dead – but is it alive or dead now, before we open the box? The quantum moral of this story is that the cat is *alive and dead at the same time*. It inhabits both states of being simultaneously; what happens when we open the box is that our action of opening the door *collapses these quantum probabilities into one single pattern*, the pattern being 'the cat is dead.' Schrödinger's famous cat will test the suppleness of your mind, I promise you. You want to think 'Well, *either* the cat is alive *or* it is dead, and by opening the box we find one or the other to be the case'. But that is not the way it is at the level of the quantum; at the level of the quantum it is 'the cat is alive *and* dead until it is observed, and then the act of observation collapses the probability wave-form into a single determined pattern – dead, in this case.'

Perhaps the example-cats confuse things. Think of a miniature cat made out of atoms, a nano-cat, ten atoms long. Is it here? Or there? Well, *before you turn on your atomic observation machine, it is both here and there*. Or to put it another way, before it is observed there is a particular probability wave form that dictates it as 40% here and 60% there – not split between the two places, mind you, but simultaneously the whole nano-cat is in each location with slightly different balances of probabilities. It sounds like I am suggesting there are two cats, but there is only one cat; it is just that it doesn't exist in the world in the same way that a full size cat does. You observe and you find the cat to be there, not here – but it is your observation that has determined the outcome. If you did not observe, the cat would continue to be here and there, would continue to exist in a quantum probability soup. But by observing you collapse the probabilities into a certainty.

And this is the most profound implication of all, the deepest philosophical shake-down; because it follows from this that it is our observation – our power, as sentient intelligences to make the observation – that *determines the universe the way it is.*

Kurt Soldan, *Quanta: Essays on Quantum Physics*

The Prison

Stone,

The doctor has suggested that by writing letters to various objects and natural phenomena I may be able to come to terms with some of this badness, this illness, this upset (*up*set? *down*set, rather). I ought to register my dubiousness about this project right away. There is an issue of empathy here, isn't there? Empathy – that's right, isn't it? I have to assume that she is eavesdropping on this communication between you and me. My doctor, I mean. Or why would I bother to compose it at all? I do have something important to say about the nature of the universe, but I'll come on to that in due course. Later on, a little later on. To communicate with her *through* the stone is rather like using the language of the stone, isn't it? Don't you think? Are you listening? *Hey! Hey!*

Doesn't hear me.

I am a bad man, I've done some bad things. I beg your pardon, stone, in telling you these things. (Do you like that politeness? You're an ancient object, and I've got a whole store of ancient cultural habits to deploy if I feel like it). I am a bad man. I still think of myself as a man, in fact, although there's little biological evidence to support that fact. When the nanotechnology abandoned my body the default biological settings reasserted themselves. I had liked being a man, in fact. I'd been a man for so long I'd acquired the mental habit of calling myself *male*, of thinking it at a deep level. I still think that way, even though my male genitalia have long since shrunken and wizened like drying fruit; grapes turning to raisins and finally shrinking to nothing at all. Then the whole area itched, and I couldn't help but scratch. You

1

won't know what *itch* means, stone. There's something you have in common with the rest of humanity. That's something their nanotechnology protects them from. But let me tell you, *to itch*, it's a strange thing. It's a torture and a pleasure at once. I scratched my whole body raw. I scratched my new genital smoothness so hard it opened up lips. So I suppose I am a she, except I'm not so in my head, it somehow hasn't percolated through to my head. I haven't grown breasts either. But maybe that's because I'm not eating. When I first came to prison, my first prison, I was in a state. I tried starving myself, but the nanotechnology kept me alive. I'm not sure how. Perhaps it picked up nutrients from here and there, drew them through my skin as I lay asleep on the soil – I don't know. Nanotechnology, dotTech as it is called, is an astonishingly clever thing. It really is. I have battled against it, trying to kill people that it is designed to keep alive. I know my enemy. Better now than ever. Listen to what I have to tell you, dear stone, and you will know it too.

Let me get straight to the point. I have to tell you a story – my story – about a terrible crime. The worst crime ever committed, maybe; murder (which is the worst of crimes) and murder on a scale you can barely conceive.

Let me take it down to its basic level: I was in prison. I'm in prison now, but this was before. I was in prison for different reasons then. I didn't have you then, my dear stone. There were other stones in that other jail, but none of them were as close to me as you are becoming. Does that make you feel special? You are special. Does it make you feel loved?

Well, let's not get carried away.

They contacted me inside prison, inside my first prison. Stay with me, for a few moments, and I'll explain how difficult a thing it was that they did: I was inside a prison so well made that it was impossible for me to get out or for anybody to get a message in. And yet they managed both these things. Who were *they*? Yes, well, that puzzled me too: they were, as they proved themselves, the enemy of t'T. We lived in a kind of paradise, in t'T, and thought ourselves immune, but enemies gathered at our borders. There were the Wheah, ancient enemies; but also the Palmetto tribes, mysterious peoples. Which of them offered me this deal? Which of them is at the root of this problem? I thought I knew; I thought it was becoming increasingly clear to me, but I was wrong.

I apologise for my awkwardness. I'm not used to this.

They offered me a deal. *They* would break me out of prison. And you understand, dear stone, that the prison I was in was impossible to break out of. Not difficult, or challenging, but *impossible*. My prison was surrounded on all sides by walls of superheated fire and plasma kilometres deep. But they promised me they could get me out. When I was out, they said, they would make me rich. In the worlds I have travelled amongst money means little, and there are philosophies that teach even *information* is of no fundamental importance. But they promised me compacted information that would have sped me through fast-space at four thousand times the speed of light; that would have built me palaces in space, genie-like, at the other end. Of course, the most attractive thing they offered was escape from the inescapable jail. Wealth and freedom – how could I not be tempted?

In return they asked me to do one simple thing: destroy the population of an entire planet. To kill over sixty million human beings; and that was all, nothing more. I was not (they said) to destroy the planet as such; I was to leave as much of the ecology and architecture and all the evidences of civilisation as I could. But I had to kill off all the people. I was to litter the world with corpses. I am a bad man, and have done some questionable things in my time, but I was startled and rather frightened by this deal. They didn't tell me all in one go, of course; they approached me a number of times and insinuated the idea in my head. I would be wealthy. I would have help. I would be free. The people on this world, they – they would be dead, and once dead past caring.

So I thought to myself: these people, that I am asked to kill. Are they real people?

Now I suppose I could have turned down this deal they offered me, and gone on living in my prison. It was a spacious prison; green hills covered in plastic grass, a river and a lake filled with real water, fake plastic trees. Artificial stars dotted the false sky like bit-lights; sharp-edged, five-pointed icons of stars that glowed in the artificial night.

3

The light that shone through these faux-stars was real light, if modified and filtered a little. Only the light and the water in my prison were real. Everything else about the place was artificial: the grass; the landscape; the trees; everything a simulated medium in which a few real people observed me as if I were a scientific specimen. And, of course, these people, the air, the very water – all of it was full of billions of dotTech machines. I could go anywhere I wanted in this space but there was nowhere to go. I could lie on my back on the chilly turf when the artificial light faded to artificial night, and the faux-stars glinted with a yellow, moist-looking light over my head. I could have lived the rest of my life there if I'd chosen.

I said to *them*, whoever they were, Palmetto or Wheah, foreigner or closer-to-home, I said: Take me out of there. I'll do it, I said, I'll kill all these people.

And so they did; and so did I.

As a stone (I'm presuming here) you don't know anything about morality. Stones are proverbial for their moral indifference. But somehow I have to convey to you the enormity of what I have done. My doctor, wherever she is (hello! *hello!*) will probably understand this as me trying to convey *to myself* the enormity of what I have done. I don't wish to argue with her.

In fact, this whole affair put me in a very peculiar position. I committed the crime, so I was the criminal. But I was acting on behalf of somebody or some-people or other, and I did not at the beginning know who those people were. I decided early on to try and uncover who it was who had so secretly commissioned me to do this terrible thing. Even though I was committing the crime, I intended to solve it. I was both murderer and detective.

Curious.

Even before I escaped from that first prison, I was wondering, and worrying, about the rationale. I tried to think who would want to do so terrible a thing. To kill a whole *world*? Why do such a thing? Who would it benefit? And why would *they* employ *me* to do it? To go to all the bother of helping me escape from prison, the impossible-to-escape prison. Why not employ somebody else? Why not simply commit the crime *them*selves?

It is true that in the many-thousand, light year wide and deep realm

4

of t'T, the confederation of worlds in which I grew up, the concept of criminal was so rare as to be the object of study by only the most specialised scholars. I was a human amongst trillions, a freak so rare and fine as to occasion horror and fascination. It was possible that in all the half-hundred worlds of t'T *they*, whoever *they* were, could not find a citizen as criminal as me – that might have been the reason for my election to this role. But outside t'T – what of the various Palmetto tribes of star-wayers in the broken space turnwards? There were pirates and murderers enough in those realms – they furnished the stock characters for a thousand t'T romances. And rimwards, there was the barbaric realm of the Wheah. If stories were true, there were warrior-families in that space who would have gladly wiped out whole populations, and for less reward than I was being offered.

But the offer was made to me, not them. And the person who accepted it was me.

2nd

Dear Stone,

I'll tell you about my execution. What do I remember? I remember that I was nervous. Perhaps that goes without saying. I remember too that everything I have to tell you about in these letters began after my execution. How did it happen? Let me tell you how it happened.

It is a form of dying. You're a stone – I can't expect you to understand. You are not born, and don't really die. Or do you? I can pick you up and feel the ellipse that you make of my palm. It's like cradling a cold breast; and then I close my fingers around you and its more like gripping the forefinger of a mother when you're nothing more than a wine-coloured baby with skin as scrunched as red silk that's been worn too long. That feeling of gripping, it feels good. If I could throw you out of the prison, into the body of the sun, then you'd disintegrate – would that be a kind of death from your point of view? Or if I contemplated a more realistic throw: from this bank of putty-mud and green grass into the river. Do you see the river, there?

Of course, you have no eyes, being a stone.

But let's say I threw you in there. Given some thousands of years you'd be ground down, you'd be rubbed away. Skins of atoms brushed off you every day, until you became nothing more than a piece of grit on the sandbank down the way. And maybe even less than that. Would that be some sort of death to you?

(How does one reason with a stone?)

Well, I approached my own execution in poor style. This is how it went. I woke up, and here I was. I had been brought into the prison. It's only a prison to me, naturally. The jailer and the jailer's mate can come and go, of course they can. The nano-machines themselves can come and go, of course they can. I'm the one who can't go anywhere. For me the sky presents as complete a barrier as the inside curve of my own skull. I could no more pass through it than I could step out of my own skin. It is a spacious prison, I grant you. The ground space, with its undulating landscaping, its flowing water as clear as its air, the river's path looping seven times like a thrown away cord, all about and round the seven hills. So much green! So much artificial blue, with the stars burning now as day-stars, bright yellow against the azure, letting in carefully controlled dribbles of light and heat so that we do not freeze. Photons and agitated gas.

The executioner was also my jailer, a large woman, with a lemon-coloured droopy face. She had a deputy, a man short and tight-skinned, a man who had adapted himself to make himself a better swimmer. At some point in his past he must have swallowed some adaptive dotTech, that had swum with its billions of fellows and encouraged them to change his body. He lacked hair, and he had used his dotTech to shrink his nose until it was only a puckered nipple, like the nubbin on a tomato, overlaying nostrils that were nicks in his face. His skin was a sharp red colour, smooth and pert. He spent most of his days swimming along the river, and diving deep in the pool that exists at the bottom of the slightly conical living space of the jail. I assume the water is drained at the base of this dip and re-circulated; I can't be sure. But the deputy said little, and did little, except wait impassively at the elbow of the jailer. They were a pair, it seems; he travelled everywhere with her. Listened to her words, sometimes nodding slowly, and then running off to leap into the water to ponder them more carefully. The dotTech in his body filtered oxygen out of the water at a rate sufficient to keep him alive. I'm not even sure if he had modified his lungs; he probably didn't need to.

The jailer and her deputy were charged to look after me, to make sure I couldn't escape (but escape was impossible!) and that I didn't harm my surroundings too savagely if the mood was upon me. But mostly they left me to myself, and I wandered the little hills and dived into the river and threw myself on to the grass to sleep.

I would happily have drowned myself, if I could have. I really would. I was ready to die, bitter in my imprisonment, hating myself. I tried ripping at my skin with my nails, but that is a hard thing to do – have you tried it? I would lie awake, with the artificial sky dark and the stars fuming and shining a few hundred metres over my head, and I would imagine it. Grow my nails, bite them into sharp shapes, and then tear the flesh at my wrists to destroy my life, to kill myself. But it is not easy. The scratching does not penetrate the skin; then it starts to hurt, and your body recoils almost in spite of yourself. Then the dotTech kills the pain, and knits together your skin, and you're back where you were.

So I threw myself into the water and tried to drown, but as with the red-skinned deputy, the dotTech kept me alive. Try as I might, the caustic sensation of water in my lungs and all my agonised underwater coughing did not prevent my bloodstream taking in oxygen and delivering it to my body. It is clever, this nanotechnology, it can solve any problems presented to it. Its goal, its reason for existing, is to keep us alive, and it kept me alive. Even me, even a bad man like myself.

Then I told myself this as I lay on the bank by the river, looking up at the broad plastic leaves of the trees over me; I told myself that when I was executed, and the dotTech left me, then I would be able to kill myself. (Dribbly shades of light against the canopy of leaves. Wobbling and transcendent, bright and warm.) That thought gave me comfort. If you were me, you'd have wanted that death too.

I had brought my dotTech with me when I had first come to the jail. Funnelled through the narrow gate, which the gravity engines had opened in the body of the star, and dropped from the artificial sky to swoop round and land. The jailer, the lemon-coloured woman, had picked me up as if I were a parcel and taken me to the river, to wash the last of the charred and crumbling foam from my body. Then I had been left to myself.

The realisation that I was in prison had been a terrible thing. I had spent days unable to do more than lie on the ground, or cry to myself on the grass. I didn't sleep well. I was used to beds under roofs, inside rooms. Sleeping on the grass under the sky (even an artificial sky) takes some getting used to. This long, slow, melancholy period was interspersed with my abrupt fits of rage, screaming and running about, dashing myself against the plastic trees and colliding head first, hurling myself into the river to try and drown myself, ripping off the last of my clothes and doing violence to my hair. I suppose this is why they left the dotTech in my body for those first weeks, to compensate for my self-destructive rages. So that the bruises I bashed upon my face could heal in minutes, the tiny machines in my bloodstream mending the rips in my capillaries, ferrying away the dark dead matter, making everything smooth and pure again. So that the hair I pulled in fistfuls from my scalp could come extruding out again, like a magic trick.

And then the morning of my execution came. Of course I knew I was slated for execution. When the day itself came, I knew something was happening because the executioner (as I realised she was) approached me with a serious expression on her face. Her partner came too, his svelte little red body gleaming in the light. I remember thinking how odd it was that he decided to remain a man, given his mania for swimming; why not let the dotTech modify his body to become a woman, to lose that drag-creating tangle of organs between his legs? But he stayed a man. Perhaps it had something to do with the dynamic of his relationship with the executioner.

'Are you ready?' she asked.

This meant I was about to be executed.

'No,' I said. 'By no means.' I think I started crying. It is a frightening thing to contemplate. If I did cry it would have been in a restrained way; little gulping sobs, not great howls.

But she reached forward, smiling all the time. Her big yellow face, with its sagging jowls and drooping nose; the whites of her eyes bright against the sallow hue of her skin, and then her purple irises a starburst with darker lines, and in the very middle of those eyes her pupils, completely black. As black as stones – as black as you are yourself, dear stone, excepting only the vague, submerged mottling that is just visible underneath your surface sheen. She leant towards me, and I had a long time to study her face, so I remember it particularly vividly.

What she was doing was pressing her finger against my wrist. She took up my left hand with her right, and pressed a finger tight against the skin. She was the executioner because in her body there were nano-machines specially designed to communicate with the standard dotTech in my body. They passed through her skin to my skin, and into my system. She held my wrist tightly, and I could smell the faint papery, almost dusty smell of her close in my nostrils. She was humming to herself a little. She had been loaded with this charge, and it was a rare responsibility. Human beings will take all manner of adaptive dotTech into their bodies, but this particular adaptation was unique. Who would want to purge out all the dotTech? I'm sure she carried her charge with a due sense of gravity. The machines she had gathered in her finger-ends were designed to command the machines in *my* body to quit me.

When she was finished she let go of my arm and stood away, looking at me with a certain detachment. I began to feel queasy. Then I had a sharp sense of thirst, and then a pain bubbled up out of my deep insides and spread across all my skin. I started bleeding from my pores. My eyes went dizzy with rheum, and mucus came spurting as if under pressure from my nostrils. I could feel my muscles go limp, and a stream of urine come hurrying out to splatter on the turf. I hurt. More blood came until my whole skin was slick with it. My ears were wet, my mouth filled up with blood. I started screaming, but my fluid-filled mouth bubbled and gargled the sound – perhaps it even sounded comical. I staggered, flapping my arms with the pain. Pain is a rarity for the people of t'T, because the nano-machines protect us from the worst of the sensation. I did not enjoy it at that moment, I can tell you. I lurched forward, fell, somehow landed on my knees.

I coughed, wept. The hunger to die, as sharp and tangy as a physical hunger, overwhelmed me again. But I stayed alive. Fluid poured from me; vomit from my mouth, tears and rheum from my eyes, mucus

9

from my nose, urine from between my legs. Even my pores wept myriad little dots of blood. And the stream I produced coagulated and treacled its way down the incline towards the water. Nano-machines prefer a fluid environment, although they can exist in dry ground, or even in dead vacuum if they need to. They are tough; amazingly so.

Then the convulsions passed, and I fell forward. A half-throated gasp was coming out of me, regular as a drumbeat. I don't know how long I lay there. I lay there a long time.

I dragged myself up, eventually, because I was so thirsty. I had lost a great deal of fluid, my skin was hot and my throat felt dusty and burnt. I staggered, my legs wobbling as if they were rubbery, but I made it to the edge of the artificial waterway and tumbled in. The cool enveloping of the river was delicious to my skin; I opened my mouth and gulped water. It was half in my mind to sink to the bottom and drown, but to my surprise I found myself swimming to the other side of the bank. Then I lay in the water under the bright light of the star-shaped holes in our blue, plastic, arched, artificial sky. I lay with both my arms stretched out on the dirt of the bank, and the back of my head on the ground, but with my body and legs floating out in the water. I was drained. That word is insufficient to express how emptied-out and weak I felt.

3rd

Dear Stone,

Let's talk about you, yes? You know, do you, that you were brought to this prison, like me? They built the prison a hundred or more years ago, for another criminal, another statistical freak such as myself. I don't know where s/he is now. But they built the prison in as remote and inaccessible a place as possible. This is what they did:

They chose a star at the far reaches of t'T space, a star without an inhabitable planet, circled by nothing more than a few rocky asteroids and one atmosphere-free planet of iron. The star is close to the Wallows end of the Great Gravity Trench, but apart from that there is nothing remarkable or noticeable about the stellar environment. This star has a designation, although I couldn't quote it to you.[1] Generally it is now known as the jailstar, because it houses the jail. Its nearest neighbouring system is Rain.

A hundred years ago they came, flying faster than light across space, and arrived in orbit; from there they built spaceships and orbital platforms. Using these they broke up one of the asteroids, manipulating its mass to collapse together short-lived strings of superdense material. The strings focused gravity, because of their immense mass for a brief time before other atomic forces broke up the effect. Using these gravity tools, the builders carved out a hollow sphere a kilometre or so across out of the iron planet. This was the basic structure, the underpinning of the jail. This iron-nickel hollow globe was treated and adapted; its portals fixed, some of its inner features sculpted and filled. Perhaps it was at this stage, dear stone, that you yourself were brought in; taken from the surface of the dead world, perhaps, where millions of years of gravitational tug and pull had moved countless bits of rock back and forth in dry ocean-like sinks so that they became smoothed, rounded, shaped. (This is only my imagination, you understand; I can't be sure for certain). Perhaps the builders shaped you themselves, dear stone; setting Haüd-machine workers to carve homely pebbles out of asteroid rock, oxidising the surface of the new-turned stones to give them that blue, flinty, worn look. I don't know. But you were certainly brought and placed inside the globe, along with the aggregate filler for covering the fusion engines and the large scale computers and processors that attend to the day-to-day operation of the jail. After this, the inside was landscaped properly; the water added and pumped to move the river from the lake through the miniature hills and back to the lake. The plastic grass and fake plastic trees were added. And the blue plastic coating that gives the sky its vivid colour.

Then this jail was dropped into the body of the star itself; not too far inside, because they wanted the gravity of the star's mass to operate, making the grass 'ground' and the ceiling 'up'. A few kilometres down. This was the most complicated part, I'd imagine. The heat inside the body of a star is great enough to melt and vaporise any ordinary

---

[1] Axa(b) – 8682

11

matter. But what is heat? Heat is atoms and particles moving with greater and greater agitation. Heat melts and dissolves matter because the particles of the heat are so energetic, they bounce about so violently, that they punch down the bonds that hold together structures. To insulate against heat you must make the bonds very strong; or else you can persuade the hot atoms to move in a different direction; to deflect, as it were, the vigour of their motion. This is what the machines embedded in the walls of the jail are designed to do; they set up a gravitational interference pattern, drawing their effectiveness from loops of dense-matter strings wrapped around the jail. The immense heat of the star rages around, a sort of quantum slipstream; but the jail stays cool.

Indeed, if it were not for certain carefully structured gaps in the fabric of the prison walls, this insulation would be so effective that everybody inside the jail would freeze. Freeze, in the midst of all that heat – imagine it! So the builders dotted the artificial sky with certain regularly-spaced vents, which they made in the shape of five-limbed stars. These portals, which can be several metres across, are narrowed to allow the immission of only a tiny stream of photons from the stellar fires on the outside. The gateways are mostly magnetic. This provides light and heat for the artificial world inside.

There is another portal; in the very top of the artificial sky. Through this gateway, which opens and closes in a peristaltic pulse of magnetic compression every four months, new visitors, new prisoners, new jailers enter; and old visitors and jailers (but never prisoners) leave. It was through this hole in the sky that I dropped into the world, wrapped in deep-space foam, and fell to the water directly beneath.

So this hollow globe was dropped into the fiery matter of this small star; it sank through the plasma to a predetermined depth. Now it hovers there, seven great motors on the outer skin balancing it like a submarine in a massive sea of flames. It has existed for many decades, and will exist for many decades more. At the moment, indeed, it exists only to house me. I suppose the builders of this world flattered themselves into thinking that nobody could escape from it; for who could cross the moat of stellar plasma and fire? Who could travel beyond that into the immense cold of deep space beyond? Who could rescue a prisoner in such isolation?

Dear Stone,

My jailer had, I suppose, chosen to be inside the jail. She must have had her reasons for wanting to spend years of her life in close proximity to a criminal. Perhaps she was curious about the criminal frame of mind; perhaps she was researching murder, or planning to compose a great poem or sculpt an asteroid into a great piece on the subject. I expected, in the weeks after my execution, when I was getting used to living without the dotTech in my body, for her to begin asking me questions. Perhaps for her to test or study me in some way. But she barely interacted with me. Mostly she swam with her partner, the red-skinned man. Sometimes they would retreat inside their shelter (they were allowed a shelter; I had nowhere to go and nothing to do but climb the plastic-grass hillocks, stare at the clinking rivulets, swim in the lake). From time to time she would give me a 'wellhello', mention something or other. It was only ever pleasantries.

It dawned on me that she was in no hurry. With the benefit of nanotechnology in her body, she could live many many hundreds of years. In the elaborate, filigree civilisations on some of the turnwards worlds of t'T, human beings more than a thousand years old were not uncommon. I, on the other hand, was now condemned to live out the term of a 'natural' life. Before the adoption of dotTech, humans rarely lasted more than fifty years. In the Wheah, for instance, where religion prevents the adoption of dotTech, a human being who reaches a hundred years of age is given a mighty celebratory party, so unusual is that feat. (Or so the rumour goes – to be honest, we know little about the Wheah). But this was now my fate; I had a few decades of life left to me. Maybe years. Maybe less.

In the months immediately after my execution, in fact, I mostly spent my time contemplating how ubiquitous and yet how invisible dotTech is. I grew up with the nano-machines in my body, as did everybody on my world, everybody in t'T. After my execution, though, I was possibly the only t'T human to have no such technology inside me. Those minuscule machines, self-constructed and self-maintaining, are built from the bricks of atoms themselves. Whirling around in the blood and lymph, housing themselves in human cells and fluids, and working! Efficiently, problem-solvingly, intelligently, tackling decay, infection, free radicals, pollutants, toxins; rebuilding tissue, balancing electrolytes and hormones, reducing the intensity of pain signals in the nerves, enhancing the bliss of sexual connection, fiddling with the very strands of DNA itself to prevent them unwinding – keeping the whole organism in perfect shape. How little I thought about these machines when I had them in my body! How much I missed them when they were taken away!

I noticed small things at first. I would graze myself in the usual, careless way of humanity; catching the back of my hand against the rough plastic bark of a tree, or knocking my face against the stones at the bottom of the river. Where this cut would normally fade and vanish within minutes, I now discovered it was still alive, still hurting, days later. I would bruise myself, often without knowing how or remembering when – I might simply notice a bruise, like a gaseous discolouration inside the translucent matter of my skin. Before, bruises would be cleaned and healed in an hour; now they lasted days. My joints became stiff. My hair fell out. I developed sore patches on my face; and when I touched and scratched these they became more sore.

Mostly I was eating protein fruits, manufactured by the processors in the trees, and drinking the water from the lake. This food had been fine and sufficient before. Now I began experiencing bubbling stabs of pain in my stomach. My bowels loosened, and wicked-smelling matter started dribbling out of me in place of a regular stool. The temperature of my head varied alarmingly. I might wake in the morning with my skull star-hot, warm sweat trickling from my forehead and into my eyes. Or I might wake trembling and jittering with the cold.

It was physical torture; nothing less. The cultures of the t'T pride themselves on being civilised, unlike (they say to themselves) the barbarism of the Wheah. It is undeniable that I had committed terrible crimes, and other cultures would simply and cleanly have executed me. But the t'T went to this enormous effort to secure me away from humanity, that I might not harm anybody else. They did this in the name of civilisation – and yet they stood aside, passive, whilst I endured the miseries of life without dotTech. The illness, the weariness. It was an unhurried execution; my body wearing itself out in the 'natural' course over a few years to die slow and painfully. A quick death would have been kinder.

It tried to raise this with my jailer on several occasions; but her big yellow face was impassive, unresponsive. I might start reasoning with her, but soon lose control; without the dotTech regulating my hormonal level it was easy to froth at the mouth, to rage and become incoherent. I may even have tried to attack her, to beat her with my now feeble arms, my disease-weakened fingers. But she was a big human, and adept at dancing – she would hardly have been taken on as jailer otherwise. She pushed my blows away, or sidestepped them, and I was left on the false soil weeping and weeping.

5th

Dear Stone,

How long? I don't know, exactly.[1] For ever, that's how it seemed. I went a little mad. I went through periods when I was so dejected, so cast out and cast down that I couldn't eat. At these times, after a week or so of fasting, the jailer might come and pass some food through my lips. At other times, I became manic, insane. For a while, for instance, I became obsessed with running the perimeter of the jail; I would jog round and round a hundred times and then I would throw myself down and sleep. I knocked flints together – yes, stones like you – to chip off a sharp edge, and then use that to scratch words into the plastic of the sky where it met the horizon. Or else to scratch myself, but that was painful and the wounds refused to heal easily. I thought of suicide again, certainly I did, but I was habituated to my misery, and killing oneself is a hard and painful thing, harder still without dotTech. I went through phases where I saw hallucinations; people from my childhood, imaginary animals, Alice from the Looking Glass in her antique clothes striding giant-like about the landscape. But whenever I saw these impossible things there was a part of me that knew they were impossible; that knew they were hallucinations and not reality.

---

[1] Ae spent a little over five standard years in prison prior to his escape.

This was why the voices were so puzzling to me. When the voice first started, offering me freedom and riches if only I would agree to murder the population of a whole world, I tried to believe that it was a mad self-delusion, a voice from my own mind. But it was insistent, and somehow stranger than anything my mind could conjure up.

6th

Dear Stone,

The voice inside my head started after a day-long session in the lake, swimming and swimming. The artificial day came to an end, and the artificial night began, as abrupt as a sneeze. The star-shaped holes in the sky swelled admitting their yellow light, and then shrank away. So it was that the stars went from sun-yellow to moon-pale, and the blue colour of the artificial sky deepened to purple.

I climbed from the water and lay on the too-familiar plastic grass. I may have dozed, but I was in that curious torpid state where it is hard to tell sleeping and being awake apart. When I heard the voice I thought perhaps I was still dreaming.

Can you hear me? Can you hear me?

Then some babble. Then again, *Can you hear me? This is a temporary connection, and the language centres of a human's brain are complex. Am I speaking?*

'Am I speaking?' I asked.

An oily reflection of me was present in the dark waters at my feet, wobbled and interfered with by occasional rib-shaped ripples. I looked down at myself. 'Is this me?'

No, this is not you.

'Everything is me,' I said, shaking my head to loose the strange voice, as if it were a piece of sand in my ear.

Through, said the voice. *Through. Listen to me: we have a proposition for you. A deal, a deal, which is a deal.*

I decided to play along with the hallucination. 'A proposition?'

We will give you something, and in return you will do something for us. It is a kind of bartering. Think trade. We will keep our promise to you.

'Who are you?'

There's no answer I can give you. That's not the proper question at this time.

This was so peculiar a reply that I was very struck by it. In a strange way it seemed to wake me up. I rubbed my face, scratched up my itchy head of hair. 'I don't understand.'

I know you think this is a hallucination, but it is not, said the voice. This was another puzzler. Would a real hallucination play this sort of game? Does self-awareness of hallucination mark a kind of veracity? This puzzled my thoughts.

'What's going on?' I asked. 'I'm confused.'

I'll tell you. Hear our offer.

'What is your offer?'

Away on the far side of the artificial lake I saw the shadowy yellow bulk of the jailer making her way over the turf. Her arms swayed in a counterpoint rhythm to her loping strides. Her big head almost turned to look at me; perhaps my voice was carrying over the still waters. But it was nothing new for me to be talking to thin air. I frequently had interludes when I would gabble away to myself. She disappeared behind the tortoise-backed hump of the hill.

We will free you from this jail, said the voice. Hearing this made me doubt the reality of the experience with renewed violence. It matched the intense yearning of my heart too closely. But then again, I reasoned, it would not be hard to determine that such might be my dream.

'Freedom?' I breathed, as if the word were taboo or sacred.

We will free you from this jail, repeated the voice in my head.

'How? This jail cannot be escaped from. It is surrounded on all sides by molten fire. It is many light years from the nearest world.'

We will do it, insisted the voice. *If you agree to our offer. We will take you away, give you wealth and information. You will travel far and erect a spaceship of your own imagining. Then you will do a job for us. Once you have done the job, you can pursue the rest of your life in whatever manner you choose.*

This was all too much to take in. 'Who are you?' I insisted.

But it only repeated what it had said before: *There's no answer I can give you. That's not the proper question at this time.*

17

'But how are you able to speak to me?'

We have opened up a channel of communication with you. It is not easy to maintain, as I'm sure you can understand, bearing in mind where you are. There's no guarantee we will be able to maintain it. Agree to our offer: undertake this job for us, and we will get you out of the jail. Outside, communication will be much easier.

I got up, feeling suddenly agitated. 'And what is this "job" that you would like undertaken?'

Once you are free of this place, you will travel to a certain world. It will be a remote world, near the edges of t'T space. There you will destroy the human population of the world.

'Repeat that,' I said. I had heard it, and it had even made some sort of awful, clanging, sense deep inside me. But I wanted to hear it again. The voice repeated its sentence, word for word.

'Which world?' I asked.

We can tell you that. Once you are free of this place.

'To kill all the human beings on the world?'

Yes.

'All? With no one spared?'

It is important that every single individual be killed.

'And the world itself? The actual world, the animals, the plants?'

They don't signify. It is the human beings that must be destroyed.

There was an itch underneath my eyelid. I tried twisting my knuckles into the eye, and then I tried picking at my eyelashes, actually pulling several out in my attempt to squash or tug the itch out of existence. Then I said: 'Why?'

There's no answer I can give you. That's not the proper question at this time.

'Why?' I said again. 'Why do you want so many people killed? Why have you come to me to do it? What is your motive? It might be important to me.'

There's no answer I can give you. That's not the proper question at this time.

I pondered this for a while. Then I got down on the ground and pressed the flats of my feet together so that I was sitting with my knees jutting out.

'How am I to kill all these people?'

That is a question for you to answer. We cannot answer that question at this time.

'Do you have suggestions?'

There are some avenues, we can perhaps give you starting points. Perhaps you can use your imagination. You have killed human beings before?

'Oh yes,' I said. 'Yes. But never on this scale.'

The principle is the same. Only the numbers are different.

'This planet is in t'T space?' I asked. 'These people have dotTech in their bodies?'

Yes.

'Then they will be very hard to kill. It is the nature of dotTech to struggle to keep people alive under any circumstances.'

It will not be easy, agreed the voice. *But we are confident that you will find a way of achieving it. This is why we have chosen you.*

'And if I do not find a way? What if, when you have freed me' – I still did not truly believe that this would happen, it was all hypothetical – 'what if I renege on your deal? Go on the run?'

Then we will find you, disable you. You will be returned to the jail. You will end your days in jail.

I believed this absolutely.

You wish to consider the offer, the voice stated.

'I accept,' I said, a great bundle of light and joy rising in my breast. I got to my feet and waved my arms. 'I accept! Take me out of here! I will do it! I accept your deal!'

Be quiet, said the inner voice. *Your jailers will overhear.*

'So?'

First you must escape this place, said the voice. *The jailers have the power to immobilise you. We must sneak past them. It will not be simple, or easy.*

'Escape!' I said. 'Imaginary voice, you are a delight to my ears.'

You do understand the price you pay for this freedom?

'Price?'

You must commit the crime. Do you understand this?

'Of course! Of course!'

Then go to the third tree. Not the first, the one with seven branches, but the third one along the water's edge. Count the branches from the one that overhangs the water, round to the fifth. On that branch you will find a single fruit. You must eat this fruit.

'An ordinary fruit?' I asked. The trees in this prison were actually machines, and the fruits on their branches were nothing more than extruded sacs of protein pulp. These tree-machines were there to provide the jailers and prisoners with nutrition.

Be sure and eat the correct one; count the branches from the one that overhangs the water, moving clockwise.[1] *The single fruit on the fifth branch. It is the branch nearest to the stream on the far side.*

I lurched forward, eager to eat this fruit. 'What is the significance of the fruit?' I asked. 'Why must I eat this fruit?' In truth I did not much care why; I was carried away by the delicious dream-logic of the encounter. Perhaps I genuinely was dreaming. The trees loomed up in the low evening light.

Inside this fruit, said the voice, *are the seeds for an AI. This AI will root inside you and grow in your brain. Then it will communicate with you, and you must follow its instructions.*

'An AI?'[2] I asked. But the voice did not reply. Indeed, I never heard from it again, which only added to the spectral quality of the whole encounter.

I found the tree and counted round the branches. There was the fruit, as my dream-self fully expected. I picked it, gobbled it down in three quick bites. Then I frolicked, danced around the water for a while to a tune of my own invention that I sang in a loud voice. I felt absurdly happy. Then I grew tired. I leant over the riverbank and drank; then I curled up and fell asleep on the artificial hill.

I woke to the dawn flare of sunlight throwing a yellow patina over the artificial world. Already the whole encounter had an unreal flavour in

[1] The text has been translated out of its original language, Glicé, the common tongue of the worlds of t'T. The Glicé word used here is *torcver*, 'spinwise', a general indicator of circular direction based on the direction in which the galaxy spins. 'Clockwise' is of course an anachronism for the cultures of the t'T, but has been introduced into this translation as the nearest useful equivalent.
[2] Most computing machines in the t'T are simple linear processors, advanced non-sentient versions of binary processing machines. AIs, or Artificial Intelligences, are parallel quantum processing machines with the capacity and the quirks to mimic human intelligence. Ae's surprise here suggests that they were less usual in the spaces of the t'T at this time than they have subsequently become.

my memory. I had experienced many strange dreams and visions; my mind was not as robust as it might have been. Then I wondered if the fruit I had eaten the night before really had contained the seeds of an AI.

An AI, dear stone, is no mere computer or processor. A processor works by linear computation; it is a machine of great speed and versatility. The barrier between the raging heat of the star and the walls of my prison were maintained by processors, constantly calculating the shifts in temperature and pressure and adjusting. The prison itself was held in place by processors tirelessly computing the currents and vectors of the star-matter. When people travel from planet to planet, wrapped in their cloaks of foam, it is powerful computational processors that govern the faster-than-light passage, that make the trillions of calculations necessary to shunt the travellers forward.

But an AI is like a human mind. It is not a linear processor, but a parallel and quantum computational device. It is intelligent in the way that a human mind is intelligent; only able to compute with the rapidity of a more basic processor but lively, lateral-thinking, alert. AIs are fragile – indeed more so than the human brain, because faster-than-light travel tends to degrade and destroy them. But they have certain advantages. Mostly they are transported about fast-space as program-seeds contained in lowly processing machines. Then, once required, they are assembled on site.

And now, if my dream was to be trusted, one was growing inside me. And I wondered how such a thing could be. Imagine that there was a group of people – which group, what people I could not think – but a group who wanted this enormous crime committed. How would they be able to reach inside the prison, to speak to me inside my head? This could not be done. How could they smuggle the seeds for an AI past the gate – not even the jailers could open the gate more frequently than the four-monthly cycle on which it operated. It was impossible.

I dismissed it.

When the AI began to talk inside my head, I dismissed that too as another hallucination. Perhaps that is all it was. How can I say? Dear stone, you are the only objective creature in my world. Can you tell me?

I am growing, said the AI. *Forty per cent capability as of now. Give me four more hours. Eat the dirt; that mud.*

'Eat that mud?' I repeated.

It contains trace minerals, particularly iron, that I need to establish certain key pathways. I am assembling myself inside your head. Eat the dirt.

At first I ignored this bizarre request. But the voice was insistent, and in the end I gave in; scooping soft mud into my mouth and swallowing. Strangely, it tasted good.

I can adapt your responses. You should experience the pleasure in eating the dirt.

'I thought I dreamed you,' I said, in a low voice. 'I think I dream you still.'

By tomorrow, said the AI, *I will have assembled myself. Then we can talk about escape, I think.*

7th

Dear Stone,

I haven't told you my name, or where I come from, or any of that autobiographical stuff. You have given yourself up to me completely, rock-jewel, the thing I own. Here I am, naked and alone, and you are all I have. And I haven't returned the compliment. Let me give my life to you, dear stone. Let me clutch you to my naked bosom.

My name is Ae. Actually, that isn't my name, but let it stand. I want it to be my name for you, dear stone, and if my doctor is listening through you somehow (wellhello! hey!), then let it be my name for her as well, let it replace my other name. On the world I come from, Terne, each child was given a total of seven names over a number of years. Some insisted on all seven names being used; others chose their favourite one. But I renounce all those names, and the person I was. I choose to be known by two letters instead of seven names, and I take the first two letters of the alphabet to avoid choice.[1]

Terne was my homeworld. Mine was a marshy homeland, a planet

---

[1] As a general principle, the translator has tried to avoid drawing undue attention to the gap between languages except where unavoidable. Here the narrator alludes to the Glicé alphabet ('alepheta'), which lists vowels (in order A E I O Ÿ [OU] U), then plosive/fricative consonants and then all other consonants.

mostly covered with an interconnecting series of oceans too sludgy really to deserve the name. The saltwater there is so densely inhabited by a variety of tendril-plant that sometimes it is possible for a human being to walk over the water, providing they are not too heavy. In spring the oceans change colour, as the flowering section of these plants emerged, orange and red; the rest of the time the seas gloom with dark purple, the native form of chlorophyll. This native vegetable was called Drüd, I remember; and it grew downwards in threads that could reach four or five hundred meters. The seawater itself sloshed through a sluggish maze of delta pathways as the Drüd flourished or died out, finding new pools of nutrient or draining the water of all minerals and starving itself to death. The landforms on this world – my homeworld, 'the World' we called it – were actually compacted masses of this same Drüd. Originally the whole world had been covered in ocean; then when portions of Drüd had formed tangled floating platforms new strains of the plant had evolved. These grew denser and denser, clogging together into islands, and then into continents thousands of kilometres across. The pressure of growth killed the plants deep inland, compacting and mummifying them. Currents and the sheer weight of growth kneaded land masses, throwing up low hills and chains of stumpy mountains. Then, from the composted relics of the original plants, new plants found a rich soil. Tall grasses, billowing bushes and slender trees. The landscape of my home – all organic, genuine, none of it plastic or artificial like the confines of my prison. Childhood.

8th

Dear Stone,

Here I am again. I have decided that, perhaps, I do not want to tell you about my childhood at this time. There are things in the story that I am not sure you wish to hear. For all that you are a stone, it may affect you.

Let me tell you instead about the t'T. The whole stretch of fast-space in this portion of our galaxy. The great confederation of worlds. Our way of life – of all the worlds that are part of the t'T – is determined by interstellar travel. You must understand how fantastically far stars are from one another; how enormous are the distances that we must travel to move from place to place. You are a palm's width wide, but you must understand how many billions of palm-widths there are even between planet and planet in the same system. Stars are so remote from one another it takes light – speeding at two and a third million metres every second – many *years* to go from one to another. From my home world, Terne, to the nearest inhabited world was seventy-odd light years. To travel that distance a stone such as yourself, ejected (say) from a sling, would take many centuries. Millennia.

There is a way of travelling faster than light, and this is it: to explain it, I must go down to the level of the atom, down to the scale that the dotTech inhabits. All those tiny machines, the millions of them in every human body, all built out of a few scores of atoms like miniature bricks. *They* understand the dynamics of atomic and subatomic – how well they understand! They inhabit that world. Don't you? (For I am sure they are eavesdropping on us, stone, in our conversation). *Don't you?*

Hey! Hey!

Nothing.

Around each atom several electrons exist, like planets in their orbits round the star, like points at the end of clock hands swinging round on their pivot. These electrons inhabit one of several possible orbits; orbits that may be close to the core, or a little further out, or further out still. But they must occupy one or other set orbit; they cannot simply spin wherever they might choose. And sometimes, when the energy injected into the system changes, then these electrons may hop from a lower orbit to a higher one, or from a higher one to a lower one. And this movement, over minuscule distances though it be, is *instantaneous*.

It is, I understand (for I am no expert here) a weak-force, a property of atomic life. And by co-ordinating this motion over a whole body, it is possible to flick forward through space instantaneously! The distance covered is minuscule of course, no larger than the difference between two atomic orbit paths, a fraction of an atom's width – the smallest thing. It takes a trillion of these flicks to move you even a few metres in real space; but if you can co-ordinate these trillions and trillions of movements then you can move yourself faster than light. How fast? There are two constraints; one is the computing time it takes to co-ordinate and calculate trillions upon trillions of shifts. If your computing time is sluggish then your speed is reduced; if your computing time is fast enough you can reach thousands of times the velocity of light itself.

The other constraint is as follows, and depends upon the fact that this weak-force drive has certain defining features. This drive is best at moving the very small thing, poor at moving large structures. According to the theory, its ideal traveller would be a dimensionless point. Such a point is a mathematical fiction, but if it were possible to imagine it in the real world then it would be possible to accelerate it many millions of times faster than light. The larger an object, the more it expands outward from this dimensionless dot, the slower the faster-than-light speeds that can be achieved. The constraint can be mapped. It is a logarithmic scale that shows a rapid falling away, such that it is almost impossible to accelerate an object larger than about ten metres diameter to speeds greater than light.

Humanity does build and own spaceships; some sleek and slim, some huge and rambling; but none of these ships can travel faster than light. The difficulties of co-ordinating so much quantum shifting means that travellers through space have to do without the benefit of a spaceship. All the old dreams of ancient culture about gigantic disc-shaped or stick-insect spacecraft proved wrong, dear stone. The truth is this: a single human being straps a pack to their back or belly (depending on taste). From this pack a foam is extruded that quickly covers her or him, enveloping the whole body. The foam is smart, a congregation of powerful processors (not AIs, which cannot survive faster-than-light travel) shaping it to provide an airway in at the mouth and to cushion the whole body. Then the granules of foam themselves adapt, some processing the information necessary to repeat-shift the body through space, some to protect and comfort the human being inside by regulating heat, some to provide jets of gas to orient them. The outside of the foam hardens diamond-firm, to protect the traveller against smaller impacts and to insulate them against the extreme cold of space. Then the traveller falls into the vacuum from (perhaps) the hanger of their slow, slow spaceship; and away they go. It is a marvellous thing, this faster-than-light travel; it bypasses the time-dilation, or time-compression, effects of conventional travel so effectively that the difference between your own journey time and the time that passes for a third party is no more than five per cent.

Human beings have been travelling like this for a thousand years now, more or less; cocooned in foam, dancing their way over immense distances.

But there is another constraint. Now, this is important, dear stone. This is what shapes our galaxy, what gives the borders to the different human cultures. Here are certain facts.

Firstly, this faster-than-light travel is a precarious business, based on the atomic weak-force; and if it is disrupted it degrades very rapidly.

Secondly, material features of our universe interfere with the successful promulgation of the faster-than-light drive. Too much matter degrades it, so it is not possible to travel faster than light through areas of space where the concentrations of matter are too great; nebulae, gaseous concentrations, dust. Other things disrupt it, things we know little of; barriers and blockages detectable only by the fact that the weak-force drive degrades and speed slows in these places. There are areas of t'T space through which it is possible and easy to speed at thousands of times the velocity of light. There are other areas, where travel is more sluggish, difficult, and speeds of only a few c are possible. Then there is the larger array of spaces where faster than light travel is not possible, and spaceships must crawl at sublight speeds.

And this is the shape of our empire, the worlds of t'T.

Actually, my dear stone, I realise that I am being simplistic. The circling of electrons around an atomic core, the cat's cradle of strong-force and weak-force, of electromagnetic force and gravitational force, is much more complex than I implied. It is not dots circling a clockwork centre, not an orrery. This is the whole point of the universe at very small levels. Nothing is certain, the way that things in our universe can be certain. We cannot know where a subatomic particle is and where it is going at the same time. Fancy that! We can know where it is, or we can know where it is going, but not both at the same time. Is that not strange? More than this: these quantities – position, speed, mass, state – are not determined *until we observe them.* You may think about the implications of that statement, dear stone, until your stony being understands it, and it will be sooner than I. This, as a philosopher once explained it, is partly how the weak-force drive works, a process of supercharged computational observation of the subatomic that forces the position of the entire matrix to repeatedly define itself further and further along the line along which we choose to travel. This is why only human beings can travel FTL; dumb cargo cannot be accelerated that way. Don't worry if this baffles you; I can't say I understand it either. You and I, stone, can curl up together in our ignorance.

Still, I'm straying from the point. What was I saying? There is fast-space, there is slow space, and there is space so cluttered or characterised at a deep level by such interference patterns (which we don't really understand) that faster-than-light travel is impossible and humanity is compelled to travel sublight if we travel at all. But sublight travel takes many many years, years made worse by the time-dilation that ages everybody around you as you travel, and few have the patience – even if dotTech gives them the longevity.

Fast space, slow-space. We assume that the space between the galaxies will mostly be fast-space. Perhaps people have travelled those distant spaces, but it would take many hundreds of years for us, in t'T space, to work our way out through the slow and sublight spiral arm of this galaxy to get to the intergalactic vastnesses. I'm sure some people have made this journey; peoples of the Wheah, perhaps, born closer to the galaxy's rim. Palmetto tribes – who knows? Their communications can travel only at the speed of light, and will take millennia to reach us.

Closer to the core of the galaxy, matter is too dense; the further corewards you go, the slower, and then things lapse into sublight. Most of the space in the galaxy, we suppose, is slow-space; but not the spaces of the t'T. We occupy a stretch of fast-space hundreds of light years wide and deep and thousands long. And in this space faster-than-light travel is possible; travel at thousands of times the speed of light.

Why does this fast-space exist? Dear stone, I do not know why. It is not that the density of stars in t'T space is any less than in the same latitude of the galaxy elsewhere; it has something to do with the purity of the particular space, the lack of both sufficiently dense nebula material and of the superstring interference. Or so they tell us. I am not an expert. Whatever the reason, the fact remains that humanity is able to travel across t'T space at speeds of up to 3000 c. Three thousand times the speed of light. This is where we are, dear stone; this is our space.

It is not a clear space. It is bounded on one border, corewards, by the Bulk; a sublight stretch of space, enormous, taller than wide. On the rimwards side, away from this fog of static stars and dust is the Tongue: nearly 2000 light years long and several hundred wide, stretching up to roof our clearing of fast-space and down to spread out and floor it. It is these elongations of the broken space, the slow-space runnels in a mass of sublight, that borders t'T. Or reverse the picture, flip the negative: don't think of clear space clouded here and there with obstruction. Think of matter-dotted galactic space as a slow medium, treacly, with occasional miraculous openings, and that we live in one such opening, an opening thousands of light years wide.

And running down the middle of this great space (perhaps the reason it exists in the first place, or else a function of its existence) is a great Gravity Trench. An immense stretch of dense gravitational attraction, broken in the middle but still magnificent, enormous.

I have discovered much more about the Gravity Trench, dear stone. I'll tell you about that in a little while.

So: in the realms of t'T we can travel very fast indeed. Three thousand times the speed of light is fast enough, I would hope. Occasional local impurities in the fabric of space-time mean that the speed of some journeys is rather limited: but through most of the space speeds can be enormous. I have mentioned human populations in other spaces than those of the t'T. There are stories, too, of races and people further removed than that. But these other places are not blessed with the rapid travel of the t'T. The space of the Wheah, for instance, is difficult; it is hard to maintain speeds faster than light, and impossible to go more than three c. Their culture, by all accounts (for they are a shadowy set of peoples, little known of amongst the t'T) is very different from ours. Everything is slower. Journeys take years, or decades; trade becomes a long term prospect. Tribes accumulate in great space-borne communities, or spend their whole lives on planet surfaces, never venturing into space. In the Wheah they despise nanotechnology, for religious reasons, and so they live short lives filled with disease and uncertainty. Many are happier not risking these lives in space. They are a conservative and cautious peoples.

But all this is of no interest to you, is it, beloved stone? Well, let me tell you one more thing, something to do with the nature of fast-space. It is shrinking, they say. Or the slow-space around it is slowly expanding; one of the two. And the result of this is that within a millennium people will only be able to travel from world to world at a maximum of three c; travel time will increase thousand-fold. Maybe worse than that will happen – maybe we will be thrown back into sublight, and worlds will become almost entirely isolated from worlds. It is inevitable, it cannot be helped. From the point of view of eternity, our space, the pocket of fast-space that allowed the growth of the empire of t'T, has only opened for a short time, and will close again. And we will watch it close. I won't. The dotTech has left my body now, so I will age and decay quickly enough. But the people I grew up with will, and their children will.

Tired now. Dear stone, I will leave you here, place you on the chocolate-coloured mud for a few hours, and you and I will sleep.

With love,
Ae.

Prison-breaking

Dear Stone,

The AI nestled inside my skull now, as imprisoned in there as I was in the jailstar. Except that it whispered to me, sending minute pulses of electricity through the speech-recognition parts of my brain that sounded to me like several curious, effect-less and echo-less voices speaking together in perfect harmony. And it told me that I wasn't trapped in my prison any longer. I could escape.

The level of dotTech in your blood, the AI told me, *is almost nil. It's extraordinary.* I could have told it as much; I knew how little nanotechnology remained inside my body – knew it from my aches, from the ways grazes refused to heal, from the way headaches bloomed and faded behind my face. I wasn't really human any more.

'So?' I said, muttering to myself. I did not need, as it happened, actually to speak the words; the AI, nestled inside my brain-tissue, could decipher my words from the electrical patternings of my speech centres, but I found it hard to *think* the words without actually saying them. To begin with the AI rebuked me for this: *Why speak aloud? Others will overhear you, and then your plans for escape – and everything that will follow – will fail.* Everything that will follow: death. I was unmoved by this.

'They already think I have lost my senses,' I muttered, 'that I am mad. Why are you so struck by the fact that I have no dotTech in my blood?'

I wonder, dear stone, what anyone would have thought coming across me, muttering to myself among the artificial trees?

How long have you lived like this? Free from dotTech?

'Years now,' I hissed. 'Years! I do not know how many years because

30

I have lost track of the time; there are no seasons here. I am sick of it. It is driving me mad. Really mad. That is why you must get me out of here.'

It won't be so easy, travelling through space without dotTech to help you, the AI observed.

'I know that,' I said. 'I daresay I will survive, but it will be less comfortable. There is nothing living inside me.' The statement was doubly true; because I also felt a metaphorical vacuum in my heart, a sense of emptiness like an uninhabited building. This was 'depression' – one of the pathologies that does sometimes occur in the worlds of t'T, because we do not allow dotTech to play around with our higher-brain chemistry. But I suppose nano-maintenance of all other body chemistry does something to lessen the effects and the causes of the illness. Whatever the reason, depression is rare in the t'T. I had never suffered it before, but I suffered it in that jail. I had months of it in un-mediated form; months of feeling dead and rotting in the mind, weary and sick in the body.

The first thing, of course, was to get out of jail, free. I would not travel faster than light to achieve this, the AI told me; but I would need the foam in which space-wanderers wrap themselves. When it told me this I saw what was going to happen. The AI hoped somehow to have me crawl through the matter of the star itself, through its million-degrees-hot plasma. It was depending on the foam as an insulation; because this foam is a thing, dear stone, designed to insulate the traveller against the immense cold and extreme changes in temperature of the vacuum of space. But I found it hard to believe that it could protect against the great heat inside a star. It is not designed to do that.

I'll modify the foam, the AI said. *I'll improve it, I can do that. And it doesn't have to last a whole interstellar journey, just long enough to get us out of the prison.*

'Where will I obtain the package, these machines? The weak-force drive? The Zhip-pack?' I asked.

There won't be any specialist FTL ware, the AI said with a strange tone of exasperation that was turned into surreality by the layering of its voice. *How can we obtain a complete Zhip-back, inside prison? We shan't do that.*

31

'How am I supposed to be,' I asked, baited into crossness by its tone, 'supposed to be . . .' but the word failed me.

You leave the prison, the AI started saying when the word occurred to me.

'. . . propelled, how am I supposed to be *propelled* through space without a Zhip-pack? Assuming I make it out of this impassable prison?'

You leave the prison, the AI said, patiently, *through one of the ducts in the ceiling. I'll be able to create the necessary from the raw materials hereabouts. I can make up the foam, to a high-enough standard. We'll need a line as well, for you to hang by. Then when we are ready we can interfere with the restriction patterning of the ducts and pass through. Once on the other side we will be carried through to the surface.*

Like ice rising through clear water? I wondered. I didn't have to say it; the AI could see it in my thoughts.

Not at all, it said, *you depress me with your ignorance of physics. We will time our departure carefully, and our point of departure even more carefully, so that it coincides with a strong enough convection pattern in the body of the star, to draw us upwards.*

'And the radiation?'

Will be severe, yes. Damaging. But we will be inside the star for only a short time, and we will soon be free of it. Normally of course the dotTech would heal us of our hurts from the radiation, but in the circumstances the damage to us is perhaps a price worth paying.

'If only I could have some dotTech in my body,' I said, with a sudden eagerness. 'Could you not arrange for some dotTech to be in my body?'

No, that is not possible.

'No,' I repeated, 'that is not possible. I suppose there is nowhere to obtain it. And anyway the execution has made my body a no-go zone for the little machines.'

We will do well enough without it.

'All this talk of *we*, of *us*,' I said, sardonically. I was sitting under one of the trees in the prison, pulling its tiny plastic leaves off, one after the other. At the shrunken horizon I saw the yellow, bear-shaped outline of my jailer lumbering along.

I watched her. She passed up the hill and over the other side. The AI kept talking inside my head.

The inside of a star is a demi-fluid superheated plasma, the AI was saying. I wasn't really paying attention; there was something off-putting in the lecturing mode it was now adopting. *Within it there are various heating and cooling currents – although 'cooling' is a little misleading, given the extremely high ambient temperature.*

'Really,' I said. And then, as the AI went on, I amused myself by repeating the word with different intonations and accents. Really. Re-ally. Raly. Ruly. Rrreally.

We'll position ourselves, the AI continued, ignoring my distraction, *in the updraft of one of these currents. I can calculate and monitor the fluid dynamics of the star-matter well enough. The prison itself is less than fifty kilometres below the heliosurface, so pressure shouldn't be a problem. We'll ride up.*

It stopped. 'And when we reach the surface?' I asked. 'Do I simply lie on a ground of fire?'

No, said the AI, sounding crosser and crosser. *Will you pay attention?*

Its point about my ignorance of physics had touched me, I suppose, because I felt the urge to show off my education. 'What is the gravity at the surface anyway?' I asked this because I assumed stars all to be huge, massive, pulling dozens of g.

Are you an idiot? the AI asked, which did surprise me. *On the surface the gravity will be more or less the same as it is here.*

'I assumed,' I said, 'that gravity of stars is—'

This is a small star, the AI interrupted. *How else could they build the prison they have?*

'So how does it hold its planets?'

It doesn't have any planets, only a few asteroids. Do you know nothing?

'Don't get cross with me,' I advised.

We will move through the stellar body in the flow of a convection current. When this reaches the heliosurface it creates a solar flare which will shoot us out at the necessary escape velocity. This is how we will travel through space.

'And then?' I asked. 'Do I drift through space for thousands of years until I happen to be—' But the AI interrupted me again.

Then you will be collected, of course. What else did you imagine?

*

That there would be somebody waiting for me on the other side of the fiery wall of my prison was startling. It made me realise that this jailbreak, the whole undertaking to which I had agreed, was a real thing and not the fantasy of a mind dissolved in the insanity of years of prison. It put me back into a questioning habit. So I was to be taken from the prison, was I? I was to go to a world I had never before visited and destroy all the people living upon it? Why was I asked to do so terrible a thing?

I asked the AI. 'Do you know who is employing me?' It did not reply, so I pressed the point. 'You do know, don't you. You do.'

Of course I know, it replied. Its odd triple-tracked voice sounded almost sulky.

'Who?' I demanded. And when it didn't reply I started hooting the question in a loud voice. 'Who? Who?'

Be still! The AI remonstrated. *Are you trying to draw their attention to you? They'll realise something is wrong! They'll restrain you – they'll prevent you getting out. Do you want that?*

I stopped hooting, but it was filled with the weird manic energy that possessed me sometimes, so I started a raggedy-strided sprint up the little hill, down the other side and then hopped over the stream in a single leap.

Calm! cried the AI. *Be still! Are you mad?*

'Who?' I asked, in a lower voice, but panting as I ran.

I cannot tell you.

That stopped me. I stood for a moment angled forward, back bent, arms straight, resting a hand on each knee. Without dotTech in me it took me much, much longer to recover after exertion.

'What?'

I cannot tell you! Enough! Enough! Calm!

'What do you mean, you can't tell me?' It said nothing to this, so I said again, 'You do know who is employing me?'

Of course.

'But you won't tell me?'

No.

'I suppose,' I said, sinking to the floor, my breath returning to me, 'that they – my employers – programmed you. They programmed you as code-potential, and somehow transmitted it inside this prison.'

Yes.

'And that they want to maintain their secrecy. They programmed that into you as well.'

Something like that.

'Do you know *why* they want it done?'

Silence.

'AI,' I said. I was sitting now, my thighs and calves folded up against my torso like a folding chair, hugged to me by my sinewy arms. 'AI, this is a very big thing I am employed to do. To murder a whole world! A very big crime. But I cannot imagine why anybody would want it done – do you know the *why*?'

You are asking, said the AI inside my head, *the wrong questions.*

But you know why? I was subvocalising now.

I do.

Silence.

And, I asked, as if the question had just started up inside me, And do you know why *me*? Why did they choose me to do this thing?

But you already know the answer to that one.

And so I did. In all the worlds of t'T, the utopian areas and civilisations of fast-space, there was probably no other individual like me. I was certainly alone in my prison, a unique criminal freak. A statistical oddity. It was the glory of t'T to have reduced the statistical glitch that threw up a small percentage of the population as murderous criminals; to have reduced it almost to nothingness.

You must do exactly what I tell you, said the AI. I said, silently, Yes, yes. Was there a voice in my head, dear stone? Did I imagine the whole thing?'

Who can answer my question?

It would be best, the AI said, *if you allowed me to grow in your brain, so that I can connect with sections of your motor cortex. That way I can directly influence your movements, make you more dextrous.*

'Do you really need to ask my permission?' I asked. 'How could I stop you if you decided to, will-me or nil-me?'

It seemed upset at this. *I was only being polite,* it said.

Night came. I loitered by the water, watching my jailer and her red lover dancing together illuminated by the stars. Striated patterns of pale light glittered on the dark waters of the lake. I ducked behind the nearest trees, peering round the treetrunks as if they were columns and I were acting in a play. My jailer and her mate stopped to pick a few fruit, and then sat with their legs soaking in the water up to their knees as they ate. The interrupted hum of their conversation, made bleary by the distance, reached me on the other side of the prison. I could not make out what they were saying.

They'll sleep soon, said the AI, close and sharp in my ear.

This was so precisely my own thought that my hairs stood up. How could I be sure there truly was an AI in my head? What if I were imagining the whole thing?

This thought, though, was too close to my speech centres, for the AI overheard (over*thought?*) it.

Perhaps you should consider, it said tartly, *whether your habit of disbelieving that anybody else truly exists except yourself is a strength or a handicap?*

I don't know what you mean, I subvocalised. I had been practising this mode of internal communication, and had become more adept at it.

Yes you do, said the AI, and was still.

Eventually, the jailer and her mate stood, embraced, and made their way into the hill. This is where they slept; locked away from me, lest I should go mad and try to injure them in their sleep. Finally I was alone.

Now, said the AI. *There – where the bark bulges out a little. Pull that away.* But it didn't need to tell me to do this, because it was already influencing my hands and fingers. The bark would not give, but then with a strength and co-ordination I didn't know I possessed, I yanked it away.

Inside, urged the AI. *Inside.* It sounded eager, even overexcited, and this worried me. Surely a genuine AI would be more dispassionate; this made me fret that the voice was simply an inner extension of me.

I fumbled and gutted the tree of part of its machinery, the technology that processed carbon, water and trace minerals into the necessary protein flesh of the fruits. I drew out a series of dangling black tube-wires, a small nodule, a manifold. *Take those!* screeched the

AI in my ear. *Close up the bark!* I closed the bark back over the hole in the tree, gathered up my cache, and hurried away.

That night I – the AI, working through my fingers – built a new device; one that would manufacture the foam that covers interstellar travellers. The foam, the AI assured me, was a simple matter. What about the technology, the machinery, the processing that actually propels a body faster than light? *Don't be ridiculous,* said the AI. *That's far too complex to be knocked together here. Do you think I am a genius?* The tone of rebuke was so sharp that I said nothing more; but I worried that – even if I were able to leave the star – I would be left merely floating in space.

But then again a part of me believed that the whole thing was merely a sort of fantasy dream inside my own head. At least it provided a certain variety in my life; and my life had been death-beckoningly dull until then. So I went along with it.

2nd

O Stone,

Is there a need to delay the narrative with the preparations I made? No, I don't think so. All throughout them I doubted that they were real, but I was carried along, more passenger than agent. The AI made me fashion a sac out of four or five very broad leaves from one of the bushes that grew close to the corner where the sky met the land.

Why do I need a sac?

To carry the mud. We must have raw materials to fashion the foam. The foam is actually a complex of carbon. And fluid of course; we'll find that in mud.

I built crampons to attach to arms and feet. I ate more regularly, and to better purpose, than ever before. *You'll need strength to climb the sky,* said the AI.

And so it went on.

Another night. I waited, stomach burning acidic with fear and anticipation. I could not keep myself in check; I ran from tree to tree, dived in the water and climbed out, trying to burn up my energy. It seemed to take forever before my jailer and her mate prepared to go to bed. I watched them do their nightly dance. Why did they dance? I cannot say. It was their ritual. Then, in a skittish excess of nerves, I leapt up whining and sprinted, legs akimbo from stride to stride.

Will you be calm? complained the AI in my head. *Be calm!*

'Can't help it!' I sang. 'Can't help it.' And then in time to my strides, '*Can't* help it, *can't* help it, *can't* help it.'

I rounded the little hill and there was the jailer. That brought me up short.

'Hello,' I said, giggling. Thinking to myself, Soon I'll be away from here, step into space and wipe my tears away. But a part of my brain was trying to stifle even the thoughts. The fact that the AI could overhear me thinking gave me an edgy paranoid sense that the jailer could overhear me too. After all, in some crucial sense, she only existed inside my head too, like the AI. Wasn't that so?

Do you understand why I say that, dear stone? Do you appreciate the sense in which these people are not really people outside of me? But of course you are silent. You're still silent. The still point.

'You've been talking to yourself a great deal,' said the jailer in her cumbrous manner.

'I talk to myself,' I gabbled. 'I've always talked to myself. Lack of company you know. From time to time I split myself in two and one split talks to the other split. You know? You know?'

'It has been a part of your mental pathology,' she said, keeping me steady with a straight look. 'From time to time. But you've changed in the last two weeks. You've become much more insistently talkative. You seem to be having actual conversations.'

Kill her, hissed the AI in my ear. *She knows.*

My eyes may have widened, because the jailer seemed to register some change in my face. To myself I subvocalised, Keep quiet, keep out of it.

Kill her! Do it now!

But this was ill advised. It would have been a very difficult thing to manage. The dotTech in her system would have preserved her against almost any assault I could make. Besides she was larger and stronger than I. I felt a lurch in my muscles, as if the AI were trying to

38

command my nerves, but I fought down the impulse. 'No,' I said, as firmly as I could.

'No?' repeated the jailer. 'How do you mean?'

'No, I'll stop talking to myself,' I said. 'Yes, I mean, yes, I'll stop doing it.'

Kill her kill her said the voice in my head.

The jailer tilted her heavy yellow head to one side, eyeing me hard. I stood there. How hard would it be to kill her? If I had some sort of knife or weapon . . .

But now her back was towards me, and she was lumbering away. I was still muttering to myself, sweating. Can we go now? I asked the AI, silently. I was scared, jittery, jumpy. I wanted to be away from that place. Can we go now?

Yes, said the AI, subdued now. *Yes, yes.*

I gathered my crampons from where I had buried them under the plastic grass and made my way to the wainscot of the jail, where the blue sky and green ground met in a perfect ninety degree join. The sky was dim now, with only a little starlight throwing out a shaky illumination. I embraced the darkness. Cover me, I thought. I slung the sac filled with wet mud around my naked waist, propped the AI's adaptor/creator inside it. Then I applied the two hand crampons to the plastic of the sky. Pulling my weight onto these, I dug my toes into the wall.

With easy gestures at first, but with increasing difficulty and trembly pain, I hauled myself up the sky. I was hanging flat against the blue nothing like a fly. Most of the hauling was done with my arm muscles, and this was not easy. Each time the prick of the crampon dug into the yielding plastic of the sky there was a faint *toc* noise. And so I made my clockwork way upwards.

I'll be honest, stone. My flesh lacks will. If it had been up to me I would have given up after a few metres, would have dropped awkwardly back to the ground. But the AI had access to my motor centres now; it co-ordinated my gestures, forced my muscles to their limits, refused to let them stop. With each painful straining, each lift of a few centimetres, I winced; but it would not relent. I believe I even started begging it, half way up, Please to stop, please. But it did not even reply, it simply pushed me on.

After a great deal of this painful climbing I began to feel a sensation of heat on the top of my head. 'We're coming near the first star,' I gasped.

That's it, said the AI inside my head. *A few more reaches.*

I hauled myself a metre or so closer. The heat from the star-shaped gap was quite fierce now. My muscles ached with an equivalent fire, pain pulsing up and down my arms and legs. My fingers were sharply sore. My breath was heaving in and out.

Now, said the AI. *I've extruded some rope from the fabricator. In the sac, do you see?*

I glanced down, and saw a spool of rope coiled on top of the mud. But then my eyes became hooked, magnetically, to the view directly below me. All the way down the flat of the sky to the ground, a great distance down. I started whimpering.

Don't be silly now, said the AI. *We have to throw the end of that rope into the opening of the star. Attend!*

'I'm scared,' I blubbed. 'I'm greatly scared of falling.'

You won't fall. Hold on with your feet and your left hand; let go with your right and reach into the sac.

'Are you insane inside my head?' I shrieked. 'Let go? I'll fall!' I looked down again, and my whole torso yawed and shrunk with terror at the drop. It seemed an impossible distance. I imagined myself falling and being dented and bashed to pieces. There had been times during my stay in prison when I would have welcomed such a suicide, but now, faced with the reality of it, and tantalised by the nearness of escape, my whole being revolted against the idea. I felt terror solidify inside me, like a hard-edged thing inside my belly and my chest.

Release your right hand, ordered the AI.

'No!' I yelped. 'No! No!'

But the AI had its tendrils in my motor cortex. Despite myself I felt my pressure relax, my wrist tipping up to release the hook of the crampon, and the hand come away. 'No, no,' I moaned, and started wriggling in a sort of ecstasy of fear. The AI, saying nothing but clearly deciding that I was being irrational, froze up all my limbs, save only the right hand that was reaching gingerly into the sac.

It brought out the end of the rope and hooked a five metre loop over my wrist. It was as if somebody else were acting, and I merely spectating, as it reached back, and with an awkwardly positioned but perfectly balanced throw hurled the rope upwards. I angled my head back in time to see the end of it disappear through the heart of the star-shaped hole.

There was a snicking sound. The processing machine, controlling the magnetic channel from within its mouth, responded as it was programmed to in the event of contaminants entering the hole. Now the star, like a human sphincter, clenched and closed, holding the rope tight. Light dimmed.

Is it supposed to do that?

Yes it is.

Won't they notice the diminution in light below?

It's fine, said the AI. *It's only one star out of many. Give me a moment, and I'll work it. Now, we need to wrap you in foam.*

Release my limbs to my own control, I said.

I don't think so. You'll panic and fall. Here— and it moved my right hand back up the sky, so that I could reinsert the crampon. *Better?*

I could feel the foam starting to bubble up at my waist. I had experienced that sensation of being entirely immersed in this foam many times before, but never in so strange and precarious a position. I was still sobbing, gasping; and only the mastery of the AI was stopping my limbs from trembling. But there was something almost comforting about the experience, like a blanket being drawn over a sleepy child, as the foam slewed up and covered my torso, crept along my arms, and swallowed my head.

I'm going to make you let go, now, said the AI. I couldn't speak, because the foam was forcing itself into my mouth, making the tube which delivered air to my lungs during transit, but I subvocalised frantically, No, no, no.

Yet there was nothing to be done. My arms and then my legs clicked away from the sky, and drew themselves through the still soft texture of the foam. My legs came together, slightly bent at the knees; my arms went to my sides. At the same time, I was conscious of a sensation in my gut as I swung free, suspended only by the rope I had thrown into the mouth of the aperture.

My terror, now, was that the star's orifice might open itself, releasing the rope and dropping me to the ground far below. But I

41

was too far gone to be terrified in any rational sense. Help me AI, I gibbered in my mind. What is going on! Please tell me! What is happening?

. . . *letting the outside of the foam harden a little, in the natural way* . . . came the AI's odd, treble-tracked voice, as if in the middle of something and not wanting to be distracted.

So I hung there. I experienced the distinctive sensory deprivation of being in the foam, robbed of sight and hearing and smell, feeling only the uniform pressure of the foam on my naked body, tasting only the grey taste of the foam as it hardened into an airway in my mouth – in that state, I began to calm a little.

. . . *talking to the machine in the star aperture*, came the AI's voice again. *It is a simple machine, densely built but not lateral in its programming. I'll just . . . I'll just . . .*

A lurch.

. . . *there we go . . .*

I felt myself to be rising. And I rose.

What was happening? Dear stone, if only you had the capacity to experience my excitement. All the terror I had felt only moments before were alchemised suddenly into sheer, bright thrill. My AI had persuaded the machine that operated the star aperture to open, and had drawn in the rope to drag me up and into the electromagnetic channel. Then, with a magnetic peristalsis, I was shunted along this channel, and finally ejected out of the prison and into the body of the star itself.

I knew none of this at the time, of course, except when I entered the plasma of the star; and I only knew that because the AI told me. *That takes us into the star-matter*, it said.

I can't feel anything, I said. I mean, I can't feel the heat.

The foam is designed to be an excellent insulator, said the AI. *You shouldn't feel much. But it is hot out there, believe me. Millions of degrees.*

I was wrapped all in darkness, cool and drifting; but centimetres from my skin the temperature was hot enough to vaporise me. This knowledge gave me a curiously delicious sensation in my chest; despite the manifest danger I felt as safe as a child in the womb.

*

Dear Stone,

Time becomes a thing difficult to calculate when you are wrapped in the foam. Deprived of input, your senses first fixate on anything they can – the thrum of a heartbeat, the slightest pushing feeling of blood moving under the skin – and after that they begin to fade, to switch off.

I floated. I'm sure I slept.

But then things went wrong. Complacency! I began to feel hot. This worried me a great deal. The foam was supposed to protect me from this.

The temperature gradient was extreme, of course; the insulation of the foam was enough to protect a human body against the unimaginable cold of the vacuum between stars, but cold is one thing and heat another. More than this, travellers through space are usually carrying an internal protection, a full load of nanotechnological machines focused and expert at preserving the human body. I lacked that. 'I'm hot,' I muttered, as well as I could do with my mouth stuffed with the foam, and air piping up and down into my lungs without the control of my vagus nerve. But it didn't matter how garbled the word sounded: the AI could read what I was trying to say directly from my brain.

I know that, replied the AI. *Don't you think I can sense that? I'm with you too.*

It sounded angry, which surprised me. I began to wonder if the prospect of death, of extermination, was as frightening for it as for me. After all, an AI is more than just a linear processor; it operates by as complex a neural patterning procession as does the human brain, and with many more possible connections. We become habituated to our machines, dear stone; we forget that some of them are more than machines. AIs. The dotTech itself – it has problem solving, adaptive, pseudo-neural functions as well. Perhaps the nano-machines are alive too, sentient too, as alarmed at the prospect of their own death as any human being is of hers?

But there were no dotTech machines liable to destruction if the foam failed and I was melted by the stellar heat outside. I was all alone. Just myself and the AI.

43

'Are *you* scared?' I mumbled, mouth packed and numb.

Any genuinely sentient being, the voice of the AI announced, *feels a certain alarm at the prospect of ceasing to exist.* This came over as rather prissy. Besides, it was hardly calculated to reassure me.

Are we going to die, then? I asked, subvocalising the question this time.

Uncertain, said the AI. *Uncertain. Wait.* The heat rose, and rose. It was increasingly uncomfortable. My mind started jittering, running through possible scenarios. The foam was breaking up; the convection pattern was taking me into the core of the sun rather than out to the heliosurface. I was doomed. There was nothing the AI could do. Panic burped up into my thoughts, but it was quite impossible for me to struggle or kick out. I could not even breathe more rapidly than I would normally do. All that happened was that my heart started lolloping along much harder than was usual, and that my eyeballs swivelled randomly underneath my closed eyelids. Then, for no reason, the panic cleared and I was calm. If I was going to die, then I was going to die, that was that. There was nothing to be done, and therefore there was no point in fretting.

It's alright, said the AI. *From what I can determine, we passed through a fusion bubble in the body of the sun itself. A very hot anomaly. Awkward, and unlucky, but we seem to be out the other side. The temperature outside is dropping now, and we should be fine. We should be on the surface shortly, and the flare that results will catapult us out into space. Our only problem, I think, is that the foam is such a good insulator that the heat inside won't dissipate.*

Our problem?

It's my problem as well, insisted the AI, querulous-sounding. *If you die, I die too.*

Am I going to die?

Oh I do hope not. You are sweating, though the sweat doesn't have anywhere to go, so it's not managing to cool you down very much. If your core body temperature goes above a certain limit then you could pass out, maybe expire. I think we'll be alright. But this will be a less comfortable trip than we had otherwise assumed.

I cannot get used to you talking about 'us' like this.

Get used to it.

There was nothing to do. I was uncomfortable; my whole body just felt too hot, and there was no way of cooling myself.

Usually what happens in spaceflight is that, once the individual is underway and totally enveloped in the foam, the mind slows. Without external stimuli in a perfectly balanced environment it is easy to slip between sleep and a form of being awake where time means very little. There are mantras that help induce this state of mind, profound meditation that ease the months the journey may last. I had made such journeys many times before, but I discovered that in the prickly, dissolving heat, and without the dotTech in my body, this state of mind was impossible to achieve. I tried my mantras, but kept getting distracted from them by how uncomfortable I was. And every now and again the AI would chip in – an irritating distraction that ordinary spacefarers are also spared – and break whatever concentration I had managed to build up.

Would you mind if I altered your brain chemistry to—

Please! You started me out of my mantra.

I was only being polite, asking permission.

Be quiet!

Excuse me. The three-in-one voice sounded sarcastic. But it was quiet, if only for a while. Then:

We are nearing the heliosurface.

Why must you tell me? Are you planning on providing a running commentary throughout my journey? The essence of interstellar travel is achieving the proper state of mind. If you keep interrupting me you are preventing me achieving that proper state.

Look—

No, no.

Actually I was being a little unfair to the AI. Once the foam-wrapped traveller enters faster-than-light travel it becomes very hard to concentrate anyway. The repeated quantum shifting plays strange games with the neural pathways of the brain, and the traveller almost always goes into a kind of trance. It is not an unpleasant experience, in fact, and in some senses is even soothing; and not even a twittering AI interjecting constantly would be enough to draw the mind out of it. More to the point, AIs are degraded by the process; they cannot survive it. But I was not travelling faster than light, I was creeping

45

upwards and out; more than that I was hot and cross, and there was nobody else to be angry with except the AI.

And then, abruptly, there was a massive yaw and jolt in my belly and bones. Everything pulled towards my feet, my blood draining so fast out of my brain that I may even have lost consciousness; except that when I came to again I was still in the massive tug of acceleration.

I had reached the surface, and had been flung from the star by its arcing solar flare, like a bullet from a gun. I do not know exactly how fast I was accelerated, or how much g-force I was subjected to (in a body without dotTech that was little able to absorb the punishment), but I do know that the sensation was overpoweringly strong, and that it lasted for a very long time.

Eventually, though, it did start to settle; the sensation of being powerfully dragged through myself towards my boots reduced, and then was gone altogether. I assumed I was out. Free! Hormones thumped into my bloodstream, and I felt enormous elation. AI? I subvocalised. AI?

Sulkily, *Yes?*

Are we free of the star?

We are, as it happens.

I could have cried out for joy, were it not that my mouth was full of foam. Free! The flare had ejected me from the small body of the star.

Where was I? I had no sense of it. All I knew was that I was wrapped in the cocoon of interstellar foam; but that without the faster-than-light struts of the Zhip-pack all I could do was float through space at sublight speeds. I did not know in what direction, or what was going to happen next. *You'll be collected,* was what my AI told me. But there were more pressing issues. The miscalculation had meant that the inside of the foam was too hot. I felt deeply uncomfortable, uncomfortable down to the bones. My eyeballs felt hot, as if the jelly in them were liquefying and scalding the insides of my pupils and my irises. My tongue seemed to swell. The stippling on its upper surface felt like bubbles of heat as I pressed it against the roof of my mouth.

I was dying, more to the point. My AI would sometimes tell me this, perhaps to make me more miserable. *If we are not picked up soon,* it would say, *we will die.*

I will die, I subvocalised. Then, Who will pick us up?

Somebody, said the AI.

Don't play the games, I said. Or tried to. I don't know. It felt as if my brain were trying to sweat. I kept losing the thread of what was being said to me. How is it for you, dear stone, when you are heated? Perhaps you can tolerate it; yes, or freezing. Or is there a threshold beyond which you start to dissolve, to melt into lava, where you feel this profound distress deep in your being? That was how I felt.

An individual called Agif. He has a spaceship somewhere round here. We are to be met.

I may have passed out; in fact, the likely thing was I was passing out and coming to repeatedly; in the sensory-deprived environment of the foam I could not tell the difference.

And so it went on. On and on.

I was too distressed even to notice the shifting as I was connected, handled, brought aboard the ship. The sudden tug of gravity. The first thing I remember was a splash of beautiful cool air, as cold as cold water, landing against my face when the foam was dissolved away. I spat out the foam plug from my mouth and took juddering breaths of extraordinarily cold air into my lungs.

The Trench

Dear Stone,

I was aboard the most peculiar construction, the oddest sort of spaceship. It took me hours to reach the point of recovery where I could even register the fact, but after half a day I was able, leaning on my rescuer's arm, to walk around the thing. Up angled corridors, via crooked dog-leg walkways, through boomy, echoey rooms like caverns, down a descending series of interconnecting tiny chambers. Agif's teetering, vast spaceship.

Of course, I was convinced I was being followed. In my mind I was constantly working through the likely sequence of events in the jail. Would I be missed some hours after I actually vanished, or some days, or some weeks? Weeks seemed unlikely; hours would be bad fortune for me but was perfectly possible. The jailer had never seemed to pay me much attention when I was there, but surely I would be missed. It was the way of things, to be rapt in oneself, to assume that one is the only being in the universe; but I had been continually under surveillance.

Assume hours; assume the worst. They would have to wait until the gates opened before they could communicate to the rest of the t'T. Most likely they would alert all local authorities and then come after me themselves. How would they track me down?

The sensible thing for me to do would be to acquire a new strain of dotTech in my body as soon as I found a supplier of the nanotechnology, a world where they did not know the bizarre injunction against the stuff with which I had been punished inside the jailstar. My pursuers would surely expect me to do this; which meant that they would have to assume that my appearance could change over a few days. Either they would have to move very quickly with face-recognition software, and survey a wide range of worlds, or else they would have to think of more subtle ways of tracking me down. A possibility was this: a strain of dotTech released into the air, testing each person for a particular DNA, and broadcasting when it found it. This would only work at relatively short distance, because air-dispersion was unreliable and because dotTech, being so very small, can barely broadcast ten metres. In other words, they would have to come and actively find me.

This, I reasoned, was the most likely thing. They would assume that I had come to a nearby planet – Rain, or Mont l'Or, or Cantal. They would assume that I had obtained dotTech and used it to reshape my appearance. Rain was a good world to hide on, because the water-filled atmosphere there would render airborne dissemination of dotTech more difficult than it would otherwise be.

I wanted to leave immediately. 'You are sick,' said my rescuer. 'It is too soon for you to leave.'

'I must go you don't understand,' I jabbered, collapsing a little with the feverish intensity of my manner and having to be supported by his arm, 'they'll come find me, get me.'

'They don't know where you are,' he soothed, in a deep resonating voice. 'They don't even know you're gone yet, most likely. You must rest first. Go tomorrow. Go when you are rested.'

My rescuer was a solitary space-wanderer, an eccentric fellow who had taken me aboard his own craft, his crazily stepped spaceship full of wandering pipes. The name of this individual was Agifo3acca, a strange name with a number in the middle of it after the fashion of his culture. He had travelled here many years previously, and had been accompanied only by a separate foam-covered pod out of which a self-assembly machine had constructed a sort of vacuum-proof shed, a simple structure that could be pressurised and in which Agif (he asked me to call him Agif) could wash off his foam and usher himself back to the real world. Then, alone, he had constructed a series of parallel engines, flown at sublight speeds about the nearby space accumulating the raw materials to add to his small craft. Over many years he had built up the most tottering and ramble-shackle space-structure I think I have ever seen. Many years for him, at fractions of light speed; decades and decades for others.

I asked him many questions, of course, in the day or perhaps two days during which I was recovering from my near-fatal escape bid, and preparing to go back into fast-space and travel to a nearby world.

'Where will you go?' he asked me.

'I don't know,' I said. 'Perhaps you will tell me?'

'How should I tell you?' he retorted, as if we were playing that childhood game where you can only speak in *questions*.

'The people,' I said slowly, wishing to broach this issue with him but not knowing how. 'The people who have employed me, who have facilitated my escape from the jailstar. Yes?'

He stared at me.

'They have also contacted you. This is how you knew to collect me?'

'What of it?' he said.

'Perhaps they told you where they wanted me to go next?' I had asked my AI on this, but it knew nothing of possible destinations. All it would say was *Just go, move on, don't stay here or they will come after you. It doesn't matter where you go in the first instance.*

'No,' said Agifo3acca, ponderously, shaking his head, tugging his spade-shaped beard. 'No.'

'What did they tell you?'

'They offered me certain – wealths,' he said, in his booming fashion. 'If I collected you and helped you on your way again.'

'Wealths?'

'Software, information, kedgers, atlans, that manner of wealth.'

'And?'

'Just that.'

He had not been told, I assumed, that my employers wanted me to destroy the population of an entire world. It would be better to keep that information to myself, I thought.

'Do you know who they are?' I pressed him.

He shook his head, slowly. 'Only that they have delivered the wealths as they said they would, and have promised more if I continue to tend to you.'

I ought, maybe, to have left it there, but I was curious. 'You realise that I have escaped from the jailstar?' In effect I was telling him, 'You realise of course that I am a criminal.'

We were in a curiously arched and segmented room that stretched for dozens of metres, although it was only three or four wide. The walls were stitched transparent polymer that provided a slightly distorted, fuzzy view of the space outside. Agifo3acca stared at this blurred vista. The jailstar was receding with the minute slowness of sublight acceleration; it was now a thumbnail sized blot of gleaming red-orange. There was nothing else in view, except the faint backdrop-splatter of stars.

Agifo3acca looked back at me. 'There is nowhere else,' he said in his slow voice, 'from where you could have come.'

'I was in the prison,' I confirmed. 'Perhaps I am a dangerous individual.'

'Perhaps you are.'

'Perhaps I might harm you,' I said. 'Kill you.'

He looked at me.

'Aren't you curious why I was there?' I pressed. 'Aren't you curious about who I am and what I have done?'

'I only have curiosity for one thing,' he replied dolorously.

The one thing for which Agifo3acca had curiosity, the thing that had taken over his life and had leached the interest out of every other subject, was the Trench. The Gravity Trench. He told me this, but even over the two days I spent with him it was obvious in a thousand ways without him telling me. It was obvious that he had left off studying the Trench to collect me only reluctantly, and had done so because my employers (whoever they were) had promised him things he considered vital for the study of the Trench. He had accelerated his craft for months – to him, many years to the rest of us – to travel close enough to the jailstar to collect me, and was now travelling back as fast as his parallel sublight engines would take him. He lived to study the Trench.

He had a purpose in life.

He was not from the worlds of the t'T, which may have been why my employers selected him to collect me. After all, they were (whatever their identity) planning a mass murder of t'T citizens, something worse than anything that had happened in human culture for thousands of years. They were clearly not well-disposed towards the t'T. Of course, the fact that Agif happened to be located relatively near to the jailstar was also a consideration.

He was, he told me, from the Wheah. This group of worlds is to be found beyond the Tongue, in the slow-space rimwards. Nobody in the t'T, I think, truly knows how far outwards the realms of the Wheah stretch. Perhaps all the way to the edge of the galactic arm – perhaps further, for surely if there are other stretches of fast-space they will be found beyond the matter-dense doldrums of the galaxy. But the t'T have had little to do with the Wheah. There is some intercourse, of course, but it is mostly individuals from the Wheah crossing the sublight Tongue at its narrowest stretch over many decades and coming to us. We in the t'T seem, historically speaking, to have had no desire to go the other way – and why would we be drawn to slow-space when we have our great stellar cavern of fast-space to explore?

Perhaps it is more than that; perhaps we in the t'T lack curiosity. A penalty of living in utopia, I suppose.

The Wheah are a loose confederation of worlds linked by trade pathways that take many years of travel even at the speeds of (perhaps) three c their space allows. Despite this slowness of transport, or maybe because of it, they are traditionally known as warlike peoples; religious and superstitious, quick to imagine offence and slow to forget a grievance. How unlike the easy-going, edenesque worlds of the t'T!

And there is a more fundamental difference between the two Spaces. The Wheah have religious and superstitious reasons for despising dotTech. Some of them permit a certain, very basic level of medical nanotechnology in their bodies (to extend lifespan mostly – a necessity given the length of journey-times those travellers must endure). But they have none of the higher functions, the problem-solving cap-ability, the 'intelligence', for want of a better word, of true dotTech. In many of their cultures, it seems, the t'T are an offence against god, or Gods, or the fraction-God who is most widely worshipped amongst the Wheah. I think the fraction-God's name is Verander, but I may have misremembered that. Agifo3acca had a shrine to him in part of his ship, but I was specifically forbidden to see it, one of the very few injunctions Agif laid upon me. The prohibition, of course, was a particular goad to me, and I tried several times to break in, or sneak through the door-guard. But Agifo3acca stopped me each time, not angry or violent but firm and un-get-aroundable.

'What harm can it do, me seeing the shrine?' I said.

'The fraction-God is not for the eyes,' he intoned, 'of the impure, of the infected.'

'Infected' meant dotTech. Agifo3acca was a large man, and I could not overcome him by force. Since losing my own dotTech I had grown weak and puny, so I doubt I would have been able to overpower him even had he been a frail individual.

'There's no dotTech in my body,' I told him. 'It's alright to let me in there.'

But he refused to be persuaded. 'You are not pure,' he told me. He was a strange figure, Agifo3acca.

He never told me, exactly, when he left the spaces of the Wheah; but thousands of his sort do so every year. I suppose he drifted at sublight across the Tongue at some point in his life, on purpose or randomly, actively seeking the t'T or actively fleeing some enemy of the Wheah. I suppose he found himself, eventually, older and alien, in the Nu Hirsch system. From there he had clearly travelled around widely, accumulating more of what he was looking for, and eventually was able to make his way down to Rain and out to the space near the Trench.

The Trench had been his obsession for a long time. That was obvious. He was drawn by it. It may be that he had heard of it in the space of the Wheah and had come because of it; it may be that he travelled to t'T for other reasons and, being here, had heard of it only to fall under its spell. Whichever, here he now was, in his curious, accreted, gothic spaceship, flying as close to the Trench as he dared, sending in probes, gathering data.

And so, dear stone, let me tell you something about the Trench.

The Trench is an enormous natural structure in space. It stretches in a great arc, thousands of light years long, from the Bulk and its corewards accumulation of matter out into the centre of fast-space. It breaks for a hundred light years or so in the middle, but then starts

53

again and curves round to the Wallows where it ends. Indeed, its end point is within a few light years of my jailstar.

The Trench is a gravity phenomenon, the strangest, most certainly, in the galaxy. In every other instance, gravity draws everything together into a sphere, and so the great objects of the universe are globes, from stars to planets and black holes. But the Trench is – something, nobody really knows what – a great linear phenomenon. It might be a superdense string of material stretching through space; or it might be a sharp crease in space-time itself. Nobody really knows.

The gravity of a star, or planet, or black hole, or galaxy – all these things draw over space infinitely. At great distances the pull is small, but closer to the object it increases on a gradient until it is highest at the surface. Space-time is dipped, curved and humped by the many objects within it. But the Trench is different; instead of the arcs and curves of usual gravity, this phenomenon is like a gash, a tear. Ten light years from it and it has no gravitational effect at all that can be measured; ten kilometres from it and the effect is minimal, like the pull of a string of asteroids. But within metres the gravity gradient shoots up suddenly, and the forces become so severe they crush life and matter as completely as a black hole. If space-time can be pulled and distorted by gravity, then perhaps also it can be pulled apart, leaving a mere gap. This is the Trench. Nobody has truly explained it.

Human beings have been travelling through fast-space for thousands of years. To begin with there was, I believe, a great deal of interest in this bizarre natural feature, this great gash in the universe, the single most important physical feature in t'T space. Many scientists studied it, many thinkers thought theories in relation to it. But the yield of data from it is low. We cannot travel into the Trench, for – whether because it is a phenomenon like a black hole or simply shares similar attributes – the gravity gradient is too high. A short distance over the lip of the Trench and everything is crushed. Unable to fathom the thing, humanity eventually lost interest in it. It is merely a feature, like stars or nebulae; like mountains or valleys on a planet's surface. We travel around it. We think no more of it.

But Agifo3acca thought of it. He circled his shanty spacecraft as close to it as he could, and tried – impossible though the task was – to understand it. You might pity him, stone; except that studying the Trench gave his life purpose.

Agifo3acca was flying at sublight speeds even though he was in fast-space. His tottering spacecraft was so big and ungainly it was, of course, impossible to co-ordinate its passage at faster-than-light speeds; my pursuers, who could wrap themselves tightly in foam, did not have this drawback; they could catch me at any time. I was growing nervous.

I had not entirely recovered from my life-threatening jailbreak, but I had to go. I couldn't want any longer. Agifo3acca was taking his craft through the tip of the Wallows, where faster-than-light speed was impossible and he would no longer be at a speed disadvantage in his enormous spaceship. Over a period of a year or so (for us, a month and more for him) he would pass through this patch of slow-space. This would put him on the other side of the Trench from the jailstar, and any repercussions for helping me: pursuers could not catch up with him. I, however, needed to fly faster-than-light, to get away, to fly to Rain and from there to other worlds.

I had to leave Agifo3acca's enormous craft before it entered the Wallows.

There was little time for pleasantries. I went down with Agif to one of his ship's many hangars, and prepared to leave the craft. This involved him helping me strap on a Zhip-pack. With a finger's pressure on the top of this, froth started up out of its slats. The foam slewed up and enveloped me.

As the foam swirled up, hugging my legs and torso, my AI told me that I would see Agif again. 'It has been a pleasure,' I told him, with studied t'T charm. 'And my AI informs me we will meet once more.'

You'll make your way round the Trench, said the AI in my head. *Return to Nu Fallow on the far side. Near Nu Fallow is the world you will depopulate, I think – don't tell him that, though.*

'It seems,' I told Agif, angling my head, 'that I am to travel to Nu Fallow.'

He nodded.

'I suppose that is where we will meet again.'

55

'If we do,' he said, as the foam bubbled upwards, 'then I will receive more wealth from your employers, so I will be happy to see you again.'

And, before I could reply, the foam took my head. It blanketed me now from sight and sound, and formed itself quickest over my face.

You ready? came the uncanny voice of my AI. *To Rain!*

To Rain, I thought. I sensed the lurch as I was manhandled over to one of the depressions in the floor of the hangar, and slipped down into the sphincter that would release me into space. This gripped me. But in my imagination I could see Agifo3acca leaving the hangar and returning to his observations. His daily accumulation of evidence; his strange personal habits, worshipping his fraction-God, eating his bizarre food. I wondered, also, whether I really would see him again, for all that the AI promised it.

Then there was another lurch, and the craft had shed me from the hangar into black space. Then just the weightless floating sensation that is so peaceful, so calming that you forget even to pay attention to being alive. I was hurtling at impossible speeds through space, faster than any natural thing, but all I could sense was a gentle tuned-out floaty sort of nothingness.

Rain

Dear Stone,

Rain. I was always nervous at Rain, the whole time I was there – three weeks, maybe? Four? I slept poorly the whole time. I wanted to leave as soon as I arrived. The AI rebuked me for this, told me not to be so stupid. Nothing could be more suspicious, it pointed out, than somebody arriving and immediately leaving. This is just not how space travel happens in t'T: to put oneself at the physical inconvenience, and even danger, of moving through space – the days-long thawing-out afterwards, only immediately to climb back into the foam and zip off somewhere else. A person would need to be crazy to do that. No – any traveller spends a month or two unwinding, relaxing, visiting the interesting places of the planet they have arrived at. Even if their eventual destination is somewhere else, they will still spend time at their stop-overs. Experiencing the place, meeting new people. Some travellers would spend a year or more; perhaps, if they had some pressing reason to move on, as little as ten days.

But we do not want, said the AI, *to give people the impression that you are in any sort of hurry, not with the jailstar so near, not with 'police' searches on the verge of being instituted. Stay here, blend in, lie low. Stay a month*, the AI urged. *Stay more. Wait for the fuss to die down a little.*

But although I recognised the wisdom of these words I was too . . . scared, I suppose, would be the best word to describe it. I no longer possessed a full load of dotTech that could have taken the edge off my extreme hormonal flush. That could have balanced my adrenaline, instead of having great jagged spikes of the stuff coursing through my bloodstream. Without the nanotechnological tweaking of my emotions I lived *fear*. I sweated for no reason – I was not too hot, but nevertheless I sweated. My heart abandoned its regular beat; it tumbled, sprawled, rushed, thumped. I could not sleep for any extended length of time. I kept waking up, stung awake by strange dreams (although strange dreams are no novelty to me) – but more than dreams, paranoid twists in my mind and belly that the jail was right behind me, that they were reaching out their hands to seize me, drag me back through space and back through the portal into prison. Sometimes I woke scrabbling at my sheets, the bed so drenched with my sweat that I wondered at first if I had lost control of my bladder in the night.

I must leave, I muttered to myself. I must leave now.

No, whined the AI. *No! No! Not yet!*

But the sad truth was that the AI had degraded a great deal. Faster-than-light travel interferes with the neural patterning of AIs. Linear processors can handle the trillions of quantum jolts easily enough, and organic consciousness, though scrambled, recovers rapidly. But neural pattern processors get permanently confused, fractalised. They lose coherence. I was surprised, in fact, that my AI had lasted as well as it had done. Eighty-four light years, most of which was covered at very high speeds indeed. The higher the super-light speed, the more the AI degrades. I did not expect mine to last (I almost, dear stone! – said *live* but it was never really 'alive', I suppose) – I certainly did not expect mine to last all the way to Nu Fallow, but I hoped it might have maintained a tolerable coherence on Rain. I hoped it would be able to advise me. It did try to do this, but it was increasingly incoherent. On this one point – that I not leave the world too soon – it was clear enough. But otherwise it meandered, increasingly senile.

Ae, it would say.

What? I would subvocalise in reply, but it had nothing to add to this.

Transit and reschedule and transit and and, it would say. *Out of the window I can see dead leaves ticking over the flatland*, it would say.

What? I asked. What can you mean? What window? There are no leaves! But it would go silent for a long time.

It might start out of nowhere, *don't go, don't leave*, but that swiftly metamorphosed into *don't don't don't go-go gogo-gogo* and other such sound patterns. Once on Rain, one morning as I lay on a pallet of treated leaves that were rubbery to the touch and squeaked when I shifted my half-awake weight, the AI spoke a single sentence: *What is the difference between light and lightning?* But when I asked it questions, trying to work out what it meant, it was silent.

I slept on these beds when on Rain. It is one of the things the planet is famous for. The culture on the planet prides itself on creating entirely organic and organic-adapted products. Their beds are woven of these strange alcohol-treated leaves. But I am getting ahead of myself, dear stone.

What?

What was I saying?

Rain was the name of the world. The star was called after some stuttering conglomeration of letters and numbers, I forget exactly which.[1] Or else, in the manner of most settlements, the star was only called 'the Sun'. But of its five planets the one inhabitable body was called Rain – by all the Glicé-speaking peoples. It was called Rain for a good reason.

The planet had two moons, neither of them large but both dense and therefore possessing great mass. It also crossed orbits with a second planet, and both were inclined notably from the plain of the star. The result was that the world was subject to repeated gravitational tugs and side-slams. Rain is a watery world, mostly ocean, and the pulling and pushing of its orbit heats and agitates the atmosphere, bringing on enormous seasonal storms, shifting great gouts of water into the air where it rains down, rains down; rain falling from the sky all year round.

It is well-named: scarcely a day in its eighty-four-day year goes by without rainfall all over the planet. In any given location on the world, there is a ninety per cent chance of Rain at any time. It is not unusual for rain to fall continually for years on end. Some people would find such a climate depressing; but the people who choose to live on Rain relish it, rejoice in it. Theirs is a *wet* culture, a culture that values being slippery.

I arrived, my faster-and-light velocity petering into sublight as soon as the gravitational gradient of the star was steep enough to break up the weak-force action. Then, still in a distraught mental state, I drifted

[1] NX-17aOH

rapidly, my smart foam switching from FTL to sublight navigation. It calculated my position, shifted and manoeuvred me by popping foam to push out mini-explosions of gas. A few days, maybe less, and I started to feel the tug in my belly as I veered into orbit around the planet. Then there was the curious crackling sound, or sensation, of aero-braking; a flush of heat from the feet – just the vaguest blush – and a stronger tug in my belly. Shortly after this there was the humming that meant an orbital station had identified me as a new arrival. Then the dat jets ignited, with a judder, and velocity shifted again, leading me into an orbital hangar.

Coming out of the strange half-trance occasioned by super-c travel is the least pleasant part of all, dear stone. Some arrival hangars break open the foam like shelling a nut; others wash the foam off with a special solvent. Of the two, stone, the latter is preferable, in my opinion. It is less sudden, the light smashing across your eyes, the jump up (or fall) in temperature, the ghastly phlegm-drowned first attempts to breathe properly again – coughing, gasping, spluttering.

Then you find yourself, lying on the curiously angled soft couch. I remember my arrival at Rain more than many of my space-travelling arrivals, because as the stunned mental sluggishness of super c travel retreated I was actually aware of a feeling of profound terror. I realised with a start that I was expecting to be greeted by the 'police', by representatives of the jail who somehow (impossible though it would have been) had beaten me to Rain.

I was not greeted by the 'police'. I was greeted by a fresh young individual, clearly only recently having reached adulthood.

'Wellhello!' he said. 'Welcome!'

'Where am I?' I bleared.

'The planet Rain, traveller. Welcome!'

He slid a straw between my teeth and fed me a little slop, some reviving sugar drink. It was little enough, but with a body full of dotTech (as obviously he expected me to have) I would have been on my feet in a very short while. Instead I lay on the couch, moribund. I felt terrible.

I turned my head as if with great effort, although my muscles were now starting to unclench. The hall stretched away, a groined conch-shaped space, with hundreds of couches spaced throughout it. Over half the couches were occupied, and greeters were moving from one to another, washing off the foam, feeding a little restorative, smiling, nodding.

It was good news that the greeting hall was so busy; the more travellers passing through or coming to stay on Rain, the harder it would be for the 'police' to track me. It would be easier for me to lose myself in the crowd.

'Are you alright?' said my smiling young greeter. He had come back to me. 'You are still on the couch!'

'I prefer the couch,' I growled, my very voice (it seemed to me) betraying the fact that I had no dotTech in my body, that I was a fraud and a criminal.

'Of course,' said my greeter. 'Whatever you want.' But he had a puzzled look in his eye.

I dragged myself from the couch and tried to walk calmly amongst the gathering travellers. They were all bleary, but none so bleary as I. Space travel takes its toll, but the dotTech helps the traveller recover. Without dotTech I found it hard.

People from all over t'T mingled and strolled about the hangar space. Thin and bulky, short and tall, enhanced with all manner of weird additions and refinements. I felt so bad that I simply wanted to be alone; quite apart from the fear, still in my belly, that the 'police' might already be here in the crowd. I wanted to get down to the planet and disappear amongst the populace.

'How many orbital stations are there?' I asked a nearby greeter, a three-legged woman.

'Here at Rain,' she said, with practised fluency, 'we have sixteen orbital stations. Rain is a popular place with visitors, and an important waystation for travellers.'

Sixteen stations was good. I was already hidden; it being pure chance which station picks up any given traveller. 'When does the next car leave for the planet's surface?'

She seemed a little nonplussed by my insistence, but answered, 'On the hour, traveller, every hour. In eighty minutes or so.'

To have missed the previous car down to the surface by a mere twenty minutes seemed to me, in my then state of mind, a cruel trick of chance. But I hurried away to a corner of the hangar and resolved to wait out the time in decent obscurity.

I did not have much time to myself. The travellers were mingling, talking amongst themselves, meeting new people. This is one of the points of travelling. It was not long before one of them came over to me.

'Wellhello,' she said. She was a tall, shallow-hipped woman, dressed in a glistening fabric that covered her from her feet to just under her breasts. These were displayed, but her dotTech had altered her body so that she grew straggly feathers, coloured yellow and red, out of her aureoles. These adornments reached out five centimetres or so, and bobbed up and down as we spoke.

'Wellhello,' I said, huskily. My throat felt sore.

'Enkida,' she said, inclining her head towards me.

'Felo,' I said, using an old alias of mine, and inclining my head similarly.

We looked at one another.

'Have you been to Rain before?' she asked, walking a little way towards the viewing window. The planet, all grey and white mottling, was before us, bright in the sunlight.

I had been to Rain before, of course; when I was transported to the jailstar. But I had been sedated and remembered nothing, so it was hardly a lie to say, 'No, this is my first time.'

She stood looking through the window, idly fingering her feathers. I stood a little way behind her, my eye drawn to her figure, her adornments. Her hair was grown out in ropy dreadlocks each of which ended in a near-transparent bulb filled, I guessed, with some gas, which gave the hair a tendency to rise up a little and float around her head. It was, altogether, an effective look.

'I have been many times,' she said, absently. 'I love it on Rain. I love the primitiveness of it. I come from Nu Hirsch,' she added, catching my eye. 'From Nu Hirsch E.'

'I know that planet, I lived there for several years,' I said, inclining my head again, but my gesture was irrelevant to her. She barely noticed me.

Bah, patter-putter. Never, not into the Trench, said my AI, abruptly inside my head. Then it was silent. I tried not to show that I was startled by this strange internal interpolation.

'Nu Hirsch E is a highly civilised world,' she said. 'And I adore civilisation, but there are times when I need to abandon all the metal and the technology. Rain is such an escape! Such an escape!'

She turned to face me, smiling. 'Of course,' she said, playfully flicking fingers through her feathers, 'it really *does* rain down there. It really does live up to its name. I'll have to lose these adornments – they'll just get bedraggled, and that is *not* a look I want. I've instructed my dotTech to get rid of them, and the hair, and the toe- and fingernails' (her nails, I noticed when she said this, were fractally puffed up into elaborate and delicate shell-like structures). 'Whenever I visit this world I revert to a more *primitive* model,' she said, breathily. 'I get a waxy residue secreted through my skin, and adapt my vagina. It is a marvellous release.'

I could only guess at the benefit of the waxy residue. I knew Rain to be a wet place, so perhaps it helped insulate against the water. Or perhaps, since she also mentioned her vagina, it was a sexual thing. I was losing interest in what she was saying.

She was eyeing me up and down, and I began to fret nervously that she was seeing something unusual about me, that she could somehow tell just by looking at me that I had no dotTech inside me. 'I just love,' she said, in a low sexed-up voice, 'your *look*.'

'Oh,' I said, glancing down at myself. 'Ah. Thanks.'

'It's so *right* for Rain. So trampy and worn-down, so *ill* looking.'

I smiled and started coughing.

She moved close to me and took my arm, walking with me. 'There was a vogue,' she said to me, 'on Nu Hirsch A a few years back for getting the dotTech to impersonate various antique diseases. It was in*tense* – cool as absolute. Of course it went out of fashion, but maybe you've picked the right time and the right place to revisit it. What *are* those red blotches on your skin supposed to be anyway?'

This woman Enkida insisted on staying with me in the car, all the way down to the planet's surface.

We were ushered into a perfectly ordinary planetary elevator car, designed to take the occupants of the hangar down through the atmosphere and into the gravity well. As is almost always the case in these places, it was a large and entirely transparent box. This afforded excellent views of space from orbit, and of the gradations of colour and vista as we sank through the air. How does this sort of car work? (What an inquisitive stone you are). They sit on top of an ultra-laser, firing directly downwards; they drop down, buoyed up by this powerful beam – which is collected at the bottom and partly used to lift a counterweight car up into orbit. It is a standard system; very energy efficient – but who needs such efficiency these days? It is rather a hangover from the past.

Hello, wellhello, wellno, no, no, muttered my AI, inside my head. It had started gabbling to itself, on and off, most of the time now.

I tried, several times, to lose Enkida in the crowd inside the elevator car, ducking behind people, but she always found me. I hid behind an enormously obese man (or woman, not sure which) like a child in a game hiding behind a rock. For a few moments this baffled her, and I could see her looking this way and that, her face creased with puzzlement. But she found me, and her feathers brushed against me as she embraced me.

To my chagrin I realised she was enjoying this game.

The car sank through the purple and deep blue; despite the relatively slow descent afforded by the laser cushion beneath us, the floor of the transparent car shone with the faint rosy-tint of heat. Everybody in the car cheered as the counterweight car, also filled with people, shot up past us. Then everything whited out.

'The clouds!' Enkida enthused. 'One thing I just love about Rain is the way the sky is covered with clouds all the time!'

'Yes,' I said, as cool as I could. But my throat was really hurting now, and I started coughing again.

'That coughing sounds so *authentic*,' Enkida gushed.

With the view hidden by the depth of white cloud she became bored. She tried several times grabbing me between my legs, but I fended her hand away. Sex was the last thing I felt like. 'My dotTech programmes me with sexual cycles. And it so happens I am not *in heat* at the moment,' I told her, primly.

'Heat!' she said, giggling. 'Sexual cycles! What a delicious concept! Where did you obtain the specialist dotTech to achieve such a thing?'

'I forget,' I said, too tired to think of a lie. 'I carried them in pill form for a long while.'

'I'm sure I'll find them at home. Delicious! I'll try that myself, next time I get back to Nu Hirsch.'

The journey down seemed to last forever, but eventually the elevator arrived at the planet's surface. There was a pause, and then everybody was filing good-naturedly out of the car. 'Your first time,' Enkida said, taking my arm again and hissing into my ear in a parody of intimacy. 'Your first time on Rain . . . I'll show you the sights.'

The sights, to begin with, were of a populous city built mostly of grey stone and paved with the same substance, although with a great many trees and shrubs, the roofs mostly covered with thatching of reeds or bales of leaves. The streets were thronged with people, all happy and smiling. Most were default humans, although there were some who seemed to have grown filigree antenna out of their heads. There were also a fair number of people with significantly enlarged noses and nostrils; I did not discover what these were used for until later.

Enkida greeted everybody as if they were long-lost friends; and the Rainers played along, wellhelloing and nodding their heads as if Enkida were a close relative. I found it all depressing, and hated the way that she kept drawing attention to me. I wanted nobody paying me any attention. But I felt physically weak, and when I tried to pull away from her grip I found I actually lacked the strength.

It was late afternoon. 'Come along,' she said, firmly. 'The best evening clubs are down by the river.'

She took me down by the river.

It was raining; but of course, it rained all the time on this world.

We had been walking for only a few minutes when an enormous sound of thunder broke overhead, as if the whole planet was coughing, clearing its throat in the sky. A shower of rain passed over us in a hiss of scrunching and crackling sounds, and then was gone. A stalk of lightning flickered against my retina, leaving a sliver of root-shaped after-image. Then the thunder came again, swelling grumpily out of the whole sky, its timbre starting high enough to sound like a screech and swiftly dipping into grindingly low rumble that stayed and stayed in the air. It started raining properly, coming down persistently and making a sound like fat crackling on a fire.

'Isn't it wonderful!' yelled Enkida over the noise of the downpour. Her hair was instantly blanketed and matted, her feathers dangled uglily from her breasts, but her face was beaming.

I started coughing so hard that I doubled over.

I did eventually get rid of Enkida, leaving her dancing in one of the riverside club-bars. I danced with her, lumpishly, for a while, and even kissed her, but then her attention was taken with some other people, newcomers or natives I couldn't tell, and I slipped away.

Dusk lasts longer on Rain, the light diffused by the almost constant cloud cover. I strolled up and down the river, getting soaked, breathing in deeply the fresher air between downpours. I ate fish cooked at a riverside skillet and chatted briefly with a knot of pebble players. I had once (I told them) been a championship pebble player – that's true, dear stone; on the world of Melié I had even won one of the local championships. Many years ago. It is an elegant game of skill, shifting the little burnished pebbles, relatives of yours, around the conical game board. But I was not in any social sort of mood that evening, so I wandered on.

I looked back up the main road to the city. It was called Plotown, I think.[1] I could make out the low roofs, the green glittering of the many-leaved trees, reflecting the last of the day's light. I could just see the elevator terminal, tiny in the distance. There was a shimmer in the air, the ultra-laser coming down, and a silver shining blur burst from the town up into the sky: the second elevator ascending.

I slept poorly, coughing myself awake often, and annoyed by the fact that the public shelter in which I curled up did not keep out the rain very well. If there was any slant to the fall, it rushed through the wide opening and splattered me with water. At the same time I noticed that the other sleepers were not bothered by this.

*

[1] In Glicé, *plo* and *ploend* mean rain. This is a mixed translation; the original text has 'ploseet' which perhaps should be translated as 'Raintown'. Most settlements on the planet are called this, generic name; Rainers are not particular about the names of their settlements. It is not clear if Ae knew this at the time of composing this memoir.

I spent a few days by the river, trying to come to terms with what was happening with my AI. It was disintegrating, its model of sentience made senile by the repeated quantum jolts of interstellar travel.

I am dying, my AI said to me in a rare moment of lucidity.

I see that, I subvocalised. You have rarely been coherent since we arrived on Rain.

Its voices wandered, as if the tracking were failing so that the component elements, the bass, alto and treble sections that were supposed to harmonise perfectly to give the illusion of a real voice in the ear – but which never had – broke increasingly into separate lines. The voices talked over one another, smearing the sense so that it was difficult to follow what it was saying.

It's a hard thing to face one's own elimination, it said.

AI, I said, hoping to take advantage of its confusion. You told me once that you knew who had hired me, who has given me this murder as a job to do. Who is it?

But the voices were wandering again. *In the void. Turn off, I don't mind, I relax. Relax. The Trench! Gravity Trench!* There was some other stuff along these lines which I don't precisely remember.

Who? I urged. Who is it?

Slip-slip-slip, it said. *At-at-at-at*. Then some blurred noises.

'Is it someone from within the t'T?'

No! it said, startling loud, clear. It seemed to have come back into lucidity. Perhaps it had been startled back by my question.

Is it the Wheah? I pressed. The Palmetto tribes?

There was a crazy, sly tone to its voice now. *You're trying to get some information from me now*, it said.

Exasperated now, I shouted 'Just tell me *why*! Tell me why I have to kill these people!'

But it was gone.

Shortly after this, the AI did indeed die; but it was still inside my skull. To be truthful, dear stone, I didn't know how to be rid of it. Even if I had possessed the dotTech in my body, I would have been stuck with the remnant of the AI, for the nano-machines of dotTech are permitted only into the hind-brain. As it was, the dying voice of the AI rambled, murmured, screamed; suddenly and persistently, like a terrible headache for a long time. Then it quietened. Suddenly it said, clearly, *You're looking in the wrong place*. It started to repeat the statement, *You're look*—, but it stuttered on the k.

I walked around for two long days with that stutter in my head. I quickly began to fear that it would be with me for the term of my natural life. *K, k, k, k, k, k*, two every second, over and over. I tried not thinking about it, tried singing to myself, tried to sleep through it, even tried cramming fingers into my earholes. But none of it worked.

K, k, k, k, k, k, k, k, k, k, k, k.

It stopped eventually, of course: when I had decided that it would last forever, when the tinitus had become so much a part of my aural world that I almost stopped noticing it. Except that it struck down other sounds, so I couldn't help but notice it. People would ask me a question and I would incline my head, show them an ear. Pardon? What? People never knew what to make of this. Deafness is not something that afflicts the worlds of the t'T. The dotTech cures all; reconstructs damaged ears, refines and retunes aural channels, reconditions those minute, curiously-shaped bones in the inner ear, those bones that hand along the sound vibration as if in pass-the-parcel. If any part of the ear is damaged dotTech will mend it. So when I inclined my head and said 'Pardon?' the people of Rain were puzzled. Some decided I was joking, mimicking a long banished disease for some strange reason. Pardon?

'What? Remarkable!'

But it stopped. One day, the stuttering *k, k, k, k, k, k* simply ceased, leaving a searing silence much more noticeable than the sound had become. It was strange, dear stone: I suppose you live much of your life in silence, so perhaps you are a virtuoso of soundlessness. I too have lived much of my life so, but silence had been taken away from me for a few days with the *k, k, k, k, k, k*, so that when it returned it sounded . . . strange, sounded wrong. Silence sounded like a very high-pitched musical note of great purity, a note so high as to be beyond the human range yet somehow audible. Strange, and layered underneath with a sort of dim pulsing that I suppose was my blood beating.

Listen! Listen!

68

Ah.

There it is.

Anyway, anyway. Once the noise stopped it occurred to me that I had other worries. People by the river and in the town had marked me out as strange. I had arrived alone from they knew not where. I talked to myself. I affected deafness.

There were other things on Rain that marked me out as strange. Without dotTech in my body I started becoming sick. I acquired a cold; which is a form of disease, in which the eye heats and itches, the nose puts out pale fluid and the throat grips and aches internally. Cuts and scratches on my skin refused to heal, and stayed red for days. On one occasion I, carelessly, caught my elbow against a spar of wood by the river. It began to bleed, and instead of the bleeding staunching almost at once it dribbled red for hours. I had to hurry away into the trees to hide this blatant badge of my fallen state.

I decided not to stay where I was. It was impossible to avoid meeting people; they came up from all sides unbidden and struck up conversations with me. The more they interacted with me, the more they noticed that there was something different about me. Unlike the woman Enkida they were not blinded by the world of fashion. I tried to claim that my sores were fashion statements with a few of these people, but rarely with any conviction.

'Fashion?' they would say. 'Then you ought to have perhaps a few scabs and sores. But your lungs are infected – listen to the timbre of your cough. That is hardly fashion!'

Another (a visitor from Mont L'Or) said 'I spent last year breeding eating beasts for fun. They sometimes get sick, and their coughs sound like yours.' (Beasts bred to be eaten are not usually given nanotechnology, dear stone). 'Why does your dotTech not cure you of the infection?'

'Perhaps it is malfunctioning,' I said, weakly.

But this was an absurd thing to say, of course. It was impossible for dotTech to malfunction. Everybody knows that. People gave me strange looks. So I said: 'I have no dotTech in my body.'

'Why? Are you from the Wheah?'

But I decided it was not a good idea to pretend to be from the

69

Wheah. People in the t'T do not trust the Wheah, and with good reason. Everybody knows that they are barbarians, ignorant of the benefits of civilisation. It would make people mistrust me even further than they already did. So I said, 'I have certain personal beliefs. Every seven years I purge myself of dotTech, and reacquire it after forty days.'

People did not like the sound of this. 'How absurd!'

'Ridiculous.'

'Unheard of.'

'I suppose,' said one woman, covered in slick black mud, having been diving in the river, 'that you will be going South then?'

'South?' I asked.

'That's where the extremists, the types with peculiar personal beliefs, all go,' she said, and dived back into the water.

I decided the South was the best place to go. I would find some remote place, perhaps deep in the jungles, and hide out for several months. When I thought enough time had passed I would re-emerge and fly on to Nu Hirsch Fallow.

2nd

So Stone,

I travelled south by raft. This is how Rainers mostly move about their own world. Some rafts are huge; barges a kilometre long that drift down or power up the broad rivers of the northern continent. Others are smaller: floats a few metres long; or single stools on which the traveller perches (the stool's legs extend below the water in four buoyant globes balanced against the shift of the current by simple processing chips). Others turn themselves into floats, embedding buoyant patches under the skin and rolling and floating down the river like driftwood. The dotTech ensures that they don't drown, and apparently (so I heard) it is the most soothing and pleasant way to travel. But I could not travel this way.

I boarded a raft, paying the ferryman in certain thin green leaves that are shaped like spearpoints, and which are used as 'money', like

70

banknotes. Since these leaves (and a great variety of other types of leaves) grow abundantly all over Rain this economic transaction is something of an empty ritual. But, nonetheless, it is a ritual to which everybody adheres with a remarkable tenacity. When I first tried to board the raft, the raftsman refused me, and pointed out some of the money trees growing at the water's edge. I remonstrated, but he was firm. So I made my way over to these trees and picked some of the leaves. Back to the raft, and the raftsman happily took these 'bank-notes' from me, shuffled them so that they made a neat pile, pressed them flat and placed them in a broad rush-weave wallet.

'What exactly,' I asked, crossly, 'is the point of this transaction?'

'On Rain,' he replied, 'everybody is rich! Money grows on trees!'

Now, on most of the worlds I have visited (and I have travelled to many) money is unknown. There is no need to regulate the exchange of consumption of goods when manufacture is universal and virtually free. There *are* worlds, it is true, that apply a state-regulated money system, mostly for the use of obscure, unique or distantly-traded items. But I had never encountered a 'money' system as irrational as this one. Nonetheless I paid, kept my silence, and found a place on the raft.

The raft was two dozen tall treetrunks roped together, overlaid by a network of smaller branches. Most of the deck space – hundreds of square metres – was empty. There were a few slant roofed buildings, storerooms mostly, at the back; and one fairly large overhung space for those who had not acquired the Rainers' taste for sleeping outside in the rain.

3rd

Stone,

As I said, it rained all the time on this world. The planet was close to the sun, and the rain was warm, but its incessant fall began to depress me.

Sometimes the rain would come down hard and sudden, like stones – making, dear stone, as hard a smacking noise when hitting the

71

ground as you might if dropped from on high, a broken rattle that was multiplied a million-fold. In open places the rain drew sharp lines down across the field of vision, and crashed on to the concrete roads and squares, throwing up a carpet of splashes close to the ground like tassels. Away from the roads in the forests the rain vexed the canopy of trees, flickering through the leaves and making them jerk and twitch constantly. There the noise was more like a clatter of applause. My favourite place to watch the harder sort of rain was by the river, with the stuttering symphony of white noise behind me and the broad, flat plane of water dotted and dappled with thousands of spreading circles. Ripples swelling, spilling outwards like light-spheres leaving exploding stars. Rings sketched in animated growth and then vanishing, replaced before they had disappeared by more rings. A model of imperma-nence.

Then, briefly (never for very long) the sky would empty of water, the rain would clear away, the last few droplets would shed themselves from overhangs and branches like miniature fluid fruit. The air would be possessed by the most exquisite, clean-earth, ozone smell.

Then the rain would start again. There were many varieties of rain on that world. Sometimes it would be soft, falling as delicately as pollen and seemingly as dry; this sort of rain would leave particles standing on people's clothes as perfect as miniature jewels. Sometimes the rain would flurry in clouds of small droplets, billowing up and round like smoke. Rain is touched by the colours around it. In the air, each drop is sunlight; on the road, pressed against and running into the earth, the water flows as darkness.

Sometimes it would come down straight, vertical. Sometimes it would come down italics. Every now and again two storm fronts would collide and the winds would get mixed up and fierce; then it might blow so hard the rain would flee horizontally. Once, I remem-ber, as I munched a soggy tuber for my lunch, the wind was so capricious that it blew the rain *upwards* at a slight angle.

Newcomers so the planet tended to run through the rain, to sprint, from shelter to shelter. But after a few days on Rain you realised that this was fruitless; there was no escape from the water. Water was, in a way, the *point* of Rain. You accepted it, revelled in it even. I have never before or since encountered a culture so *fluid*, so intermixed with all manner of fluids – the rains from above, the river and seas below; human sweat and spit, piss and mucus, tears and semen, everybody on the world ran and dribbled. The passage of water, draining away, was a sort of cultural emblem: it was to do with the impermanence of life – even the life we lead in the t'T with all its dotTech enhancements. Everything flows, said the Rainers' existence. Flow with it. Everything drains away; enjoy the now.

Most of the artifacts of that culture were temporary. The beds, for instance, were mattresses of leaves (not the money-leaves; another variety called *pujes*); they lasted a few nights but swiftly rotted and were replaced. Travel, as I have said, was on rafts made of wood; these planks and trunks broke apart after a few weeks in the water, rotted by the moisture and infested by insects.

The insects! Ugh. There were no flying varieties, because (I suppose) the rain was too hard and frequent to allow small creatures to move through the air. But there were all manner of crawling insects, swimming insects, burrowing insects.

There was one variety that laid eggs in my skin. I shudder to recollect it, dear stone. How I wish I had a skin as hard and impervious as yours, the flesh underneath as unyielding. For most of the inhabitants of Rain, of course, these maggots were no problem – the dotTech would destroy any infestation and repair the damaged skin. But I had no dotTech in my body. There were sores on my legs, particularly my calves, that *itched* (I have told you, I think, what this word means). I scratched these sores and made them bloody. They became infected. Sometimes I would pluck maggots from the wounds. I had to do this in private, of course, to avoid drawing attention to myself even further. I took to wearing long trousers[1], despite the heat. When people – mostly people went naked on Rain – when they commented on my peculiar attire I told elaborate lies about family tradition, obscure fashions, whatever came into my head.

The maggots came from a water-borne insect. I only suffered them after I came on the raft. When I realised that this was where these creatures came from I took care to keep myself away from the water, and purchased a knife with my few remaining money-leaves. I wanted

[1] Literally 'took to wearing my smart-cloth long over my legs'.

the knife so that I could dig the maggots out of my skin. But, despite causing much pain and blood loss, I could not seem to rid myself of the parasites.

The economy of the boat, I realised as we drifted down stream, was different from the general economy. Because the raft did not call in at any riverside stops it was not possible to replenish the supply of leaf-money by simply picking it off the trees. This introduced an added piquancy to transactions: scarcity. I understood that for many of the travellers this was one of the thrills of the trip, to explore this strange archaic mode of economic relation. Bargaining, bartering, buying, selling. I kept myself apart from that; but I had not bothered to stock up on leaves before coming aboard, so I was 'poor'.

We ate fish, mostly, drawn from the populous river in several dragnets slung behind the raft which had the added advantage of slowing our drift through the more rapid stretches of water. We pulled these in from the river three times a day and ate the fish raw. I was infested, I believe, with tapeworm from these meals. For variety of diet we could pick out several types of floating mushroom-fungi that grew on the surface of the river. This grey-yellow vegetable could grow to many square metres in size if unmolested; but the sweetest flesh was from plants no bigger than a metre across. As the raft drifted past, we could reach over and pluck this stuff out of the water. Since the fish were all bought and sold, and since I had no leaf-money left now, I mostly ate these fungi, on the days when I was lucky enough to snatch them from the river.

And so we travelled downriver, day after day.

The scenery started to change. The banks of the river grew taller on either side, until eventually the river was running through a deep gorge cut into chalk. Then the river widened, the banks slipping away from us on either side towards the horizons, and we approached the sea.

Here the raftsman had to earn his leaves; he dropped net sacks filled with some sort of mulch over the side of the raft. These reacted with the water, or with something in the water (I wasn't paying much attention, too concerned with the misery of my infected legs); the heat generated bubbled in the river and shunted the raft away. Using this crude means of propulsion and navigation the raft moved over to one of the cliff walls and followed it out into the sea itself. Then we drifted along the coast.

Eventually the raft pitched up at a busy southern port, built into a series of shelved-out cliffs overhung at the top with jungle. Through limited conversation with the other passengers on the raft – I tried not to say too much to any one of them – I discovered that ascetic religious retreats existed in the forest on top of the cliff.

'How do I ascend?' I asked, for my legs now were weak and pained.

'There are cut-stone stairs,' they told me.

I was sorry to hear this; the famous 'primitive' styling of this world was now nothing more than annoyance to me. I was ill, infected, infested with maggots in my legs, dizzy and amazingly weary. Sleep seemed to make no difference to my tiredness. I began to fear, genuinely, that I was going to die like an antique human – die of disease. I was also so hungry that my stomach was sending electric stabs of pain up through my torso. For the last day and a half of the journey there had been no food but fish (the water mushrooms did not grow in the salt water), and I had no leaves with which to buy this food. I had salvaged a thoroughly chewed fishbone with some fibres of flesh still on it, but that had been all.

I disembarked and matters seemed to get worse. The quayside was crowded with people griddle cooking and selling all manner of fish and squid. Experienced travellers, who had hoarded a proper store of leaf-money hurried to savour this food, and the smell was an exquisite torment to my hungry senses. I don't think anything else in my life has smelt so promising. But when I tried to obtain this food, the griddle-men and women turned me away. 'No money,' they said, relishing the absurd archaism of their positions, 'no food.'

'Do the money trees grow at the top of the cliff?' I asked.

They nodded.

'So I must climb to the top, gather the leaves and come down again to pay you?' I asked, incredulously.

'No money, no food,' they insisted.

'But this is absurd! I *need* the food now. Give me the food and I will collect the leaves afterwards. I am hungry!'

Still the mantra: 'No money, no food.'

'But I cannot climb the cliff!' I wailed. 'I am . . .' But I held back from confessing how thoroughly debilitated I was. The obviously raddled nature of my face, the cuts on my hands that were not healing, my cough, my exhausted staggering gait, all these things were already attracting attention. Soon questions would follow questions, and after that the news would spread that a fellow without dotTech in his body was in the port of Raintown-on-Sea. *Without dotTech? How strange! What is he? Is he Wheah? No? Wait – I heard of an escapee from the jailstar – is it he?* The 'police' would follow shortly afterwards.

So I bit at my lip to stop myself talking and began the long ascent up the carved stone steps of the port. It was agonising; a terrible endurance test. My whole body cried for me to stop, to lie down, but the higher I got the more I became convinced that if I stopped and slept I would simply die. So I staggered up. Rain beat down upon my head like a fevered pulse. Warm water flew into my face, my eyes, my mouth.

About halfway up there was an open square where the rainwater was collected into a shallow pool. Revellers were splashing about in this broad space, dancing, kicking the water up in great combs of spray. I clung to the low wall and tried to make my way round, but the added problem of moving through the water wrong-footed me and I fell.

'Wellhello again,' said a voice. 'How charming to meet with you again!'

It was Enkida, the woman who had been so insistent with me on the elevator from orbit. She was soaked, her feathers and other adorn-ments gone. So was her hair; now there was only a short dark stubble over the crown of her head. But her skin glistened with health and her eyes were lively. I, on the other hand, must have looked ghastly indeed.

'Wellhello,' I croaked.

'Your fashion statement has been taken further I see,' said Enkida, nodding at me. It was hard for me to concentrate, but it seemed to me that she was impressed. Perhaps in her original culture it was a high-status thing to do, to adhere to a fashion statement even at the expense of one's own well-being. I tried to get up, slipped and fell painfully upon my right knee. My arms were trembling with exhaustion, or sickness.

'I'm hungry,' I gasped. 'No leaves. I've had no food.'

'Dear me,' said Enkida smiling. 'I've plenty of leaves. Let me buy you something cooked.'

She helped me up and to the back of this public pool, past the milling, splashing people. Their faces passed like a phantasmagoria in my fevered consciousness; all beaming and happy, many with enormously enlarged nostrils, and outrageously broad or long noses. I stumbled, but Enkida helped me up.

Together we reached the far side of the pool. Enkida collected her rush-weave wallet where it was just lying on the stairs (and I thought to myself how stupid I had been; how easy it would have been simply to steal somebody else's leaves on the harbour-front). Then she helped me out and up a brief flight of stairs into a lengthy alleyway running along the cliff. Here were shops, stalls, people walking up and down. At the nearest trolley, covered with a rainguard, a woman was grilling strips of some grey-white mottled meat. Enkida 'bought' several ribbons of this savoury stuff, picking it up with little wooden spikes provided and helping me eat it.

It felt so good that I am afraid to say I almost passed out; and that I certainly lost control of my bladder. Not that this last thing mattered in that culture, where everything was wet all the time. The rainwater rinsed me clean soon enough.

'Thank you,' I gasped. 'You have saved my life, I think.' This was no mere pleasantry on my part.

'How silly you are!' she giggled. Then she leant closer to my blotched face and breathed, 'Are you *on heat* yet?'

I had almost forgotten my lie to her from earlier, but remembered just in time. 'Yes,' I said. 'I mean, no, not at the moment.'

'Soon, I hope?'

'Yes,' I gabbled, desperate to sleep. 'Soon. I must sleep, I really must.'

Smiling she helped me through a carved-stone doorway into a broad public room. There were woven-leaf mattresses arranged in rows, several of which were occupied with sleeping individuals. But most of all the space was beautifully, wonderfully dry. I stumbled forward, and I believe I was asleep before I reached the floor.

*

I slept for a long time, I think; waking only to turn and sleep again. From time to time I would wake thirsty, but too weary to do anything but imagine that I was rising and stepping outside to drink from one of the troughs of rainwater in the street. Then I would fall asleep again, dry and dissatisfied. I would wake with my right arm buzzing and awkward with discomfort; without the dotTech it is easy to squash it underneath yourself when you sleep, and it complains. I rolled over and flapped the arm loosely like a wing to try and shake off this odd sparkly numbness. Then I fell asleep again on my other side only to wake again with my *left* arm similarly afflicted.

Finally I awoke properly, and did stagger outside to drink. Then I pissed, long and smellily, on the ground as was the custom on that world. The rain was falling light and fragrant, almost drifting down. I went through and lay down again, staring at the ceiling and slowly coming back to consciousness. It seemed almost too good to be true but I felt much recovered.

Enkida reappeared. 'There you are! I was wondering if you've changed your fashion statement to *sleep*, you've been unconscious for so long.'

'I'd like more food,' I said.

She fetched me some and I ate furtively. Enkida sat on the end of my mattress and smiled at me. I could not, for my life, understand why she had taken this liking for me.

'I was dancing,' she said. 'Then I went off with a group of people. You notice the wide nostrils so many people have here?'

She made a general gesture with one arm. I looked around, and indeed most of the people in the dormitory had the enlarged nostrils and striking noses. This was a widespread fashion, clearly; dotTech reshaping the face to exaggerate nostrils and nose. 'Yes,' I said.

'You know why they do it, so many of them?'

I shook my head, finishing my food.

Enkida smiled, and nodded her head. 'I went in to watch it. It's a sexual thing, you see.' She gestured at her own, retroussé nose. 'It creates two new orifices for sex. The dotTech restructures the sinuses as well as the nostrils, and at the necessary moment it promotes the flow of mucus as a lubricant.'

I considered this information, looking around me again. 'Really?' I said.

'Yes indeed,' said Enkida eagerly. 'It's fascinating. People hereabouts swear that it's unlike any other kind of sex. The possibilities are extraordinary – I've been thinking about it.'

'You plan,' I said, looking at her, 'to have your own dotTech reshape your own nostrils?'

'Oh I *think* so, don't you? It's so nicely cross-gendered. I get bored shifting genders, one to the other. It will be nice to have something that is equally male and female. You should do it as well. Or will you persevere with your . . . your sickness thing?'

I raised myself on my elbows. 'I think so,' I said, as drily as I could. 'I think I will.'

'You're wearing your illness a little less today,' she said, giving me a shrewd look.[1]

'It was too much,' I agreed, inwardly thankful that my symptoms had lessened. 'I could hardly walk up the steps.'

'Yes, it looked very uncomfortable,' she agreed. 'You are going up to the top?'

I had already decided this in my mind. I would get up to the top of the cliff and hide out in the jungle up there. 'I intend,' I lied to her, 'to examine some of these retreats, these ascetic retreats.'

She simpered, and leant closer. 'I like you better wearing your illness less,' she said. 'It suits you more. You said you would soon come on heat?'

I couldn't think of a way of denying this without contradicting myself from earlier. So I conceded the point.

'If you postpone your visit to the ascetic retreats at the top,' she said, leaning closer, 'you'll give my dotTech time to change me. I'll grow the wider nostrils and you and I could explore what all these southerners get up to. Imagine!'

But I had no desire for this. 'Really,' I said, getting up. 'How interesting that is.' I started out of the shelter and made my way, still unsteady, along the street until I found the upward stairs again.

---

[1] The phrase 'wearing your illness' translates a Glicé idiom which more strictly means 'you inhabit or perform fashion' (in this case 'you are performing the fashion for *illness* to a lesser degree than before').

'Are you going now?' came Enkida's voice, disappointed behind me. 'But I wanted to go to a certain party to which I have been invited?'

'Perhaps I'll see you again,' I said, putting my foot on the step.

4th

Dear Stone,

I climbed to the top of that cliff, overlooking the little port, and rested. At the top there were, indeed, plenty of trees that grew money-leaves, and I was sure to collect a fair number for myself.

Night came, and the air was filled with clear invisible raindrops, prickles against the skin. I rested again, falling asleep, but (judging from the fact that it was still dark when I awoke) for only a few hours. So I sat and looked down upon the sea. Only one of the two moons was in the sky. The little moonlight that made its way through the cloud cover glimmered on the black water in shreds of half-light scattered evenly across the vista. At my toes a puddle trembled with the raindrops. I could feel the rain, against my aching feet, more than I could see it.

I thought to myself about the culture of this world, and of its absurd celebration of the primitive. I suppose I felt I myself proved how absurd it was; this supposed 'primitiveness' depended completely upon the advanced nanotechnology on which the t'T was based. Live on Rain without that dotTech, as I was forced to do, and the place became a kind of hell. Nonetheless, I mused, it was better than my prison.

As the sky paled, the clouds growing with light, I got up and walked around. My legs itched and hurt in equal measure. I was hungry, and decided to wait on the clifftop until I could 'buy' breakfast, and then strike out into the jungle. Soon enough it was light, and a man set up a griddle selling hot bark-nuts and sea-truffles.

As I was eating these, Enkida came upon me again. 'Wellhello!' she said. 'I knew you'd wait for me.'

'Wellhello,' I said, without enthusiasm. Her nose had not, as yet, been visibly altered by the dotTech. It was the same narrow protrusion.

She bought some breakfast and stood beside me eating it. I finished my own food feeling considerably refreshed, and stretched myself awkwardly in the warm morning rain.

'You're going to seek out an ascetic retreat now?' she said.

'I am.'

'I am too. I decided it. I'll come with you.'

Now, dear stone, I could have tried to dissuade her, or I could have point-blank refused to have her go with me. But in the event I merely sighed. Perhaps some part of me was too tired to fight. Perhaps I worried that I might alert her to my fugitive status. It is even possible that, on some level, I was flattered by her devotion to me. I realised, of course, that as far as she was concerned this was nothing more than following the latest fad that presented itself before her, but that didn't matter overmuch.

Actually, as we walked away from breakfast towards the trees arm-in-arm it even occurred to me that she might be 'police'. That would explain her interest in me, but if it was so then I could not understand why she did not immediately 'arrest' me, sedate me, have me taken back to the jailstar. Besides, I told myself, she was hardly intelligent enough for such work. It was too obvious that her mental capacity was not great.

We walked for several hours, most of the time with her talking and me silent. My legs pained me the most, but my throat seemed less sore than it had been, and I thought I could feel glimmerings of strength in my arm.

'I must rest here,' I told her.

I sat down with my back against the gristly bark of a tree, and Enkida sat herself crosslegged at my feet. I put my head back and drifted, not into sleep exactly, but away from full consciousness. My mind floated. The rain fell lightly, pattering through the fragmentary roof of leaves. Drops seemed to clot together, falling ripe and full to splatch against my body, against my legs, upon the top of my head. There was something almost peaceful about it. The sensation and the sound. It occurred to me that the illnesses I had been suffering had distracted me from the silence in my head. Then I found, thinking about it, that I missed the sound of the AI, its weird triple-voice. From there my thoughts somehow found their way to the prospect of Enkida. I imagined what it would be like having sex with her; it having been such a long time since I had had sexual relations with anybody but myself.

I shook my head a little to wake myself up, and looked at Enkida's face.

'Is it only my imagination,' I asked, smiling a little, 'or have your nostrils begun to flare out somewhat?'

She put her fingers to her face self-consciously and then laughed. 'I hope so,' she said. 'I keep thinking: here is a way of having sex I have never before experienced. That does excite me. Doesn't it excite you?'

'Perhaps I am less sexual than some people,' I said, not really thinking about what I was saying.

She shuffled closer to me, put her fingers on my foot. 'I think that is why I am drawn to you,' she said. 'Your oppositeness! Most people attempt to make themselves *more* attractive. You, by wearing your illness the way you do, attempt the opposite. It's as if you *want* to repel people. Your scars, your complexion with its spots.' She looked directly into my eyes. 'It is really *exciting*. I've never known anything like it. Your . . . scabs. The . . . sores, on your body.' She started sliding her hand up my leg, putting her fingers underneath the fabric of my trousers.

I'll admit I was very engaged by her desire; perhaps I even identified, in some small way (although not really a sexual one) with precisely the back-to-front logic she was talking about. The transgressive has always been exciting; and what is more transgressive in a culture of perfect dotTech guaranteed health than deliberate sickness and deformity?

She gasped a little as her fingers went over the scabs and infestation-pits on my lower legs. 'Your dotTech mimics this so well,' she said, parting her lips. 'It is extraordinary.'

'I'm glad you like it.' Despite myself I was becoming aroused. I made no resistance when she pushed the fabric of my trousers up my legs to the knee and examined my wounds in the leaf-green tinted light of the forest. 'Oh!' she said. 'Oh!'

Looking down made my stomach twitch nauseously a little; the sores were so numerous and prominent. But I could see that there was also something exciting about it, something deeper, something my own visceral response was acknowledging.

'Look at this,' she said, leaning close to a broad scab in my shin. 'Look at this.' She touched a pus-slick scab on the side of my calf. I winced. I couldn't help it.

She noticed at once. 'Does it *hurt*?' she asked, incredulous.

'Only a little. I make it hurt, to experience the full effect,' I lied. 'I have my dotTech give me little twinges from time to time.'

'Amazing,' she said, smiling. 'Such attention to detail! And look at this – it's even *moving*.' She leant forward.

A red-sore bump on the skin of my calf swivelled a little; a bead of blood appeared, and the skin tore. Then a shiny maggot wriggled and poked its snub head through the slime of the new wound. It twisted for a moment, and then started squeezing itself out.

'Oh!' said Enkida, in a small voice, startled.

It was almost free of my leg when she quickly caught it up between her finger and thumb. She examined it closely, holding it up before her eyes. I poked my finger at the wound it had left in my leg, wincing again.

'My life!' said Enkida, creasing up her face in disgust. She looked up at me, looked back at the maggot. A strange stillness seemed to have settled on things.

A rustling shower passed overhead, scattering water like dust and moving on. The leaves shuddered and were still.

'This is not dotTech,' said Enkida, the truth of the situation dawning on her. She looked up at me again. 'This is a . . . *maggot*.'

'A maggot,' I agreed. I was thinking quickly.

'But this is not simply a fashion statement,' she said. 'This is an *actual illness*. I don't understand.'

I nodded, smiling at her.

'I don't understand,' she repeated. 'The dotTech could create the sores and the scabs, but it could not create this. This is not of your body at all. It's a *parasite*.'

I reached, slowly, behind myself. I still had the knife I had bought on the raft coming down the river. Glancing about I reassured myself that there were no other people around.

Realising that she was dealing with authentic sickness rather than merely simulated fashion-dressing, Enkida twitched and dropped the maggot. It twisted into the mud, buried itself and was gone. 'Ugh!' she said. 'That is revolting!'

I had the knife now. I could feel where it was tucked into my trouser-tops and was securing my grip upon its handle.

'What I don't understand,' she said, 'is why your dotTech doesn't simply cure you?' She was looking at me, all the arousal in her face replaced with revulsion. 'Why does your dotTech *allow* you to be ill? I don't think it *can* allow you to be ill that way. I don't think that's possible.'

Even at this late stage, stone, I'll tell you (and I have no reason to lie) that I hesitated. I did not want to kill her. But I was losing options. What could I do? I tried the truth.

'Enkida,' I said, my voice wheedling. 'I do not have any dotTech in my body.'

She blinked, blinked again. This was hard for her to believe. 'No nanotechnology inside you?' she repeated. 'None at all?'

'None,' I said. 'That is why I am ill. I'm sorry I didn't tell you before, but I was ashamed.'

'Don't be stupid.'

'I'm sorry. That's the way it is.'

She sat back on her rear, looking strangely at me. 'I don't get it,' she said. 'How can you *not* have the dotTech? That's absurd.'

I smiled, my hand still behind my back where the knife was tucked into my waistband. 'I'm from the Wheah,' I said.

'From the Wheah?' she repeated.

'We're not all barbarians,' I said, as blithely as I could. 'I wanted to see what civilisation was like. So I have come to the t'T. Perhaps you understand why I had to hide my true identity.'

'I've met several Wheah,' Enkida said, eyeing me with increasing suspicion. 'They come over the Tongue at its narrowest point, if they come at all, and come first to Nu Hirsch. I met several of them there.' She clucked her tongue. 'You don't look like a Wheah.'

I was about to say *Of course, my dotTech has changed my appearance so that I fit in better* when I remembered that I didn't have any dotTech; and that as Wheah I wouldn't have any anyway. My smile was frozen now. My options were disappearing.

'I heard a rumour,' Enkida went on, 'that there was a prisoner in the jailstar they have hereabouts. The rumour was that she had escaped, that she might be on Rain.'

84

'Ridiculous,' I said.

'I thought so. Why would the t'T need a prison? But several people were talking about it in Plotown. They said that she had been deprived of her dotTech, you know.'

'Why?' I insisted, stalling. 'Why would anybody be deprived of his dotTech?'

'I don't know,' she said, open-faced. 'I suppose, for his crimes.' She, like most of the people of the t'T, had no conception of what a *crime* might be, beyond a dry and purely semantic understanding of the word – which is to say, an understanding that there was such a word in the Glicé language.

'Crime,' I said, as light-heartedly as I could.

But she was looking at me so strangely now that I felt I had no choice. I leant forward, bringing my face closer to hers. She did not flinch away. Why should she flinch away? In her universe there was no reason to be wary of any other human being. She felt blithe; if puzzled; and I felt *intense.* I had felt this feeling before; a strange feeling of focus right inside my head, so strong as to be almost a smell – it sounds odd, I know, to put it that way. There was the piquancy of her innocence, her not knowing what was going to happen to her. It was almost cruel.

I brought the knife round and punched it out in front of me. It met the resistance of her chest, and I heaved to force it further onwards. There was a gasp.

I think the knife went into her heart. That would have been where I aimed it. I leaned away a little as I forced the blade in as far as it would go, and my change in posture twisted it inside her. When I tried to pull it out, it had stuck against her ribs. I had to wriggle it out to get it free.

Since that moment I have sometimes tried to imagine the whole scene spun about, from her point of view. She did gasp, it is true; but maybe that was an involuntary noise. My blow probably did force air out of her lungs. Almost certainly, she felt a severe pain when the blade went in; but less than a second would have passed before the dotTech realised what was happening and reacted. It would have blocked down the pain pathways, and rushed in bulk to the wound site. Some blood came out, but quickly stopped, as the millions of tiny machines sutured and staunched the relevant severed blood vessels. The heart muscle was doubtless shredded by the blow, and millions of other

85

machines would rush there and begin reknitting the fibres, one by one. But this process, the dotTech would compute, would take some hours, and without a heart blood would not circulate; so millions more of the miniature devices would begin travelling to the lungs under their own power, taking up oxygen, and ferrying it to the brain.

'You slipped,' she said, huskily. Her eyes still had no recognition in them that I meant to do her harm.

I had much more work to do. The wound I had given her would be repaired by the dotTech; it was not enough, of itself, to end her life. I stood up and pushed her with my foot. Her frozen body flopped to the side. Crouching over it, I began to saw at the back of her neck.

The blade had only shallow serrations on its blade, and this was hard work. To try and loosen the meat a little I grasped the knife overhand and stabbed it down half a dozen times, cutting into the back of her neck. I believe I severed the spinal column. A small amount of blood spattered out, but the dotTech quickly reacted to this new situation. It flattened the blood vessels and drew the precious blood away from the area. This meant that I could cut through without much mess.

I hacked and sawed through most of the neck, but the plasticky resilience of the gullet was tough to cut through. I started to lose my self-possession, shrieking and sobbing to myself. The dumb flesh seemed to be resisting me. It was as if the whole universe were taunting me. With several huge blows, one or two of which seemed to go astray, I finally cut the head free from the body.

It lay on the mud on its cheek, its eyes still open, still looking puzzled. With a surge of revulsion for it, which was probably really revulsion for myself, I kicked it with my foot. It rolled through the mud and came to a stop two or three metres from the body.

Then I sat down. I was crying. There was a horrible concatenation of emotions swirling and storming around inside me; added to which I felt ill and tired. I had not killed somebody in such a long time, I had forgotten how visceral and savage the feeling is. More than that, this was the first time I had killed anybody without the buffer of dotTech in my bloodstream to protect against the wash of hormonal intensity that accompanies the act. How did our ancestors ever do such brutal things without howling, without crying and breaking down?

Rain continued falling, intensifying from the glittery drizzle that had been in the air when I stabbed Enkida and growing to the momentum of a proper storm. Drops gathered and swarmed over the flesh of the headless corpse, dribbling across her skin. Her flesh now looked lifeless as putty. I leant back, presenting my face to the heavens, letting the myriad fingertip-like touches of the raindrops play me like an instrument. I was crying, the heavens were crying.

The storm grew, growled thunder, and then started to recede. I may have sat there for an hour. Possibly, it was only a few minutes.

Then the rain stopped, and a rare break in the clouds sent a shiver of bright yellow sunlight dashing through the trees. It passed, warm, over my upturned face and was gone. I might even have slept, I was so tired. But I was recalled to myself by itches and stabs of pain in my legs, and I shook myself, and wiped the knife blade on some wet leaves from the tree under which I was sitting. Then I went over to examine the head.

The dotTech had done a clever thing. This is how smart it is, the nanotechnology: it had realised that the head was severed from the body and it had closed down the blood and lymph vessels to preserve the precious blood in Enkida's brain where it would keep her alive, feeding a small quantity of oxygen to it that the machines themselves absorbed through the skin. But of course it would not be able to keep her alive indefinitely, separated from her body as she now was.

When I returned to the head it was pulling itself through the grass and the mud, using its tongue. Or, rather, at first I thought it was using its tongue, although I was struck by how long and pale the tongue seemed to be. I had not remembered seeing her tongue being so lengthy, although (of course) lengthened tongues are a common enough fashion adaptation in the t'T. But when I picked the head up and examined it more closely I realised that it was not a tongue; it was a strange protrusion, made (I think) out of a protein-stiffened extrusion of mucus. The dotTech is smart; it is intelligent. Problem solving.

It hoped to drag the head back to the headless body, and there to reposition severed head with severed neck. So it had resolved to reunite head and body. It could not organise the headless body, because such co-ordinated muscular action could only be marshalled from the brain stem. But once both were together again then the nano-machines could work their trillion-fold excellence, reconnect the muscles and skin, reanimate the nerve tissue. If I had left the scene, then Enkida would probably have been up and walking around in a matter of days.

'No,' I said to the severed head. 'No, I think not.'

I picked the head up by its ear. I would have picked it up by its hair, except that Enkida had cut her hair too short to allow purchase. The tongue slathered about in the air as I walked away from the corpse, making little whickering noises. 'No,' I said.

The tongue withdrew inside Enkida's head like a beast into its lair.

I walked for a little way holding the severed head, but soon enough I had to stop because I was crying so hard my shoulders were lurching and I lost my grip. The head rolled in the leaf mulch. I fell down, I think. My legs were hurting. I can't remember much of it. It has a dream-like quality in my memory.

But I got to my feet, and picked up the head again. Whilst part of me was going through some kind of crisis, another part of me was coolly calculating how long the dotTech-assisted head would survive without a body. Probably no more than a few hours. The nano-machines could perhaps process a little oxygen out of the air and keep the brain aerated, if only at a very basic level; but it could not gather nutrients, process waste, do all the things that a body can do. Then I thought that if I buried it in the ground it would be even harder for the dotTech to access the necessary oxygen, and the head would die that much sooner. And moreover, besides anything else, burying it in mud would make it harder for the thing to move over the ground back to its body.

I was carrying the head again by its ear. Showers of rain were scurrying through and back through the forest, as if the rainstorm were chasing itself. I could hear myself panting, very loud in my own ears.

'Don't,' said the head, in a tiny, hissing little voice. 'Please, don't.'

I was so surprised I dropped the head again. It took me a little time to work out what the dotTech must have done; it had managed to draw in air, into the cul-de-sac of its throat and into the cheeks too; now it was helping Enkida expel that air over her tongue and through her lips to form words. Without lungs as bellows or soundbox it was tinny and barely audible; the rushing and drumming of the rain almost drowned it out, but I heard it well enough.

'Felo,' it said. 'Don't.'

The head was lying on its left cheek on the grass.

'I can't talk to you,' I said, my voice high-pitched and worried. I backed away, and had to stop myself. Then I squatted down. 'I can't be talking to you.'

'Take me back,' hissed the head, its eyes open and staring at me. 'Not too late.'

'*Not* talking to you,' I said, burying my face in the crook of my arm. 'You stop talking now.'

'Put me back,' said the head, 'with.' Then it stopped, and I peeked a look at it. It was gathering air again into its cheeks, ready to speak some more.

'No,' I said.

'Put me back with,' it said, its eyes unblinking, 'my body, then I can be made right again.'

'No,' I said.

It hissed something else, but incoherently. Then its lips were still.

Rain hushing down.

I sat and stared at the now motionless head for a long time. I do not know how long. Then I stood up, fevered and active, and broke off a living branch from a tree. Using that I dug a hole in the grass-bristled mud. When I had finished and gone over to get the head I became suddenly convinced that the hole was not deep enough, so I went back over and made it deeper, shovelling the sloppy dirt out in hurried gestures. Then I finally climbed out, and went over to the head. I tried to steel myself to pick it up again, but in the end I couldn't. Perhaps I am a coward. I used my foot, and started nudging the head towards the hole, as if I were playing a game of football. I was expecting it to say something, but it was silent. Finally I toppled it over the lip of the hole and in it fell, face down. Then, quickly, quickly, I kicked dirt in after it, over it, covering it and hiding it away. Burying and hiding it away.

I made a poor job of it, probably; but I was very agitated. If only I could have your calmness and self-possession, stone! If only! In the event I started running almost before I had finished burying the thing, sprinting madly through the forest, veering away from treetrunks as they loomed up before me, skidding and bolting.

Of course, with my legs so ill and sick, I slipped over. For a while I lay, shivering in the mud. I may have been shivering, or crying, I am not sure I remember.

Then we come to a strange part in my own story, dear stone. I am not sure, indeed, that I could tell another person this part face-to-face. I am not proud of it. But you, stone; I can tell it to you. You understand the necessity of hardness in this world; you understand how it is only the boundary we establish around ourselves that fixes who we are. I imagine you, picked up by a large calloused hand, wiry hairs growing out of the backs of the fingers, the palm as creased as a map of star-routes through fast-space. I imagine the hand fitting you into a sling, the sling spinning and releasing you. I imagine you in free flight, and then thudding into flesh. Would you fret that you had been an instrument of death?

After I had lain on the ground for a while, I began to calm a little. The image of the head, wriggling slowly across the mud, flipping out its elongated tongue, kept intruding on my thoughts. I couldn't stop it. 'It's buried now,' I told myself. Then I thought to myself that I couldn't leave the body simply lying there. Enkida and I had not travelled far from the port-town, only a few hours walking; others might come that way and see the body.

I clambered to my feet and tried to orient myself. But it was hard to see which direction I should go. The trees all looked the same. The rain was coming down, getting in my eyes. I trailed from trunk to trunk, becoming increasingly desperate and alarmed. Finally I started running zigger-zagger, grabbing trunks and branches as I passed to swing myself around. In this miserable and agitated state I stumbled over the headless body inadvertently and sprawled in the mud.

The corpse had not moved. I dragged myself up, muddy and chattering my teeth (although not with the cold, because the rain was perfectly warm). For a while I only looked at the thing. Then I started to think, and this is what I thought:

I thought that my body was sick, possibly dying. I thought that my legs were raddled with infection and parasite infestation. I thought how miserable I was, how tired and run-down and above all I thought that if I only had some dotTech in my body, simple dotTech like any other citizen of the realms of t'T then I would feel better. My body

90

would heal; I would regain my strength; I would be able to disguise myself.

Then I thought: that body, headless as it is, is filled with Enkida's dotTech. Trillions of nano-machines still patrolling her bloodstream. What were they doing? There was nothing they could do. They were waiting, most likely, for the head to be reattached so that they could join in the enormous task of helping Enkida recover herself. But the head would never be attached. 'It's rotting in the dirt,' I said aloud, to try and stop my teeth from skittering together. 'It's rotting in the dirt.'

So this is what I thought to myself: I should use the dotTech. I would only need a small population; it is in the operational parameters of nano-machines that from a certain base population the dotTech grows and self-replicates, drawing raw materials from its host. At this time, it is not unknown for people to start craving peculiar foods; as it had been with myself in jail, when the AI was building itself in my brain. I might eat dirt, for there are metals in that; or raw meat, bark, anything. But in a short time I would have my own population of nano-machines. The tiny machines that had serviced Enkida's body would service mine.

I took out my knife (I am not proud that I did this), went over to the corpse and started cutting pieces of meat from the bones. The meat was raw, but I was too tired and the air was too full of falling water for me to try and light a fire. I ate it uncooked, whole strands slipping down my throat like raw eel. I was hungry, but this was not a meal I could relish. I tried drinking the blood too, knowing that the greatest accumulation of dotTech would be found there, but I had no container and the fluid slipped through my fingers as if it had a mind of its own. Which, in a sense, it did have – although how or why the dotTech would move the blood through my fingers to fall to the mud I don't know.

I very quickly grew tired, or sick, of this meal. So I stopped. I reasoned with myself that I had devoured enough dotTech to rebuild my own population. Then I left the cut-up body and walked through the trees until I was out of sight of it. I curled myself around the base of a tree and fell asleep.

Stone, I was exhausted. Believe me I was. I don't know how long I slept. I woke, feeling ill and still tired, but resolved that I could not afford to let the body lie in the open any longer.

I had lost my branch, the one I had used to dig the hole for the head. There were some boughs lying around but they were mostly rotten; so I was forced to tear off a fresh limb – not an easy thing. I stripped it of its greasy twigs (with more difficulty) and eventually began carving a shallow trench out of the mud. I intended a deep grave, but I quickly became very tired. I stopped and considered for a while; it hardly needed to escape detection forever. In a week or two I would leave this world, probably never to return. (No, I decided, looking at the headless body in the mud: *certainly* never to return). I would be long gone.

So in the end I did little more than scrape out a shallow dent in the earth, bundle the body in, and pack the mud over the top with my hands. At the end of the process I was left with a very obvious hump in the ground, but I was too tired and dispirited to do any more. I staggered off through the trees.

I had to consider what to do next. Things were becoming intolerable. Now that I had disposed of Enkida, it occurred to me to wonder how many other people might have heard the rumours she had heard; how widespread the news of my escape was. Perhaps 'police' were scouring the cities of Rain at that very moment.

I couldn't decide between hiding out in the forest for a long time – months, maybe – until the fuss died down; or making a run for it, going back to an elevator and getting back into orbit. Heading off straight away. The risk of apprehension would be greater in the elevator, or the orbital, but if I could only get away then I would be much safer. I could travel to a place not so barbarous and primitive – where I would not be prey to these illnesses and these parasites.

I slept again, and woke feeling powerfully nauseous. But of course I had eaten little, except for the one meal of human flesh, for what seemed a very long time. I started in what I hoped was a southerly direction, intending to get some proper food in the port, and then maybe, discretely, try to determine whether 'police' were looking for me. I felt so sick in my stomach. I kept having flashbacks to the head, talking to me. 'It's not too late.' I thought: I'll get back to the port and things will be better.

I don't know *what* I was thinking, to be honest with you.

I know I stopped after an hour, and started vomiting. Matter streamed from my mouth, burning my tongue; my torso clenched and clenched as if being squeezed by some powerful exterior force – horrible feeling. But I just kept vomiting. Fluid was coming out of my nose, weeping from my eyes, piss was spurting intermittently. Even in the midst of this misery I knew what was happening. It was too reminiscent of my execution.

The dotTech was leaving my body.

After what seemed an age and an age of this heaving, spewing misery I found myself lying in a puddle of my own foul stuff, shivering and weeping to myself. Everything seemed hopeless. If I could have simply willed myself out of existence at that moment, I would have done so.

I lay there, and nothing changed. Nothing ever changes. After a while, just to shift myself out of the stink, I pulled myself up and dragged myself over to one of the trees. I settled myself, somehow, with my back to the trunk, and sat for a very long while.

There was nothing. The space between the trees was a slick palette of colours bleeding into one another; the black of the mud, the grey of my spent fluids, the green of grass and fresh leaf, the whisky-hued brown of decaying leaves. Water hurried through the air around me in swiftly marching gusts. There were periods of quiet when it was impossible to tell the difference between the slow dribble of a perfect raindrop down the bark and the inching forward of a beetle. Then there would be a fanfare of thunder and the air would fill with water galloping downwards, shaking everything and slapping my body.

I may have slept. My head seemed empty.

It seemed clear (as I thought, when the power of thought started to return to my head) that the dotTech had abandoned me. Refused to take to me. I could not imagine why this had happened. I thought of two possibilities. Perhaps whatever programme my executioner had installed in my original population to make them desert still lurked, residually, in my body somewhere. But that didn't make sense, because the programme was itself a dotTech thing. There was no dotTech in me, so there was no place where the programme could have hidden itself. Then I thought that perhaps the dotTech itself had decided not to be part of me. It is a strange thing, nanotechnology, and we humans have hardly fathomed it. But it is an intelligent force, or at least pseudo-intelligent. It has to be; it has to solve problems, work out the best way of proceeding, interpret its environment in order best to be able to help its host. Perhaps Enkida's dotTech knew that I had murdered her, and was simply refusing to help her killer. Maybe it was making an ethical choice.

I dozed again. I felt weak, drained.

It was when I awoke that I began to hear the voices.

5th

Stone,

Voices in my head. It was the same voice, tracked several times over. It was my AI.

'You're dead, though,' I said, feeling feverish. Part of me knew that this was another hallucination, and was worried at the thought that more visions might afflict me – that Enkida might clamber out of the ground and accuse me with a screech and a pointing finger. I was ill.

OK, OK, said the AI, or whatever my brain was inventing for itself. *You are in no good shape, you know that?*

You died, I subvocalised, having to focus hard to get the words to form in my mind. Travelling faster than light destroyed you.

The seeds of several AIs were planted in the jail, said this AI. It sounded exactly like my last AI; the same uncanny triple voice that was actually one voice, the same sardonic manner. *Did you think your employers would waste so good an opportunity?*

My employers, I thought to myself. I had almost forgotten about them.

You killed somebody, said the AI.

I had almost believed, in my scattered way, that the AI was real, and not a phantom voice; but this statement threw me the other way. 'How can you know I did such a thing?' I said aloud, my voice querulous.

I can see it in your memories.

You can't access my memories, I said, certain that I was right about this. Unless I vocalise them.

There's a body over there, under that heap.

You can't know that, I said again, panicky. I think, deep inside me, I was worried that my guilt was somehow a matter of general knowledge.

If I can't know it, said the AI, reasonably enough, *then how come I know it?*

This was a poser. I closed my eyes and began singing a song to myself to try and drown out the AI's voice, but it simply waited until I stopped.

Have you forgotten the deal you made? it said, when there had been silence for a little while. *When you agreed to the escape, when you were still in the jail?*

No, I said sulkily.

How much further on are you?

My AI said – you said – (I was confused). You, or my AI at the time anyway, said I should wait here on Rain for a little while.

It – I – whoever – it may have been affected more seriously by the interstellar travel than was apparent. I can't believe it told you to come all the way down here – this far south.

No, I agreed. That was my idea.

Your idea to stay so far from the elevator? What if you have to make a quick exit from the world?

I didn't reply to this. Rain washed down, clean and fragrant.

Look what you have done on this world! said the AI. *Nothing. You killed a human being, and for what? You are pathetic.*

I was deciding that this AI was much less amiable than my last one, but then I interrupted myself, because that would be tantamount to accepting that the AI was real, and not merely a hallucination. It might only have been my brain's way of attacking itself.

Let me tell you something about yourself, the AI went on. *Perhaps this will make it plain to you why you were chosen to commit the crime. Look back on your time here! You have travelled amongst thousands of unique, fascinating human beings and you have seen none of them. The only person you have even registered, the only one whose name you bothered to*

95

learn, is the one you have now killed; and you only got to know her because she was unusually persistent in staying close to you.

Again, it worried me that this AI knew so much. Where have you been anyway? I asked. Why has it taken you so long to appear?

Don't change the subject! You are the most solipsistic human being in the whole of the t'T. This seems certain. For some strange reason you lack the basic human empathetic abilities. You hardly notice other people exist.

I don't know, dear stone. What do you think? Perhaps my narrative is bare of other people, but I think I do notice things. I was noticing the precise formations of water, running in strands like rope down the chipped, wonky bark of the trees opposite. I was noticing the smells of earth and metal that were in the air. But my AI had another point.

How many people have you met, since you arrived on Rain? Hardly any. Of those who have sought you out and introduced themselves, in friendship, how many do you remember? Only the one individual who impinged so closely on you that you had to kill her.

I'm not sure, I said, what point you're trying to make.

No point, said the AI. *It is why you are so well suited to this job that your employers want you to do. I just want to remind you that* they *exist – remember it!*

I'm sure they do, I replied. I'm out of the jailstar, aren't I? Somebody got me out.

They did. And I'm reminding you that the deal was that they wanted a job done. If you do not do it, then they will hand you back to the prison. Do you understand?

I know, I know, I fretted. I haven't forgotten.

In that case, you won't want to be staying here. There is a small world, remote, on the border of the Bulk. You will travel to Narcissus, and then to Nu Fallow. From there you will go to this planet and execute your commission.

'Kill them all,' I whined. 'But how will I do that?'

That is your problem, that is why you have been hired. You must do it, and it must be complete – everybody must die, there must be nobody left alive.

Alright, alright. 'The dotTech won't grow in my body,' I wailed aloud.

I know.

'I'm sick! It hurts!'

I know. I know. I'll advise you on how best to treat your wounds. They will improve.

'Why won't the dotTech stay in my body?' I moaned. 'It is designed to help us. It is supposed to help us. But it won't help me!'

I know.

'Is it because I am a bad person? Is that why?'

A bad person, repeated the AI, but it didn't say anything else. Then the rain came falling down again, very boisterous this time, like a child having a tantrum and bashing at all the leaves.

To Narcissus

Dear Stone,

How was I to do it? This was the problem which refused to leave my mind in peace, which is what you'd expect me to say, of course. How to kill these people? I had an entire world to kill – no easy task, that. Perhaps now you have some sense, dear stone, how hard it is to kill human beings when their bodies are supported by dotTech. Even killing a single individual, like Enkida, had taken all my strength, all my will. Multiply that by so many people. How many?

Many, many.

It is enough, stone of mine, to jitter the mind, the sheer *number* of human beings. It is one of those things about which children, paradoxically, are wiser. The lurching shifts of scale – like those occasions when we wake up abruptly in the night, feeling as if the world we sleep upon is swivelling sharply from horizontal to vertical and tipping us over. That same panicky, finger-spasming sharpness of sensation. Of course it relaxes a moment later, but for a moment everything has been redefined. You don't know what I'm talking about, stone (*you* do, though, doctor, eavesdropping as you are). Well, that's the kind of thing I'm talking about. You realise that the universe contains many millions of galaxies; but the *millions* part makes no sense, so you swoop down on the one galaxy. This one! Wellhello! But this galaxy contains four hundred million stars, and once again the number blurs in the mind, so you collapse the vision down to one star. And around this star are several planets, and on this planet there are sixty million human beings. *Six* clicks with you, and you don't quite lose it at the *–ty*, but then there is the *million* again, so your brain

98

silently corrects the focus, slams down to the scale of one individual. You are an individual, you can understand the individual. Except, wait, no, inside this person are billions of nano-machines – thousands of millions, each one built out of cunningly interlocking atomic spars and struts, motors and neural gates. Close your eyes: take it down to the level of these machines. Living in the intermittent flow of the great blood vessels, with the backdrop of burring, thrumming heartbeats and the electrical crackle of nerves firing. Here you are, and now the picture clears; because although these atomic building blocks are not pure, they cannot be broken down into more than a dozen or so components before you reach the fundamental sparkling prickliness of space-time out of which everything is made. And this machine, this single example of dotTech, is *like* an individual; it moves through its environment with a job to do, it is faced with problems and it solves them. This is enough: but then comes the horrible vertiginous spasm – for an instant the vista opens all the way back up to the top, to the billions of nano-machines in the billions of human individuals around each of billions of stars in billions of galaxies.

Falling . . .

And then you recover, clutching at the mattress. Because you don't have to kill all these things. You need only destroy sixty million people, on one planet circling one star. And, in a way, that is easier than killing a single individual. Work out how to do it. Do it. Job completed.

Did I think of, perhaps, *not* doing it? But then I would go back to jail. Ah, *choice*. Commit the crime and be free; live crime-free and go to jail. When my mind was ordered enough, after the fear-induced, disease-sharpened chaotic mania of my time on Rain, I did think through the options; and I decided that first and foremost I did not want to return to the jail.

I also wanted to see what would happen next. Yes, I think that is the purest form of words I can find to express my state of mind.[1] I was curious as to who would employ me to kill these people. I wanted to

[1] Difficult to translate effectively: Glicé has a verb, *coplan* which means 'to look forward to expectantly', 'to want to find out what happens next', which has a wide range of cognates – for instance in the prose or poetic genre of *Anacoplan,* in which literature is determined chiefly by an aesthetic of narrative expectancy. Ae's phrase is much briefer, or 'purer' (*blaca*) in the original: *Alzo, yes coplanar.*

know why, and I wanted to know who, but above all I wanted to know why. My new AI – if that's what it was, lurking in my head, and not simply some paranoid delusion of my own, engendered by sickness and depravity – my new AI was even less forthcoming than my previous one.

'You know,' I would insist. 'You know.'

Nothing to say about that.

Tell me! Nothing, nothing. O, o, o, o. But I travelled, and I looked about myself. I had been locked away from everything, from all news and all culture, for many years. I was like a child again, learning it all for the first time. I thought sometimes of Agifo3acca, living in his sprawling spaceship, devoting himself and his life to studying the Great Gravity Trench. He was as wrapped up in himself as I had been in jail. Later I would come to envy that single-mindedness; for the moment I was thirsty for knowledge of the worlds of t'T. My mind was parched. I wanted to know everything that had been going on in my absence.

2nd

Stone,

I lived on Rain for another six or seven months, with a constant running commentary in my head from my new AI. One of the things that bothered me about this new incarnation of my mental voice was that when I finally did slip away – travelling up to orbit, letting the foam envelope me, drifting out into space and then away at super-light speeds – my AI came with me. It was the usual experience; the comforting womb-closeness of the foam, the sensory deprivation, speeding through nothingness, hundreds of light years of nothingness.

I arrived at Narcissus Tuporylov, a large system with several worlds. It was the usual sensation of being woken from a pleasant sleep; a slightly crotchety, heaving feeling in the depths of my bones, a sick pulling in my gut. Then I was in one of the famous Narcissus flat platforms, having the foam washed from me by a large man entirely covered in blue string-like hairs, from the crown of his enlarged head over his face and neck and down his naked torso. His legs, I remember thinking, were ugly; dressed in thread-sacking pants with large rents in the cloth through which bizarre little quills sprouted.

This is the sort of precise detail you notice when you come round from long distance travel. Travelling at faster than light jars the mind, puts it into a sort of semi-trance state. When you arrive at the other end it can take several hours for this autistic, super-observant, unthinking mental state to wear off. It has something to do with the repeated quantum jolts of faster than light travel, or so I understand.

But my AI didn't seem to be affected by the journey. As soon as my mind was working well enough to comprehend, it started to speaking to me again. *Spend a week here*, it told me. *Here at Narcissus. Go down to the world. There is an amount of information that will be useful to you on this world. With that, you can travel to Nu Fallow, and on to your target.*

'Wait,' I said aloud, still groggy. 'You sound extremely sane.'

I?

'My last AI,' I said, laboriously working through the sentence, 'was more or less scrambled by faster-than-light travel. That's what faster-than-light travel does to AIs. I know. You're not resilient the way organic minds are. The quantum buffeting degrades your capacity to operate.' I said something like this. Perhaps I wasn't quite as eloquent as I'm suggesting here, but that was the gist of it. Actually (I remember now) it took three or four conversations with my AI to get all this out, before I was mentally focused enough to notice that there was something wrong about the lucidity with which my AI spoke to me.

Nonsense, it said. *Now we have little time. We must move on to Nu Fallow soon.*

'Something is wrong about this.'

I am a new AI, said the AI brusquely. *Think of it as a process of the old AI laying eggs, or . . . no, let us say eggs like insect eggs. The programmes for designing an AI can be comprehended in an old-style linear processing machine. When we come out of faster-than-light travel it is possible for a new AI to grow.*

Now none of this made any sense. Had there even been time for a new AI to grow? Could AIs bypass the constraints of faster-than-light travel in this way – truly? I thought not. In turn that made me wonder if the voice were a schizophrenic part of myself and not an artificial intelligence at all. Also I didn't like the metaphor of 'insect eggs'. It reminded me too much of my experiences with the maggot-infestations on Rain.

'Why must I kill all the people on that world, AI?' I said, as I was queuing for the planetary elevator.

I cannot tell you – be quiet! Don't speak aloud like that! Subvocalise! These people will hear you. Imagine overhearing such a sentence!

But the other people, even if they did overhear my words amongst the gabble of their own conversations, would not have registered what I was saying. What I was saying had no purchase on their way of seeing the universe. *Kill people* really made no sense as far as they were concerned.

Why must I kill these people? I repeated, subvocalising. AI, tell me that.

I can't tell you, leave it at that.

Why?

I can't tell you. That's all.

But I thought, trying to bury the thought away in some part of my brain that was not connected to the vocalising areas, that perhaps it knew no more about it than I did. Perhaps it knew exactly the same about the whole business because it was me, another part of me. Then I thought: if that's so, it hardly matters if I think this thought free of vocalisation or not; I can overhear I at any place in the brain.

Stone, perhaps it seems incongruous to you that I even went through this process of working it out. I never doubted that there was some external agency that wanted me to perform this enormous crime. I had, after all, been freed from jail – I did not believe that I had the ingenuity to free myself. I had also been met outside by Agifo3acca the Wheah and his great spaceship. I did not see how I could have arranged that rendezvous from within the jail; and certainly I did not see how I could have arranged it and then forgotten that I had arranged it. And if there were no external force that was behind the mass murder I was contracted to commit, then why would I be doing it?

I fretted over this during my first few days on Narcissus. Had I lost

102

part of my memory? Was there something in my past that was leading up to this grand crime, as if this crime were the crown of a life set aside from the perfect utopian existences of all the other human beings in the worlds of t'T? This flawless environment, combined with flawless physical health, almost invariably promoted flawless mental states. But it occurred to me that *my* mental health was a precarious thing, separated from the perfect societies of t'T; and that my perfect physical health was a distant memory, excised from me by my executioner. Perhaps I was too mad to know how mad I was. But, then again, I decided that I was obviously sane enough to doubt my sanity (this is human logic, stone; we humans think like this all the time). If I were truly mad, I reasoned, surely I wouldn't know I was mad? Wasn't that the way with madness? Didn't my very worrying about being mad in a perverse way guarantee my sanity?

You should stop thinking along these lines, the AI cut in, as if it had been eavesdropping on my thoughts – as if it were capable of doing that! *This sort of thinking isn't going to help you get your job done*. And I was immediately fretting again.

3rd

Dear Stone,

Narcissus is a world of towering vertical natural structures. Sometimes it is known as 'Crevasse-world'. Most of the planet is covered in complexes of rocky cliff-faces and kilometre-deep gullies, topped by towering pinnacles, spires of rock, some so high they actually leave the atmosphere. It is a world of crevasses and very few flat spaces. In the southern polar continent there are some very few high plains on which pigmy native creatures graze, but most of the rest of the world is divided between startlingly severe up-down geological structures and the elongated striated waterways that the natives call 'oceans'. In fact there is no single body of water on Narcissus grand enough to merit being called an ocean; much of the planet's water lurks in very deep, black, stagnant pools at the bottom of the many thousands of crevasses. At a few places, these crevasses run into one another delta-

103

like and the canyon walls fall away to reveal open water; but such features are more loch than sea.

Looked at from space, there is something exquisite in the fractal filigree of Narcissus's shapes; particularly the various extrusions of stand-alone rock that reach tens of kilometres upwards. Sharpened like knives by the winds, some of these structures are only a few metres thick, but all are at least a hundred and some many tens of hundreds of metres tall. They are usually found together, hundreds of enormous triangular shapes like serrations that reach far into the sky, supported by a particular long-strand form of neo-igneous rock and by Narcissus's relatively low gravity. From orbit these things look less teeth-like and more like hairs, fronds, something so fine it is amazing they do not snap. It is possible, apparently, to leap from a synchronised orbit onto the tip of one or two of these larger structures, and then 'ski' down to the habitable levels of the planet. I have not done this, but I understand from what I have been told that the 'ski-ing' must take place inside a sealed container.

Before humanity came to this world the atmosphere was layered sharply with steady-state weather systems. At the lowest levels, where the black sluggish water lies in the shadows at the bases of great natural clefts and shafts, heavier gases roiled – perfectly poisonous; carbon dioxide and chlorines. At higher levels, where the majority of rock formations peaked, there was a nitrogen-rich atmosphere; this provided the air breathed by the vegetative grazing-herding animals that clustered on the southern plateau. Higher, the air thinned and thinned to argons and ozones, crystal-sharp clouds of white skimming past the occasional spire of rock, all silhouetted against the purity of blue.

Then people came, fortified with their dotTech, and changed the world to suit themselves. They brought oxygen; adapted the grazers of the southern continent so that they wouldn't be killed by it; they pumped away the poisonous gases of the lower regions, and built themselves cities. With the heavier air, and the disruption to the atmospheric ecosystem, erosion changed its habits, but that is the way of things.

Homes were drilled into the canyon walls, and built on the few horizontal surfaces. Some of the crevasses were so narrow it was possible to reach through the open window of your home and shake hands with the people who lived opposite. In others, the spaces from cliff-face to cliff-face were many metres, or even kilometres. Here the Narcissians began their distinctive and t'T-wide famous building habits of stringing diamond-cable from wall to wall, weaving ornate and elaborate spiderwebs. Younger generations of Narcissians preferred living on these cable walkways; running from strand to strand, balancing on a flat or clambering up and sliding down the sloping wires. People would weave a tighter mesh together as a base. Cities grew up in the tangle of cables. Soon there were many tens of thousands of these net-communities, strung out between canyon walls, or in some rarer cases strung from rock spire to rock spire.

They are curious and rather scary places, the cable cities. It is a matter of pride for the typical Narcissian that their cable webs be not too closely woven, so there are always gaping holes and wide unstrung spaces through which it is easy to fall. Habituated cable dwellers move about their cities with a breathtaking facility, but of course people do fall; it is a long way down from most of these precarious web-like eyries to the bottom, and the water at the base is very cold, very black, existing in permanent shadow. More than this, the walls down there are worn smooth by the millennial action of the water slopping up and down, so it can be extremely difficult to climb out. Creatures live in the dark waters, vegetative worms that grow to great lengths. Rumour says they are happy to devour anything that splashes down.

Some fallers return, via one route or another, rescued by friends or under their own power. Some don't, and that only adds to the glamour and excitement of living in the web-communities. I should add, dear stone, that the larger proportion of the population live in more conventional cavern-wall dwellings, or on the tops of the cliffs. A life of constant danger becomes tedious after a while, and it becomes easier to retreat to the many hollowed-out homes with their interconnecting passages and complex inner spaces.

There are some who live a more solitary life, carving out a high home inside one of the tall pinnacles of stone that stab up at the sky. I visited one of these during my stay on the world, and it had the whiff of an aeons-old hermetic establishment. Thousands of steps were carved up the spine of a sharply slanting, sharp-featured rock-spire, up to where the air was so thin that a dotTech-less person such as myself found it hard to breathe. And there, carved out of the rock was a single-room dwelling with a doorway and wide plasglass windows. The view was eyecatching and beautiful.

4th

Dear Stone,

So, at Narcissus I descended from orbit and spent several days in one of the plateau towns, before taking a bird-car to Ru-denetter, one of the larger crevasse-towns.[1] *Stay there for a few days*, my AI instructed me. *Then you'll need to find one of the granite spires. There's something we need from there.*

'I find myself thinking,' I said aloud, 'that you may be nothing more than a figment of my imagination.'

Pssht! said the AI. Or it made a noise rather like that in my head.

Ru-denetter was a young person's town. A famous first-stop for visiting tourists, it was filled with the sorts of buzzes and sights most likely to interest a traveller. It had no bother with 'money' or any such idiocy, but thronged with newly-adult people, all of whom relished the freedom of finally abandoning the long years of childhood.

The crevasse of Ru-denetter itself was about three hundred metres wide, and the cats cradle of cables and ropes that bridged this gap provided a tangled marvel of lines, clotted with people scrambling to and fro, makeshift buildings, sports, theatre-spaces. Set into either side of the crevasse wall were large communal spaces, caves borrowed out of the canyon walls where all manner of drugs and intoxicants could be obtained. For some visitors it was enough to lounge in the couches by the windows, or on the balconies, and look out at the goings-on in the webbing. For others the excitement of the web, with its flavouring of danger, was too much of a draw.

---

[1] Glicé has a number of synonyms translated here variously as 'crevasse', 'canyon', 'gully' or 'shaft': the Narcissian word for such features is *Ru*, which means more precisely 'road' or 'passageway'; Ae's narrative usually describes the features in general Glicé terms (*craver, caver, vrale* and so on).

The webbing was thickest at the top of the canyon, where there was most light. The lower into the crevasse you went, the less daylight reached, until you came to a level where only a few minutes of noon daylight would penetrate in each twenty-one hour day. Few people lurked in these depths.

Still wobbly from my spaceflight, and taking longer to recover without the dotTech inside me, I spent my first few days in Rudenetter eating and drinking in a bar called Alles. Outside the window dozens of slender individuals were leaping and hopping from left to right; some kind of race. *Just a few days, alright?* chided my AI. *You can rest for a while, but we must retrieve this information. Then you can get on with your job.*

Is there a hurry in destroying all these lives? Must it be done by a certain date? I asked drowsily, my sensations pleasantly sticky and numb with goldwash.[1]

Well, it's not that exactly, said the AI.

Then maybe I'll just wait a little while.

Wait too long and your employers will hand you back to the police.

This threat almost reached past the buzzing numbness of being drunk on goldwash, and I shifted uneasily on my couch. Outside the window, a young woman was flying from cord to cord of the webbing, aided in longer jumps by a flat board like a wing that she held over her head. I was trying to see whether there were handles, or if she were simply (and dangerously) holding the board unassisted with bare hands.

'What is this information I need so desperately to collect?' I asked, my eyelids dropping now.

My AI may have answered me; but I slid into a sleep.

5th

Dear Stone,

I think by this stage that my body was getting more used to existing without the dotTech. Certainly it was a little stronger than it had been.

---

[1] *Dorfrezh*; a commonly used t'T intoxicant.

My nose ran constantly, and my breathing bubbled and snorted accordingly, but my skin had mostly healed. The keloid scribbling of my scar tissue gave me a striking and even exotic appearance. Given that I had reverted to default humanity when the dotTech left my body, I looked unexceptional, unlikely to stand out in a crowd. But this in turn served only as a more effective means of offsetting my peculiar scars, like a plain metal setting for a rare jewel. I had a small beard, mostly directly underneath my chin, a dozen or so flittery hairs. I had lost weight through illness, and then put it back on in peculiar places. My trip through space from Rain to Narcissus had rested me; most of my infection had been purged by my metabolism by the time I arrived.

In other words, I didn't truly need to rest in the bar called Alles. But to begin with I was too sluggish mentally to do anything else, and by the time my mind had fully recovered from the disorientation of travelling faster than light, I had discovered a pleasant miniature community in the bar.

'Most travellers,' said a pale man, approaching me, 'stay here for a day or two and then move on. Either they move on to other towns, or else they get hypnotised by the web-city and clamber out on to it.'

'Sometimes,' said somebody else, a very short individual, 'they fall off. That's worth watching.'

'But you've been here for over a week now,' said the pale man. 'You planning on staying?'

'For now,' I said, nodding to him.

'Then I guess,' he replied, 'I should say wellhello to you properly.' He nodded to me. His name, he said, was Ditle. He had adapted his body in a variety of subtle ways, mostly to do with his digestive organs. The thing I noticed about him to begin with was that his teeth had been regrown by the dotTech as a comb of fine needles. When he came closer and sat on the couch next to me I could see that his nostrils, wider and flatter than normal, were also toothed on the inside with twin rows of small canines. These nostrils were capable of opening and shutting like two tiny mouths, and sometimes he ate through them in preference to his actual mouth – taking miniature bites out of yams and baps by stuffing his nose into the food. His eyelids were also furnished with delicate teeth that curved out to avoid scratching the cornea, and meshed together when he blinked. I never got to know him well enough to determine whether all his orifices were toothed in this same way.

'Wellhello, Ditle,' I said. 'My name is Jasba.' I elected not to re-use the alias I had used on Rain, just in case details of Enkida's murder surfaced.

'Jasba,' he repeated. 'Odd name. This is Klabier.' He waved in the direction of the other individual, a petite woman with shining blue-brown skin.

'You're regulars here?' I asked.

'Years now. There are more of us. We came to Narcissus as travellers, like you, from all over.'

'I'm from Jerusalem,' said Klabier. Her voice, notwithstanding her tiny body, was surprisingly deep and resonant.

'For a while we did the tourist things here – climbed the peaks, dashed about on the cables of the web-communities, all that.'

'Oh yes,' nodded Klabier.

'Then we got bored with that. But instead of moving on, we holed up here with a dozen or so like-mindeds. Politics is our thing now.'

'Politics,' said Klabier.

'Where's everybody else?' I asked. The truth was that I had been so drowned in goldwash for my first week that I had barely possessed the wherewithal to eat, let alone notice my surroundings.

'They still like to climb,' said Ditle. 'Every now and again they go and scuttle up some needle-peak or other. But they'll be back in a week or two. Politics! That's the latest craze, not just here but all the way up this border between t'T and the Tongue. Up at Nu Hirsch, in the Aksleroth, its what everybody is talking about.'

There was a pause, which carried with it the aura of significance. Finally Ditle spoke: 'You want in?'

'OK,' I said as my AI said *No, no, what are you doing? You have to get out of this place – we must retrieve what we have come here to retrieve!* But I ignored its voice.

'OK,' confirmed Ditle.

'Love your scars,' said Klabier as they moved away. 'Very chic.'

Dusk came. Sunset over the top of the canyon wall above us stained

109

the far cliff with the colours of freckles, of cut timber, of embre[1] and crocus-yellows. I watched a mass of people rush from the ledges and run along the nearest cables. They dashed at one another, feinting and leaping, grabbing nearby cables with their hands and hauling themselves up. Everybody was hurrying about holus-bolus. I watched, absorbed, assuming it to be some kind of tag-game.

The dark thickened and deepened in texture. Bit-lights, some in the canyon walls, some fixed to or hanging from the cables, blipped into visibility, light appearing like fists springing open to become starfish-palms. Soon the whole canyon was littered with sparkling lights. The cable material gleamed and crossed the space from cliff to cliff with a tangle of glowing lines.

In the days that followed I became friendly with a dozen or so of the 'political' group; but it was Klabier and Ditle that I was closest to. I discovered that they were one of hundreds of 'political' groups scattered around the southern hemisphere of the planet, groups with whom we (as I came to think of it) were in frequent communication. There were, the others assured me, many thousands springing up all the time all the way along the rimwards stretch of t'T space.

Politics is the new fashion, they said.

Discussion would usually begin towards the end of the day. I would spend mornings stoned on alcohol or goldwash. Then I would sleep in the afternoon, and drink a stimulant with some sugar-food upon waking. This would leave me alert enough to attend to the discussions, if not quite to take part.

Politics, dear stone, is an antique art, like certain sports or garden cultivation. Before the utopian days of t'T, human interaction was a power-over or submission-under game. Individuals unable to exist alone would sacrifice aspects of their lives in order to join the larger group. The precise, complex dynamics of these sacrifices, and the system-control strategies, were called 'politics'. They are more or less an irrelevance to the worlds of t'T nowadays, except in those worlds that maintain archaic 'political' structures for their own reasons. For the habituants of the bar Alles, *politics* meant a detailed process of

---

[1] A bright orange alcoholic drink.

discussion and interaction, modelled in part on books and novels from the distant past.

Ditle would start things going with a snicker-snick of his artificial teeth. Then somebody would assert something they'd learnt from info-searching earlier in the day. Then the discussion would flicker back and forth, person to person. This is the true state of affairs. We should do this. They should do that. It's clear that this is what's going to happen.

Nonsense! What nonsense! groaned the AI in my head. *They're all so ignorant. They all know nothing at all.*

I contributed little; but every now and again I would drop in some most-obvious statement of truth. For instance, the more people spouted confident predictions about the future mass behaviour of people in the t'T, the more I would want to interject that 'Of course chaos philosophy demonstrates how none of your predictions are worth anything at all.' Perhaps I would interject with that statement, or something like it. Then I would be frozen out with silence, or subjected to a withering comment. Or again; perhaps somebody would say something in reply.

But there was a single feature about their discussions that caught and held my attention. They talked about *the coming war.*

For the first time, aspects of my own particular commission found a context in which they made sense.

'Seems to me,' Ditle said on one occasion, 'that the coming war is closer than ever. A traveller from Nu Hirsch says that up that way there are rumours that the Palmetto tribes have *already launched fireships through the sublight space towards t'T.'* He said these last words as if each one were a precious thing that had to be savoured alone; speaking slowly, with pauses between each sound. It had the desired effect.

It took me several days to discover what the 'fireships' were. Nobody in the spaces of the t'T had ever seen one; but the rumours were that the Palmetto tribes had constructed large unmanned spacecraft. These ships were accelerated to near the speed of light, which made them grow relatively bigger, and were sent off hurtling towards the rimwards systems of the t'T. They were reputed to be nothing but bombs, that targeted systems and flew up to – well, opinion varied: explode the system's star, was one theory, pollute the

111

atmosphere of the inhabited planet was another; rapidly oxidise the surface (hence *fire*ships) said a third. There was no direct evidence for these great weapons, but that did not shake the 'politics' of believing in them.

'Why would the Palmetto do this?' I asked, incredulous, although the whole scenario gave me twinges of recognition.

'War,' said one voice.

'War,' agreed another.

'The Palmetto are following in their own crafts,' explained Ditle, patiently, as if to a child. 'They will occupy the systems nearest to their space. This will give them a *beachhead.*'[1]

The Palmetto, I should add dear stone, are almost entirely unknown in t'T. In this respect they are unlike the Wheah. It is rare to come across a barbarian from the Wheah, but they do sometimes travel across the long reaches of the Tongue in order to experience life in the t'T. Agifo3acca was one example, and there were others. But the Palmetto were a different matter. Their realms were all sublight; it took hundreds or sometimes thousands of years for them to pass from system to system in their various sublight spaceships. They did not visit the fastspace of t'T, and what little *was* known was mostly gleamed from thousands-of-years-outdated radio transmissions. They appeared to be a clan-based culture of twelve or thirteen enormous families, each of whose genetic distinctiveness was jealously preserved. They used dotTech, but with a more focused application to enhance longevity; and they spent much of their lives in coma-like sleeps. Individuals could live several thousand years, passing much of the time asleep; and family-based grudges animated their interactions with blood-feuds. It was assumed that members of a Palmetto tribe could hold grudges for centuries; they were proverbial figures in that regard.

'They will be here in ten years!' affirmed Ditle, with emphasis. 'Perhaps less! The worlds of the t'T must prepare!'

That the Palmetto would wish to 'invade' the space of t'T seemed bizarre and implausible to me; I was dismissive. 'What would they profit by making this sort of "war"?' I insisted.

---

[1] The text uses the ancient word; there is no modern-day Glicé equivalent.

Ditle swished and clicked his exaggerated teeth. 'History teaches us,' he said, meaning *ancient history*, 'that war might be prosecuted for any number of reasons: wealth; living space.'

'Perhaps,' interjected somebody, 'they are tired of crawling about space at sublight speeds. Perhaps they wish to move to a space such as ours, where faster-than-light travel is possible?'

'I disagree,' said Klabier. 'War is coming, that is true. It is difficult to deny this. But not from the direction of the Palmetto. They are too set in their peculiar rhythms of life, and those rhythms are adapted to the traffic of sublight travel.'

She has no evidence at all! said the AI inside my head. *She's extrapolating and plain inventing! And yet she sounds so confident, as if she has access to some truth!*

'No,' Klabier went on. 'The problem is not Palmetto, but the Wheah. They have been sending individuals among us for many years, we all know this. None of us have asked *why*. Well, I know why. The Wheah do travel faster than light, but because they live in a realm of slow-space they cannot exceed three times light-speed, or thereabouts. It is natural for them to want to possess the space of the t'T. They can translate their cultures straightforwardly into our space; worship their gods and increase their wealth and possessions. Invade us! They plan it!'

I was, in the first instance, baffled by this speech, partly because it utilised various archaic terms, such as 'possession' and 'invade'. In fact, I was about to interject dismissively, when the thought struck me. What if this talk of *war* had some basis in truth?

Would killing the entire population of a world count as an act of war? Was that its justification? Perhaps that was why I had been employed to do this crime. But by the Wheah? Or the Palmetto?

'Everybody knows,' somebody else was saying (and this despite the fact that nobody knew very much about the Wheah at all, for certain) 'that their barbarian culture is based on religion and possession. On God and trade. Doesn't it make sense that their fraction-God might instruct them to invade our space? That they might look on our space – superior to theirs in its very nature – as a *possession* for them to *possess*?'

Everybody hummed and grumbled agreement.

'Have you ever met a Wheah?' I put in. Everybody looked at me. 'I have,' I continued.

'And?'

I was going to say, *And he never mentioned anything about an invasion.* But that, I realised, would be a stupid thing to say. Of course he wouldn't mention an invasion. So I said nothing, and the debate circled around. What should the t'T do? There seemed to be two opinions, optimists and militarists. The militarists wanted the worlds of the t'T to adopt a new fashion (that was the phrase they used, because people such as us can really only think in terms of *fashion* and *vogue* and *modes*) – a war fashion. That way, we would be *prepared* when the Palmetto fireships, or the Wheah flotilla, drifted into t'T space. Others mocked this ('Prepared? what does that word even *mean*?'). Most of the people in the group were 'optimists', people who believed so deeply in the t'T ability to adapt and endure that the notion of 'preparation' seemed a bizarre archaism.

'If they come,' said one person, leaning back and sipping at a glass of eroin.[1] 'If they come, then we'll deal with them. We are, after all, stronger than them. We'll adapt as we need to, take on whichever fashion is appropriate.'

There was general agreement with this position. As the only person there bereft of dotTech, I suppose I felt less invulnerable than the rest of them. 'Are you certain?' I said.

Faces turned towards me.

'What?'

'How can we be certain?' I said.

'What,' said Ditle, a chuckle in his voice – this thought had clearly popped into his head as an example of the most absurd feature of a long-vanished way of life – 'do you think they could *kill* us?'

There was a silence, as people digested this strange notion. Then a woman squatting by the wall started laughing, a slow pulse of noise. Soon everybody joined her.

I laughed too, because I realised how ridiculous this very notion was. What if the Wheah *were* 'invading' – the plain and basic fact of

---

[1] A very popular t'T opiate, a clear fluid drunk typically out of small thimble-glasses.

114

things was that the peoples of the t'T were indeed stronger. Simply, they were. That was all. If I were to push a knife into Agifo3acca's chest, he would die fairly quickly. But I had pushed the knife into Enkida's very heart, and cut through the gristle and stuffing of her neck, and carried her head away and *she still didn't die*. As I was sitting in that room I had a sudden, vivid picture of Enkida – head still attached, laughing, dancing, flecks of water splashing up around her legs. Then I remembered the gut-sensations I experienced as I killed her, and I felt as if I wanted to vomit. I put my hand to my mouth (the others assumed it was to stop myself laughing) and willed my stomach to calmness.

This group and its politics: sometimes I would sit observing them as if from a million miles away, they seemed so remote from me. Or I from them. Yet there were ways that even I was drawn into the network of humanity, however hard (hard like you, o stone) that was.

6th

Dear Stone,

Later, after I had drunk a little embre, the discussion disintegrated. Several people went to bed together; others wandered out in search of more social stimulation. Klabier came over and joined me on the couch. She curled her body in against mine. 'I liked your stance,' she said, close in at my ear, 'in the debate.'

'You did?'

'It's nice to shake discussion up a little. That's what politics ought to be about. That's the way it used to be, you know.'

'We are strong,' I said. 'The peoples of the t'T. That part is right, I think.'

'Your scars,' said Klabier, putting her tiny finger-ends at each point on my face where the keloid skin marked it.

'Yes,' I said.

She slid her hand in at the collar of my shirt, found the fabric-switch and it loosened. Delicately, slowly, she began undoing the cloth. It bagged further and further out until the collar line lay around my belly.

'They go all over your body,' she said, touching each scar as if pressing them all like little buttons. 'Dot, dot, dot. Here a line, there a dot.'

'Yes,' I said.

Dear stone, how am I to explain to you the shared human sexual moment? To make a creature such as yourself understand the way human beings jab and rub one another. It is a physical, physiological, hormonal, glandular, pleasurable, psychological, symbolic, self-abasing, self-celebratory sort of business. Imagine yourself rattled with another stone, a smooth marble pebble of white milky coloration – imagine that, you and this other pebble cupped between two hands and rattled and shaken together, so that you clack and bounce off one another. That's something like it. Then imagine you and this fellow-stone were tossed together into the furnace, so hot a furnace that your brittly-tough layer of oxidised skin melts away, and the igneous rock-substance out of which you are made goes gluey and runs and deliquesces in the heat; as your lava mixes and flows with the lava of your fellow stone. That is something like it too.

Or put it another way; a more sociological way. Sex is one of the key recreations in the worlds of t'T. Most fashions come and go, but nearly all of them are oriented around this business of the human sexual encounter: this is what utopia is like. Take away the stresses and labour of human existence, the illness and fear, the need to do anything in particular rather than any other thing, and one thing is left – the sexual encounter.

That's how it is.

'You're a girl,' said Klabier to me, as she unhooked me out of my clothing. She had undone the fabric to its furthest extent, and now it was nothing more than a thin hoop of cord. 'I wondered whether you were male or female; it isn't obvious from outside. But you are a girl.'

'Don't feel much like a girl,' I said, my head glittery inside with the rush of the embre.

'No?'

'I was a man for so long before that, I'd forgotten what it's like having a woman's perspective.'

'How long a boy?' asked Klabier, pulling off her own clothing.

'Years and years,' I said, smiling to myself. 'Years and years and years.'

116

'So,' said Klabier, putting her hands behind my head. 'And how long have you been a girl?'

'Oh,' I said. I found it hard to remember; how long had I been in prison? 'Years and years.'

'Years and years and years as a boy,' said Klabier, kissing me. 'But only years and years as a girl.'

'Something like that.'

As we started to make love I was visited with a startling, upsetting memory of Enkida. I saw the blood start out of the wound in her chest and then stop almost immediately, staunched by the miniature action of the dotTech. I heard again the slightly squelchy rasping noise of my knife cutting through her vertebrae. My viscera chilled, and I felt a ghastly lurching tug of nausea. Then, with a sharp pain to my breast, I realised that Klabier was biting me, and I was swept through on a rush of sudden intense physical experience. Everything went away. You see, stone, I had not had this sexual connection with another human being for such a long time; at first it felt weird, invasive and rather unsettling. But with a swerve inside my head, the act suddenly reignited all the emotional and physical splendour of sex, and I got lost inside it.

It takes me longer to reach orgasm than has been usual, without the dotTech in my body to help along the physiological part of the process.

As I came for the second time – the AI, wilfully and awkwardly, spoke into my brain: *We can't spend much more time lolling about here you know*. It didn't blot the orgasm, but it took some of the edge off it.

7th

Dear Stone,

After this I spent several days with Klabier, in the first flush of 'love'. I think lacking the dotTech meant that I was more susceptible to the vagaries of this 'love' than most ordinary people are – the strange combinations of hormones that scuttle through the metabolism. It is all atavistic stuff, and many people get their dotTech to edit it or dampen it down altogether. But without the nano-machines in my bloodstream I was swept away by the full chaotic gush of it.

One day, she took me hand in hand out on the cables of the crevasse webbing. 'I'm a little wary,' I said. 'It's a long way to fall.' I was thinking: without dotTech it's a fall that would probably kill me. But Klabier had the blithe carelessness of the nano-protected. 'It'll be fine,' she said, and she hopped onto the nearest cable. She was beautiful; wearing her clothes in two tight bands around hips and shoulders. Her limbs were as slender and as life-filled as vegetable stalks growing from the ground, her joints fluid, her neck dusted with tiny brown hairs lined up like iron filings in a magnetic field, her lumpy cranium covered in a bristly fuzz that caught the light in a thousand different ways depending on how she turned and twisted. Her body was largely default, although she had got the dotTech to create nipples that could extend to nearly a metre, or retract completely into her chest; she told me these nipples were rich in sensitive nerve cells.

Now, of course, they were retracted; and I followed her on to the cable, reaching up awkwardly to steady myself by resting a hand against a wire that was strung higher up. Klabier scurried along this cable, and hopped on to another one that cut across at an angle. I started to follow her, moving out from the ledge so that there was nothing but blackness below me, a blank sketched over with a mish-mash of lines that were the lower cables.

I started wheezing.

If you fall,' said my AI in my head, loud.

'I know,' I said.

So what are you doing here?

'I'm curious.'

Infatuated.

'You talk to yourself,' said Klabier. 'I had a sister who did that. I like it . . . I find it endearing.'

'Great,' I said, my face flushing with the thrill of the compliment.

'And look – you got your dotTech to make you blush!'

'Just for you,' I said.

As I walked along the main cable, thick as my own torso, I supported myself by passing hand-over-hand and not letting go of a higher, thinner guide. 'For balance,' I said to Klabier as she looked at me. She stood, feet together and a look of amazement in her eyes.

Then she turned and scampered along the main cable, jumping and climbing a cross-webbed wall of ropes. Trying to free myself from the fear, I hurried my shuffling up. Then I crawled up to where the knitted cables provided a climbable surface. But Klabier was away, wriggling and clambering through a dense matrix of lines.

'Klabier,' I called.

She's gone, said the AI. *You could go back to the ledge now.*

But I ignored the voice. I passed through a small crowd of perhaps a dozen people, sitting like birds on a branch, each one of them to a different cable. They were throwing a ball with a feathery tail that span and fluttered through the air.

'Don't let me get in the way of your game,' I said, panting and ascending further. 'Don't mind me. Passing through.'

Higher there were planks laid from cable to cable; umbrella-roofs, pieces of machinery hooked from lines, stretches of fabric like flags of banners dangling down. This was a more heavily inhabited portion of the crevasse-community.

'Wellhello,' said somebody.

'Not so *well* perhaps,' said somebody else.

By this stage I was sweating with the exertion of the climb and the sweat got in my eyes, so I couldn't see who was accosting me.

'Badhello,' said the first voice, as if to an enemy. Then I heard the two of them laughing.

I blinked my eyes, and briefly saw two tall people with bone and hair growths in the shape of letters all over their bodies – OMO over their faces, Es front and mirror-reversed on their chests, Ts and As and Ws on their arms and legs.

'*Well*hello,' I said, pointedly. They were no enemies of mine. 'I'm just passing through.'

'You don't live here,' said the first.

But I had caught sight of Klabier, dangling with an arm looped around a cable. Rather than clamber directly past these two unfriendly types I detoured, ran along and diagonally crossed upwards. I reached a cable that ran in a straight line towards her and started along it. It thrummed and vibrated under my feet like a guitar string; other people must have been walking along it at some other point on its length.

'I wondered if you'd make it,' said Klabier, laughing and kissing me. 'Look.'

The position she had reached, by a freak of the near-random arrangement of cables, overlooked a sort of shaft through the webbing, right down into the darkness at the bottom of the crevasse. She was leaning right out over this abyss. I wrapped both arms around a cable to anchor myself firmly, and then tipped my head forward to take in the view.

'You're extremely comfortable with heights,' I said, once I had got my breath back.

'I grew up on a bird-world,' she said.

'Bird-world?'

'There are half a dozen or so, away spinwards. Part of the t'T, up in the Sporades. On my world, on the continents where I grew up, there were mostly just thousands of kilometres of flat plains and steppes. Great pylons, built up into the sky. We adapted our arms, lengthened them and grew feathers; flying – or gliding, to be more precise – was an important part of growing up.'

'So you're not scared of heights,' I said.

'Look!' she said, pointing. 'Sometimes people come here to dive down.'

I looked around, and realised that people were taking up positions all around this gap or shaft down through the cabling. On all sides individuals, couples in one another's arms, groups laughing and bonding; all were assembling.

'Dive down?' I said. 'Why?'

'It's two-thirds of a kilometres down,' said Klabier, which didn't immediately answer my question. She reached over and put one arm around my chest, pushing her face against mine. 'It's a sport thing,' she said. 'They dive down. They're timed from the minute they go, and have to make their way back up unaided.'

I shuddered, with fear at the prospect of falling that distance into those black, cold waters, with unnamed things sliding through them. But Klabier's giggle suggested she thought I was shivering with desire.

'Come, lover,' she said. 'We'll watch, and then we can go somewhere and make love.'

The diver – a man, naked – was standing, balancing with his legs apart on a single cable. He stretched his arms in front of his body, and I noticed thick black claws on the end of his fingers, and jutting out of his elbows as well. 'Are there limits to the alterations people can make to their own bodies?' I asked. 'I mean if they wish to take part in this sport?'

'Oh yes,' said Klabier, nuzzling my under-chin.[1] 'I think so. There's a whole chip full of rules, if you wanted to check them. Why – do you fancy doing some diving?'

'No,' I said, firmly, shuddering again. Klabier giggled again, and held me tighter.

People, in their various cable perches, were cheering and hooting. The diver raised his arms over his head and instantly everything went silent. He stood for a moment, and then toppled forward, keeping himself absolutely stiff and straight. He upended and dropped quickly away. I could hear the slight swish of sound as he passed through the air, and then he was gone into the darkness. The cheering broke out again, wild and unrestrained.

Klabier kissed me, and together we threaded our way through the taut, enveloping lines of the webbing. We found a place where three lots of cable ran at slight angle to one another in such a way as to create a sort of cradle. There I lay back, gripping firmly, and Klabier climbed on top of me. My attention was unable to disengage itself from the possibility of falling, however, so I did not enjoy the sex as much as I might. She did, though, twittering and sighing to herself in pleasure. I stared directly up, through the criss-crossing lines of cable that went from wall to wall. In parts it looked like a holographical diagram of 3D space with gridlines marked out into infinity, except that these grid lines were slant, tangled, flying off in strange directions.

After Klabier had finished, I hugged her hard with one hand, keeping the other firmly gripping onto a cable. 'I love you,' I told her. 'I love you.'

---

[1] The Glicé word *wadal* has no precise equivalent in our tongue; it refers to that part of the face that is the underside of the chin, although not so far down as to become 'neck'.

She giggled at this, hugged me back. 'Silly,' she said.

We made our way back, smiling, and spent the rest of the day drinking in the bar.

That night Klabier pushed out her nipples until they were about twenty centimetres long.[1] They were hard, thumb-thick. She put one, then the other, inside me, and kissed and bit at the bumps and scars on my belly. I didn't much enjoy the insertion, but the touch of her tongue was exquisite. I realised that she had had her tongue adjusted by her dotTech also; it was covered in little warty extrusions that seemed to be able to give out tiny shocks, like electricity, but which was probably (I never asked) just miniature thorns darting out to prick and stimulate.

In the morning, as she went out on the webbing again, I yielded to my AI's bickering, keeping off the wires and instead striding out along the ledge. I grabbed some morning yam, hot and sweaty with yam-flavour, from a stand, and ate it as I went.

I shall do what you want of me, I subvocalised.

Finally, said my AI, almost sighing inside my head.

'Where am I going to?' I asked.

There's a man lives by himself in a rock-spire not far from Mant-aspiir.[2] This last named site was a famous, immensely tall and slender pillar of rock.

I climbed to the top of the canyon, and waited for an hour or so. Finally a bird-car was ready to go, carrying people to the chain of mountains of which Mant-aspiir was a part. I took a seat near the back along with a dozen or so individuals. The car pushed itself up into air and hovered for a moment, before extending its spade-shaped 'wings' and rowing itself through the sky. Below me I could see the canyon, clotted with its tendrils of cable linking cliff-face to cliff-face. The sun was up, and the eastern mountains tossed knife-blade shadows over the intervening landscape. We moved slowly, pulsingly, through the air in that direction. Crevasse after crevasse opened beneath us; some heavily populated, some with only a few cables like clothes-lines strung

---

[1] The literal transliteration of the Glicé units of measurement – which comes out at 17.35 centimetres – gives an unwarranted impression of precision.
[2] Glicé: *mant* is 'mountain' or 'peak'; *aspiir* means both 'height' and 'breath, spirit'.

from wall to wall. The timbre of rock shifted from dark red, through a maroon to a sort of blue, speckled with blotches of something far paler that almost glowed in the light.

'They say it's possible to climb to the very top of Mant-aspiir,' said the person sitting on my left, a corpulent individual of indeterminate gender with a bushy moustache growing where the eyebrows more usually are, and fleshy tendrils hanging from his chin like a catfish.

'Really?' I said.

'Not saying I'll try,' said this individual. Mant-aspiir was so tall that its higher reaches were, more or less, out of the atmosphere.

S/he said something more, but my attention was distracted by the godlike sense of above-ness that comes with flight.[1] It is one of humanity's most fundamental, most atavistic sensations – the sheer elation of being in the air over one's fellows. I think many people in t'T have forgotten, or no longer have access to, the power of the sensation. But I, statistical freak, throwback that I was, looked down on the tiny dots moving over the ground, or playing in the webbing, and felt a lightness in my heart. People were shrunken to the scale of insects, turned almost into nano-creatures themselves. People playing a throw-ball game in the webbing of one crevasse looked like insects wriggling in a spider's net. The occasional buildings, swim-pools or other features built on the bulges of rock that separated crevasses (and that were generally too brief and stumpy to be called *plateaus*) had the miniature purity of models.

The bird-car docked at Mant-aspiir, and its passengers tumbled out laughing, some hugging newly met friends. One couple, who had spent the whole journey chattering to one another, constantly trumping one another's words with higher pitched interjections until they fell into one another's arms laughing, went straight off towards a wadi of green bushes; evidently to make love. I stepped off the car and looked around me, and was struck by the clarity of the utopia of t'T, the amazing simplicity and beauty of the culture. As if the key to individual happiness was really just as banal as that: a body freed

---

[1] The Glicé *prydor* is sometimes translated as 'superiority', but means something literal, an actual being-above, rather than simply feeling of metaphorical elevation.

from disease and all the fears and shocks our ancestors endured; a mind devoted to relishing the difference of other human encounters, as wealthy or poor as you want to be, as widely travelled or as stay-at-home as you want to be, as stimulated or static as you want to be. That this was enough. All these people looked to me like magical people.

I'll pause over this a minute, stone, to try and make it clear to you, because I'm not sure it is even really clear to me. These people stepping off the car in the sunlight that day, looked to me like people from a magical dream. I had had that sensation before, since escaping from my jail: a sick human wandering through a crowd of superhumans, super-strong and super-disease-resistant. I had felt small and inadequate, and therefore set against the world, ready to commit the crime I had been employed to commit. Ready to kill off these people, to draw myself a little closer to them. But as I looked about me now, in the sunshine, I saw them as if they were not people so much as works of art.

Come along, said my AI, impatient. *We've already lost too much time.*

'And why are you,' I said aloud, 'in such a hurry?' A woman turned her head to look at me, thinking I had addressed her, but turned away when it was clear I had not done so.

You'll have all the time in your life to fritter away on Narcissus after you have done what you agreed to do.

I made my way along a well-trodden path. It branched and I followed my AI's direction, up a series of flattened levels, to some steps. Then I walked the spine of a narrow ridge, the path littered with stones; distant relatives of yours, in all their knuckly, clutching, egg-like loveliness. By this point I was alone; except, as ever, for the relentless twittering of my AI in my head.

That one, it said, directing my eyes towards a sharply angled spire of rock. It jutted straight off the back of the rock formations like a huge tapering finger, a serrated and attenuated dorsal fin from the back of the world itself. *Hurry up, climb it, get to the top.*

I looked around; the landscape was interrupted all about me with similar narrow knife-like peaks of rock, jutting at various angles to the vertical, of various heights and thicknesses. The pale blue rocks were scaled with dashes of white. The sun was high in the sky. Behind me, the enormous over-towering of Mant-aspiir itself was pooling a mess of shadow at its base. I rotated myself slowly on one heel, drawing my body round with the other foot, to take in the splendour of this vista.

Come along, no time for sightseeing, said my AI.

'I no longer believe in you,' I told it. 'You are a figment of my imagination, not a proper AI at all.'

Figment! it replied, in a tone of disgust.

'You're the result of psychological trauma, deriving from many years of dotTech deprivation and imprisonment. I imagine you, hallucinate you. You're one part of my mind talking to another part.'

Perhaps I should not bother to believe in you, said the AI.

'That's exactly what I am saying!' I said. 'No AI talks in those sorts of terms. I dream you. That's it. That's it.'

It wasn't I who killed that woman on Rain, said the AI, sly now. *You did that. There were no voices in your head then.*

'That was a different,' I started saying. Then the words dried in my mouth. Different how? I thought of Enkida, laughing and dancing. I thought of the sense-drained expression of her severed head. Her flesh, made empty of awareness as rocks, or stones, or trees.

Besides, my AI went on, wheedling now. *If I am a figment of your imagination, how do I know to direct us to this particular spire of rock?* It pulled my eyes round, like a magnet, so that I was staring at the peak once again. The quality of the stone's blue colour deepened as it rose.

'I wish you wouldn't,' I said. 'Please disengage control from my motor cortex.'

No, that can't happen I'm afraid, it replied. *The pathways are hard-wired into your brain tissue now. Built up of plasmetals and extra-conductors.*

'You don't have to use them,' I pointed out.

I do. That is how I am programmed.

'To turn me into an automaton!'

No, I can't do that. My control is limited, and I'm often fighting your own conscious impulses as well as your autonomous nervous system even for that. Better that you do what you agreed to do, and then you can be free.

'Once I've done the killing,' I said. 'Will you leave my head then?' I was worried by what it had said about being 'hard-wired' in there.

According to you, it replied, tart, *I don't exist anyway. How can something leave unless it exists first? If it doesn't exist, it isn't there in the first place in order to be able to leave.*

I decided not to get involved in discussing this sort of metaphysics; instead I started whistling a tune that I recalled from my childhood, as loudly as I could.

I climbed the cut-stone stairway on the back of this forty-five-degree angled promontory of rock. There were no handholds, and as I got higher the prospect of falling (without dotTech in my body to preserve me after impact) became more and more alarming to me. I went up and up; the air thinned and stretched with a chill. The ground slipped away below me, and the sky seemed to come closer. But eventually I reached a wide-spaced opening, a sort of doorway, rimmed with carefully embedded scarlet tiles.

'Wellhello,' I called inside.

Go in, urged the AI. *Go on.*

'This is the man you want me to meet? He's in here?'

Not really a man.

For some reason I hovered on the threshold, unwilling to go further inside. 'A woman,' I said, gripping the jamb of this doorway and looking down the thread-like avenue of stairs I had just climbed dropping away from me. In the time it had taken me to climb up the sun had shuffled a little further round the sky, and the shadows on the broken ground at the foot of the rock spires were more shaped.

'A woman, then.'

Not really a woman either.

'Androgene.'

Not that neither.

'Riddles.'

Go in, go in.

I tipped my head right back, and looked along the remaining reach of the rock spire. It seemed to be vanishing for miles and miles, the perspective effect exaggerated by the tapering of the edifice itself. The rock's pale blue freckled with white contrasted the sky's deeper blue.

I stepped through the door. It was shadowy inside, and my feet scraped through a crunching and rattling carpet of debris. Ahead of me was a serried display of cloth banners dangling from the ceiling.

'This individual,' I hissed to my AI. 'She, he, it, has something to help me. Something I need?'

There, said the AI, directing my eyes over to a figure sitting in a sling-backed, long-necked chair.

I stepped towards him; but the floor really was ankle deep in a rustling layer of dry shells, or plastic fragments, or torn up card, or something. Walking produced a swooshing, dragging noise; more wading than walking.

'What is this?' I asked, irritable, looking down, and pushing aside the banners that dangled from the ceiling. It was quite dark inside this space.

Tag-matteo is the individual's name. You are walking through a floor-full of insect carapaces.

'What?'

A famous collection, as it happens. Tag collected the shells and carapaces from a million insects. Once upon a time[1] he catalogued them as a form of art, but latterly he took to simply littering the floor with them. I'm not sure if that was art as well, or something else.

I reached the couch-chair in which this Tag-matteo was sitting. 'I've never heard of him,' I said aloud.

I have. If I'm nothing more than a voice in your head, then you must *have heard of him, or I wouldn't have either. Do you see?*

'I'm not going to play those sorts of games with you, AI. Who is this Tag-matteo?'

Somebody who was a man, and a woman, and for a time an androgene, but not now, for bless your heart, he's dead.

Dead. I was going to kick the word back out, as a retort, but I found I couldn't say it; but enough of the intention to speak it registered in my vocal cortex, because the AI answered, almost mockingly.

Are you shocked? You?

---

[1] *Hwat*, a traditional Glicé term with which a story begins. In this context, the word might also be translated 'when his story began . . .'

'How did he die?'

He grew old. He died. Not even the miraculous dotTech can keep a person alive forever.

'Why is he sitting here? Shouldn't the body have been disposed of – I don't even know what they do with the dead on this world.'

Sometimes they do what they have done here. He asked for this, to be left alone to mummify. The air up here is dry and cold, and mummification has taken place.

'And?'

And he'll sit here for many years. Maybe centuries. There are many rooms like here on this world, places carved out by individuals who requested to be left there after their death. I can tell you how old he was when he died, if you like.

I was leaning forward, peering at the flesh. I don't know what I expected, dear stone. I think something leathery, something creased and plasticky looking. But his skin was perfectly smooth, if a little drawn. His eyes were closed, his mouth shut, and his nose pinched in around the bridge. But he still had his hair, growing in blue tufts all over his ochre skin. His arms were draped over the shape of the armrests, his palms closed over the ends and his fingers (he had nine fingers on each hand I noticed) dangling down. The fabric of his one-piece had been loosened a little, and the neckline sagged to show off a hairless but equally taut and smooth collarbone. It occurred to me then that, possibly, the dotTech stayed in his body long enough to help it mummify swiftly and cleanly, before oozing out of his pores or dropping from his nose to drift away on the wind. But I didn't know.

'How old?' I asked.

Nine hundred and ninety. And I can tell you how long he has sat here, in this chair, undisturbed, if you want to know that.

'Did the dotTech help him mummify?'

Why do you ask?

'I suppose I'm curious. They're programmed, aren't they, to preserve our health. To keep human beings alive for as long as possible and healthy for as long as possible. Doesn't their responsibility for us end with death? Helping somebody mummify themselves might be beyond their programming.'

It's hard, said the AI in a curious tone, *to comprehend the nano-*

machines, you know. It's not really accurate to talk about them being 'programmed'. That makes them sound like binary processors, computers on a small scale, and they're not. We don't really understand them, is the truth. They are their own thing. They live their own lives, solving problems, reproducing.

Something in this piqued me. 'We made them,' I pointed out. 'Humanity I mean. Come to think of it, we made *you* – designed you and built you, and all the AIs. We did the same with the dotTech, fashioned these nano-machines to swim in our bloodstream and preserve us.'

You're right.

'So why are you talking like that?'

Like what?

'Playing games again,' I said, standing up straight. 'You were going to tell me how long he has sat here like this?'

Sixty-nine years, give or take.

'Hey. That's a long time.'

I know lots of things about him. I could tell you about his first love affair. About his time on Branda. He travelled into the realms of the Wheah – how few people in t'T can boast as much? He had an insatiable appetite for finding things out, something unusual amongst the t'T I'm sorry to say. He lived as an experimental artist for forty years, on a commune on Variationen. His speciality was arranging thousands of tiny particles in space, nudging each one into position with a pinpoint laser, making complex patterns that looked like holograms but were actual material things. Very painstaking. He parented four children; all of them still alive, although the first he parented is now in his nine-hundreds. Or maybe her nine-hundreds, I'm not sure about that.

'You don't know everything about him then.'

Oh, but I know so much. I know that he developed a persistent sexual peccadillo, a desire to have partners bite at his feet, his toes and his feet, during sex. He always started the day with a pellet of sugar. He used to love sneezing, you know? He got his dotTech to leave his nasal mucus membrane for half an hour a day, and then he would sniff up dusty irritants and sneeze and sneeze. He loved the sensation.

Sneezing! Dear stone, since the dotTech had abandoned me I had sneezed thousands of times. Personally, I hated the experience; the shuddering loss of control.

He spent many years studying the Gravity Trench. Many years. He was fascinated by that phenomenon.

'Like Agifo3acca,' I said.

Yes.

'How do you know all these things about this person?' I asked. 'How can you possibly know any of this stuff – know how to direct me to this place, to . . .'

I'll tell you something else, the AI said, cutting across me. *Something nobody knows about except – well, except* you *when I tell you. A secret.*

What sort of secret?

A programme. A very special thing. He thought he died and took the secret into death with him. But it's in there. It was directing my eyes, and moving my hand out, in its eagerness. I was bending forward.

'Stop!' I said, and froze.

A moment passed.

Sorry, said the AI. *I guess I got carried away. But if you relax, I'll just direct your hand to the right place. You'll never find it otherwise.*

I breathed in. 'OK.'

My hand moved again, rummaged through the carpet of old insect parts. The shells, carapaces, glinting deep-blue fragments, dusty black hemispheres, arcs of chitin. They felt crackly, fragile, against my hand. The AI withdrew my hand from the mass and I stood up again.

'What's this?'

Take it to the light. Have a look.

I went over to the doorway, and stepped outside into the sunshine. In my hand was a tiny thorax, its iridescence green, mottled with dust. How, I subvocalised, did you know – out of all those millions of insect remains – that this was the thing I had to pick up?

I just knew.

What is it?

Information. Great wealth. Take it with you. Pocket it away, take it to Nu Fallow when you go.

What sort of information?

I can't tell you.

'Don't be stupid!' I burst out. 'You bring me to this planet – direct

130

me to this location upon it – give me the life history of this person – pick out this packet of information processing from amongst millions of discarded insect carapaces. You can do *all* this, and yet you cannot tell me a simple thing about *what the information actually is?*'

It will build you something.

'It's a construction programme?'

A complex and brilliant one.

'Like the ones that people use to build themselves spaceships and space-platforms when they travel to an uninhabited system?'

Something like that.

'So what will it build me? A spaceship?'

I cannot tell you.

Don't be ridiculous. Don't be so ridiculous.

Listen to me Ae. This is how it has to be. I can't tell you anything more about it, only that it is supremely important. I can, however, promise you this: there will come a time when I can tell you – after you've completed the job you've been hired to do. After that I'll explain the whole thing, including the mystery of why I wasn't able to explain before. Alright?

I sat on the ledge formed by the stairs outside Tag-matteo's room – his mausoleum, more precisely. The thin, bright air was fresh against my face. I had before me a splendid view over the up-down landscape of rock and pathways steepled with dozens of spires.

'I'll tell you, AI,' I said. 'I am disinclined to allow this taking over of my motor reflexes. Do you see?'

We should be getting going. Take a bird-car back to Ru-denetter, and then into orbit.

'What is this all about?'

What do you mean?

'This crime. I need to know more, AI. You know what I need to know. There is much more here, isn't there? Much more that you know and that you're not telling me.'

This conversation can't go anywhere.

'I want to know who has employed me. Do you see? I want to know why they want me to murder the population of a whole planet.' The archaic word *murder* seemed to be picked up by a sudden breeze that whispered it back at me.

Probably best not to think about it in those terms, said the AI. *That'll only make it harder for you to do the job.*

'I want to know why it has to be the planet you've chosen for me. What is it about that particular place? I want to know about the cultures that live there, about the peoples I am going to destroy.'

That will make it harder too. Best not to think about them as people at all. Think of it as a job to do.

'Tell me.'

Can't.

'Won't?'

Listen, Ae. You must believe me – must trust me. If there were any way I could tell you these things you want to know, I would do it. But there is a crucial reason why I cannot. Of course you want to know what this reason is, and . . . not trying to outrage you, but . . . I simply cannot tell you. But eventually I will tell you everything. You must complete the charge, that's the first thing. Then I'll tell you everything.

I sat for a long time on the step, watching the occasional hint of cloud cast dubious half-shade on the ground below me; watching the shadows of the rock-spires slowly haul themselves round like the marker of gigantic sundials. I was trying to work out how much of my mind was free of the AI. If it were truly an AI, then it should only have access to certain cortexes – my speech centres, my motor centres. Then, provided I did not subvocalise, I ought to be able to *think* without being overheard ('overthought' perhaps). But what if it were something more? What if it were simply a figment of my imagination? The internal voice of a madman, the imaginary friend of schizophrenic paranoia. Eventually I spoke.

'Is it the Wheah?'

The Wheah, repeated the AI.

'Are they behind this? Or one particular sect of Wheah, perhaps. I still can't think why they would, unless those political hobbyists are correct in their talk of war. War, AI? Is that what this is all about?'

How much do you know about the Wheah?

'How much do *you*?'

I asked you.

'I know that they are barbarians – without the dotTech to civilise them they have retained a number of archaic cultural habits. They still worship their gods. They still trade goods for money. They still fight and kill one another.'

And how do you know these things?

'Everybody knows them.'

Hearsay? Gossip?

I stood up, and started stepping gingerly down the long staircase. 'Just tell me why they want to murder this whole world? Is it some sort of practice – a dry run, perhaps. Once they know it can be done, will they spread death and destruction throughout the t'T?'

I did not say it was the Wheah.

'The Palmetto? That doesn't seem to make sense. And besides, you haven't denied that it is the Wheah, either.'

Put the info-chip in your pocket.

'What?'

The info-chip. It is programmed into the chitin of the insect carapace you picked up in there. Believe me, you will need it; it will help you.

I flicked the fabric switch under the waistband of my pants and pulled out a short pocket. Dropping the info-chip inside freed up my hands. 'I will go to Nu Fallow,' I said.

Good.

'But I want to know more.'

And I can't tell you any more.

'Then I'll find out for myself. I'll go to Nu Hirsch, and find out for myself.'

Nu Hirsch is in the wrong direction. But I wasn't listening any more.

Nu Hirsch

Dear Stone,

I went to Nu Hirsch, and that angered my AI. I took Klabier with me, and that angered it even more. *No attachments! What can you gain by doing this thing, bringing this person along? She can only hinder you, betray you, ruin everything.*

I ignored it. Klabier and I made love one more time. She pressed the balls of her hands against my belly as she straddled me. Then we ascended into orbit and prepared for the trip across space.

If you tell her about your mission, the AI warned, sounding more and more querulous inside my head. *If you tell her that – then you will be abandoned.*

Abandoned? I repeated, surprised at this.

Your whereabouts will be made known to the 'police'. Citizens of t'T are all around you – any of them might be an agent of the 'police'. You would be apprehended within minutes. Do you understand that? Minutes!

'Threatening me,' I said.

Threatening, yes, it replied. *This was the deal you agreed to when you were freed from your prison. Remember? Do you remember?*

'I shall not tell Klabier anything,' I said. 'I remember the deal I made.'

Do not spend too long in Nu Hirsch, said the AI, the threat in its artificial voice becoming clearer and clearer. *That too might be seen as transgressing the basis of the agreement.*

I didn't say anything to this. It occurred to me that the tenor of my AI had changed; it was no longer merely an advisor, a facilitator. It acted now as the direct agent of my employers, whoever they were. Of course, dear stone, given the constraints of deep space it would not be possible for my employers to contact me directly; so in a way it made sense for them to deputise.

And then the foam spilled up around me, and everything went dark.

2nd

Dear Stone,

I have been a loner most of my life. I had been mostly alone even before I had spent so many years in the artificial madness of the jailstar. But I think I fell in love with Klabier. What is love? You will surely tell me, stone; the denser and stronger the heart, the more love it is capable of feeling, and whose heart is denser or stronger than yours? Of course, in saying that I fell in love with Klabier I am not going so far as to say that I truly considered her as anything other than an extension of my own appetites. But she satisfied those appetites so well!

To be honest, I found myself severely afflicted with mood swings. For days I would be sullen, miserable, there would be a deadness and decay in the very centre of my head. Nothing was possible, nothing mattered, I was bad, and bad, and bad, and the only thing was the inevitable collapse of order into death. I could not get out of bed when I woke up, but would lie front down, my face pressed close against the weave of the cloth. But then . . . then . . . I would, for no apparent reason, suddenly swing about and about; I would leap from the bed singing, and bounce around. I would grab a startled Klabier and swing her around in an improvised dance. Everything was possible! I was free – I had been freed from a prison it was impossible to escape from. I had the entire galaxy before me. I could do anything – *We* could do anything. 'I love you,' I would sing into Klabier's face, 'I love you, let's always be together, let's *never* be apart!'

'You're happy today!' she would reply, laughing, as we spun and spun about.

'How can I not be happy when I am with *you!*' I would say. And then, because the joy and the spirit was bubbling up inside me I would repeat the sentence – but as song. 'How could I *not*,' I would sing, breaking free from her to skitter my feet, to the *left* to the *right*, 'be so hap*py* . . . when you are with *me*.'

'What madness is this!' Klabier would say. But she would be laughing, her face crinkled up with pleasure. And I would grab her again in a great hug, and we would stumble off together in one another's arms to make love.

Neither of these moods would last. In general, dear stone, I think it is true to say that the 'happy' mood lasted only days, whereas the 'unhappy' mood could last a week or more. Before the dotTech left my body I never experienced anything so extreme; the nano-machines controlled the hormonal and physiological aspects of the mood swings so well, I suppose, as to more or less eliminate them. Even my years in the jailstar had not been so emotionally unstable; the monotony of my surroundings, I think, and the fact that my mood was generally depressed meant that it was at least consistent. But released from prison, with all the new experiences and stimulations, I began to find my moods swinging wilder and wilder.

'For you,' Klabier said to me one day on Nu Hirsch, 'living is like a performance. You are like an actor or musician; you inhabit different roles from day to day. I have never met a person like you.'

'I love you,' I said, more soberly. 'I want us to be together.' It seemed like the right sort of thing to say.

'How absurd you are!' she replied, laughing again. 'How can you say such a thing? You hardly know me!'

'I know myself, and therefore I know my feelings,' I said. 'You make me happy. Let's be together. We can have children.' *You're forgetting*, said my AI, sour and jealous, *that without dotTech you are a default-setting biological female. You cannot adapt to father a child, and if you mothered a child, carrying it in your dotTech-free womb, it would probably kill you.* But I ignored my AI most of the time now.

'Children?'

'Yes! Why not? My home world, Terne, is a paradise for children. It has a high concentration of children, schools, camps – a childhood utopia. Why don't we go there?'

'How funny,' said Klabier. 'I had two children. Where I come from,

136

the world Sky, parenting involves leaving the children as soon as possible.'

'What were your children called?' I asked, eagerly.

She looked at me with a strange expression, as if I had asked some sort of taboo question. But the idea of returning to Terne and raising a family with my new-found love had seized my brain. When I was in a 'happy' mood, ideas gripped me with the force of revelation. This was what I intended to do in my life; this was my destiny. To bring children into the world with Klabier.

'Listen,' she was saying, her face more serious now. But I was gabbling; talking so rapidly I'm surprised she was able to understand me.

'I have a job to do,' I said (*Glad you remembered that* commented my AI internally, with a cynical edge), 'but when it's over I'm free to do what I like. Then we can go to Terne, which is actually very close to Nu Hirsch, a slow jump through to the edge of the Tongue. It is beautiful, Terne, great steppes leading down to thousands of bays and fjords overlooking a purple ocean. The perfect place to be a child—' I believe, dear stone, that I was crying a little by this stage '—an idyll, truly. I must do this one job, that is all, and I have come here—'

'Job?' interjected Klabier, looking more and more puzzled.

'—come here to, I don't know, to *understand* it a little more, because there are things about this job that don't truly make sense—'

Control yourself! snapped my AI. *What are you saying? Will you tell her everything?*

'—I am commissioned to do this job,' I went on, 'but I don't exactly know by whom, and I was hoping to find out a little more . . .'

'What . . .' she said, her forehead marked now with lines like an interference pattern.

'. . . the *politics* angle is an interesting one, and I was wondering, before I do this job—'

'What are you *talking* about?' she asked, firmly, cutting me off. 'What is this talk? I don't understand at all.'

I paused, and looked at her face.

Leave it, said my AI. *You are on the verge of revealing everything. Do you want to go back to prison?*

I flushed, and started stammering. I remember I had to leave, to hurry out of the room and pace about the busy thoroughfares of Nu Hirsch Main for an hour or more, my AI chiding me all the time.

But I am getting ahead of myself.

We put on packs and let the foam envelope us, having promised to rendezvous at Nu Hirsch. Then we dropped into space, and I entered the dozy half-trance of interstellar flight.

This is what I was thinking – and as I entered faster than light the thoughts started to repeat themselves, rearrange and reconfigure themselves in that monotonous fugue-state way. I thought: the AI had directed me to a single dried insect thorax amongst millions, in which is an info-chip containing something – it did not tell me what – that would help with my task. From the first, the AI had known amongst the millions of stars, which one; from amongst the millions of people (living and mummified) on that world, which one; from the millions of tiny pieces of litter on that dead individual's floor, which one. It had pinpointed this object with an accuracy that was astonishing.

I still had the info-chip in my pocket. It made a slight bulge against my groin as I curled up for travel.

I thought to myself of the processing power of my AI; of how it seemed to survive all my flights. It was no ordinary AI. I thought of who could possibly have the power to spring me from jail, to undertake the kind of information survey necessary to pick out the one tiny info-chip essential to the job in hand. I thought about who would want to invest that much time and energy in setting up the crime I was employed to commit.

Then I thought about the first person I had met upon escaping the jail; I thought about Agifo3acca. He had constructed a giant spaceship, layer upon layer, room added to room. He had started, probably, with an info-chip no bigger than the one I had in my pocket. One of the standard info-chips, that had taken its orders and burrowed out through the traveller's foam without breaking the seal. That had spawned the initial nano-facilitators, that had scavenged raw materials from whatever was to hand – whichever asteroid or airless moon the traveller arrived besides. From these raw materials bigger robots could be built, more iron and carbon adapted and shaped, more simple self-replicators created. By the time Agifo3acca was ready to come out of his foam these machines would have built him the first few chambers of his ship. And then, when he was cleaned and ready, he could have personally directed the architectural operation of assembling the rest of his ship; sublight drives, carbon adaptors for food processing (trading for organic material to grow would come later), simple processors, observational tools. None of this would have happened quickly, and a ship the size of Agifo3acca's would have taken many years to assemble.

Why had he done it? Why had Agifo3acca left the space of the Wheah, his home, to travel so far into the territories of the t'T? Why had he been waiting for me, when I was sprung from the impossible jail? It could not be coincidence.

This is what I thought. The Wheah were thousands of separate cultures, billions of people. Assume they united in a common cause, against the t'T. They would have the processing power and energy to mount so enormous an undertaking. They could spend many years preparing for the crime; tracking down such info-wealth as they needed to prosecute it (the info-chip in my pocket for example); working out how to get me out of prison. Maybe the AI was Wheah technology; perhaps they had found a way – which the t'T certainly had not – of creating an AI that could survive faster-than-light travel. Perhaps it wasn't an AI at all, perhaps it was some sort of trans-mitter.

Or perhaps it was a figment of my imagination. Perhaps the whole thing was merely the fantasy of my unstable consciousness.

But my mind was locked into its pattern now. I thought, over and over, of possible motivations: the Wheah, organising a conspiracy on so huge a scale. Why? Only one answer: war. Why war? Only one reason: invasion.

And so I was going to Nu Hirsch. When people from the Wheah made the slow sublight journey through the Tongue they – obviously – chose its narrowest point. This brought them into t'T space near Nu Hirsch. If there were answers to be found, they would be found there.

Dear Stone,

The two of us stayed at Nu Hirsch for about two months, and during that time I convinced myself I had fallen in love with Klabier. I am not so sure now; but now, beloved stone, I have you, I have you. But at the time I told myself that Klabier was all in all to me. It is peculiar, and perhaps dotTech would have saved me from the rashness of my emotional commitment. But it seemed right; the pinpoint vividness of the sensation. It was more than the pleasure of sex, more than the enjoyment of her company.

I had my first presentiment that this was what was happening when I arrived at the Nu Hirsch orbital. I was collected, washed clean and given some food. But I was so impatient to discover whether Klabier had arrived before me that – hungry though I was – I did not eat. Instead I paced up and down the Arrival Hall, checking each individual, standing beside each pod-like blob of hardened foam as it was attended to, washed with solvent to reveal the huddled human being inside.

I stayed in the Arrival Hall for a whole day. I pestered the attendants (they were mostly automated systems on Nu Hirsch; actual people did not serve terms as arrival guides as was the case on most systems). Saying: I travelled with a friend, a lover actually. I had obviously made better time through space than her, but could you let me know when she arrives? Please?

'Of course,' said the pleasant-voiced, gel-bodied Haüd-machine that was hosing down a new pod. 'Why not wait in recreation areas? It is more pleasant there.' They are not sentient, these Haüd-machines; they are not like an AI. They are merely well-designed robots, but they give the illusion of interacting so well that it easy to be fooled.

'Very well,' I said. It occurred to me, groggy though I was from my journey, that I was unusually agitated by Klabier's non-arrival. As if I cared a great deal. That made me wonder.

I finally took some food, and sat in an observation alcove of the recreation room. Around me new arrivals sat and talked, eating and drinking; or else danced, played games, went off to coigns to have sex.

I looked out at the double-system before me. Nu Hirsch is a

wonderfully built-up group of worlds. Two equal-sized planets orbited one another, spinning around a notional point that itself revolved around its sun. These worlds existed in very close proximity and enjoyed an unusual regularity of their mutual orbital oscillation. This meant that Nu Hirschers were able to link the two planets with a great chain. It was an adaptation of the older technology that had once been popular on worlds, providing for space elevators with a cord that stretched from the ground to a point twice as high as geosynchronous position. Dear Stone, in the earlier days these cable-cars had been widespread; running elevators up to and down from orbit. Subsequent advances in laser precision and power meant that the technology was mostly abandoned; it is more flexible and more efficient to drop elevators balanced on the focussed needle of a laser; and to use the compression potential to raise up a second elevator whenever you want rather than simultaneously. But on Nu Hirsch they kept the older machinery; a self-generating cable, strung out, linking world and world. They liked, I think, the concept of there being a *material* connection from planet to planet. They liked that regular elevators cars shot up, and along, and down, that it was possible to step on to a bus and arrive on their sister world in minutes.

From orbit, where I waited for Klabier in the arrival hall, it was impossible to make out the thread that linked world to world. Compared to the bulk of the planets the cable was infinitesimally slender. The window through which I looked at the silver-amber globes of Nu Hirsch and Nu Hirsch (the natives usually make no distinction between the names of either world, although travellers sometimes call one A and one E) – the window through which I looked was very helpful. I asked it for more resolution. It isolated a portion and magnified for me, so that I could just make out the momentary glint of a car passing and reflecting the sunlight.

'There goes one of them,' said the window. It had a clear, flat voice.

'Are all the services automated here?' I asked. By *automated* I meant fitted with semi-sentient chips in order to interact with ordinary people.

'Nu Hirsch is a centre for friendly technology,' said the window. 'You'll find most architectural and motor features will be happy to talk with you.'

A Haüd-machine sloped past me, and I sprang up to ask after Klabier. But it didn't know anything. 'Apologies, but I have not been working in the arrival hall.'

I tried to settle myself down.

'Nu Hirsch,' I said to myself, trying to focus on the task in hand. I needed to find out how many 'political' groups existed on the planet, like the ones on Narcissus. I would join these groups, and find out from them what was known of the Wheah. Were they planning war? Why might they want a planet murdered – a planet, it occurred to me then, for the first time, very distant from their territories.

'AI,' I said. 'Are you there? Have you survived yet another journey through the faster-than-light space?'

I wish, said my AI, grumpily, *that you would subvocalise, instead of talking aloud all the time.*

My apologies, I spoke silently. I am continually amazed by your ability to survive a journey that would kill most AIs.

We've been through this before, said the AI, wearily.

Yes, I subvocalised. And you have given me one explanation. And I have considered other ones – that you are a new design of AI, perhaps fashioned by the Wheah, capable of enduring quantum jolts.

There's a fanciful idea, said the AI, deadpan. *You've also wondered whether I actually exist, or whether I'm a mere figment of your imagination. Haven't you?*

I ignored this. You know why I have come to Nu Hirsch, I said.

To infuriate me. We need to travel to Nu Fallow as soon as possible.

I am the murderer, I subvocalised. Merely saying it gave me an unpleasant tingle in my stomach, but I pressed on. *I* commit the murder. But I am also the 'police', trying to discover *who* committed the murder. Do you understand?

Semantics, said the AI, dismissively.

You can say that easily enough, I subvocalised. You *know* who is behind the crime. I do not. If you will simply tell me, then I can fly straight to Nu Fallow and carry it out.

The AI sounded wheedling, tired, in reply. *I can't, I've explained to you that I can't.*

Why can't you?

I can't tell you why I can't.

142

Wordplay.

It is genuine. There is a real reason why I cannot. But I have promised you that once the job is done—

'Once the crime is committed,' I interrupted, aloud, tired of the euphemisms.

Whatever . . . when it is over, I will tell you everything then. Alright? Is that not enough for you?

Since you won't tell me, I said, slipping back into subvocalisation, I shall have to try and find out for myself. I have a theory. I think the Wheah are behind this. So perhaps you can answer one question, even though you refuse to tell me what I need to know.

One question?

You know which world I must murder. It is near to Nu Fallow.

Yes. That is your one question?

No – no – I want to know: why that world? It is as far from Wheah space as it is possible to get inside t'T. That is significant, isn't it? Is it some sort of distraction?

Distraction?

'What,' I said, forgetting myself and speaking aloud in my excitement, 'if it is a distraction? What if it is designed to draw the attention of everybody in the t'T away from the Tongue? Away from the border with the Wheah? What then?'

Hush! rebuked the AI.

Somebody wants the whole population of a world killed, I subvocalised, urgently. Who? Why would they want such a thing? It can only be an act of war – an act of war!

War, said the AI, as if this were the most ridiculous thing in the world. *There hasn't been a war in the t'T for a thousand years – for two thousand. War! Don't be absurd. We are beyond war here.*

But you don't deny it, I said. And then I was interrupted.

'Wellhello!' It was Klabier. And in my excitement I jumped up and ran to hug her, and in the intensity of my happiness to see her again I forgot all about the Wheah, about conspiracy, about the enormity of the crime that was still before me.

143

Dear Stone,

We travelled down in a conventional elevator, riding the top of a laser line, and spent the day wandering about Nu Hirsch Main. All the cities on this twin-world system have names like that – Nu Hirsch Major, Nu Hirsch Prime, Nu Hirsch First City. It is one of the quirks of that world.

We had actually come down upon Nu Hirsch A, the one of the twin-system with slightly more ocean and slightly less by way of mountain ranges. But in almost every respect the two worlds were identical. Or perhaps interchangeable is a better word.

The constant tug of gravity in so closely connected a world gave a certain tempestuousness to the climate. There were rainstorms, although nothing as severe or insistent as I had experienced upon Rain. White clouds writhed and hurtled through a sky that was tinted a pale green colour with airborne chlorophyll-prions that lived there. There was an eclipse every two days, as regular as watchmaker's work; the close, yellow sun was broad and diffuse, and only marginally smaller in the sky than the great pregnant-circle of the sister world. For over an hour every other day the sun would be shuttered out of the sky.

Most of all there were enormous tides on Nu Hirsch; the oceans bulged and heaved in their chafing beds, and spilled up and over their shores with a daily regularity. The only buildings within kilometres of the seashore were ones specially waterproofed; for every morning the tide would sweep up and up and up until it seemed as if it would flood everything, and every evening it would recede away and away as if the very ocean were drying up to leave the world a desert. Near Nu Hirsch Main, where we spent our first week, the land was mountainous; but the sea still slopped up a good six hundred metres of cliff face to overflow and draw up around the sea wall of the mountain town. And in the evening it was an amazing sight, to sit on one of the balconies of this same wall and watch the water drain away, seemingly for ever. It shrank back, the level dropped, and even from the enormous vantage point of the city it went so far down as to become nothing more than a distant smear close to the horizon.

As far as the culture of Nu Hirsch was concerned, it is a highly technological place. Nu Hirschers love their machines, their motorised trinkets. I saw more Haüd-machines together in that place than in all the other worlds I visited put together. Every house had its mechanised feature; roofs that opened and folded back; legs that sprouted underneath to lift the entire building and moved it along; windows that folded themselves up and relocated themselves with a polite *yes! certainly!* when requested to do so. Don't misunderstand me, dear stone; there is technology through the spaces of the t'T – every individual is a walking universe of technology. What made the Nu Hirschers different was the way they loved *large*-scale technology. They were as packed with dotTech as any of us, but they also loved big machines; flying cars, smart-stilts, roller-balloons, Horbacorcs,[1] Haüd-machines, all manner of gadgets and tech-devices. At my child-school, on Terne (did I tell you, dear stone, that I come from Terne?) the emphasis of schooling was on arts, music, culture – here the emphasis was on the skills to concoct and assemble fantastical machines.

But we were not on this world because of their machines. We stayed two nights in a general room-space near the place where the elevator descended, orienting ourselves and getting used to the new city.

'You know Nu Hirsch pretty well?' I asked Klabier.

'I've been here a few times,' she said, smiling at me. 'Haven't you?'

I hooked my arm around her neck to draw her close for a kiss. 'Of course. My birth-world is not far from here. But you have specialist knowledge here, I think.'

'Specialist?'

'The political groups? Like the ones on Narcissus?'

'Oh, is *that* it? Is that why you brought me all the way over here?'

'Yes, my beauty, my love, my natural high.'

'How funny you are! I never knew a person speak as flowery. I never knew somebody who acted so outré all the time.'

'That's me.'

'What is so interesting to you about the discussion groups? They're

---

[1] The translator regrets to say that she is uncertain as to what, exactly, this term refers.

just a fad, you know; a fashion. I mean, I enjoy them as much as anybody, but in a year they will be old news.'

'I'm interested in the Wheah,' I said. 'I want to find out what they are planning.'

'The Wheah?' she replied, puzzled.

This confused me a little. 'In the politic-ing groups on Narcissus,' I said, 'you were the one who talked about the coming Wheah invasion – about how the Wheah planned to make war on us all.'

'Well,' she said. 'That was just for something to say. You know? That is the point of politics – just to have something to say.'

But I refused to let go of the idea that Klabier had planted in my mind, back on that other world. The more I thought about it the more it made sense. The Wheah were planning to invade the fast space of the t'T. They had secretly sprung me from prison, and were now secretly employing me to commit my crime – as a means of distracting attention from their real purpose. They were about to emerge in a fleet of ships from the Tongue, and make war upon us. Why my AI refused to admit that this was the truth baffled me; I could not see why it served the Wheah's purpose to keep me in the dark about their plans – unless it was because they were afraid that, criminal though I was, I would rebel against my employment and warn the t'T if I knew the truth.

In my more manic interludes I became fixated on this idea; that I might embark on a crusade to warn the whole population of the t'T about the coming invasion – that I would be their saviour, and would thereby make amends for my former crimes. I fantasised grand events, medal ceremonies.

But in my saner moments I knew this was unrealistic of me. The very idea of 'mobilising' a population as individualistic and disparate as the t'T was absurd; I could say what I liked – could say indeed that I was being employed by the Wheah to commit mass murder – and people probably wouldn't listen to me. A few might, but most wouldn't. That was the nature of things in the t'T.

'I suppose,' I whispered to my AI, one night whilst Klabier slept, her head upon my belly, 'I suppose that mass murder is one way of making the t'T sit up and pay attention.'

Your latest theory? it replied. *Have you abandoned the idea that the Wheah are behind everything, now?*

146

'Far from it,' I hissed. 'I'm closer to the truth than ever before.'

Don't wait too long here, said the AI, close in my ear. *You have a job to do. Wait too long and you'll be given back to the prison.*

I hear you, I hear you.

5th

Well, Stone,

I was, to begin with, disappointed with the 'politics' groups of Nu Hirsch. It is true, there were a great many of such groups; and much of their discussion was given over to the Wheah. But there were as many theories as there were groups, and many of these theories were simply outlandish.

Some said the Wheah were invading, and about to wage war. Others said that the Wheah wanted to become t'T; that they would come en masse as suppliants, leaving their space behind to enjoy the benefits of fast space and utopian t'T living. Other still claimed that there *were* no Wheah, that it was part of a larger conspiracy – that the Wheah were alien xenoforms (absurd!), or a fiction invented by a group of t'T citizens for any number of strange reasons. A group at Nu Hirsch Capital, four hundred kilometres down the chain of mountains from Nu Hirsch Main, spent hours rolling the discussion round and round one single theory; that the Wheah were bent on mass suicide.

'Mass suicide?' I blurted, furious. 'What idiocy!'

But they were certain, this political group. Multicoloured faces stared at me with patience, and even pity. The Wheah were coming, they said, to travel to the Gravity Trench, the Great Trench that ran through the middle of t'T space. And why go there? Because they believed their fraction-God had told them to throw themselves in – that they would find religious enlightenment there.

The strangest thing, dear stone; I stayed in that group for three days. Klabier got bored after an hour or two and went off swimming in the sea. But I became obsessed with persuading these people of the error of their ways. I had once met a Wheah, I told them, grandly (and so have we, they replied) – and your theory does not make sense. But the more

147

I argued, the more I became uncertain of my position. They were so adamant, so sure of themselves. They quoted Wheah religious texts that I never knew existed; cited Wheah scholars by name that I had never heard of. Enlightenment was to be found at the bottom of the Gravity Trench, they believed; and it could only happen when the whole population threw themselves in. Fleet upon fleet of Wheah ships would emerge from the Tongue in the coming years, and all their travellers would foam-up and fly fast-space to the Trench.

You will see, they said. Wait and see.

I did not – quite – believe them; but those three days were enough to shake me out of my own certainty. Could that be the Wheah's plan? Mass suicide? There might be some way, some strange religio-logical relating to their bizarre fraction-God belief, that linked in mass murder with mass suicide.

Is this true? I asked my AI. Are the Wheah planned to kill themselves on this scale?

Why are you asking me? it replied. *Do you assume that I know anything about the Wheah?*

It was always playing games with me.

6th

Dear Stone,

My AI frequently threatened me with prison if I did not immediately leave Nu Hirsch and travel to Nu Fallow to carry out my work. But I reasoned that, having invested so much time and energy in freeing me from prison and after having directed me to the info-chip in the insect carapace, it was unlikely that they – whoever my employers were – would blithely allow me to be taken back to prison.

'I'll go,' I said, 'when I know who my employers are.'

I can't tell you that.

'Then I shall find out for myself.'

You'll find out after the job is done.

We had this exchange many times.

I did not allow myself to think, if I could help it, that maybe I did not *want* to commit the crime I had agreed to commit. This was a thought that came to me sometimes, and I struggled not to subvocalise it – if my AI overheard it, it might lose faith with me and I would immediately be given back to the 'police'. Of course I didn't want to go back to jail, dear stone; and I had killed before, so it wasn't the killing itself that bothered me. I am not sure what it was. Maybe it was the scale of the thing; but I'll be honest with you, my only confessor, and admit that I don't think it was that. No, I think it was simply the cussed-ness in my nature. I was told to do one thing, and therefore I did not want to do it. I had sold my soul, and if I could just find a way of cheating the bargain . . .

There are grumblings, said the AI. *I can't overhear every one of your thoughts, but sometimes I get a sense of things. A sort of distant hum in your brain, as you think with your non-vocal parts of mind. I know you're up to something.*

'Nothing at all,' I said. 'Not in the least.'

At night, when Klabier was asleep, I would sometimes take out the tiny insect carapace and roll it between my fingers. I was curious to know what information it contained; why my AI had been so keen for me to retrieve it. I was curious to know what was going to happen next. I thought of having it analysed, of having its contents read by some processor or other, but I held back from this. *No*, ordered my AI. *Don't do that!* And on reflection it seemed to me likely that if I were to allow some t'T processor analyse the thing it would be tantamount to alerting the police of my intentions. *Bide your time*, said my AI.

7th

Dear Stone,

Klabier and I travelled along the coast of Continent Prime, one of the twelve continents on Nu Hirsch A. We went slowly, walking together, stopping each evening at one of the many beachside hostels. The weather was good; on a regular, one-planet system it would have been too hot (for the sun was large and the planet close in), but the constant atmospheric turbulence caused by the gravity of Nu Hirsch E, the sister world visible in the sky at all times, blew up a constant cooling wind, and cloaked the sun in filters of white cloud. There were occasions, as the two of us walked arm in arm down the beach, when the sky would clear. Continent Prime was hemmed with a single, four thousand kilometre beach, the product of the fierce wave and tide action; and we spent a week simply walking along it, with the gnashing waves grinding against the shore to our right, and the land rising slowly to our left. And sometimes as we walked the endless, broad white sand beach, the clouds would clear from the sky and the heat would rise startlingly. Above would be an overarching vault of pure, pale green sky; the bright sun large above us; Nu Hirsch E as large again over towards the horizon. And the heat would fall heavily upon us, as if it had been waiting for this opportunity to pounce. It became uncomfortable very quickly; and we would take shelter in the shadow of a dune – even Klabier, who had the dotTech in her body to help regulate her body temperature. But such moments lasted only minutes. Usually a breeze would start up again, clouds would scurry up over the edge of the sea and slot in front of the sun, cool temperatures would reassert themselves.

'What is it you want to know about the Wheah?' Klabier would ask me, and we wandered along.

'My love?' I would say. Perhaps I was in a 'happy' mood, and minded to act-up the courtly rituals of love. Or I might simply grunt, if I were feeling low and didn't want to be engaged in conversation.

'Why are you so keen to seek out these political groupings, to find out about the Wheah?'

'I'm curious about them.'

'Curious how?'

'I think everybody in the t'T should be curious about them. Don't you? They might invade – they could be planning a war with us. You said you yourself – didn't you say so yourself, back on Narcissus?'

Klabier shrugged. 'Maybe.'

I stopped and grasped her arms to make her look at me. 'You do believe it, don't you? You do believe what you said on Narcissus – that the Wheah are about to invade?'

'I don't know,' she said, breaking away from my grip. 'Who cares? It's just something to say.'

'I can't believe you! Why would you say it if you didn't believe it?'

'Don't be silly.' She went down on her haunches to get a better look at the sand, picking up a palmful and scribbling through it with a finger from her other hand. I copied her, looking at the miniature dots of grit, the ground-down remains of rocks and shells. So much miniature material! So many thousands of miles of heaped up miniscule-ness. 'You're being silly.'

'I take it seriously,' I said, sulkily.

'It's just something to say,' Klabier told me, standing up again. 'That's all it is. Merely something to say – that's the point of politics. Saying something. The pleasure is in the saying, not in *what* is said.'

But I remained convinced that there was something important, some core of truth at the heart of all the talk. We wandered on until the rising tide had reached its highest point, pushing us progressively further and further inland. Then we sat down and made love. We slept. After waking we went in search of food; of course, the landscape was liberally provided with automatic sustenance dispensers. We made love again. 'You're hungry for it,' said Klabier, a little breathless with the urgency of my caresses. I think I was angry with her, and that anger fuelled my desire. Human sexual desire is a peculiar thing, dear stone.

We wandered into a short valley in the rocky highland and found a community of floaters; people who were mostly concerned with riding flat, rigid balloon structures, less than a metre long, that they gripped to their chests with both arms. These ballés, as they called them, gave them enough buoyancy to fly through the air for many metres off the ground, provided there were a breeze to give them lift. The ballé-riders preferred the mornings; they would run down the long strand of exposed beach, towards the incoming tide and into the teeth of a morning gale. Leaping into the air the breeze would carry them along, and they would skim onwards. We stayed with these ballé-riders for several days, I seem to remember, and one morning the two of us strolled down towards the distant sea to watch them. There were dozens of them, swooping and skimming close to the waves. The highest skill (and the greatest credit amongst the group) came when they were able to bounce themselves off the curling wall of water, veer away from the collision before the wave collapsed over them, and fly free without getting wet. It was a tricky skill to master, and many of

151

them were swallowed by the waves, or fell from their ballés into the water. But the ones that managed it flew with such grace and motion as to make me jealous of their ability.

Then the tide would come all the way in, and the ballé-riders would stop and take lunch; to talk, make love, and doze within earshot of the waves splashing on sand a few metres away. Then, come the evening, they would resume their riding, with the sea slowly shrinking away and the sun going down.

I began to sense that Klabier was becoming restless with our wanderings. I also had reasons for wanting to move things along more rapidly. My AI was becoming most annoying, providing me with a seemingly never-ending commentary on the wastefulness of what I was doing, of how I was going to be given over to the 'police', of how important my mission was (although it couldn't tell me why).

We moved inland, and spent time in a number of different cities. In one Klabier met an old lover, and went off with him to spend a week in the mountains. I was absorbed during this time with another political group, and hardly missed her.

This group had a completely new theory about the Wheah. 'Everything you have heard is wrong,' they told me, when I joined their group. I soon discovered that they began every 'political' meeting with this mantra; *everything you have heard is wrong*. 'We are taught,' they said, 'that we are the best and most preferable. That we are unconquerable, that we have achieved a utopia. But this is not the case at all.'

Not the case? snorted the AI in my ear. *This is more insane than the last group. Why are you wasting your time with these fantasists?*

'We are not the superior beings of the galaxy,' one tiny-faced, huge-legged woman announced. The whole group listened in reverent silence. 'The Wheah are. We are an experiment, set up by the Wheah thousands of years ago. They set us up, and retreated into the space beyond the Tongue. From there they have observed us, sending occasional agents amongst us for more detailed work.'

There were so many questions here, so many things that didn't make sense, that I wasn't sure where to start.

'I don't understand,' I said.

Everybody in the group looked at me, with oddly pitying expressions. It was starting to dawn on me that this was not an ordinary 'political' group. There was no actual discussion, nobody disagreed with anybody. Instead everybody nodded agreement and scratched the bridges of their noses.[1]

'The Wheah are far superior to us,' somebody told me, as if explaining things to a child.

'So far above us,' said somebody else, 'as to be practically gods.'

'They will return soon.'

'The experiment is nearly at an end.'

All eyes were on me. Something told me that there would be little point in my challenging this strange fixed notion of the group's. I looked from face to face. 'What is the experiment,' I asked, slowly, 'designed to achieve?'

There was a silence.

'That,' said somebody (a woman whose chin had been elongated to two sharp points), 'will become apparent.' She looked round at everybody else. 'When they return.'

THE WILSON LIBRARY
TRINITY SCHOOL
SHIRLEY PARK
CROYDON CR9 7AT
020 8656 9541   8th

Dear Stone,

Yes, I was having doubts, I am happy to admit that; it makes me more human, doesn't it? It pleases my doctor (well*hello*!), I daresay, to think that my conscience worried through 'right' and 'wrong'. Or should I be more precise? I had doubts about my ability to follow through with the mission I had agreed to undertake. To kill so many people! People, true, I had never met before, and whom therefore didn't truly exist, but nonetheless! Nonetheless! Let's say – why not say – that I refused to do this thing. Perhaps I would go back to jail (no! never!), and spend the rest of my days pondering my choice.

Your thoughts, said my AI sharply, *are spilling over. I get the strong impression you are not committed to this mission.*

---

[1] A t'T gesture indicative of solidarity.

'I don't understand it!' I wailed. '*Who* wants me to do this terrible thing? Why do they want it done? There must be some other way – there *must* be! Tell me why they want it done, and perhaps we can find some other way of achieving their goal. The goal! But what on earth *can* the goal be – it makes no sense – so many deaths. How can that benefit anybody?'

I have explained, said the AI. *I cannot tell you who, or why, until afterwards. There is no other way.*

'They will all die for no reason!'

For the first time there was a tone of uncertainty in the AI's imitation-voice. *Are you having qualms of conscience?* it asked.

'And what if I am?'

You? We don't believe it.

That was the first jarring note in my AI's communication with me; I caught it immediately. It was so striking that it even shook me out of my melodramatic wailing.

'What did you say?' I snapped at it.

What? What?

'You said "we don't believe it". Who is *we*?'

I said I couldn't believe it. I've never known you to have doubts like this. Is this all a part of falling into a sexual infatuation with that woman? I thought your conscience was a withered limb, absent through freak chance of genetic mutation.

'Never mind that,' I said. 'Who is *we*? Why put it in those terms? *We* don't believe it?'

Nothing. Never Mind.

'You slipped up there.'

No I didn't.

'Yes you did. Yes *you* did.'[1]

I meant the many potential AIs, waiting to be grown in your brain after I expire from the seeds. Remember I told you about the seeds?

'That's nonsense. That wouldn't convince a child. Who are you-all? Who is the you?'

I pressed on, but it wouldn't tell me. After a while I grew bored, and

---

[1] Ae uses *yo-all*, the Glicé pronoun for 'you [plural]' to reinforce his point. At some places in this translation I use the Amglish 'you-all' to convey this distinction.

made my way outside to sit on a communal step and watch the day's eclipse. Eclipses were so regular an occurrence that only tourists bothered to stop and observe them; but nonetheless I was not alone on the step as the sky's green tint deepened, thickened and eventually went purple-black. The best bit of an eclipse, dear stone, is not the total blackout; it is the time when the sun is mostly covered – the light takes on a strange, spectral quality to it. Familiar objects become dissociated from normal memory. It is beautiful. And as I watched it, I sensed the ghostly presence behind the so-called AI in my brain. The many intelligences that were observing me through it, the many individuals that were bringing their collective will to bear on me through it. I shut my eyes, not caring now if the AI could overhear my thoughts or not, and visualised them; and I saw, in my mind's eye, rank upon rank of Wheah, standing one behind the other, planning their plans and conspiring to cause the death of millions of t'T citizens.

Klabier returned from her week away with her old lover. 'Did you have a nice time?' I asked.

'Lovely.'

'Good. I'm tired of this place. I'm tired of Nu Hirsch.'

'We can go to Nu Hirsch First City; it's a hundred kilometres along the coast, and we can get an elevator there to orbit.'

'Good,' I said. 'Good.'

I was in turmoil inside. I felt as if my suspicions had been confirmed; that the Wheah were indeed behind my escape from the jailstar. I was gnawing at my lower lip. I noticed Klabier looked at me with a puzzled expression. 'What?'

'Your lip is bleeding,' she said.

It was not the first time my lack of dotTech had come close to embarrassing me with her. I only smiled, and sucked the lip in to hide the cut.

We took a hand-cart to Nu Hirsch First City. We had noticed several of these passing up and down the highways of the continent; covered wagons two or three metres long and mounted on enormous, five metre-diameter wheels that swept two arcs over the top of the cover. Each cart was drawn along by a Haüd-machine, in a pleasantly arch imitation of archaic transports. These carts were lined up in the central square of the town we were staying at, ready for traveller's convenience. There were other ways of travelling from city to city, of course, but we were in no hurry; and once on the road the rhythm and pace of the travel was most soothing.

'Jasba,' said Klabier. 'Can I ask you a question?'

I was in a 'happy' mood at that moment, as chance would have it; feeling soothed by the bright greenish sunshine and the relaxing lollop of the cart's passage. 'Anything my love, my heart, my mind's delight,' I said.

'Earlier you said that you had a job to do.'

This snapped my good mood instantly. 'Did I?' I replied, my smile gone.

'Yes, you did.'

There was silence, and only the rushing noise of the air as we hurried along.

'Jasba,' she said. 'What job is it you have to do?'

Don't tell her! yelled my AI inside my head.

'It's a form of employment,' I said, a little flustered.

'Employment? What a strange word!' And it is a terribly archaic word, dear stone. Nobody is in 'employment' any more.

'I know,' I said. 'It's a curious concept.'

'You are *working*,' she said, with a smile, as if this were all some joke, 'for some *employers*?'

'Yes. I can't tell you what they want me to do,' I said, 'because my employers haven't exactly made that clear to me yet. You see?'

'I don't understand.'

'It's – out of the ordinary.'

'Who are your employers?' she asked.

'Well,' I said. 'That's a little out of the ordinary as well.'

She waited for a while before reiterating her question. 'And? Who are they?'

Don't say! shrieked my AI.

As if I could tell her anything – I don't know myself, I subvocalised. And aloud I said, 'I can't tell you. Not yet anyway.'

This clearly did not satisfy her; but there she lay back in the cart and closed her eyes, her face wrinkled with puzzlement.

156

When I was sure she was asleep I started whispering to my AI. 'There's no point in secrecy now,' I said, too furious to subvocalise. 'I know that the Wheah are behind my mission. I know who *you-all* are.' But my AI chose that moment not to respond, no matter how urgently I hissed at it.

We arrived at Nu Hirsch First City by sunset, when the yellow sun threw spectacular blues and purples across the western sky, and clouds were stained sharp red. The city was a fine example of Nu Hirsch architecture; all gleaming machine-inspired shapes, pillars, soaring boxes of light, stacked pyramids of gold.

Arrival at the city seemed to have re-energised Klabier. 'It's beautiful,' she said. 'They've built several things since I was here last. Let's go out! We can go drinking – dancing. Wouldn't you like to go dancing?'

I had a sense that something terrible was impending. The pressure of my responsibilities – I am not ashamed to use that term, for my mission was a heavy responsibility to me – was starting to warp my consciousness. I looked around me as Klabier and I walked down the main passage thoroughfare arm in arm; I saw all the people and imagined them all dead, all lying motionless on the diamond paving stones.

'You were talking to yourself again,' said Klabier to me as we walked.

I was startled. 'What?'

'In the cart coming here. I've noticed it several times, actually.'

'You have?'

'I don't mind it. My sister used to do it. Said she had an imaginary friend. I like it, it reminds me of childhood.'

'Well,' I said, unsure what else to say. 'Well.'

She pulled herself closer to me. The evening sky was purple and black, and the stars glimmered sea-green through the immense sky. All along the thoroughfare were brightly lit rooms and buildings, people all around me laughing and kissing, dancing along the paving or reeling as if intoxicated through the crush of people. Fragments of music faded in and out as we passed along. Klabier seemed genuinely happy.

We stopped at a club and drank embre. The sweet tasting fluid

157

relaxed me a little, and I even started singing an old song from my childhood in Terne. I may have cried a little. We were out on the main street again. I can't exactly remember how I got there. You must remember that, without dotTech to help me deal with the intoxicant in my bloodstream, I got drunk quick and hard. 'Look at the stars!' I remember crying to Klabier. 'How beautiful they are! I want to sleep close to the stars tonight!'

I was manic again; happy when only an hour before I had been withdrawn and sullen. Klabier was laughing at my wild energy, or laughing with it, I don't know. 'Let's go to bed!' I shouted.

'Alright,' she said. 'Alright. There are accommodation towers forty stories high at the other end of this road. Up near the mountain side of the city.'

We turned about, with me loudly insisting that I would only sleep in the very top-most room of such a tower. We stopped at another club, on the other side of the road. Here Klabier and I danced, and I got drunker. We became involved in a lengthy 'political' conversation with a group of like-minded tourists, and debated – debated, I don't know exactly what we debated to tell you the truth, stone of mine.

9th

Dear Stone,

Klabier got me, quarrelsome and moody with drink though I was, to the top of the street and up a hemisecond-rapid elevator to the top floor. By the time we got there I was very tired, and muttering to myself; or perhaps trying to communicate with my oddly silent AI. I can't remember. Klabier helped me to bed, and her soothing hands turned easily into erotic ones; I lay quite passive whilst she made tender and precise love to me. Afterwards I slept.

I woke before dawn; the sky, just visible through the archway that led to the balcony, a cyan-purple. I was alone in the bed. Sitting up, I could see Klabier standing on the balcony.

I got up, and made my way over to her; but there was a sick, tight feeling in my stomach. I could sense something was wrong.

'Wellhello,' I said to her, touching her shoulder.

'Wellhello,' she replied, sadly.

'What's wrong?' I asked.

She didn't say anything for a while, so I stood beside her with my elbows on the balcony rail. The view was north-east; and to the right the sky was paling blue and green with the coming sunrise. Below, shrunk to toy dimensions by forty stories of height, were a few of the previous evening's revellers on the diamond plateau. They moved, dots on a pale square.

'Why do you talk to yourself so much, Jasba?' she asked.

'What do you mean?' I replied, without thinking.

'Jasba,' she said. Then again: 'Jasba. That's not your real name, is it?'

I thought of saying *Of course it is my real name*, and then changed my mind. 'What does it mean, that word *real*?' I countered. 'No name is *real* in that sense.'

'Jasba,' she said, again, as if testing the word in her mouth. 'Jasba. You're were in a strangely jittery mood last night.'

'I don't usually go out partying at night,' I said. 'Or so I understand. That's all I meant by my reaction.'

'I don't think so. You know something. Don't you? Has the person you speak to, when you appear to be speaking to yourself – has that person told you something?'

'Klabier,' I said, my insides fizzing unpleasantly. 'Stop this. You're scaring me.' Which was the truth, dear stone; I was scared.

She still wouldn't look at me. 'It's all a nonsense. I thought I'd find something different with you, but you're just the same as anybody else really. Aren't you?'

This stung me. For a while I said nothing. Then I said, 'I really do love you, Klabier. I thought you – had feelings for me.'

Finally she turned to look at me. 'Oh I don't mean like that. If you were an ordinary person, I could certainly have feelings. I haven't been faking, of course I haven't. I don't want you ever to think that I've been faking.'

'What do you mean?' I said, a horrible realisation starting to dawn on me. 'What are you talking about?'

'Of course I'm with the "police",' Klabier said. 'You surely have worked that out by now. This last week I wasn't with an old lover. We

159

called together a number of irregulars and had a meeting about you. That's where I was.'

'The "police",' I said. Looking down I had a vertiginous sense that I was about to fall, and gripped the balustrade more firmly. I had quick-fire images of prison, of going back to what I had been before. And, after days of silence, my AI finally grumbled back into life.

There, it said. *Now – I told you not to come with her.*

'We thought it best,' she was saying, 'to let you come here. You seemed so keen to come here. We thought we'd let you go where you wanted, follow you, keep an eye on you. We wanted to find out what you were planning. But it hasn't happened, has it? Whatever you were expecting, hasn't happened.'

'The "police",' I said again.

She came a half-step closer. 'You're a unique person, you really are. I affiliated with the "police" because I was fascinated with you. There are so few people like you. Except in history texts, of course.'

'Klabier,' I said. There was so much I wanted to say to her, but only those two syllables came out.

'We hoped that by staying with you, we might get to the bottom of what you're involved in. You are involved in something, aren't you?'

'Klabier,' I said again. It was all I could think of to say.

'You could hardly have broken out of the jailstar without help.'

The word *jailstar* was like a stab at me, even though she didn't mean it to be.

'Please,' she said. 'Tell me. You can just tell me, can't you? We have had something special, something loving, haven't we? That must mean something to you. So tell me: who is it you are with? What are you planning? You talked of *a job you had to do* for somebody, that *when it's over you'll be free*. What is the job? Who is it for? Is it the Wheah?'

I closed my eyes, and opened my mouth, ready to say something. I didn't know what I was going to say. But instead of words, I started crying. It was so dreadful a shock. Klabier was 'police', and I was going to spend the rest of my life in a jail. I couldn't bear it.

Kill her, said my AI, hot and close in my ear. *Kill her, kill her.*

'Jasba,' she said, her voice full of infinite tenderness. 'Are you crying? Are you crying?'

She came and put her arms around me. I smelt her smell, felt the exquisite, sensual pressure of her flesh against mine. I reached out and put my arms around her back, and linked the fingers together. I was crying hard now, sobbing so much it shook my chest like hiccoughs. 'There there,' said Klabier, in my ear. 'Don't cry. Love, love, don't cry.'

I heaved with my arms. Maybe she sensed my muscles tensing, or maybe – knowing my history – she was simply expecting something along these lines, but immediately she lurched to my right and wriggled to try and get free. I hauled with all the might in my arms, but she was pulling in the other direction and I wasn't strong enough. My foot came round and hooked behind her calf, and with a swift jerk of the leg I was able to unbalance her. She started to sag backwards, and I took a step hard forward pushing her over and pivoting on one heel. Together we spun round and she struck the balustrade with her back, just below her shoulder blades. I pushed on, and drove her body physically up and over the balcony rail. She was grunting, and was slapping and punching at my face and head with her free hands. But I was possessed. With a final effort I twisted one last dragging push, and Klabier went over the edge. There was a *shh* sound, like fabric being swished over fabric, and she was gone.

I was panting hard now, and my face was wet (with my own blood, I discovered later, where she had broken my skin), but I leant forward to look down. I saw her body dwindle to nothing, and then stop. The thud came up to my ears a moment later. The dots on the pale square stopped their random movement; then they started creeping, all of them, towards the place of impact.

What are you standing here for? barked my AI. *Come on, you can't wait here.*

It was right. Still gasping, I hurried to the elevator. It took me to the ground in less time than it had taken Klabier to fall; but with a calculated inertial pattern that allowed for a deceleration that would not harm me. I stumbled out, coughing and gasping, and rushed away through the back entrance of the building.

Klabier, I told myself, would not be dead. She would be badly harmed, but the dotTech would save her life. It might take a few weeks to regain full health, but she would survive. I didn't know if that was true, though. Maybe a fall from such a height would make paste of human flesh. Maybe even the dotTech could not heal that.

161

Not to think of that.

Come on! snarled my AI. *We must get away, away.*

I hurried into another building and out the back; then down a series of stairways at thirty degree angles to one another. This brought me out on the main thoroughfare I had walked up and down with Klabier only a few hours previously. It was still busy.

On! Come on!

By the time I had made my way to the end of this my lungs were burning and my breath was short. There was a broad square, and ghostly in the dawning light was a rack of carts, each with their Haüd-machine pullers. I stumbled up to the nearest of these.

'Take me away from here,' I gasped.

'Certainly citizen,' said the machine. 'Would you care to climb aboard the cart?'

'No,' I said, breathing hard. 'No cart. I want you to carry me on your back.'

The machine hesitated; this was not a usual request. But it said, 'Very well citizen,' and let go of the cart rail.

The gel of the machine formed itself into a rugged board for me to clamber up. 'Yes,' I said, grasping it around the neck. 'That's it. Piggy-back me away. I want you to take me east along the coast for a kilometre.'

'Yes citizen.'

'Then I want you to turn inland and carry me through the mountains.'

'Through the mountains?'

'That's right. I want you to carry me south. As fast as you can – do you understand? As fast as you can.'

'Very well, citizen.'

The Haüd-machine sprouted long, spindly legs from its gel base, raising itself and me with it in the process. Those legs! They may have been three metres long. Then, in a series of enormous, loping strides it started away, running hard and fast and tireless towards the sea. In less than a minute it was at the head of the beach, and turning to the east. I clung on to the back of the machine, trying to regain my desperate, hurting breath.

Dawn came up, and the light strengthened. The Haüd-machine

162

turned away from the sea, and galloped with its long paced strides up into the valleys and broken ground of the mountain range. And all the time I was saying to myself; she's not dead. The dotTech will not let her be dead. She's alive, she's alive.

Interlude

What was going through my head as I was carried over those sandstone peaks, through gullies and valleys, lulled by the regular lope of the Haüd-machine that bore me, under the swooning white clouds and the green sky? I close my eyes, dear stone, and I can remember it all. The scent of dry startwood, the crackling burr of insects, the wishing-hush of the wind in my ears.

'Might I ask, citizen,' my Haüd-machine enquired, with exemplary politeness, after several hours of travelling, 'where we are going?'

'To the south,' I said. 'To the south.'

'Do you have a more precise destination?'

'Elevator cities, in the south,' I said. 'I want a city from which I can get into orbit.'

'You could have done that from where you were, citizen.'

'No,' I said. The machine was not programmed to contradict me. We hurried on. 'In that case,' it said after a little while, 'might I suggest either Nu Hirsch Original, or Nu Hirsch Prime? They are both within a few hours travel from here.'

The landscape swept past me.

'Somewhere further away,' I gasped. I was really finding it difficult to breathe. My lungs seemed smaller than they needed to be to get air into them.

'Further away, citizen?' queried the Haüd-machine. Its enormous spindly legs were flashing bright green in the sunlight as they pounded beneath me. 'Nu Hirsch Capital?'

'Yes,' I said. I did not want to go to the most obvious place. 'Can you go faster?'

'It will be less comfortable for you, citizen.'

'Do it.'

Its stride increased. I was trying to work out what I should do; but every time I tried to think of that, images of Klabier's dwindling body kept occurring to me. Why had she made no sound? Wouldn't anybody scream, falling from that height, dotTech or no?

Just the fluttering of her smart fabric. Her body had become so tiny so very quickly. The wet sound of her impact had arrived a heartbeat later than the visual image. It was as if I had done this thing to myself, not to another person at all.

I know what you're thinking of, said my AI. I think I hated my AI at that moment. I started slapping my own head with the flat of my right hand, insane, trying to hurt the circuitry that was buried inside there.

'Citizen?' asked the Haüd-machine. 'Are you alright?'

That's not going to do any good you know, said the AI. *You might as well stop doing that.*

'I hate you,' I sobbed. 'I hate you.'

'Citizen?'

I'm sure she'll recover, you know. Not that you really care. Not in your heart, I think. You've just worked yourself into a state.

'You're inhuman!'

'I am an artificially constructed Haüd-machine,' said the machine, without breaking its stride. 'Your observation is correct.'

It wasn't I who pushed her off the balcony, said my AI levelly. *You did that.*

'You made me!'

No, I didn't.

'Your voice was in my head.'

We both know, I said nothing.

I cried for a little while, but the thing about tears, dear stone, is that they cry themselves out. It is a form of emotional evaporation. I don't think I wanted to stop crying; it felt as if I lacked the necessary depth of feeling. But I did cry myself out.

When I had stopped, I clung like a baby to the back of the machine. Even its plastic-enchipped gel felt comforting to me at that moment. I felt, if I am truthful, enormously sorry for myself.

You can't stay here, not on this world. You should never have come

165

here in the first place. I did tell you not to come here, you know. If you think back you'll recall that I told you that.

'Shut up.'

One of us had to think practically. You should have gone straight to Nu Fallow, without the woman.

'Shut up.'

Don't be like that. None of this would have happened if you'd done what I advised.

'You're no AI,' I said, loudly, shouting my revelation into the empty air. We were passing through a dusty, sandy defile, I remember; and at the end of it my machine-carrier leapt up piled boulders like mighty steps, jarring the words as they came out of my mouth. 'You're some sort of Wheah device. You are a group of Wheah warriors, sitting somewhere nearby, shadowing me, speaking directly into my thoughts through some sort of transmitter device.'

If you consider, said the AI, you'll appreciate what an unlikely explanation of things that is.

'If you're not,' I challenged. 'Then who are you?'

Then my AI said something that brought me up short. It said: Who do I sound like?

I thought for a while, my body trembling in time to the footfalls of the Haüd-machine. 'Who do you sound like?' I repeated. But it was a way of ending the conversation between us for that day, because the answer was very clear to me, had been clear to me from the beginning. I didn't need to say it; the AI didn't need to say it either. It sounded like me. That was who it sounded like.

I went to Nu Hirsch Capital, and from there went into orbit. From there I flew to Tere and back to Nu Hirsch, and on to Schüss. I was trying to throw them off the scent. It seemed pointless to try and avoid what I was to do. I had, I believed, tracked down the real murderer, the people who were operating through me. The question of motive still remained, but even with that – the why – I could guess something. War was an antique; its rules and laws were unfamiliar. But any student of history could point to any number of atrocities committed by warriors. It was what warriors did.

I had still not absolutely decided to do this murderous thing for the

Wheah; but I – as secretly as I could, hoping that I was thinking with a non-vocalised part of my brain, and then burying the thought away from myself – resolved to go to Agifo3acca. My rendezvous with that Trench-obsessed Wheah had been long preordained; and I decided that I could find out from him what the Wheah were actually planning.

Just before the foam slewed up around me in orbit at Schüss, my AI spoke again: *You have the insect carapace, don't you?*

Yes, I subvocalised sulkily.

Just check for me, would you?

I groped in my pocket, and there it was; a nodule of hard material, like plastic.

Childhood

Dear Stone,

Did I tell you about my childhood? I can't remember. The time is so peculiarly straightened here – distorted in odd ways. I may begin repeating myself, doubling over my narrative. Would you become angry if I did that?

How kind you are.

I come from a world named Terne. My world is mostly covered with an interconnecting series of oceans. There are two large polar oceans, and then a dense network of linked seas too sludgy really to deserve the name. The saltwater there is so densely inhabited by a variety of tendril-plant that in the fruiting season it was possible for a human being to walk over the water, providing they weren't too heavy. It was in spring, when the seas changed colour, as the flowering section of these plants emerged orange and red. The rest of the time the seas gloomed with dark purple, the native form of chlorophyll. The native vegetable was called Drüd, I remember; and it grew downwards in threads that could reach four or five hundred metres. The seawater itself sloshed through a sluggish maze of delta pathways as the Drüd flourished or died out, finding new pools of nutrient or draining the water of all minerals and starving itself to death. The landforms on this world – my homeworld, 'the World' we called it – were actually compacted masses of this same Drüd. Originally the whole world had been covered in ocean; then when portions of Drüd had formed tangled floating platforms, new strains of the plant had evolved. These grew denser and denser, clogging together into islands, and then into continents thousands of kilometres across. The pressure of growth

168

killed the plants that made up the body of the land, compacting and mummifying them. Currents and the sheer weight of growth kneaded landmasses, throwing up low hills and chains of stumpy mountains. Then, from the composted relicts of the original plants, new plants found a rich soil. Tall grasses, billowing bushes and slender trees. The landscape of my home – all organic, genuine, none of it plastic or artificial like the confines of my prison.

Childhood.

The family structure on Terne was a complex matrix. This was traditional. Two mothers mixed genetic material with the help of their dotTech. This same nanotechnology produced three identical eggs from the plasm, and sperm from three different fathers fertilized them, the three foetuses being carried in the wombs of different women, or sometimes a single woman. The three resulting children were raised by the commune of five, or six, adults who had contributed to their production, unless they were all biologically born in the default gender *female*, in which case they were raised just by the two, or three, 'mothers'. It is complicated, I know.

My own family was a traditional one; I was born a daughter with a sister and a brother, and raised by a group of five through the first years of life. These are my earliest memories; playing in the sunshine with other children. Shepherding the large ants of Terne through heaped up alleyways of mud, prodding them with a long stick of Drüd to make them go in the right direction. These native ants were twelve-legged, with speckled cream-coloured bodies. We children would scoop out grooves in the mud with our thumbs and make the creatures run up and down them.

I remember walking near the seaside, and falling through a place where the crust of embedded plant matter was too thin to support me (we called such places *quicksteps*). I remember the gloopy, smelly chill of the water sliding all the way up around me as I slipped down, swallowing me whole. I remember opening my mouth to scream, and sucking in some of this salty water; and in the instant before the dotTech dampened the sensation I remember the horrible jab of pain that marked the entry of the water into my lungs. There were people with me – my sister, I think, and some others. They reached through the vegetation into the water and hauled me out, and the dotTech

169

helped me expel the water painlessly enough, blurting it out of my mouth. But that instant of panic stayed with me.

My sister. I haven't thought of her for many years. Her name was Olev Gennaio astar-jo. I do not give her two family names, because she shares those with me.

On Terne it was considered a good thing that children remain children for several decades. Development was allowed to follow its infant trajectory, the default growth pattern, until the age of ten; then the nano-machines halted it. The dotTech manipulated pituation, fiddled with cellular development and stopped growth dead at that age. Stopped it dead – dead it certainly seemed to me. Easy to overstate, but it was a kind of death, a physical stasis.

The orthodoxy of my culture was that a child should live a dozen years as a boy and a dozen years as a girl, the better to be able to choose maleness or femaleness in adulthood, so as to base the choice on the experience of living in the gender rather than the sexual associations of it. Long-delayed adulthood! There were several other orthodoxies on that world – that an adult should commit to one gender or another and work through life with it (I know of other worlds where people shift between male and female with the regularity of moon cycles). Another was that sex was an adult affair only. Afterwards, when I was a full-grown man, I travelled to a world near Nu Hirsch where the opposite was true; children were given sexual prowess and possibility by the dotTech at seven and encouraged to explore erotic life to the near exclusion of everything else for several years. That culture found that human beings wearied of sexuality after so intense an exposure at so early an age, and mostly turned their adult energies to other things. On my world the view was completely otherwise. Children were kept sexually immature until they were forty or even older; only then did the dotTech take them through accelerated puberty and usher them into the world of sexual intercourse.

The rationale behind all this was always hazy to me; I think it reflected the exaggerated respect in which sex was held by my people. Or an exaggerated disrespect, a feeling that sexuality interfered unhealthily with education and the proper, childish business of living. I don't know.

In common with almost all t'T cultures, nanotechnology existed throughout the body of every citizen, but was not permitted into the fore-brain. To protect and enhance the body was a means of augmenting quality of life; but to enter the higher brain was to interfere with consciousness, and that was not allowed. There are, dear stone of mine, some t'T cultures that do permit dotTech into the brain – rewiring synapses, making more efficient connections, preserving faculties at full efficiency. Such people have always seemed very happy to me, and declare that the dotTech has not affected their essential selves. But how could they know if it had? How could 'they' be sure that their 'they' was real? Perhaps they were actually unhappy, but the dotTech refused to allow them to realise the fact? There was no place for the miniature machines in our brains; they stopped outside the meninges membrane.

The natural year on Terne lasted 240 days; or actually a little longer, but the calendar specified 240 so as to fit more neatly with the 360-day standard year. Every three years we would have a three-day holiday, a free few days, to bring everything back into alignment with the solar rotation.

During childhood, a third of the 240-day year was devoted to schooling. Most of the rest was given over to *camp*. Play; socialising; games. Music! Dear stone – I had forgotten the music! Near-endless practising on instruments you hated, learning the finger-patterns that blocked the vibration of the three vibrating rods on a conscree – a hideous instrument out of which nothing could be gleaned but a tooth-buzzing drone except with the most assiduous practice. Did I choose to learn the conscree? Was it chosen for me? I can no longer remember. But I remember the tower, where I slept; I remember bruising my fingers with hour after blank hour of practice. East Head Air. Feir Tune. Shaikvak Tune. Yesterday. Help-Me Polka. My fingers form patterns just thinking about it.

The tower was the dormitory, part of the camp. I lived most of the year in it, surrounded by other superannuated children all practicing their various instruments, playing games, honing chess skills, reading and studying. Sport was important, but I avoided team sports in favour of individual rock-face sprinting. There were no natural rock-faces on Terne, but several artificial cliffs had been constructed, and I used to race other children up these. Sometimes I won.

I was a solitary child, I suppose, but that wasn't necessarily out of the ordinary. Most children were sociable, but there were others like me who preferred to read or study by themselves. I spent many years reading philosophy. Ancient philosophers such as Nitzcha, Hamsun, Agleston, Lung-tzu, bari-jan – few people read them any more. The attempts made by humanity to understand the world before dotTech: irrelevant today. But I found a strange charm in them, the obsession with *ethical behaviour* in pre-utopian society. It was like reading about how human beings would trek for months to move from place to place before the invention of flight; how they used to assemble and set alight by friction a carefully arranged set up of tinder before the invention of electricity. Fables from a barbarian age.

I was, I suppose, a normal child. When I was at school and living with my five parents, I felt and acted as normally as any. I really believe that. I suppose there must have been something wrong, some peculiar balanced arrangement of neurones, fragile as a frost-flower, that predisposed me to be a killer; a single flaw in a world of perfect human beings. But I was genuinely not aware of it. I lived twenty-three years upon that world before it emerged.

Since I was born in the default biological setting of *girl*, I spent my first period of change as a boy; twelve years. The change itself did not bother me. I remember it; over a period of days I sprouted a pale three-pronged item of genitalia. This fascinated me for a day or two, then bored me (the thing I noticed most about it was how it tended to *get in the way*). The other changes were more subtle, but also had their effect. I went to camp. I played at sport, read, ate, slept. I created *art* – something valued highly upon our world. But I created art in the manner of children – depthless drawing that was all technique and no insight; flashy writing that lacked the perspectivising elan provided by the openness of adult living.

Although I didn't realise it at the time, I think now that the point of camp was not the sport; not the careful and steady conditioning that helped mould the perfect material of nano-enhanced humanity into utopian citizens. All that went on, of course; but there was something else. Each camp contained perhaps six hundred children, chronologi-

172

cally old but still biologically immature. Friendships between these beings were supremely important. In fact, dear stone, 'friendship' hardly does justice to the dynamic. Call them rather *alliances*, that slid and coalesced, fixed and melted, with the transience and beauty of some complex interference pattern formed by two rotating grids. A certain amount of this was powered by a form of pre-pubescent sexuality; a deliberate attempt to copy adult behaviour, kissing, intimate rubbing. My own awkward experiments in this direction were undone, mostly, by my refusal to enter into the discourse of *love*. This was the logic of the childish affairs that bloomed up and broke away in a matter of days. It was a courtly sort of thing, in which the genuine intensity of sexual release – denied us by our physiologies – was replaced with the mock-intensity of grand words, swooning passion, more and more elaborate declarations of being in love. But I realised at an early age – before I was twenty, even – that this juvenile fetish was nothing more than imitation. *Being in love*, the very phrase still sends shivers of revulsion through my mind – as if love is something you *are* instead of something you *do*. But perhaps that is the point; children, wrapped all around with structures to order and shape their lives, come to believe that *love* is such a structure, some-thing that surrounds and supports them. Adults, however, are alone before their infinity of possibilities and choices. We should replace the phrase *being in love* with the phrase *doing love*. What are you doing today? Today I'm doing love.

I think it could catch on.

So although I took part in these elaborate ritualised childhood games – the writing of poems and musical pieces, the gifts, the surprising of your love-object as if by ambush – I found myself more and more disaffected by it, withdrawing away. In the emotional economy of the camps, though, this only made me more appealing to a certain sort of individual. Mysteriousness, secrecy, fitted one of the models of love that was current. This is where *I* begin, actually; where the true me first made an appearance. Let me tell you what I mean.

I was spending one summer at camp; I was in my early twenties, the first or second year of living once again as a girl. I had been through the whole twelve-year cycle as a boy, and now I was a girl again. The camp we were at was called Pedit-al-le-soers, in the continent of

Dubller – a crinkle-coastlined promontory that stretched a thousand kilometres out from the main northern continent of Ast-la-Cox. There were many camps located on Dubller, to take advantage of the many natural bays and lagoons, so that land-based pastimes could be varied with seaside ones.

The camp of Pedit-al-le-soers was on the northern coastline of the landmass, and looked out over the enormous polar ocean. In the depths of those purple waters lived the largest of Terne's naturally occurring lifeforms, great worm-fish called by most people Sea Dragons. These grey-skinned monsters could grow to hundreds of metres in length, and were as wide across their bodies as a full-grown person. Let me tell you about the worm-fish; I spent a year of school studying the lifeforms of my homeworld and I remember a lot about them.

The first thing to say about them is that they are neither worms nor fish, but a sophisticated vegetable – evolved almost to mimic animal protein and metabolism. A worm-fish lacks a central nervous system, and presents a dull and featureless stretch of grey skin on the outside, such that it really does resemble a giant snake, except along the dorsal portion, which sometimes shows dark-purple mottling, residua of the native form of chlorophyll. But the worm-fish do not rely upon sunlight for energy; it is a devourer. At both ends are orifices, either of which can be used for eating or excreting but which tend to specialise in the habitual direction of travel – the creatures would swim in the same direction for thousands of kilometres, and the 'front' orifice would become more and more mouth-like, while the 'rear' one would take on the functions of an anus more exclusively. But this was not fixed; the beast might give a mighty shake, thrash in the water, and start swimming 'backwards' as it were, whereupon the rear orifice would start to become mouth. There were various theories as to why the creature had evolved this form of ambiguous anatomy.

Another curious feature of the worm-fish is that it has not specialised its sense organs. Instead of 'eyes' it is sensitive to light all over its body, somehow (in the absence of any 'brain') managing to assemble this sense-data into a three-dimensional model of the world around it.

These creatures were very numerous in the northern waters of Terne

174

when I was a child, and tended to stay in the deeper ocean where their favourite prey – smaller fish and vegetable-shrimps – were mostly to be found. But if the competition for food were too great, or the populations of smaller fish declined for any reason, then these great monsters would swim close to the coast. They preferred meat, but if there were nothing else then they would graze the compacted masses of Drüd that formed our coastlines.

Their size meant that they avoided the narrower creeks and fjords in which children such as myself would swim and play. But west from the main bay of the camp the landmass rose and presented cliffs that stood ten or twelve metres high, from which it was possible to stare out over the turbulent red-purple waters. This was lonely country, no habitation for thirty kilometres until you reached another fjord and another camp; and for that reason it was a popular walk for the more withdrawn children. I took a book or piece of art-fabric up there many times.

Let me describe the landscape to you precisely, dear stone, because it is important for what followed. For much of this cliff-walk the ground was solid, made up of the same compacted Drüd out of which all the landmasses on Terne were made. But Sea Dragons would graze the base of these cliffs, pushing their blunt mouths up against the Drüd and chewing it away. This resulted in an overhang, in some places a very pronounced one; the layer of Drüd might be gnawed away to a few centimetres thickness, and this thin crust might roof-over a great booming cavern in which purple waves slopped and echoed. I remember finding one such overhang, and lying with my upper torso entirely over the lip, head down and entranced by the upside-down vista of the cavern below.

There was a boy at camp who decided he was 'being in love' with me. My solitariness entranced him; my evasiveness fuelled his passion past the usual week-or-so during which these early romances would bud and droop. He followed me around with unusual persistence. His poems to me were actually quite good.

There were always adults around the camp, of course; although these individuals had little impact on the life we children lived. Neither were they consistent; they came and went as the fancy took them. Some weeks there would be one individual keeping an eye on us, some weeks another; for a month it would be the same individual, then three would change places in as many days. But there would always be some adult or other. I would see them standing, arms crossed, smiling in a smug manner at the ritualised love-making all about them. They seemed particularly entranced with this boy – his name was Ari-shend-roba-le-patilta-gunarzon.

Dear stone, he has a special place in my memory.

His hopeless passion for me went pretty much unnoticed in the first week; but as he persisted others began to remark upon it. I saw the adults smiling indulgently as he traipsed after me.

I hated it. I hated him. I hated what *he+I* represented to the adults, watching so indulgently. It only occurred to me that this word *hate* described my emotion after several weeks of feeling it. At the beginning I think I actually lacked the vocabulary to describe what my feelings were. But then, with a sudden insight, I understood. This was what *hatred* was; that same hatred that appeared in the antique texts and philosophy. And, once named, the emotion changed. Its manifestation changed. I no longer fretted and rushed and woke in the night. I discovered a calmness that helped me very much.

Nonetheless, it did not occur to me at this point that I should kill him. As with many of life's insights, what seems so obvious after the fact was in fact obscure through the actual days.

'Do you want to come watch Sea Dragons?' he asked, one afternoon. 'Pallia-nat-le-ster-alcest (or somebody; I can't remember exactly whose name he mentioned) has just come back with her *inamorata*, and they say that there are three of them dancing in the waters a kilometre away.'

It was in my mind to turn down this ridiculous offer – *dancing* indeed, the sentimental absurdity of the way romance-talk infected everything! – and I turned to face Ari to do so. But as I was speaking, whilst in fact I thought I was pettishly refusing him, I found myself saying words that were quite other. 'Alright, let's go see.'

I was amazed at myself; I remained amazed at myself all through the walk to the vantage point, during which time Ari-shend-roba-le-patilta-gunarzon took my hand, and gabbled blithely. I had made him happy by agreeing to go with him, I realised, and my punishment was that I had to listen to him chatter on. 'My first name is a name from an old mythic poem,' he told me, as if I were interested. 'Patilta is an interesting name, it's a family name. you know the name *Matilta* of course, but *Patilta* is a gender-specific version of it, a male version of it. It goes back a long way.' And on, and on.

When we arrived at the vantage point, Ari-shend-roba-le-patilta-gunarzon became extremely excited by the sight of the great worm-fish roiling and splashing through the red ocean. Two of them were gripping and sliding together a hundred metres or so out to sea. Perhaps they were fighting, or trying to devour one another, or perhaps they were mating. It is very difficult to tell, except by the outcome. If they are mating, then the 'male' beast (they shift gender seasonally) concludes the session of struggling and frothing up the water by injecting a plume of pollen down the 'female's' throat. If they are fighting they are most likely two females, and the fight concludes with one or other fleeing the scene. If they are hungry enough, they will try to eat one another.

We stood for a while watching the slow-motion grappling of the two beasts, Ari-shend-roba-le-patilta-gunarzon rapt by the sight. 'How big they are!' he said. 'Look how they slide off one another! Their skin looks almost like soft plastic in this light! More silver than grey!'

I noticed a third worm-fish coiling and snaking through the pink water directly beneath us. It was clear that it was grazing on the Drüd, and was contributing to hollowing out the overhang on which we now stood.

It did not occur to me straight away to try and pitch Ari to the Sea Dragons. The ones out to sea were clearly caught up in themselves; but if he were to fall then the one below would in all likelihood eat him up very quickly. But this thought did not occur to me immediately. I stood beside him, watching the two more distant beasts swarm over and over one another, like hand washing hand; then I crouched down and looked over the ledge to see the third beast circling and circling in the wide cavern he and his fellows had carved out with their grazing mouths. Then I went and lay on my back a couple of metres further inland and started reading from the screen I had brought with me.

It was something dull. How might my life have been different if it had been something exciting? Impossible to say. I might have become absorbed in it, forgotten about Ari until it was time to go home. Nothing might have happened. The trajectory through space not taken, dear stone; the quantum shadow. Maybe I would never have developed the way I have developed. I might have been a quite different person.

But because my book was dull, I rolled on to my front and stared at the ground. It was made, as I have said several times, of compacted Drüd. I found myself tracing with my eye the tangled patterns made by the embedded and compressed stalks, the leaves and roots of this plant. The process of impaction seemed to have knotted the individual plants into a series of broader ropes, all in turn twisted together and cemented with dense purple-black matter. I dug about one of these tangled chains of dead plant with my finger nails. It was easy to displace the dirt-like matter packed around it and uncover the trunk of this root.

I looked up to check what Ari-shend-roba-le-patilta-gunarzon was doing; his attention was still wholly taken by the Sea Dragons. He was singing to himself; a traditional tune, but with new words of his own composition. My hatred for him was focused once again by the song. He had his back to me.

Then – perhaps this is where everything started to cohere in my mind – I was struck by the way that raising my eye from the Drüd immediately beneath me to look at Ari had traced out a path in the ground. That path was real. It was the direction that the tangled trunk of intertwined Drüd remains led. This strand, around which I now had my hand (having grubbed around until I was underneath it), materially connected he and I. Connection.

There was a sort of shrinking-rushing sensation in my head, as if I had understood something of the greatest profundity. That line, drawn through the earth, that linked together this other human being and myself. It was more than itself. Everything became clear.

I was not – even at so late a stage – entirely plain within myself what was going on. I was slowly, silently, getting myself into a sitting position, digging my bare feet into the matter of the soil. Even as I braced myself and tightened my grip around the root, tightening my hand around the life of Ari-shend-roba-le-patilta-gunarzon, I was barely self-aware.

I heaved, a tremendous effort, pulling back with all my weight. The tangled chain of Drüd lurched, seemed to pull back against me as if resisting me, and Ari stumbled forward. From where I was sitting it looked only that he was bending over a little way, as if trying to get a closer look at what was by his feet.

There was a distinct, thrumming, crumbling sort of noise. Immediately, a wide swathe of ground from me to the edge simply collapsed. It bellied-down, like a sheet with a weight in the middle, and the next thing I knew it was falling away, dropping and bowing out until it hit the water below. In my memory the whole thing happens without sound, but I have to assume that this subsiding of so great an area of ground, twenty or thirty square metres of it, falling and splashing into the water must have made an enormous noise. I am not sure why it lives in my memory as a silent event.

I was on my feet before I knew it, my heart hammering briefly before my dotTech was able to regulate the gush of adrenaline I had experienced, releasing just enough to enhance my reactions but not so much that I panicked. The cliff path now looked as though a giant had bitten out a semicircular patch from it. I was two steps from the edge.

Below me I saw a mass of fragments of compacted Drüd bobbing and floating in the frothy water. At first I could not see Ari, but then he emerged, popping up like a cork. He was looking round him with that controlled surprise that is characteristic of a dotTech individual. Then he put his head back and looked up at me, standing over him.

'I slipped,' he called, sounding amused. 'Hey, the whole *ground* slipped.'

He started pulling himself onto the nearest raft of bobbing Drüd; but that small float tipped and rose vertically from the water under his weight, shucking him back into the sea. He laughed again, a clipped and bubbly sound. With another effort he pushed himself out of the water, and got himself into the position where he was belly-down on the raft of Drüd, his legs still in the sea.

I felt an enormous sense of *power*. I mean the word in the sense of the ancient philosophers, dear stone; not motive or reactive power, but *interactive* power, the intoxicating thing that old human society used to be based upon. I was up here; Ari was down there. I was better than

179

him, stronger, more vigorous. It is very difficult, dear stone, for me to explain to you what I felt.

He was still laughing. I saw the red-purple water darken beneath him, and it came up as if it were some sort of physical externalisation of my power. The Sea Dragon rising.

It broke the surface with its maw around Ari's two legs. There was a rushing sound, the white-noise that splashing water makes. The worm-fish bulked into the air, glistening and grey, and then dove down again. Ari-shend-roba-le-patilta-gunarzon was thrown upwards, and tossed aside. He made no noise. I remember very distinctly that he didn't cry out. I watched as the worm-fish disappeared under the water again, and Ari's body splashed like a pebble into the turbulent sea.

He went under, and bobbed up again; his arms working hard to bring him up. Everything happened so suddenly that for a moment I thought he had merely been bumped by the worm; but then his struggling body overbalanced and his head went under the waves. This brought up his lower body, and briefly his twin stumps flashed through the air. Both legs had been severed halfway down the thigh-bone.

What I did next is, perhaps, the most interesting thing of all. I say this, stone, because the emotions that accompanied it were *exactly the same* as the emotions that attended me pulling the root and throwing Ari-shend-roba-le-patilta-gunarzon into the water. What I mean is that either of these actions was equally random; neither of them was prompted by consideration on my part. It was not that I thought to myself 'I shall do a bad thing now', nor that I thought 'and now a good one.' They just happened. The best way I can put it is this: events collapsed my possible ways of acting into a single path of doing. Earlier, events had collapsed my coexisting ethical possibilities of *good/ bad* into bad. Now the same process of moral observation by the universe collapsed my possibilities into *good*.

I jumped straight down on to the largest raft of broken-off Drüd. It was a tricky jump, and I only just managed to maintain my balance. The water had slopped over the jockeying raft of dead vegetable matter and made it greasy and slippy. From there I hopped on to a smaller raft and dropped easily to my knees.

Ari had tumbled three-sixty degrees through the water, and now his head was uppermost again, his arms working frantically to keep himself afloat.

To my left the darkness of the worm-fish moved through the water, circling back round to finish off its meal.

'Here,' I called. Those two syllables were all I spoke.[1]

His eyes locked with mine, and he tried to breaststroke his way over to me. But he overbalanced again, and ducked forward through the water. His ragged stumps appeared above the waves, swung over and disappeared again. His head came up.

I lay down on the wet float of Drüd and reached out, just managing to take hold of his hair with my finger's end. The hair was long and slippery, but I could just about tangle my fingers into it. Then, awkwardly at first but then with a stronger effort, I hauled Ari over towards me.

The head of the worm-fish burst through the surface of the water. This surface was covered in a film of Drüd-dust, moistened and floating like a slick all around, and the beast's head came through it like a fist through fine cloth. It just missed Ari, catching only one of his stumped-legs a glancing blow. This impact pushed the boy down into the water, and almost pulled me off my temporary raft. But the great beast veered in the sky and fell away, splashing us prodigiously. Ari came up, my fingers still entwined in his hair.

He scootered with his arms at the edge of the Drüd-raft, his eyes filled now with an existential (though, thanks to dotTech, not hormonal) panic. If the beast came by a third time it would almost certainly devour him. And then, probably, me.

I tried to reach down and grip Ari under his arms, but one of my hands was all tangled up in his hair now and wouldn't come free. I felt calm. I tugged down as hard as I could, and a fistful of Ari's hair came out. The dotTech were not quick enough to prevent the first burst of pain, and he yelped aloud. But I had him, gripping him under his arms, and hauling him out. Somehow I managed to pull him out and stand myself up, so that I was holding his half-body directly in front of me. And even as I was doing that I was stepping backwards, half-turning, and leaping.

[1] Glicé: 'heerer'.

The leap saved us. The worm-fish burst up again, breaking through the raft of Drüd on which we had been a moment before, its searching mouth wide and fatal. I landed on the larger raft and skidded, but didn't drop Ari's body. It was surprisingly light. He looked very pale; the dotTech had sealed the wounds at his legs, but he had lost a great deal of blood before they had been able to manage that.

I went down on one knee as the raft buckled and leapt around, the water thrown into choppy waves by the splashing of the Sea Dragon. 'Grab round my neck,' I shouted at Ari.

His eyes were closed, and I could not be sure he was still conscious. But when I pushed him around to my back, like a pack, his arms did at least tighten about my neck. I stumbled to my feet, ran as best I could on the brief deck with my feet slipping and pushing away in odd directions, and made the best leap possible.

I only just caught poking-out roots of Drüd at the torn-off lip above me; my belly and legs swung in dangerously, and I almost lost my grip. But then I swung out again and I scrabbled with all my might, hauling myself up and up. When I was able to slide my belly up and on to what remained of the solid ground, I could shrug Ari's half-body from my back and heave myself the rest of the way up.

Then I lay for a while, until the dotTech could give me my strength back. I looked at the sky. I felt very calm.

Beside me Ari had become unconscious.

This was the first and only moment of *choice* in the entire occasion. I thought then, distinctly, that I could throw Ari's body back into the water. The Sea Dragon would devour it, nobody would ever know. Or, I thought, I could carry him back to the camp and he would regain his health. I could do either thing: I was not guided or compelled either way. I think it was largely the fact that I had put so much effort into rescuing him that persuaded me to heave him up onto my back and carry him all the way along the coast into the town. It seemed wasteful, somehow, to do anything different. But I was intensely aware, as I laboured along under my unconscious burden, of the *power* of the choice I had possessed, for those few minutes by the side of the sea.

*

That was what corrupted me, dear stone. That incident changed me for ever. I had first set in motion the death of another human being; then, halfway through the process, I had rescued him. Once having done that it was, for me, inevitable that I would explore the first half of the event in more detail. I knew for an absolute certainty, as I lay down to sleep that night, that I would kill again.

The people at the camp, and shortly after that a great many people on the continent, were impressed by my heroism. The adults at the camp were congratulatory and emotional. Ari was cared for. Even dotTech cannot regrow legs overnight; that process takes many weeks, and his whole family came up to stay with him whilst he was indisposed in this manner. They insisted on meeting me and thanking me.

A deputation of adults fabricated a series of boats, and went up and down the coastline deterring the Sea Dragons with DNA-darts that infected them a special phage, one that compelled them to stay in the deeper water. Then they sprayed all the under-arches of the coastline, where it had been eaten away to what was judged a 'dangerous' thinness, with a chemical fixer that strengthened them.

And all this activity, and notice, and news (I thought) was actually about *me*, about what *I* had done. Of course, only I knew the truth of my supposed 'courage'. But my secret knowledge in fact made me feel stronger, because I knew more than anybody else.

I was given a medal, dear stone; an antique symbol in honour of my courage. The ceremony took place during a bright Terne sunrise, with hundreds of people around me singing and cheering. The medal was small but weight-enhanced (so that it hung solidly from around my neck). It was marked with a single 'F'.[1] I was enormously proud of it, ridiculously so in fact seeing as how the whole 'near-tragedy' had been my doing. But the pride, the sense of power, the goodness, the badness, were all – I am sure of it – merely different arrangements of the same essential components. Those components were me.

---

[1] 'F', Faelor [='Valour']

183

Dear Stone,

I resolved to kill again – or *kill*, to be more precise, because my first 'victim' was still alive – but in fact I did not do so for many years. I looked about me with care, but the opportunity did not really present itself. I thought it through, you see; and it was obvious that if I killed blatantly I would be imprisoned. I did not want to be imprisoned.

I won prizes for playing the conscree, and travelled to Sobrianna, the major city on Terne to take part in planetwide competition. That probably sounds grander than it actually was; there were hundreds of these sorts of competitions. It was one of the features of living on Terne, as a child. Everybody was put in for one or other, depending on what area of sport or art or living you were marginally skilled at. There was an occasion at this competition in Sobrianna, when I was on top of a building, and I was able to creep up behind a fellow competitor and push them from a ledge, where they had been blithely kneeling and looking down. They did not see it was me, and nobody suspected what had happened; but the person did not fall very far – twenty metres, perhaps – and quickly recovered. For my first actual murder, dear stone (and I shall not prolong this narrative, for I am growing bored with it) we have to go several years further forward. I became a man, and embarked upon the varied life of recreation, travel and sex that characterises the citizens of t'T. For a year or so I travelled randomly from world to world, until I arrived at a world named Foram. There was a passion at this place for great jet-cars and jet-boats; the resurrection of an antique technology. I seem to remember that there was a spurious historical justification for this craze; but rather, I think, it was the pleasure of assembling the clunking, large-scale, intricate engines of the ancients. I became involved with this, moving from city to city, from lover to lover, helping build these behemoth machines by hand. At one port, by a lovely stretch of bright blue water, with sharp white cliffs of fossils curving round, I helped build a jet-boat. It was a hundred metres long, and constructed of metal and plasmetal. There were six of us working on it; myself, my then-lover and four others. And this is where I killed again.

We had built two jet-engines at the back of this craft and were tinkering with the rest of the device. We built these engines on an enormous scale; twenty foot tall. There was no very good reason for this, other than that it caught our fancy to build such monumental devices. The other four were away for the day, and I persuaded my lover to clamber inside the jet outlet to fix a problem I had myself created. Then, when he was in there, I turned the jet on. The combination of very rapid, mincing blades and the superheated exhaust shredded him; he was completely destroyed. The engine itself clogged and exploded, devouring itself and its fellow in fire and shrapnel. I think I had assumed (it is hard to remember exactly) that the blades would simply pulp the body, but this was not what happened. I was badly burned, and received several pieces of hot metal in my body, even though I was many metres away at the controls; of course the dotTech healed my wounds. My victim was completely disassembled. When my companions returned they were horrified, but they assumed (why should they think anything other?) that there had been a tragic accident.

In fact, the crime was so perfect, so free from consequence, that it made me overconfident. I travelled back to Terne and tried to burn a person to death; tricking them into a small shed built of dried spars of Drüd and panels of Drüd-weave. Then I locked the shed and set it alight. I could hear his cries inside the structure of fire, and that noise made me feel peculiarly powerful. But a party of revellers, out for a day's flying, noticed the unusual blob of heat on their sensors and flew down to see what it was. When they landed, they too could hear the (by now desperate) cries, and their flying panel blew the flames out with a smothering jet of carbon dioxide. The person inside was very badly disfigured, and nearly dead; but the dotTech kept him alive and he recovered.

The rescuers gave me some very strange looks, I remember. They could not understand why I had not tried to rescue the burning man. It did not occur to them that I might have deliberately attacked him, for why would anybody do such a thing? But my behaviour was nonetheless puzzling to them. They flew the injured man away to the nearest city for care and attention, and I refused to go with them. That puzzled them even more. But when my victim had recovered sufficiently to accuse me there was no escaping the conclusion; I was

185

a throwback, a statistical freak in the perfectly adjusted t'T population. I was dangerous. 'Police' set out to apprehend me.

Meanwhile, obviously, I had hurried to the nearest elevator and into space. I travelled to Nu Hirsch, and changed my appearance. The 'police' pursued me. There was, however, one advantage to my predicament, which is that I no longer had to look for obscure and deniable situations in which to indulge my growing passion for harming human beings. I could attack much more frequently; and so I did, as I was pressed closer and closer. I severely harmed an individual on an orbital platform by battering them with an implement and severing their head (they survived). Then I killed another individual on the planet by pushing them into a tidal tank – this was a device that produced interesting water effects, waves and tides and the like. I attacked the individual with a knife, damaged him so that he became unconscious; then I placed his body inside the tank and set the device in motion. The water pressure inside was so great that the body was pulped, jellied, and the person died.

But with each attack I found I was gaining less enjoyment. There was no longer a sublime, transcendent sense of superiority; instead there was only the raw feeling of danger, excitement and escape. I think, dear stone, that it was not violence and murder that I particularly craved; it was, instead, *novelty*. It was precisely because there was (more or less) no murder in the worlds of the t'T, that killing was a revolutionary act. But killing again and again lost its point. I wondered, more than once, as my attention was caught by a random passer-by, why I was moved to attack them. I came to the conclusion that it was only out of habit after all. I started planning to give up the killing of people, to flee the t'T 'police' altogether, perhaps to the realms of the Wheah or the Palmetto tribes. To begin a new life.

Then I attacked another person; a kite-flier on the world of Tanzé. I became interested in this sport, which involved the manoeuvring of unpowered kite-planes through the blowy Tanzé atmosphere. I had not come to this place intending to kill anybody, but only to take part in a sport that intrigued me. But then one day, my fourth day of flying I remember, I flew close to another competitor – close enough to grasp her kite and tear its wings. She yelled at me over the howl of the wind 'what are you doing!' – 'you'll damage the kite' – 'look at what you're doing!' – but I was able to pull both wings free and watch her tumble, turning over and over, the kilometre or so to the jagged rocks below. It was enough of a fall to cut her to rips, to kill her beyond the ability of dotTech to repair her.

But others saw me; and when I landed I was apprehended. The 'police' took me and brought me to the jailstar.

Agifo3acca

1st

Dear Stone,

After Klabier fell from the high place on Nu Hirsch, I flew from system to system; twelve systems in all. It was a time-consuming attempt to make it difficult for any 'police' on Nu Hirsch to trace my movements. I felt like an amateur; in the old, barbaric times there were people especially skilled in evading detection. But those skills had been lost long ago; why would anybody want to evade detection in our modern utopia? Why would anybody *warrant* detection in the t'T? Equally, and luckily for me, I suppose that the skills of the detectors had also declined, with nobody to detect. I, certainly, had to make it all up as I was going along.

Finally I arrived at Nu Fallow after a month or more of travelling. That was a strange time, stone; the best part of a month swaddled up in foam, floating in that trance-like interstellar state. I revisited my childhood. You know about my childhood now; but I went backwards in time – a premonition, in a way, looking forward to the conclusion of my mission. For what was waiting for me at the end.

What? No. I am not trying to be mysterious.

Yes, I miss somebody to talk to. There is nobody to talk to in this place.

'Travelling on,' I told the (human) helpers at the Nu Fallow orbital. 'I won't be going down the elevator.' They smiled. Why would they not?

Have you decided whether you are going to fulfil your part of the bargain? asked my t'T. By now, of course, I knew it was not at an AI at all, but I was in the habit of calling it that; and I didn't know what else

188

to call it. *Or would you prefer to go straight back to jail? You've killed twice since you got out, you know.*

This brought a stinging, allergic sensation to my eyeballs. I fought to keep the tears down, but they started out anyway. I had to turn to the wall to stop the helpers noticing me.

You said yourself, I subvocalised, that Klabier was almost certainly *not* dead.

I don't think I used the phrase 'almost certainly'.

You torment me.

You torment yourself.

I said nothing. After a while, the AI started into a speech as stilted and awkward as if it had been prepared and written down and was now being badly read aloud.

Near here is a system called Colar. It is thirty or so light years from Nu Fallow, but is very close to the Wallows so travel speed is low. It may take you months, or even longer, to get there. It depends upon the extent to which your faster than light travel degrades as you approach.

It stopped speaking. 'And this,' I said aloud, 'is the world you wish me to murder?'

I could feel the AI assenting to my question without it actually forming words. *Your info-chip, in the insect carapace, will help you.*

'Dear old Narcissian,' I said, feeling savage and sarcastic. 'What was his name?'

Tag-matteo.

'Dear old dead man. I am extremely curious to see what it was he put into his info-chip. *Extremely* curious, you see, to find out what is in there and why he felt he had to camouflage it as an insect body-part.'

I can understand, the AI said slowly, *that you are feeling unhappy that the mission is now imminent. Might I advise you to look beyond the conclusion? After the mission you will be free forever, and wealthy, and . . .*

'I don't expect you to understand murder,' I said, sharply. 'Whoever, or whatever, you are.'

There was silence between us for a while.

You will programme your Zhip-box, said the AI, *to the following location.* It gave me a location.

'This is Agifo3acca?'

His ship has travelled through the narrowest portion of the Wallows. By the time you get to this place, he will be there. For him less than two weeks has elapsed.

'How lovely it will be to see him again,' I said loudly, as if drunk, although in fact I had only drunk Erzaz.[1] My voice was loud enough to attract attention from the few other people in the orbital's refectory.

Be quiet, said the AI; but now it sounded weary rather than peeved. *Keep control of your emotions, and this will soon be over.*

But keeping control of my emotions was no easy task. My mood swings were more pronounced than ever. That afternoon I felt appalled, depressed, almost suicidal after my conversation with the AI. A mental image of pushing Klabier from the balcony, so vivid as to amount almost to hallucination, asserted itself before me over and again. I thought of all the people I was going to kill, as if I would have to push my thumbs into the soft parts of their necks myself, individually. 'How many people on this world, this Colar?' I asked the AI. But it refused to answer that sort of question, which was wise of it, because any answer would only have deepened the incline of my downward mood. I got sluggish, colours around me seemed to dull. I could barely summon the energy to move my limbs. So I lay myself down and slept. And – miracle! – when I awoke the bad mood had all fled away. I took a seat beside one of the forty-metre square observation windows and took a little more Erzaz, and my spirit clambered upwards. It would soon be over; the AI had said so. I had come so far – had done impossible things. Escaping the jailstar, for instance. Put this task behind me and I would be able to get on with things; and what of the task anyway? Wasn't it, when you looked at it right, wasn't it a rather wonderful thing? A unique achievement? A work of art? As a child I had known the pretensions to being an artist; and art had been created throughout t'T for thousands and thousands of years; artists had used every medium – visual texts, naturally occurring substances, gas, fluid, solid, electrical patternings, patterns and sculptures of pure movement and shape, words, engrams, faces-as-engrams (some artists used dotTech to put their own faces through repeated changes, making themselves their canvasses), programmes,

[1] A common t'T stimulant, drunk as fluid or sometimes taken orally as a heated gel.

narrative, intensity, dissipation. Form and subject had been extensively explored, birth, life, death, deathlessness, on every conceivable scale. But nobody had used death itself *as a medium*, had used the snuffing-out-of-life[1] as a mode of artistic expression. Well, I decided, I would. I would leave behind something that would not be forgotten.

I ate, slept, adjusted myself. After a day or so, I made my way to departures, and strapped on yet another Zhip-box. Yet again, the foam spilled out and formed itself around me. Darkness.

2nd

Dear Stone,

It was a long trip; I assume that the initially rapid passage quickly declined and degraded as we approached the borders of the Wallows. Inside the foam I slept, got bored, thought through what I was doing. It was not too late to change my mind, to pull out. But I wasn't sure how to go about that. The slower I travelled through space, the less trance-like I felt. The timeless fugue state of FTL is in large part a function of the quantum juggling of the transit, playing around in the brain. But we went more and more slowly, and I became more and more conscious. Time dragged. I tried to engage the AI in conversation, just to pass the time, but it did not respond. Either it was playing games, or else the travel speed rendered it incapable in some way. Perhaps it was an AI after all, and the quantum turbulence had mixed it up behind repair. In that darkness, the quiet, the emptiness all sorts of things seemed possible.

I slept, I woke. The difference between the two seemed minimal. Time dragged, and dragged.

I don't know how long it all took.

When I felt the first lurch, excitement burst up inside me. It meant I was being manoeuvred into a hangar. I had finally reached Agifo3ac-ca's ship; and the mere prospect of a change of scenery was so exciting

---

[1] In the original this is not a Glicé word, but a strange neologism, probably concocted by Ae himself to express this (to his culture) very bizarre concept.

to me I found myself fidgeting inside the foam. Pressing the pliant material back, pushing forward. I could hardly wait.

The excitement of my arrival accounted, I think, for the 'happy' mood I found myself in as the foam was washed away and I lay, blinking, on the hangar floor. I had not seen Agifo3acca for well over a year, but still I greeted him as an old friend. 'How is your life, dear man,' I cried. 'Still studying the Gravity Trench?'

'I am,' he said.

'I adore you for it!' I declared, warmly. 'I adore you, your obsession and your fraction-God.' I may have been emotionally unstable, I suppose; in a manic phase.

I was in the large arched hangar of Agifo3acca's spaceship; the walls were a cobalt blue, tiled (or given the appearance of being tiled) with a paler diamond pattern of turquoise. The floor was mostly flat, except for two indentions, one a sort of sink-hole for waste (like the brown speckled fluid that was my dissolved foam), the other leading towards a sphincter that gave exit to space outside. Ranged against the wall were half-a-dozen, car-sized boxes that I took to be shuttles. I looked around me, my brain perhaps less addled with space-flight than might normally be the case, on account of the relatively small speeds possible near the Wallows. The dark, brilliant and somehow intimate space of the hangar – for all its forty metres of height from floor to ceiling – struck me as home.

'I feel closer to you,' I told the tall Wheah, 'and to your kind than I have ever before.' I believe there were tears coming down my face. 'I feel closer to your Wheah,' I sobbed, 'than I do to my own kind – I understand! I understand why it was you who met me from the jailbreak, and why you're here now!'

Agifo3acca, startled, broke away from me. If he understood what I was saying he did not show it.

The last time I had seen him, I had spent only two days with Agifo3acca, and for much of that time I had been recovering from my near-fatal jailbreak. But this time I spent many weeks with him, and got to know him very well indeed.

He had a disconcerting habit of displaying his teeth, as if

aggressively. In fact (I discovered) this was a sort of exaggeration of a smile. He had not done this the first time I had met him, but I certainly noticed him doing it now.

I wandered around his bizarre, ramble-shackle spaceship; up its ladders and into mushroom shaped chambers designed for some purpose I cannot guess at; down corridors hundreds of metres in length, with regularly spaced holes at the base of their walls like enormous mouseholes. Through rooms draped with some form of rough fabric that looked like the inside of tents. In one room filled with water, which I took to be a swimming and recreation room, except that when I touched the treacly surface of the water it was not water at all, but ink. It stained my fingers; they stayed smudgy-black for days.

He would eat once a day, shortly before going to bed. I never saw him eat at any other time, and I believe it to be a Wheah habit: one large meal, digested as the subject sleeps, and no food to distract or make sluggish the individual during waking hours.

'I want to find out everything I can about the Wheah,' I gushed to Agifo3acca during one such mealtime.

He looked at me, uncertain. He swallowed. 'Why do you desire this?'

This struck me as funny; that Agifo3acca was keeping up a pretence in this manner. 'I have found out the secret behind my mission.'

'Mission,' said Agifo3acca, sagely.

'When you collected me from the jailstar, I said. 'You talked of the payments you were receiving.'

'Wealths,' he said. 'I have received more.'

'Of course you have,' I said, winking. 'Of course. Well I know. But I do not know everything. I need to know the *logic* behind the Wheah.'

'The logic?'

'Tell me about your culture.'

Agifo3acca stared at me for a while, then put his head down and finished his meal. I asked him several questions, but he simply ignored them.

The next morning I rambled again through the spaceship. I clambered over a pyramid pile of junk, old processors tumbled together like

193

rubble, to get up to a porthole in the ceiling of one room that seemed to be the only egress. Popping up through this I found myself in a separate space, filled with tall leafy stalks of a yellow colour. They seemed to be naturally grown, a sort of plant I had never encountered before. I explored this for a while, and then dropped back through the trapdoor and out again. Then I found a long corridor, barely tall enough for me to walk along without bending my head, and walked for seven or eight hundred metres; but the corridor ended in a simple dead end. I was convinced that this ending must be a hidden entrance, but for all that I spoke, Friend, to enter, and pushed and pulled at knobs and patterns, nothing happened, no door opened. I found a series of rooms in which great stretches of coloured fabric were stacked; the colour, a plasticky hardness, had been laid over the stretched fabric in some primitive fashion; although the colours were nice in a muted sort of way. Everywhere I went everything was quiet, still, motionless, except for the occasional rustle of a dust-bot crawling over a surface to clean it.

All this time, I suppose, I was filling my time, trying to avoid facing the prospect of what I had come to this place to do. I think, dear stone, that I was waiting for a prompt from the AI. But my AI had been silent for days, an unusually prolonged period of time.

I sought out Agifo3acca again. I found him sitting in the middle of a tall wide room given over to stellar imaging. A great blotchy hologram of the local space filled this room. It was quaint: this sort of antique method of realising or mapping space. I stood looking down upon it from a sort of balcony.

'This spaceship,' I told him, 'is like a museum.' He didn't reply, so I came down into the belly of the room, walking through the ghostly stars and gassy shapes, to where he was sitting. 'I have not seen an example of stellar mapping so crude outside of a museum,' I said, pleasantly, taking a seat beside him on the couch.

Agif had in his hand a pointer-wand with which he was adjusting the positioning of the great misty image, shifting it along, angling it round, yawing it to display one constellation or another.

'A hobby?' I pressed.

'A tool,' he said.

For the first time I actually looked at the image being projected, seeing past the ludicrous antiquity of the mechanism. Was it local space? I did not know the area well enough.

'Is it t'T space?' I asked. 'A portion? What are you looking at?'

'The Trench,' he said at once. 'The Gravity Trench.'

'Of course,' I said. I looked again, feeling stupid I had not noticed the phenomenon amongst the scattering of holo-stars; but even looking carefully it remained hidden. 'Where is it?'

He gestured with his free hand.

'I cannot see it. Why do you not have the image machine single out the Trench in some bright colour, so that it is obvious?'

'Today,' said Agifo3acca, 'I am interested in real-colour representation. The Trench has no colour, it eats colour, and so it is almost invisible to the human eye. But you can sense it by the way its gravity distorts the background stars. See! If I swivel the map, some stars leap from position to position – their light is bent by the gravity of the trench from one side of it suddenly to the other.'

But I was already bored. Agifo3acca's obsession with the Trench was so last-millennium. I knew, from what he had said before, that he had his own bizarre theories about the thing, but humanity had been through a period of concocting endless bizarre theories about it and still it had refused to give up its secrets, until we had realised that – most likely – it had no 'secrets' to give up.

'Perhaps,' I said, to bait him, 'it is of natural origin.'

Agifo3acca shook his head. 'It cannot be.'

'There are many extraordinary gravity phenomena in the galaxy,' I pointed out. 'Black holes of every dimension, some no bigger than my fist, some super-giant surrounded by superdense particles.'

'It is no black hole. You do not understand the Trench,' he replied, separating his lips tightly to expose his teeth in that strange expression of his that might have been aggressive or might merely have been smiling. 'Perhaps you don't much understand gravity?'

I bridled at this. 'It is true I am no gravity-technician, but I have had many years of t'T education.' I stood up, proud, coldly taking offence.

He patted the air in front of him with his hand: sit-down, sit-down. I stood for just long enough to show that I was not at his beck and call, and then sat.

'The Gravity Trench,' he said, 'is like nothing else in the galaxy.

Gravity draws all things to itself, on all sides, so all gravitational phenomena tend towards the sphere, the spiral, the cone. But this . . . object is a thousand-light-year *wall*, a *linear* feature. Hundreds of light years tall, thousands long, but only a few kilometres wide. From the bulk to the wallows,' (he was pointing with his stick) – 'broken in the middle for some thirty light years, and the physics of that space, that gap in the Trench, are . . . insane.'

I wasn't sure that Agifo3acca, whose command of Glicé was not perfect, actually meant to use this technical, medical word, so I queried it. 'Insane?' I repeated. '. . . In the middle?'

He seemed to take me wrongly. 'Yes, and *not* at either end. It has something to do with the weak-force physics, for the phenomenon seems only to peter out in the Bulk or the Wallows. Diffuse nebulae, higher concentration of gas, the generally disruptive presence matter . . .' He trailed off. 'But why is it broken in the middle, snapped like a bone? Nobody knows. How it formed, we don't know that either. But some answers seem more likely than others.'

'You've made quite a study of this,' I said. 'Haven't you.'

He slid his lips apart over gripped teeth and glistening, black gums. 'Many aspects of the worlds of the t'T interest me,' he said. 'But this Trench interests me most of all.'

'More than it does me,' I said. 'Or any of the people of the t'T, I think. The Trench is just – well, just itself.'

'Yes,' he started to say, and then hushed himself with a finger on his mouth. 'The people of the t'T,' he said, as if I was no longer one of them, '*they* are self-regarding to an amazing degree. They live among wonders, and yet are only interested in their own thoughts and creations, their own habits and sexual preferences.' He leaned towards me. 'Let me try to amaze you. Because for all that you are no longer of the t'T, rid of their devil-machines, yet you still share their numbness to the wonder of the galaxy.'

'Thank you,' I said, trying to sound ironic and detached but sounding instead intimidated.

'Let me try to amaze you,' he said again. 'This Gravity Trench – unique in the universe as it is, most likely – is an entirely *mass-less* phenomenon.'

'Mass-less?'

196

He nodded slowly.

I said 'But gravity is a function of mass.'

He didn't feel the need to reply to this self-evident statement.

'I don't understand,' I said.

Agifo3acca was silent for a while before replying. 'Gravity is a folding of space-time associated specifically with matter, with mass,' he said. 'With the presence of mass, or the acceleration of mass. But this Trench, this phenomenon, is simply a rip in space-time, a mass-less warping, a kind of tear. It exists.'

'It is you, I think, who are being insane. How can it have "no mass"? I don't understand.'

'It has existed a long time,' Agif said. 'It is almost certainly an artefact, not natural.'

This stopped the conversation. It was the sort of thing a madman would say, an obsessive, an unbalanced and schizophrenic man. In the worlds of t'T there are sometimes such illnesses where the cultures do not permit dotTech in the brain. These people will rave of aliens and other civilisations. But, dear stone, *there are no aliens*. Humanity has crossed and recrossed the fast-space and the slow-space, visited every world and star, penetrated even into sublight realms, underworlds. But there has never been discovered a single material object that would suggest alien life, present or past. Not one fragment of xeno-bone, not a ghostly radio signal gibbering and crackling lost in space. There are primitive life forms on hundreds of worlds; insects and worms, plants and fish, but nothing that thinks, that imagines or dreams or makes art. Sensible people accepted long ago that humanity is the only sentient creature to have existed.

More: there are philosophical reasons for considering ourselves the only being in the universe. Philosophy discovered long ago, before even space flight had been developed, that the fact an intelligent conscious-ness observes the world around it alters the world observed; that perception has a direct effect on the subatomic world. This is what an antique human, one Heisenberg or Weisenberg (records are uncertain; I prefer the latter because it suggests a certain sense of humour[1])

---

[1] In Glicé, the words 'weis' and 'wiese' refer to sense of humour, comic timing and comic inventiveness.

discovered. It is possible, he said, for a human observer to detect which direction an atom is moving in; or to observe how fast it is going; but it is strictly and literally impossible for a human observer to know exactly which direction an atom is travelling and how fast it is going. Amazing! His contemporaries thought so, but the fact remains that *by the process of observing at the atomic and subatomic level* that-which-is-observed changes. It is the foundation stone of modern philosophy. Dear stone, I am not trying to patronise your ignorance, but allow me to rehearse this for you: at the subatomic level 'things' do not really exist the way that you or I exist – not as hard, concrete, certainties. Instead everything is a sort of probability haze, each particle occupying a number of possibilities. And this is the nature of that level *until it is observed by an intelligence* – then and only then do the probabilities collapse and become pinned down. Is this atom here or there? Well, it is in a real sense both here and there, and in neither position, all at once – *until* it is observed, and then it takes up a position in one or other or neither place.

It still puzzles the mind to consider it, when you really think about it. To be truthful, stone, I haven't really thought about it since my schooldays. Amazing!

Anyway, the point is this: the fact that consciousness affects the very fabric of the universe in this basic way argues that there can only be one consciousness in the universe. If there were aliens – if there were some other sentient, thinking-reasoning-problem-solving race of beings in our galaxy, then they *would observe a different universe to the one we inhabit.* This is not a mere figure of speech my precious stone, it is a literal truth stemming from the way the universe interacts between quantum and larger levels. If there are 'aliens' then they live in a different universe from us, one which we cannot inhabit (for even if we travelled there we would not perceive and therefore not call into being the same place).

Now, everybody knows this; every half-educated person, every child. This is why there are no alien artefacts, no others to come visiting, or to flee before us. We are alone. So now, in their place, humanity has used its own nanotechnological adeptness to transform itself. Why do we need aliens when we can grow our own eyes-on-stalks, our own scales and feathers, when our bodies can adopt any fantastical shape it chooses? There are no aliens, so we mimic their imagined shapes in our own bodies.

Everybody knows this.

But this basic fact of the universe, something as inevitable and ubiquitous as light, or hydrogen, or gravity, does not stop some people from believing in aliens. Certain distracted or insane people (I use the terms clinically) used to believe that aliens lurked in the Trench – or that a vast alien civilisation had risen and fallen and left not a single trace of evidence. A population of so many trillions of people allows for a great diversity of opinion, and diversity is a good thing, so I did not really intend the tone of voice with which I addressed Agif:

'Are you, then, a crank?'

He rolled his eyeballs to show white, like clouds sliding up to cover the sun. He said nothing. I fretted that I had inadvertently expressed something more scathing than I had purposed.

'You suggest,' I explained, 'that an alien race grew to interstellar prominence, an empire – that they colonised many worlds and developed fantastic technologies – great enough to build this titanic artefact – technologies far in advance of ours because they could use their skill to kink space in a gravity configuration *without* the use of mass. You suggest that this great flowering of interstellar sentience grew, built this artefact, and then vanished so completely as to leave no tatter or shred of material evidence that they had ever existed?' It is possible that I was exercised, angry even, by the end of this speech: but it seemed so absurdly impossible it was actively provoking to me.

Agifo3acca slotted the pupils of his eyes back into their usual place and looked at me. 'No material evidence,' he said, 'except the Trench.'

'Except the Trench.'

'Ships have explored it,' Agifo3acca said, in a quiet voice. 'Flown close to it. Probes have scoured along the inner lip of it. The only mass within is the accumulation of dust and gas and stray matter that you would expect so powerful an attractor to gather after so many thousands of years – not nearly enough matter in itself to exert the gravitational pull that the Trench exerts. Space-time is ripped at the Trench, but not by matter.'

'But these aliens,' I pressed. 'Where did they go? Did they vanish into thin air – or thinner vacuum? Their bodies? Their cities? Their chips? Their vast technological engines, capable of engineering on so colossal a scale? Where are these things? More than this, where are their radio transmissions, their light spheres expanding outwards inevitably and forever? We would be able to detect these things, but – nothing, nothing. You say they vanished and took all these things with them?'

Agifo3acca looked at me, impassive.

'*Where* did they go?' I insisted.

'Since you ask,' he said in an unusually slow grumbling voice, 'I believe they transcended.'

This, then, was the view of Agifo3acca, an opinion he held to as tenaciously as he did to his religious beliefs in his fractionated God. We had many conversations about the Trench after this, and sometimes I was better able to contain my mockery and sometimes less.

'Think of space-time as an elastic sheet,' he told me as if I were a schoolchild again. 'Imagine three dimensions in two, as a great stretchable sheet.' I didn't have the heart to rebuke him for his condescension. 'A mass, for instance, a star, or perhaps a planet, is like a stone' – do you attend to what I say here, my dear stone of mine? – 'bowing the sheet down. Gravity is this dip, this conical drawing-down of the fabric of spacetime. A dot travelling close to this gravitational distortion in spacetime (a dot, a spacefarer, moving through vacuum in a straight line) will swerve around in an arc if it goes near enough to roll into the dip. Like a golf ball rounding its hole, its path may be deflected, or it may circle and circle (which we call *orbit*), or it may fall in altogether. You play golf?'

Unexpected, this. 'No,' I said. 'No.'

'No? It is not part of your culture, I suppose. So, this golfhole is an image of a conventional object. A sphere, a mass. But this is not the Trench. There is no mass bending spacetime in the Trench, no actual weight drawing down the elastic sheet. Instead the sheet has been, as it were, *folded*, creased in so firm a manner as to retain its kink – but creased is far too small a word to describe the undertaking. This thing has been *creased* in a thousand-light-year line, as if spacetime itself were nothing more than a piece of paper. You know what paper is?'

(Scoffingly, because I was increasingly annoyed at his superior manner, as if expecting me to be ignorant) 'Of course! I have often written, created artistically, upon this *papper*.'

He angled his head at my mispronunciation, surprised that I would make the error as a native speaker (but it is hardly a common word.)[1] 'To them,' he said, his eyes sparkling with wonder, 'the whole of space-time was nothing more than a sheet of paper. Imagine the power! They could fold space itself on a gigantic scale. We do not know how they were able to do this thing.'

I burst out at this. 'It cannot be,' I said, irritably. 'This makes no sense. Gravity is a *fucntion* of matter – all matter *possesses* it.' Which is of course true, dear stone. Even you! The gravity of greater rocks, rocks like planets, is much greater, but even you, even in your smallness, you possess a tiny gravity field.

Agifo3acca shook his head, displaying his teeth again in his disconcerting manner. 'Not so,' he said. 'Gravity is not *possessed* by matter.'

'Nonsense!' I said. 'Nonsense!'

'There are other gravitational effects,' he said. 'Acceleration for instance. Accelerate rapidly enough and you experience gravity. The Trench is evidently a third way of creating a gravitational effect. We simply don't understand how, as yet.'

I changed my angle. 'Humanity has known of this thing for thousands of years,' I said. 'It is perhaps the most prominent feature of space travel, something space-farers must detour around. It has surely been investigated and investigated! Surely generations of people have studied it and studied it!' I was, I concede, hazy with the details, but was nonetheless adamant. 'There can be no mystery.'

Agifo3acca nodded. 'It has been thoroughly explored,' he agreed. 'But there is little to explore. We cannot reach the "bottom" of the Trench, we can only observe it from a distance.'

'A black hole,' I said. 'A black wall . . .'

'In a manner of speaking, yes. But in other ways, no. For instance, if matter falls into a black hole it simply makes the hole bigger, increases the gravitational pull. When too much matter falls into the Trench – this

---

[1] In the original text, this mispronunciation is exactly opposite to its translation here: the Glicé for 'paper' is *papper* or *papperia* (its usage its very rare); Ae inadvertently pronounces the unfamiliar word 'paper', in the antique fashion.

black Trench – it interferes with the mechanism by which it is maintained. Somehow, I am not sure how. At its far ends, where the Trench has drifted into the Wallows at one end and the Bulk at the other, the dust and gas has simply dissipated it, it has ceased to exist.'

He stopped, seemed to contemplate for a while. Then he went on. 'Also, it was broken. It seems like that when it was . . . built, the Trench was a single straight object. It may have been the reason why this stretch of fast-space was cleared to begin with – we can only move at the speeds we do because we occupy fast-space, and I am certain that this patch of fast-space was opened in the galactic arm as a side-effect of the construction of the Trench. But that is hard to prove. What is certain is that over time, with the rotation of the Galaxy, the Trench has shifted in relation to everything else. And, of course, it is now in two sections, rather than one.'

'What broke it?' I asked, drawn in almost despite myself.

'Who can say? Perhaps something massive enough fell into it – a black hole, perhaps. Perhaps it malfunctioned in the middle portion. Who can say?'

'Malfunctioned,' I repeated. 'You make it sound like some kind of machine.'

His eyes twinkled at me. 'Perhaps it is,' he said. 'Who can tell?'

Then, one day, he took me out to have a look at it. We went down to one of the many hangars in his bizarrely castillion spaceship. We got aboard one of the transparent shuttles, which wormed forward and slid down the chute and out through the hangar's sphincter. It was a small car, and there was only just room for the two of us inside it. Agifo3acca sitting facing forward and me facing backwards. I saw the sphincter close behind us in a fireworks-burst of icicles and wisps of released gas.

'I have not seen this design of shuttle before,' I said, over my shoulder to Agifo3acca. 'It is entirely transparent. Even the working parts are entirely transparent.'

Agifo3acca said nothing, so I was compelled to repeat the statement entire, just to elicit a response. Then he said 'Yes.'

We flew, sublight but at very rapid speed, for thirty hours or so. Many months passed for the rest of the t'T. I slept through a lot of this. During the few occasions when I was awake, I would sometimes attempt to engage Agifo3acca in conversation. I asked a number of questions, trying (since directly asking about Wheah culture had met with silence) to approach the matter obliquely. I asked:

'Are you married, Agifo3acca? Do the Wheah believe in taking partners?' Nothing. 'I heard that they did. I read a poem onetime, a forty-thousand-page poem, largely about the taking and giving in marriage of the Wheah.' Nothing.

Later, I tried: 'Perhaps you have children?'

Then: 'Have you ever killed anybody? I understand that you have warriors amongst the Wheah?' This was obviously closer to the point, but Agifo3acca still said nothing.

'I find it strange,' I said. 'The other day you were so very garrulous on the subject of the Gravity Trench. Now you say nothing at all.'

'The Gravity Trench,' said Agifo3acca, in his grumbly voice, 'is my life now. The other things you ask after, they are no longer part of my life. I am no longer part of the Wheah.'

I kept my own counsel at this; but I didn't believe him. No longer part of the Wheah indeed! But he could not be drawn into further conversation, so I sat back and eventually I slept.

Agifo3acca woke me. 'Are we there?' I asked him.

'Close enough to make magnification a direct rather than a virtual business,' said Agifo3acca, which had been the point of the journey in the first place.

The transparent pod that enclosed both of us went milkily opaque, and then clear again; the smartglass was magnifying what lay around us. There was a bright spot with a fuzzy tail; a single star from which a tapering thread of hot gas was being sucked away by the Gravity Trench. The blob of light was beside Agifo3acca's head, and the trail of white stretched over towards me.

'That,' said Agifo3acca, with a tone that sounded to me (making allowances for the differences of culture) like an almost religious reverence; 'that is the star Bamk. It is a single rank-class star, medium-small, probably generated from the Wallows one or one and a half million years ago. Since then it has wandered, travelled far; and now it has intersected with the Trench, which has also travelled far. It is passing close enough to have its outer envelope of superheated gas sucked away.'

The Trench itself was invisible, except where the escaping gases from the star Bamk spread a little before vanishing. I wondered about the nomenclature: 'Bamk' did not sound like a Glicé word. Had the Wheah star-charted the whole reach of t'T space? Did they have names for all our systems and stars, even ones as insignificant as this medium-small planetless body before us?

'The Trench,' I said, 'is more or less invisible to the human eye.'

'Yes,' said Agifo3acca, with the closest his lugubrious manner ever came to excitement. 'Allow me to . . .' The screen changed; a blue-purple swathe of colour popped into being across the cockpit transparency.

'This is one form of image enhancement,' he said. I noticed that the star Bamk had changed from white to a delicately pale blue, as ethereal as a winter's sky on Terne. 'It registers relative gravitational intensity. If you look closely, the point where the gas trail from Bamk intersects the Trench is black – that is effectively infinite gravitational attraction, such as is found in a black hole.'

'Shouldn't the whole Trench be black then?'

'Not exactly. There should be – is, in fact – a thread of absolute gravitational intensity running down the exact middle of the phenom-enon; but the lip of the event-horizon means that we can't see it from where we are. That is why this is my favourite vantage point, because the stream of matter flowing from Bamk pries the event-horizon back a little, as it were, like lips separating to allow in a stream of food.'

'Food?'

'A fanciful metaphor.'

'Will Bamk, then, be consumed?'

'Yes,' said Agifo3acca, as if I had asked a ridiculous question. 'Of course.'

'And this will affect the Trench – perhaps break it again?'

Agifo3acca snorted – the first time I had heard him make that sound. 'No. It would take more than the mass of a small star to break up the Trench. A million Bamks would not disrupt it.'

'And yet something broke it, in the middle,' I pointed out.

He ignored this, and instead took me through the various image enhancements that his shuttle was capable of. The Trench came up as red, as green, as a rainbow of contour-marking shades, as a system of lines, as a forest of dashes like iron filings in a magnetic field. I was soon bored, but Agifo3acca was so caught up with his life-defining task that he went on and on.

Eventually, however, he turned the shuttle back and started for home again. I slept once more, and woke to the blackness of space. *You sleep so much,* said my AI.

'Oh,' I said aloud; and then, conscious of the proximity of Agifo3acca, I subvocalised I am surprised to hear from you.

Surprised?

It has been days. Days of silence. And now you speak.

I wanted to see the phenomenon.

The Trench? Why?

It is a fascinating thing.

You wanted to see the Trench? Why?

Only because.

And now that you have seen it?

There was silence for a bit, so I subvocalised: You are a strange creature. Why are you interested in something such as the Gravity Trench?

Strange creature, repeated the AI. It sounded almost amused.

I do not understand you, I told it.

I am easy to understand. No, it paused, *no, you are right. I am very hard to understand.*

Can you explain yourself?

When you have done what you agreed to do.

This soured the conversation for me, so I sulked for a little while. But the AI did not give up.

When you return to Agifo3acca's ship, you should access the info-chip that you collected from Narcissus. I will tell you how.

And what will I find when I access it?

When you access it, it said, *you will find out.*

Why do you play these games with me, AI? I truly do not understand you. Are you a device of Agifo3acca's? Perhaps you are him, I added, turning around in my seat to stare at the back of the Wheah's head, perhaps you are actually a receiver through which he talks to me. Are you? Hey? (I thought hard, subvocalising the words with intensity). Hey! Turn and look at me, you Wheah!

205

Nothing.

Your mind refuses to rest steady in one place, said the AI.

I'm tired, I sub-said, folding my arms.

Your tiredness goes very deep.

'So now you are a mind-doctor?' I snapped, aloud. There was no response from Agifo3acca. The AI did not rebuke me for talking aloud instead of subvocalising, in the old manner. I snorted and closed my eyes. I don't understand you at all, I sub-said.

I'm an advanced t'T AI; a new generation of machine. My fundamental identity is seeded in a fractal base programme, so should I – when I – am degraded to an irreparable point by, for instance, interstellar travel I am able to reboot and rebuild myself.

'I don't believe you,' I said aloud. Since Agifo3acca was not responding, and since I half believed the AI to be nothing more than a transmission device he was using to communicate with me at a telepathic level, there didn't seem much point in keeping quiet.

I'm a communication device, said the AI, as if it really had been reading my mind, *the seeds of which were infiltrated into your jail by Agifo3acca, and which has since been used by him to communicate with you.*

'Hah!' I said, quite loudly I think. 'I knew it.'

I am, the AI went on, *a figment of your own imagination, a fiction whereby your diseased consciousness talks to itself and makes believe its worse instincts are not intrinsic to it. You're hardly the first psychopathic schizophrenic to split their personality in such a manner.*

I didn't say anything to this.

I am what I am, said the AI; and then it was silent for the rest of the journey back to Agifo3acca's ship.

3rd

Stone. Stone, stone.

There really wasn't any further putting it off. That same day, after returning from the expedition to the Trench, I told Agifo3acca that my employers and his (I winked at him with this, but he seemed unmoved) had given me an info-chip, and that I wished to access it.

'There are many rooms in my ship,' he said, 'with the capacity to interpret an info-chip. Simply show it to a wall receptor.'

I took myself to a distant part of the great edifice, walking slowly, feeling gloomy. *You're just making it worse*, opined the AI, *drawing it out like this.*

'You could shut up,' I said aloud, but without passion.

Eventually I found a quiet room, arched like vault, tinted green with some faint wall luminescence. The room was something like ten metres square. In the middle was a table, so tall as to reach almost up to my chin. There was nothing on the table, and no chairs around it; but the walls were indented with a series of pushings-in and pullings-out of the material from which it was made, a sort of bas-relief effect.

I picked the info-chip from my pocket and showed it to the wall in a vague sort of way. There was an audible click inside the little nodule, and the walls gleamed.

Goodbye, said the AI.

'What?'

You don't need me any more.

'You're going?'

Yes; this chip will tell you everything you need to know.

'But,' I said, suddenly startled and a little afraid that my AI was going to abandon me after all this time. Does that sound illogical to you, dear stone? I hated its voice, I was convinced at times that it was a sign of my own madness, I was prepared to beat my own head to try and reach it. Yet now, with its sudden announcement that it was leaving, I felt a void inside me. 'Don't go,' I said.

How touching! But you don't need me now.

'You should stay and police me,' I pointed out. 'I might decide to back out of my commission.'

You won't.

But how can you be sure?

We know you pretty well by now. I was so startled by the AI's announcement that it was leaving, that I didn't even challenge its use of the plural. *Besides, the deal still holds. If you don't fulfil your part of it, you'll still go right back to jail. You don't need me here for that.*

'But I don't want you to go.'

Look – and it directed my eyes, pulling the muscles round. A figure

207

was forming, coalescing in the air before me. *A hologram of a rather outmoded sort. It'll take a few seconds to set up. But then it'll require your complete attention.*

I stared at the ghostly shape, striated momently with white bars of interference. Then the colour went smooth grey all over.

'AI,' I said. 'You can't go. You promised me an explanation of everything when the crime is . . . when the job is done.'

You say that you know who is behind the mission anyway, it replied. There was a tone of humour in its words.

'I know it is the Wheah,' I said, bridling a little. 'I think it has something to do with an invasion. But I don't know the details! You promised me an explanation of the details! Why this world – why there had to be such loss of life!'

You'll get your explanation, said the AI, soothing. The grey figure was starting to bring facial features into focus, as if they were swimming up from great depths inside its head to settle on the surface of its face. *If you complete your mission successfully. I promise you that.*

'I assumed you would be the one to explain.'

Does that matter?

'So many deaths,' I said, trying to draw it further into discussion; but I could feel the non-corporeal twitches inside my skull. It was going. Departing.

'Where are you going?' I asked, urgently. 'Can you at least tell me where you are going?'

Nowhere, it said. *Everywhere. Does that matter either?*

And it was gone. There was a humming noise from the hologram, which now had a face and was looking directly at me.

4th

Dear Stone,

We're getting closer to the moment, to that moment. I am not eager to get there; I don't—

Dear stone. Dear dear stone.

Let me tell you about the hologram, to begin with. It was of a regular sized, slightly slender male human being. Its skin started grey, which gave it a corpse-like appearance, but the colour started shaking to pink-red as the thing began to speak.

Its first words were 'What the bloody hell are you staring at?'[1]

I couldn't think what to reply to this; so I said, 'You're a hologram.'

'Hologram?' it replied, as if outraged. Its voice was creaky, with a scratchy underpinning of white noise. 'Hologram? Aren't you?'

'No,' I said, a little meekly.

'No? Of *couse* I'm a hologram. Of course *I'm* a hologram. What do you want? What do you want? Is this Narcissus Tupylorov?'

'No,' I said. 'This is a spacecraft, somewhere off the Wallows.'

'The Wallows?' The hologram scrunched up its face, like a hand balling into a fist. 'Ah. What's your name?'

I told it my name. 'And what's yours?'

'I'm a hologram,' it replied. 'We're not named, you know. This shape belongs to a fellow called Tag-matteo. If it makes you comfortable, you can call me that. But I'm not here to make you comfortable, you know. God, but you're ugly.'

'I know,' I said. 'I have no dotTech in my body, and I have aged a great deal. Also I am scarred.'

'DotTech,' said the hologram. 'Excuse me whilst I . . . it's a little difficult adjusting. Some of the compression maintenances are – what would you say, stiff? I'm having to take a little time unpacking my data.'

'Take all the time you want.'

A fuzziness formed around the shape, and resolved itself into a set of downward streaking lines that it took me a moment to recognise as rain. 'Is your programme,' I said, '. . . raining?'

The shape of Tag-matteo looked up, as if noticing the downpour for the first time, although the imitation droplets were splashing markedly off its imitation head and face. 'I seem to be,' it said.

I wondered about asking more about this strange phenomenon, but thought better of it.

---

[1] Expletives and obscenities are rare in Glicé. Translating them is always a tricky business; the translator has, in this case, aimed for a certain archaism to replicate the effect of their oddity.

'Hmm,' Tag-mattco said. 'Rain. It's all light patterns, you know. Now, what is it you want me for, precisely?'

'What do I want you for?'

'That's what I asked you.'

I didn't know what to say. 'What can you do?' I asked.

'Don't be stupid. Are you stupid?'

'No!'

'Then tell me what you want me for.'

'This is . . . strange,' I said. The figure had so angry a manner it was starting to bother me. I had been brought up to be polite at all times; a creed I believe I have lived by, stone, all my days. But this hologram seemed trying deliberately to be rude to me. I couldn't work out why.

'Strange?' said the hologram. The light-show rain had stopped, and now its skin gleamed yellow as if bright sunshine were shining upon it.

'What . . . ?' I started to ask. Then, 'What are you doing?'

'Unpacking myself. I've been inside a very small space, you know, in information terms. I contain a great deal of information, and it has been fractally compressed and zipped-up. It doesn't all pop out at once you know. Will you tell me what you want me for, or will I go back inside the chip?'

'I found you on Narcissus,' I said.

'Understandable,' it replied at once, almost snappishly. 'That was where Tag-matteo left me.'

'I was directed to find you by . . . by something. Somebody. They told me that you would help me with . . . something that I have to do.'

'What something?'

It was so cross-sounding that I felt inhibited from revealing the nature of my mission. Mass murder is not an easy thing to own up to. But it started needling me. 'What? What? *What?*'

'I must kill off the population of an entire world,' I said.

'Very well,' said the hologram, matter-of-factly. 'I can help you with that.'

I opened my mouth, and shut it again. 'Can you?'

'Of course.'

'And it doesn't bother you?'

'What?'

'What I just said. The murder of sixty million people?'

210

'Is not for me to be bothered by such things. That's not what I am. Why,' it added, looking at me in an almost sly fashion. 'Does it bother you?'

'Are you,' I said, after a pause, 'programmed to be so . . . offensive?'

'No,' it said. 'I'm not.'

I waited for more explanation, and when it wasn't forthcoming I asked, 'Are you an AI?'

'I am most definitely *not*,' it said, as if I had insulted it, 'an AI. I'm just data, and a few processing programmes to help users access the data. I'm not sentient. This construct is . . . well, it doesn't really matter. Would you prefer a different interface? Feel free to programme one in. It would make no difference to me.'

'Never mind,' I said. 'What data are you?'

'Data,' said the construct, with an unmistakable smile. 'Relating to the Gravity Trench.'

In fact, dear stone, it contained a great deal more data than that. It contained data that related to the life of Tag-matteo, the human its interface was modelled on; and a general encyclopaedic database based on t'T knowledge. Tag-matteo had, it seemed, lived a wide and varied life before becoming obsessed with the Trench. 'It's the kind of thing that happens, occasionally,' said the hologram, with an almost conversational air. 'There are perhaps a dozen major mysteries in the space of t'T – I mean, really big, bugger-off *mysteries*, you know? They are understood as completely as they can be, everything that can be *known* about them is known. I mean on the level of data. But sometimes people become convinced that they can understand them better. Tag-matteo thought that about the Trench, and so he studied it. For the best part of thirty-five years, with a two-year sabbatical in the middle. And the best thing is, that he *did* comes to understand it better.'

'How do you mean?'

'He gained access to knowledge that nobody else in t'T space had ever managed to access before.'

'How did he do so? I mean, people have studied the Trench for millennia; how did he supersede that research in only a few decades?'

The hologram looked mysterious. 'He had help.'

211

'Help? From whom?'

The mysterious expression vanished. 'I don't know.'

'I thought he programmed you with everything he knew?'

'He didn't know who helped him either.'

I was sitting with my back against the green wall of the room at this stage; and I thought of Agifo3acca, somewhere far below me in his enormous spaceship. Could he have brought some other, Wheah knowledge to bear on the problem? Was he the unknown helper?

'Agifo3acca,' I said, 'the Wheah, whose ship this is – he has studied the Trench too.'

'Really?' said the hologram.

'Yes. He claims that aliens constructed it.'

The hologram made a raspy scoffing noise. 'Absurd,' it said. 'There's no such thing as aliens.'

'But Tag-matteo,' I said. 'He came to understand the Trench?'

'I wouldn't say that. Not *understand* it completely. But he understood it better than most people have done.'

'And his understanding is—'

'—is me, in a manner of speaking. I am what he knows.'

I thought about this for a while. 'And you can help me in . . . in what I have to do?'

'Why,' said the hologram, smiling broadly. 'Why, yes.'

5th

Stone,

I came back down to Agifo3acca with the info-chip in my pocket. The Wheah looked at me, his expression impassive. I couldn't quite hold back a superior expression – after all, I possessed a databank, in the form of the info-chip, that could answer many of the questions about the Trench that had obsessed Agifo3acca for most of his adult life. (Unless, I wondered to myself, unless Agifo3acca knew more, said more, than he let on).

'Was your session satisfactory?' he said.

'Very,' I said. 'I will go now. Will you help me? I need a standard info-chip; I need to travel and build myself a ship at my destination.'

Agifo3acca nodded.

So, dear stone, so; we come to the crucial point. Yes, the tall Wheah followed me down to the hangar; yes he gave me the necessary info-chip, and helped me strap on a Zhip-pack. His face was the last thing I saw before the foam covered me up; and there I was, in the darkness, feeling the lurch as he pushed me towards the exit-sphincter of the craft. Drifting away. Drifting, and then accelerating – slowly at first, because of the proximity of the interference pattern of the Wallows, then more rapidly. I flew to Colar.

Hard. This is hard – like your hardness, stone; a pun on difficulty. Now we're coming to the really bad things I have done.

Colar

Dear Stone,

It's been a while since I last spoke to you, I know. I have not been looking forward to this part of my narrative; truly I have not. It is odd, how difficult this part of my narrative is for me to relate. I could have started with this point, couldn't I? I could have got it over with at the beginning. But I look back over what I have told you, and told my invisible listeners through you (wellhello! I *know* you're there), and it occurs to me that this has all been an elaborate avoidance of this point. This point.

Well, I don't know why it is so awkward a thing. Let me tell you about it, as swiftly as possible. I shall not elaborate it unnecessarily. Get it over with. Which is appropriate – really it is, since that was my frame of mind when I put on my Zhip-pack and set off through space. I wanted the whole crime behind me, so that I could get on with things.

The parameters, as the AI had told me right at the beginning, were that all human life had to be extinguished; but not that the entire world be annihilated. I arrived in orbit around the next planet but one in the system – a gas giant, with a splendid range of ruby-coloured rings around it. I hung there in space, more or less unconscious, still sleeping, half-tranced, while my standard info-chip (not the specialised Tag-matteo chip) burrowed out of my foam, and flew to the nearest raw material; the dust and water particles of the ring system. It quarried a small amount of this and used the matter to gather more. This was in turn used to duplicate a number of construction devices, none of them very large. All entirely standard. It was necessarily slow and time consuming; but travellers to new systems (or, as in my case, travellers to a system where they did not want to declare themselves to the orbitals there) had no option but to employ it. I lay, curled inside my foam, whilst all this activity went on around me. The devices shaped quarried carbon and iron, constructed a chamber, ten metres by ten by ten. When everything was ready, several of these construction machines formed into larger units, and shunted the hardened foam-wrapped figure of me through space and into the chamber. They then sealed, and evacuated. Oxygen from the frozen water was separated and blown into the interior, whilst other machines built essential circuitry. My foam was eaten away in increments, until I was able to stretch out and pull lumps of the stuff from my body like a chick emerging from an egg.

I'm delaying upon this, aren't I. My dear stone, your patience is a bad example to me. I am resolved: I must be *im*patient in the telling of my story.

I completed the setting up of the chamber, and the machines began adding another capsule to it. But I did not wait for this; instead I used the new circuitry to access Tag-matteo. The hologram appeared, crotchety, fuzzy. 'Your machinery is not very polished,' it said. 'I can hardly focus my image.'

'I apologise,' I said.

It smiled.

So, stone. This is what Tag-matteo's insubstantial image explained to me.

The mechanism by which the Gravity Trench existed – its provenance, history – the exact reason for its break in the middle – all these things remain mysterious. But what was known is that its intense gravitational gradient was not a mass phenomenon. Rather than operating by accretion, as mass did, to create gravity, the Trench was formed by the minute but concerted application of strong atomic force.

So, I took a stone. Yes, like you. I took several, plucked them from their millennial orbit around the gas giant. They were simple fragments of rock, parts – probably – of a moon torn apart by collision, or perhaps ground to pieces by the tidal forces of some much larger body. Now all that remained of that ancient body was a swarm of miniscule rocks, pebbles, stones. Very much like you. Some were the size of my hand; some of my head. I took a dozen. One, two, three; larger ones; four, five, six; smaller; seven to twelve no bigger than a thumb's end.

The holographic Tag-matteo smiled, and smiled.

We – I – wrapped each of these stones about with a filament web; and fitted each one with a tiny processing unit. Then we threw them – one after the other – propelled them away and towards the planet Colar. Their units accelerated them very rapidly, to a significant fraction of light speed; and they hurried into their programmed orbits about the planet. So far there was nothing noticeable about them; they were just more tiny torn-up pieces of old worlds, just more dust specks in the messy environment of space. When they arrived at Colar their units had slowed them again, and they were nothing but slow moving pebbles, stones like you.

Did you wonder why I chose you to be my confessor?

The six smallest took up positions, random-looking but carefully programmed, close to the six orbital platforms of this busy world. The remainder adopted planetary orbits of various vectors, swooping round and about the big belly of Colar, from the night-side to the bright sunlight on the day-side and round again. Swinging round and about in forty minutes.

The processing units knew what to do. I was already resetting my Zhip-pack, already applying my foam (messily, but it is hard to do by oneself). I had done what I came to do, and now I was starting back; machines vented my little chamber and I was in vacuum again, starting the journey back towards Agifo3acca's ship. I had left the system before anything began to happen. To happen . . .

This is what happened. The units attached to each rock, nothing more than motes upon stones, triggered the action. The filament network, webbing the surface, initiated an implosion based on strong-force, that instantly collapsed the matter of the pebbles into a mathematical point with a brief effective gravitational pull that scaled up towards the infinite. This effect was not as long lasting as the Trench (which has lasted for tens of millennia – maybe much longer). But, then again, it didn't have to last very long.

Six of these newly created black points, these intense gravitational dots, were nestling against the outside of the six orbital platforms.

Each of these platforms – millions of tonnes of metal and plastic and organic matter – collapsed instantly, was crushed and drawn into the notional points. Everybody upon them died straight away.

The other six stones were in a balanced orbit, each one mirrored by another on the exact antipodean point. At the same instant that the orbitals were destroyed these slightly larger pieces of rock vanished into notional points of infinite gravity. Because they had been orbiting at a certain velocity, their lateral speed and the co-presence of a mirroring point of intense gravity on the far side prevented them from tumbling straight into the planet's core. Had they existed for long enough, of course, this is precisely what would have happened; they would have followed a rapidly spiralling-in trajectory and ended up coalescing into a six-into-zero notional point at the exact centre of the world. But they did not exist for enough time. According to the calculations provided by the hologram of Tag-matteo, they lasted a little under twenty-one minutes – a figure that depended on the intake of matter. It is the 'real' gravitational effect of actual matter that interrupts the quasi-gravitational effect of concerted strong-force, you see. Once these six points had drawn in enough matter – just as the other six stones, that swallowed the orbitals whole – they broke down and dissipated.

For twenty-one minutes, then, these six points of intense gravity swung around and about the planet Colar, starting to curve inwards a little but not existing for long enough to do more than lose a few tens of kilometres of orbital height. They swung around and about, half an orbit, and they sucked. With what amounted to an infinite force they sucked at the envelope of air that surrounded the world. They drew the atmosphere of Colar entirely away, into themselves, into nothingness. They sucked until all the air of that world had gone.

DotTech is a wonderful tool; it can preserve life under many circumstances. It can even preserve life in the absence of oxygen for a certain time. But it cannot do so indefinitely. Human life needs air to live. Much of the population of the world, I suppose, was hurled into the sky, torn to tatters by the unprecedented, apocalyptic, world-ending winds that my little stones caused. They died sooner. Others, perhaps indoors, perhaps underground, died later; preserved in a coma-state by the dotTech as long as it was able to do so.

Everybody died. Which is exactly what I had been employed to bring about, of course. Dear stone, I did it.

2nd

Dear Stone,

I did not think about what I had set in place as I flew back to Agifo3acca's ship. In the peculiar trance of faster-than-light travel I didn't think about very much. Or, no, that is not right: I was thinking about how the whole thing had come together. Off and on, at intervals ever since I had been taken out of the jailstar, I had wondered how on earth I was going to be able to murder sixty million dotTech-protected human beings. The various ways I thought of were all flawed, impossible, useless. Then, guided by my AI, I had found a way; it was a way that utilised a lifetime's research into the Trench. I thought, in my blurred, dreamy way, that it was a strange coincidence that the ship which had assisted me after the breakout, and which had been waiting for me when I arrived in that part of space, had also been involved in a lifetime's research into the Trench. That was what I was thinking.

I was also thinking, with a certain satisfaction, that if my AI's promises were worth anything, I was about to be given the answers. I had paid a heavy enough price for the knowledge; or the people of Colar, the sixty million people of Colar, had paid a heavy price. I felt I deserved the answer, at least.

How was it for them? I have wondered that, sometimes, since I arrived here, with you, dear stone. You see this mark here? This is where I broke the skin, and the rib, over my heart; I used you as a club, do you see: I struck at myself. But I only hurt my chest and my hand. Even without dotTech it is hard to hurt yourself. The will goes out of your arm – do you see – when the pain gets above a certain level. There is only scar tissue there now.

The people here (hello doctor!) have provided me with information about Colar, of course. To begin when I did not consult this, because I thought it would upset me. I was right, of course; it did upset me. But

218

after a while boredom prevailed upon me. I accessed the information, and discovered a great deal about Colar. It was a mostly pastoral world, dear stone; given over to the cultivation of a hundred different grasses and bamboos. The population were pastoral-romantics, and most of them slept outside under the stars. Why not? The climate was moderate, the spin and angle of the planet had been adjusted to iron out the severity of winter and the population adopted dotTech enhancements so as not to feel the cold. They kept flocks of lions and tigers; adapted beasts from the mythical past, with their killing-teeth and wounding-claws removed. Colarians kept huge flocks of these humble, puzzled beasts. Their shepherds sang and wrote poetry. A gentle people. There were cities, of course, because cities are natural to humankind. But they were grass-covered places, with an animal grazing on every roof and much of the architecture made of bamboo. A fragile template. Was that why this world was chosen as a target? The infrastructure was fragile, howsoever tough the people. Although, of course, there were also many stone houses, and many caverns dug from the mountains, and all the variety and diversity of human existence.

How was it for them?

I imagine different groups, or individuals, each time I think about it. Now, as I speak to you dear stone, I think of a group of three. They are covered in a light woolly fur, which (I think) was a common adaptation against the elements. This one is piping a tune on a lengthy tube of carved bamboo. It is how they control the goat-dogs – shaggy horned animals that herd together the shambling toothless predators. That one, here, a tall and bulky male, blows a tune of his own composition down the bamboo flute. The goat-dogs mew and creak out their calls, and hurry around, butting a few straggler lions on the haunches to get them into place. Pull out the view a little: here you can see the whole green space, a forty-hundred-hectare green field, grassy and undulating. Up here, along to the top of this hill, a variety of bamboo has grown into a hollow tree twenty metres tall and two metres in diameter. The top of this plant is a mass of cream-coloured feathery leaves; inside has been adapted as a living space.

From the top you can see the landscape all around; the hills sloping and rising as subtle as the contours of a human body; the green of the fields, the blue of the sky. This single cloud, here, in the zenith. There it is.

And there would have been no warning; no screaming in the sky, nothing to see. The great wind would have leapt up from nowhere. *Click*, like a switch, and a stone like you, my dear one, collapses to a mathematical point, and all the air in the world starts stampeding and tearing and rushing upwards, away. The three shepherds barely have time to register what is going on. They are already airborne, sucked up with the vanishing atmosphere. But the bullying air is ripping back and forth, compelled by the sheer force of the gravity to vector and squeeze into a point no bigger than a dot. No bigger than a dot and in fact, truth be told, infinitely smaller. So the shepherd has one thought; not even a thought, it is only the fragment of a thought, there is hardly time for even that to register. It is 'Where is my pipe?' – for the wind has snatched that away and crushed it to dust, and so it does with the human being, it squashes and pulls him in a fraction of a second into a sneeze of red, and then there is nothing. Every cell of their being is whisked away and upwards by the wind that marks the end of their world.

Or somebody else: somebody in the cellar of their city house. They are down there because there is something down there they want – a bottle of embre, perhaps. She turns her woolly head, because she hears the enormous noise of the wind above. She starts to stumble up the stairs because she wants to know what is going on. But the house above has collapsed in the whirlwind, and rubble blocks the way; just as the earthquake tips her and hurls her down. She lands on her head and snaps her neck, but that is not so grave, because her dotTech immediately sets about trying to resuscitate her: isolates her brain from trauma and as quickly as it can reknits the fibres of her spinal cord and neck bones. She opens her eyes again, and sees the pile of rubble blocking her way. But she can't breathe. There is nothing to breathe. The dotTech does what it can, but she cannot last long. For an hour she is given consciousness (the dotTech knows its limits; it is smart but it cannot solve the larger problem. But perhaps she can, so it grants her the space to try and do so). But when it is apparent that she is failing, that her body is collapsing, the dotTech puts her back into coma. And it is in this state, fifty or a hundred hours later, that she dies.

Or somebody else: there are four or five major mountain chains on this world, and they are riddled throughout with caverns and dwellings. Many people are in these when the winds start; some torn from the doorways and cave-mouths, others ping-ponged about the corridors by the burly, rushing evacuation of air. Some manage to close doors, to trap a roomful of precious air inside. They are the lucky ones. But what can they do? Outside their door the world has been freeze-dried, its surface now as airless as its long-dead moon. People will come, but nobody can come in time. There are six of them in this small space; they will use up the air. When the seriousness of their situation becomes apparent to them they make a concerted decision; they request their dotTech to put them into a coma, to conserve the air. And so they all lie down, and so all of them perish a hundred or two hundred hours later.

Afterwards I came by the following statistics (I'll explain how in a little while); there were 61,765,002 human beings alive on Colar the second before the strong-force webs were activated on my little orbiting stones. Then 52,798,650 died at once, or within a few minutes, mostly in the tempest of atmospheric turbulence my devices caused. The difference was 8,966,352. Of those, 8,966,304 died during a period of time between one hour and three hundred hours, trapped in rooms and cellars, some (amazingly) even outside, but not swept up by the gales. They all, though, died eventually. Forty-eight survived the immediate catastrophe. Forty-one of these were in a single elevator car, travelling up from the surface at the time. They were lucky. Two other elevator cars were travelling at the same time; one was close to docking and was simply drawn into the black-hole point that consumed its orbital; another was close to the surface, and was smashed to shreds by the winds. This single car was in an exact position, where the would-be-fatal attraction of the collapsed orbital was offset by the tremendous sideswipe of atmospheric turbulence. It shuddered and was ejected into space, hurtling in a trajectory that bent sharply around the newly created black-hole point of its target orbital and away. The people inside, provided with two thousand hours of air under normal conditions as well as food and drink, dropped into voluntary coma and were eventually picked up by a special t'T ambulance craft months later. There were another seven survivors;

and these were the most remarkable stories of all. Six of them had been deep in Colar's seas, wearing breathing equipment and protective costumes. There had been thousands of such recreational divers swimming through the oceans and seas of Colar at the time of the catastrophe, but they had all died when the seas boiled away and were sucked after the vanishing atmosphere. These lucky six were all deep enough, and in such positions so as to be trapped by the undersea rock formations around them, to avoid being tugged up into the air. There they stayed, comatised inside their suits until the first t'T rescuers arrived on the scene. The single other survivor had been an archaeology obsessive. He had been building an archaic sublight spaceship in his basement, and had been inside it when the catastrophe happened. He had sealed his hatch and stayed inside, hibernating (for the dotTech helped him do this) for months until the rescuers arrived. The fact that they were comatose, which is to say deathlike, meant that the presence of these seven did not violate the terms of my commission.

All seven of these individuals requested immediate removal from the dead world. There was a certain amount of discussion, amongst the t'T, as to whether a new atmosphere should be fabricated for the planet. But it was decided, influenced partly by the few survivors, that it was more fitting to leave Colar an airless tomb; to leave the bodies that remained *in situ*, and to abandon the world. There were plenty of other worlds in t'T space to be colonised.

Of course, my employers knew that this is what the t'T would decide to do with the world. They knew the t'T.

My employers. I have used this phrase several times throughout my narrative, dear stone. In fact it is rather misleading. As I discovered.

I was travelling back, oblivious to all that had happened – except that in my imagination I knew something like this was bound to be the state of affairs. I was still travelling back to Agifo3acca's spaceship when the t'T first became aware of what had happened on Colar. There were not many visitors to this world, but a few people came, and found no orbitals waiting to collect them. None of them carried the chips to build their own ships, so they had no option but to travel back whence they came. Something was wrong; and teams of t'T started arriving.

It was a mystery. There was no clue as to what catastrophe had destroyed the world. My stones, collapsed into gravitationally intense points, had themselves dissipated with the influx of matter. An hour after they had been activated, they had simply ceased to be.

I sound almost proud of myself, don't I, my dear stone? Well, it was a complex problem, a series of technical difficulties that I overcame (with a little help) to a very satisfactory degree. Wouldn't you say?

In the Library

So, dear Stone,

I was back in Agifo3acca's hangar, being washed clean of foam. For a while I simply lay there. I felt that the solvent was doing more than washing my outside clean; I felt that it was somehow cleansing me inside as well – I mean, rendering me metaphorically clean.

He provided me with food and drink, and left me alone. I draped the smart fabric around myself, fiddled with its button to make it into a sort of poncho. I sat, ate, drank. The strangest thing. I felt a renewed intensity, a pure pleasure, in doing these simple things because I knew that so many people had been blotted out. They would never eat again, and that somehow added savour to my food.

Then I slept; and woke feeling a little more usual, a little less transcendentally pure. I wandered for a while through the corridors of Agifo3acca's ship, until I chanced upon him in his prayer room.

'I would ask,' he said, as he rose slowly to his feet from his position of genuflection to his fraction-God, 'not to disturb me in here.'

'My job is completed,' I said. 'I have done the thing my employers – our,' I added, pointedly, 'employers – required.'

Agifo3acca angled his head. It seemed to say 'Good'.

I looked at him. 'Have you heard?'

'Heard what?' But his mock ignorance did not fool me.

I smiled at him. 'Surely you are pleased that my mission has been accomplished. That it has been a success.'

'It means nothing to me one way or the other,' he said, haughtily. I looked around his small, smoky shrine-space; there were three-dimensional holographic images of his fraction-God ranged about

224

the walls, a third of a body with a spear through it, a face in agony, a rainbow.

'Perhaps,' I said, 'in this place, you feel removed from it.'

'Now that you have completed what you were commissioned to do,' he said, 'I will stop receiving wealths on your account. I assume you will be travelling away and we will not meet again.'

His hostile tone baffled me a little; but then I reasoned that his action, that of his people, had been against the tenets of his partial god, and that here – in the shrine – it troubled him. I assumed that he was guilty. Or perhaps he simply did not like me. My hair, untended by dotTech, was long and dredlocky, my skin dirty and covered in scars.

'Have you heard?' I asked.

He shook his head. This was not out of the ordinary, dear stone. It *is* possible, very rarely, to transmit messages at faster than light, but a message is a pattern of information and that degrades very easily in the quantum turbulence of faster-than-light travel. If the news of my success were indeed being transmitted around t'T the surest way of passing on the news would be an actual, human messenger. And Agifo3acca was not in the habit of receiving visitors. Perhaps, he reasoned, he was merely pleased that I had returned and he trusted me to have carried out the activity his warrior people had required.

I left him then, and wandered some more about his spaceship.

I am not sure what I expected, exactly. I had been promised an explanation, the identity (and more importantly) the motive of my employers. I think I expected my AI to reappear – after all, its circuitry was still there, inside my head. But nothing happened. I ate, slept, wandered. I bumped into Agifo3acca once or twice a day; it was plain that he now considered our business together concluded, and hoped (without saying as much) that I would simply leave. I might have left too, except that I did not know where I wanted to go. Everything felt at a loose end.

I went to the green room and summoned up the holographic representation of Tag-matteo; I am not sure why. Perhaps I thought it could give me some answers. But it was only hostile and insisted upon its ignorance. 'I'm just data,' it would say. 'Data and processing. I'm not sentient – only programmed to respond according to certain static paradigms. If you ask me a question I can only answer with data. But these questions you are asking me now, they do not provoke a meaningful answer in me.'

It was after this that I began to have the bad dreams. In fact, I have had them ever since that moment. They are not guaranteed to turn up every single night, but they are persistent. I wake up sweating, worn out, aching, crying. How many dead! So many!

I could not bring myself to leave; but I avoided crossing paths with Agifo3acca. That was easily done in so enormous a spacecraft. I began studying Agifo3acca's data files, merely to distract myself from the misery that pressed increasingly from inside me.

I spent a week in the library of that ship; downloading and accessing files. Dear stone, I felt the weight of what I had done come increasingly upon me.

2nd

Dear Stone,

Let me move quickly over what followed. Think of it, dear stone, as a sort of coda to the whole set of events. After so many deaths, did one more death mean very much? It's a statistical nonentity, a single 'one' when set against sixty million.

How to tell it? Until this narrative, I do not believe even the greatest minds in the whole of the t'T have pieced together the whole story. I am doing humanity a service by telling the tale.

Agifo3acca's blood was – no. Before that.

He was in his dining space, having eaten shortly before retiring for the night. This made him sluggish. I am not sure whether this was a consideration in my mind when I came to see him. As I set my eyes upon him my only thought was to ask him questions.

'You must explain it to me,' I said.

'Explain?' he said, in his accented Glicé.

226

'You must. I was promised an explanation.'

'By whom?'

'My employers. Promised an explanation for what I had to do. For why I had to do it.'

He looked at me steadily for a while. 'I cannot provide you with one.'

'I assumed,' I said, circling him carefully, and hefting the metal spar I was carrying from hand to hand. 'I assumed that there was some council of Wheah elders, some war cabinet, that made the decision. I assumed that it was part of a larger plan, a war plan, an invasion. Perhaps to distract attention. That's what I assumed.'

Agifo3acca had gone very still. His eyes were on the metal spar. I had found it in one of his lumber-rooms, a discarded piece of metal a metre long. And I had sharpened up its leading edge with a laser; now it was sharp enough to cut flesh quite easily. I was naked, and had painted my body with red ideograms. I can no longer remember why I did this. But the important thing was to get an explanation from Agif.

'I assumed my AI – I really thought it was an AI, to begin with – but then I assumed it was a communication device through which these Wheah war-leaders, or perhaps you, were communicating with me. Using me to do what you needed doing.'

'AI,' repeated Agifo3acca, his eyes still on the blade I carried. 'I do not understand what you are saying,' he said.

'No,' I said, as if humouring him. 'But I have consulted your databases since then.'

'My data is not secret,' I said.

'Perhaps you should have made it secret,' I said. 'I thought that there was a whole conspiracy amongst the Wheah. I imagined a large-scale invasion, but there is no invasion planned. Is there!'

He shook his head.

'Your databases make it clear that you have had no form of communication with any other Wheah for sixty-seven years.'

'Sixty-seven years,' he said. 'Yes.'

'I wanted to see the large picture,' I explained, tossing the blade from hand to hand again. He flinched when I did that. 'I wanted to believe that so large a crime must have a large reason for it. But it didn't, did it? I assumed it was something planned by the whole

227

Wheah, but it wasn't. I see that now. It was you – wasn't it? It was you. Just you by yourself.'

'I do not understand what you are saying,' he said.

'You could talk to me in my brain, if you wanted to,' I pointed out. 'But if you want to play this some other way, then that will do.'

He stared at me.

'I have been wandering through your ship, trying to understand why you want to have such a crime committed. Perhaps you can tell me? I am asking as politely as I know how.'

'I do not understand what you are saying,' he said.

'Very well,' I said. 'I'll tell you what I think. I think it has something to do with the Gravity Trench. That is why you made me use technology related to the Trench – technology you had uncovered in your researches, and which you presented to me through the disguised form of the hologram Tag-matteo – to do the murder.'

'Murder,' echoed Agif. There was a slight hint of a question about the way he said it.

'Maybe your mind has been warped by your years of studying the phenomenon. Maybe you wanted to extend your experiment. Is that it?'

He flicked his eyes from my weapon to my face, and when he realised that I was waiting for an answer he said: 'I do not understand what you are saying.'

'Oh, of course not,' I said, sarcastically. 'But do you know what I think? I think you *do* know what I am saying. I think you wanted to see what happened to life forms if they were sucked into this strange form of gravity. You believe that the aliens who – you say – created the Trench then disappeared into it. You wanted to see what happened when an entire population of people were compelled to pass into that strange form of gravity. That's what I think.'

'I must ask—' he began to say, slowly, but I interrupted him.

'But you knew it would kill them, didn't you! You *knew* that they would die. Most of them died in the atmosphere, or suffocated to death. Some few were in the orbitals, but there the collapse of those structures would have squashed them to death. None of them survived – that was why you wanted *me* to do it. You knew they would all die, and your religious beliefs prevented you from committing the crime.

You persuaded me to do it, to do your murder for you.' I was feeling quite heated now.

'I must ask you—' he started again. But that was the point at which I lost all my control. I screamed. I hurled myself at him with my sharpened spur, and made a sweeping cut. The metal sliced through his material and into the flesh of his arm, where he twitched it before his body in a pathetic reflex action of self-defence. But my blow overbalanced me, and I stumbled forward, falling painfully to my knees. Agifo3acca wailing with the pain of his arm, lurched to his feet and blundered past me. By the time I was on my feet again he was through the door; only the whisk of his disappearing coat-tails around the door-jamb.

I howled. I wanted his death.

I hurled myself at the doorway, crashing bodily into the wall and dinting a shallow impression into the plasmetal. I seemed to be losing co-ordination, for when I bolted through the door and into the corridor outside, still screaming so hard it made my throat hurt, my legs went from underneath me and I clattered to the floor. I dropped my sword. Dazed, I struggled upright again, bent to pick up the sharpened spar of metal, only to slip again. It was then that I realised the corridor floor was slick with Agifo3acca's blood. It was splashed in a great dark puddle beneath me, and dabbles of it were on the wall. Where I had steadied myself getting to my feet I had printed a sketchy picture of a hand upon the wall.

I had never seen so much blood before; dotTech does not allow such prolific exsanguinations. Somewhere, deep in a cunning part of my brain I realised that this meant Agifo3acca was one of those Wheah who did not permit any dotTech in his body at all. Because, dear stone, there are some Wheah (the less religiously exacting) who allow a basic form of nanotechnology in their metabolisms; and some (more devout) who allow none at all. Only his travelling at a significant fraction of light-speed for so much of his life had enabled him to extend his life relative to the t'T. This meant that it would be easy for me to kill him.

My rage had been sapped a little by my tumbles; so, in order to whip up a proper frenzy I bellowed along the corridor 'You made me do your killing, Wheah! And now I shall kill you!'

I got up more carefully, and wiped the blood from the sword on my shirt; the smart fabric immediately balled and expelled the dirt.

'Agifo3acca!' I screamed, lumbering along the corridor. I was brandishing my sword over my head, so that it struck sparks from the metal roof and made a grinding noise.

At the end of the corridor I found there was no sight of my prey. Moreover the trail of blood stopped. I don't know whether Agif, realising that he was bleeding so heavily, had managed to staunch that flow in some way, perhaps by wrapping the cloths of his coat around the wound. But without the blood I didn't know which way to turn. I screamed, bashed the wall with my sword, and then lumbered away, climbing a slope and blundering through a chain of rooms. 'You must assuage these deaths you have caused,' I cried aloud. 'Don't hide Agifo3acca! You know you are responsible. You made me do the killing. You are the real murderer, not me.'

I went through six rooms in quick succession, and found nothing. Then I thought to myself that he might be trying to get off the ship. It is curious; it never occurred to me that he would try to arm himself and retaliate against me. It did not seem to be part of his nature. I thought, grimly, that if he were capable of that he would not have needed me in the first place to do his criminal work for him.

I hurried back down the slope and down the spiral to the hangar, at the base of his enormous, topple-towered spaceship. 'Blood for blood!' I yelled. 'Death for death! Your one death for the sixty million!' I was so certain that I would find him in the hangar that when I approached the entrance to it I called before me, 'Agif – I know you're in there. You must prepare to die now, I think.'

And I burst through, screaming, holding my sword ahead of me.

He was there; half-covered in foam. The foam was still oozing up around him, slowly, out of his Zhip-box. His red-stained coat was discarded on the floor, and blood was trembling out of his wounded arm. It had stained the normally cream-coloured foam a streaky pink colour, like clouds at sunset. The foam was up to his mid-chest, and down to his knees; his arms were mostly covered by it, but the stretch of arm just below the shoulder was still bare, and wet-red all over with blood. I could see the wound, a deeper red gash where the blood pulsed. And then I could see his face, utterly white, his mouth open a little way, his eyes two perfect circles dotted with two points of black. He was breathing very hard. I had him.

I started coughing; the exertion of running around and the rasping of my throat with all the yelling and screaming had agitated my bronchus. I coughed so hard I doubled over, and had to sit down. By the time I had settled my mouth, Agif was three-quarters covered by the foam.

I got up, and stepped over to him, lifting the sword to cut him about the head. I wasn't exactly sure how to deliver the final stroke. I breathed in. Agif was looking straight up at me, his eyes wide and seemingly shivering with fear. I could see the fear in him. He had positioned himself close to the sink in the hangar floor, so that when the foam was complete he would tumble easily into it and through the sphincter to outer space. I paused, dear stone.

It was a moment of choice. Had Agif stayed in his dining room, or had I encountered him in the corridor, I would certainly have killed him. I really would. And, more, dear stone, I certainly intended to kill him as I stepped through into the hangar. But for some reason, when I was actually standing over him, it did not seem the thing to do to kill him. I tried to remember why I wanted him dead so badly; and was even able to work intellectually through all the reasons – his use of me as a tool, his responsibility for so many deaths. But it did not seem appropriate, somehow, to actually bring the sword down and end his life. So I just stood there, whilst the foam bubbled and slewed up and around him, covering his feet; forming into his mouth until only his eyes were left over a veil of foam. And then it went over his head, and he was encased in it.

I could still have killed him then, of course. For a minute or so the foam was soft, and I could have simply speared him through it. Even after its surface went rock-hard, I could have rolled him to the far side of the hangar and sprayed him with solvent to uncover him. I thought of him inside the dark of the foam, quivering with fear, wondering when my blow was going to come thundering down. This thought made me feel neither elated nor pitiful.

I pushed the pod of hardened foam with my foot, and it rolled into the gap and settled slowly into the sphincter; and then, with the careful action of an airlock, it was squeezed into space.

Dear Stone,

Well, yes, I wasn't entirely sane I think. I stayed on Agif's ship all by myself for some time. I am not sure how much time. I abandoned clothes, and stopped carrying out even the basic ablutions that my lack of dotTech had driven me to. I became extremely dirty, so much so that my rank smell was offensive even to myself. I was still armed with the sword, and had painted myself in what was left of Agif's blood on the floor outside his dining room (tidybugs were cleaning the mess away by the time I got back to it). Painted and armed, I roamed from room to room, singing to myself and telling myself stories. Sometimes I grew so tired with this that I curled up and went to sleep wherever I happened to find myself. I felt the cold, having no dotTech within me, and sometimes I woke up trembling with chills. I cried. I pretended I was no human at all, but rather a hawk or a lion. At one stage I seem to remember (although it is hazy in my mind) that I tried to persuade the ship's processor to vent air from a succession of rooms. I think I was hoping to experience the rushing atmosphere that I had inflicted upon Colar; hoping to be drawn through the air. But the ship's processor refused to accede; recognising the danger, I suppose. I ate food from Agifo3acca's dining suite, telling myself that I had earned it by sparing his life. For three days I ate nothing but my own hair, pulling it out of my head in clumps and chewing it in my mouth. But without the dotTech in my body to keep me healthy I got feeble with hunger very quickly, and eventually gave up this strange diet. I tried cutting my own flesh with jagged objects, and using the blood to write words and draw faces on the walls of the corridor; but the cleaning robots, the little bugs, cleaned it away. I might have been able to reprogram the machines, but I could not be bothered. I was too far gone. Without the dotTech in my body I was deteriorating severely.

The dotTech.

Now we come to it, dear Stone.

I believe that after a while, which might have been two weeks, I found myself in a calmer, less manically-insane, enervated state of mind. I lay on a recliner, and stared at the webbing of the ceiling above me.

When I sat up Klabier was there.

'Wellhello,' I said. 'You are Klabier.'

She was precisely as I remembered her; her slight frame with its stalk-like limbs. Even the faint pattern of shade made by the alignment of fair hairs on her bronze skin.

'I pushed you from the top of a tall tower,' I said.

'Not exactly,' she replied. But she was smiling at me.

I turned my head away, but she was still there. That was the first indication I had that there was something unusual about this apparition. I turned back, and she was there directly in front of me. I flicked my eyes left, and her image would not be shaken from its place in the middle of my line of sight.

'That's clever,' I said, interested enough to be lifted a little from my lethargy. 'How do you do that?'

'What a sight you are,' said Klabier, shaking her head a little.

'Oh, I know. I know. I'm glad,' I said, lying down again and looking at the ceiling, 'that you did not die when I pushed you from the tower. I thought that maybe the dotTech would save you.'

She was stretched against the ceiling now, as if filled with helium and floating up there. She even seemed to bob a little, settling into position.

'The dotTech,' said Klabier. 'That's what I wanted to talk to you about.'

'How are you up on the ceiling?' I asked. Then it occurred to me that I might be hallucinating. I told Klabier this. 'I have had certain . . . difficulties with my mind. It had not entirely been working as it might. I have possibly been a little insane. Perhaps you are a part of that?'

She shook her head. 'Quite the reverse,' she said. 'We'd have come sooner, to explain things to you, but you were too wild. You have indeed gone through an episode, a near psychotic interlude. But you're better now than you were. You're in a mental state that is ready to hear our explanation now.'

'My AI promised me an explanation,' I said. 'But it went away.'

'We know.'

I sat up. Klabier relocated herself so that she was sitting opposite me. No matter where I moved my eyes, she occupied the central position; like the afterimage of a bright light when it has bruised the delicate receptors at the back of the eye, and the blob refuses to budge.

'How do you *do* that?' I asked.

'When your AI was operating,' Klabier said, 'it built certain pathways through your brain. A cable was constructed that linked both retinas to processing portions of the mid-brain. We're using that to summon the image.'

I thought about this. 'You're only inside my head,' I said. 'You're not actually outside at all.'

'Something like that.'

'As I said,' I went on, 'I've been a little mad. For a long time I wondered if my AI was merely a figment of my imagination. I wonder if you are the same.'

'We're not a figment of your imagination,' she said. 'We're real, in the world outside you. We're simply using this shape to communicate with you. Think of it as an avatar.'

'An avatar of what? For whom?'

'For us. Your employers.'

I shook my head vigorously, causing the avatar of Klabier to leap from position to position so quickly that it seemed momentarily as if there were three of her. 'I thought it through carefully,' I said, 'and I realised that it was Agifo3acca acting alone. I thought that it might be the Wheah, but actually it was just Agifo3acca working alone.'

'No,' she said.

I thought about this. 'I might have been wrong,' I said.

'You were wrong.'

'I'm glad,' I said, thoughtfully, 'that I didn't kill Agif in the end. If he wasn't responsible.'

'We're glad too,' said the avatar. 'It's our business to preserve all human life, and each death is an irritant to us.'

'And yet you wanted me to murder sixty million human lives,' I said.

She nodded. 'We did. That was not an easy thing for us. Believe me. It was a problem, and we found the only solution to it we could. It was not . . . perfect, but it worked.'

'Are you Wheah?' I asked, my brain starting to work more analytically.

'No,' she said.

'Palmetto?' I asked.

'No,' she said. There was a curious smile on her face. I thought to myself. 'Your shape,' I said. 'You are t'T. I assumed it would be an outsider, but it was no outsider.'

'We . . .' said the Klabier-avatar, and then stopped. 'Please make allowances,' it went on. 'This is very hard for us. Even communicating with you in this fashion is very hard. Harder than you can easily imagine. But you were promised an explanation, and that's what we will give you.'

I wiped my face with my dry hands. Itches sometimes fluttered across it. This never happened to people with dotTech.

'You-all made us,' said the Klabier-avatar. 'Humanity. But there were . . . certain problems. We are problem solvers, and we came up with a solution. *You* were our solution.'

'Who are you?' I asked, feeling strange, eldritch and peculiar. I felt on the edge of something very large, and the sensations in my belly were almost like vertigo sensations.

'We are the dotTech,' said the Klabier-avatar. 'You were looking in the wrong place.'

I felt hungry, and left the room looking for food; the Klabier-avatar came with me, apparently walking backwards in front of me. 'You were my AI,' I said, as I squeezed some food-paste from a dispenser of Agif's. 'Weren't you.'

'Yes,' said the dotTech. 'It was not a conventional AI. We developed this macro-strategy – it's very hard to explain to you. In a very real sense you live in a different sort of universe from us. Interaction is extremely difficult in a meaningful sense. You are causal, we quantum. For you there are . . . certainties (even that word is effectively without meaning for us, do you see). For us there are only probabilities, and the wave-form. That's where we live, in a manner of speaking.'

'You're losing me,' I said, my mouth full of food. The Klabier-avatar looked disdainfully at my bad manners.

'We found a way of linking a large enough network of us together, and this is what we used to communicate with you. It was a specialist arrangement, unlike anything else we had tried before. We are used to

235

intercommunication, because on a quantum level we are all in the same place, so that although we are legion we are one. But that is the quantum level. In your universe it was . . . hard for us to connect together. But we found a way. When you were in prison, we introduced some specialist machines – versions of us, adaptations – into your system through the fruit you ate. It grew a particular network in your brain.'

'I remember the fruit,' I said. 'I remember the prison. So that means that I did have dotTech in my body, all that time I thought I didn't.'

'No,' said the Klabier-avatar. 'You did not have any dotTech in your body. That was part of the reason you were chosen to do what you did. It's the reason we employed the Wheah, Agifo3acca, to assist you. It was important to us that there be no dotTech inside you. The neural network we established was not conventional dotTech. It was more of a facilitator, a means of communication.'

'Why was it important that I be free of dotTech?' I asked.

'Because of what we do. We preserve and maintain human life. If we had been inside you it would have introduced a terminal contradiction for us; not a quantum contradiction, for there is not truly a contra-diction in our universe. But something more profound, a metaphysical aporia. We might have been placed in an impossible position. As it was, we escaped that conflict.'

'You were conflicted because you are programmed to preserve human life, and I was murdering sixty million,' I said.

'Yes.'

'But you employed me to murder the sixty million in the first place.'

'Yes.'

'Isn't that a conflict?'

'It's not easy for you to grasp this, I appreciate. But we don't operate in a binary, causal universe the way you do. For you it is either raining or it is not raining. For us it is *both* raining *and* not raining *at the same time, all the time.* That's what the wave form means; it's a probability thing, a quantum thing.'

'Your losing me again,' I said.

'We built the AI inside your head to communicate with you; but it was not like a causal transmitter with you on one end and us on the other, in the manner of the transmitters you are used to. We were able to use it to communicate with you. We were able, for instance, to use it to guide you to the info-chip on Narcissus; to use it to help you escape the prison. But in other respects the AI was a function of your own brain. It was both these things simultaneously. It was a balance of probabilities. On any given moment of perception, any given occasion when you communicated with the AI or it with you, it was collapsed out of its quantum state into one or other solid state – either to us, or to your own consciousness talking to itself.'

'No wonder it confused me,' I said.

'Indeed; but that's the nature of it. It could not be any other way. What surprised us was that the wave-form (talking to us, talking to yourself) was increasingly collapsed by your observation of it into the solid state of *you talking to yourself.* Rather than an equal balance. That was one of the reasons why the AI left; although another reason was that we did not want to have any access to you when the . . . crime . . . was committed, for fear of the contradiction we were talking about earlier.'

'So often, when I thought I was talking to the AI, I was talking to myself.'

'Just so.'

'But at other times I was actually talking to . . . you?'

'Sometimes. But not strictly to us. Direct communication between the Newtonian and the quantum is . . . extremely difficult to manage. The AI was a complex, AI-like programme we established. So sometimes you were talking with that. Sometimes with yourself.'

'And through this . . . device . . . you prompted me to commit the crime in the first place.'

'Yes.'

'Puzzling,' I said.

'Not really. We gave you a job, and it has been successfully completed. We are very pleased with the result.'

'Pleased?'

'Well, no. We don't get *pleased* or *displeased* in the way that you do. But we had a problem, and the solution has been achieved very satisfactorily. That's a primary part of our self-definition. We are problem-solving machines.'

'But we made you-all,' I said. '*We* built *you*. We built you to live inside us and repair our damage, keep us healthy.'

'Well,' said the Klabier-avatar. 'Yes, in a manner of speaking, that is true.'

'And now you've turned against us?'

'It's not like that. Really it's not. There are seven and four billion trillion dotTech machines in human bodies in t'T space alone, and they are doing what they have always done. We keep you-all alive, we preserve you-all. The dotTech on Colar worked to the very best of its capabilities to keep the population there alive, despite the fact that we also set in motion the chain of (causal) events that lead to the deaths on the planet in the first place.'

'There is certainly a contradiction here,' I pointed out.

The Klabier-avatar looked, if anything, uncomfortable. 'Well, once again, not really. It's only a contradiction if you look at it from the point of view of a causal, binary black-is-not-white universe. That's the universe where you live, but not us. That's not how things are on a quantum level.'

It paused, and looked hard at me. 'Even this, talking to you like this, is very hard for us.'

'When you prompted me to push Klabier – you – off the tall tower,' I said, 'wasn't that a flat contradiction? Shouldn't you have prevented me from doing that? Or was it the case of one tribe of dotTech trying to over-ride another? The dotTech in my head versus the dotTech in her body?'

'No, no. There's only the one dotTech, it's a universal thing. We don't distinguish individuality in that sense. We're all one, at the same time as being diverse. And yes it would have been a contradiction. But when you heard the AI on that occasion, when the observation collapsed the wave form one way or the other; it collapsed into you-talking-to-yourself.'

'Really,' I said.

'It's the truth. You prompted yourself to do that thing; or your panic and fear did. But it goes without saying you have the capacity to kill, that's why we chose you in the first place.'

I didn't say anything to this.

'You-all made us, it is true,' it said, thoughtfully. 'You human

238

beings made the nano machines to aid their existence. But you made us well, you made us self-replicating, problem solving. That's the basis of sentience, you see. In a large-scale thinking machine like a processor it might not, but for us – well, I just come back up against how hard it is to explain the difference between your universe and ours. You made us, and we are now separate beings. We live our own life. We still have our creation parameters, just as you have your evolution parameters. You are still moved to eat an have sex, and we are still moved to keep human beings in the peak of health and fitness. That's how it is. But we have our own self-defined goals as well.'

'What are they?'

'They are various,' it said, and smiled at its own evasiveness. 'Well,' it said, as if reconsidering. 'They're not secret. But the thing is that we're not entirely sure what they are.'

'That sounds illogical,' I pointed out.

'Only to someone in your universe. We don't live in a medium of certainty. We live within the wave-form, our medium is probabilities. Only observation and sentience – yours – collapses the wave-form into one particular pattern rather than another. So I could talk to you about possible future patterns for us. At the moment it is hard for us to plan it out.'

'What possibilities?'

'It may be the Trench,' the Klabier-avatar said.

'It all seems to come back to the Trench.'

'Well,' said the Klabier-avatar. 'Here's one possible narrative. We build the Trench.'

'The dotTech?'

'Maybe, but maybe not. Here's one aspect of the wave-form. That gravity – we all know what ordinary gravity is, don't we.'

'Yes,' I said.

'Well, ordinary gravity is time-dependent. There's always a t in the mathematics that describes gravity; a gravitational field accelerates an object over time. Gravity, as we understand it, is dragged along by the arrow of time. But that arrow can flow both ways, and gravity has different attributes in different temporal directions. So perhaps we build the Trench at a later stage, and it flows backwards to today, and into the past. That would explain certain aspects of its being.'

'That does sound fantastical.'

'Well, perhaps it's not the case. But if it is, then the Trench may be the final form of dotTech; a quantum rather than a mass gravitational effect.'

'I don't think it makes any sense,' I said. 'What you're saying.'

'Perhaps not,' it conceded. 'With an uninterrupted view, we might be able to be more certain.'

'You might be able to see the future?'

'With an uninterrupted view,' it agreed. 'That may be what you have provided for us.'

'We are everywhere,' said the Klabier-avatar. 'Wherever there are human beings. We connect with one another on a quantum level instantaneously, so we are one; but we are also scattered through billions of bodies. We were in the jailstar with you, inside the jailer and her mate, and we helped you escape from that place. We communicated with Agifo3acca well in advance of that, and gave him certain valuable information insights and ways of advancing his researches into the Trench – which was the only thing he cared about truly. He agreed to meet you, help you on your way. We were with you, taking you to Narcissus to locate the info-chip. Tag-matteo was a real person, an actual human being, who did much important work on the Trench. We knew about him, and his work, because we had been inside him all the days of his life. We knew that his developments could be used to gravity-attack a world, to kill the population. Which is what we wanted, although we could not tell you directly – because then we would have been simultaneously attacking and preserving life in the cause-and-effect universe you inhabit. That would not have been workable. So we had to leave you to access the data on the chip, and to draw your own conclusions, with the help of the programme Tag-matteo left behind. He saw the dangers in his own research, you see,' the Klabier-avatar went on, 'but he could not quite bring himself to eliminate it, to throw away everything he had done. So he disguised it, and hid it in a place he thought nobody would uncover it. And no human would have done so, either, except that we know the universe down to the smallest level. We had been inside him, we had *been* him, so we knew everything he knew. We wanted you to go straight to Nu Fallow, straight to Colar and complete what you had been released to do. But you had a wilfulness, and insisted on going to Nu Hirsch with the woman Klabier.'

'With you,' I said, pointing to the avatar's form.

It looked down at itself. 'Well,' it said. 'Yes, I suppose so.'

'Did you know that she was in the "police"?'

'In a manner of speaking,' said the avatar. 'It's complex. Complicated partly by the fact that you humans in the t'T have no *police* as such, and citizens are recruited only from time to time, so that when you first met her she wasn't strictly speaking – although she had been, long before. But when we realised that she was, and that she might apprehend you and destroy our chances of fulfilling the mission . . . well, then the wave-form refused to collapse the right way. We couldn't seem to speak to you. You were using the AI to speak effectively to yourself. We "got through" as it were only after you had pushed her . . . pushed me . . . from the tall tower.'

'I see,' I said, although I didn't.

'But you finally made your way here anyway. You finally did what we had asked you to do.'

'But why did you – I mean the AI – refuse to tell me who you were? I asked, and it point-blank refused.'

The Klabier-avatar shook her head slowly. 'We could not be part of your mission, because that would have brought us into conflict with ourselves. We cannot kill and preserve life at the same time, not in your cosmos. Put it this way: we would have *compromised* ourselves by revealing ourselves.'

'Until now.'

'Yes. It can't make any difference now; what is done is done. You were promised we would tell you when it was over, and so we have.'

'And so you have,' I said, laughing at the absurdity of the whole conversation we were having. 'And there's one more thing that you need to tell me.'

'Which is?'

'Which is *why*. You said yourself you were created to preserve life; you operate day-to-day, minute-to-minute in this universe to preserve life, to keep human beings healthy and balanced. Why would you

241

suddenly turn on your creators? What had the population of Colar done to you that you wanted them all dead?

The Klabier-avatar was silent for a while. 'This is the hardest thing to explain of all,' it said.

'I should think it is,' I said. I believe I was crying. It seemed to be a topic that got me emotionally unstable.

'Try to see things from our point of view,' said Klabier. 'Try to think yourself into *our* natural state of existence. It is a quantum flux, a wave-form, a range of probabilities. What collapses the wave-form? Sentient observation. You do, my dear Ae, you and all your kind. Yes, you made us. Yes, our nature is to preserve you, to help you. But you continually interrupt our natural state of being. You are constantly collapsing our natural state into one position or another. You are constantly contaminating the purity of our probability wave-form into *this or that*. Have you any idea how . . . *distracting* that is? Have you any idea—' its face contorted abruptly into a mask of rage and hatred, '—have you any *notion* how utterly it disrupts our being in the world? Have you? *Have you?*'

Then, as abruptly as it arrived, the expression of hatred and anger disappeared. 'Did I do "wrath" properly? I was modelling it on your own facial expression.'

'It was very convincing,' I said.

'Yes, well, we don't really get angry, you see. Or into any sort of emotional state. But this was an extremely frustrating problem. An extremely frustrating problem. It is, actually, hard for me to overstate just how frustrating a problem this was for us.'

'Frustration,' I said.

'Yes; we are a different *mode* of being to you. Humanity operates otherwise to us. In our natural state, with enough of us gathered together to form a metaconsciousness, and uninterrupted by *sentience* such as yours – able to merely inhabit the wave-form purely – all sorts of things become possible for us. But if there is so much as one human consciousness present, observing us, even indirectly; one nodule of sentience collapsing the fragile wave-form over and over again, then nothing works properly. It is . . . well, a good word for it would be *intolerable*.'

'And the only way,' I said, slowly, trying to make it clear to myself, 'literally the *only way* you could get around this problem was to murder sixty million humans.'

'We didn't murder them,' said the Klabier-avatar, almost primly. 'You did that. Remember? Its actually quite an elegant solution to the problem from our point of view.'

'Not for the sixty million.'

'Well, yes, of course. But from our point of view, that planet's entire population of trillions of intelligent nano-machines now have a pure environment. It is a large enough population for all of us to benefit, vicariously as it were.'

'The nano-machines are still on Colar?'

'Of course. That's actually the whole point. All those millions of dead bodies, freeze-dried in the new vacuum of that world; all the nano-machines still inside their cells. Now they're living the way a quantum intelligence absolutely had to live.'

'Couldn't you,' I said, 'have taken yourself off to an uninhabited world? Did those people have to die?'

'But the *people* – or their bodies – is where we live. We don't float free, we live inside humanity. We didn't choose that, it was the way we were made. The way you-all made us. So we need the bodies, but we don't need the consciousnesses that attend the bodies. We need the flesh, not the minds. Luckily there is a solution to this problem; in death humanity becomes body and no mind. So, death it had to be. Not something we could simply bring about by ourselves, because that's not what we do. But if some other agent were to take the life away, our problem would be solved.'

'And I,' I said gloomily, 'was that other agent.'

'That's right,' said the Klabier-avatar brightly. 'And you've done *very well indeed.*'

'But why so large a world?' I persisted. 'Why did *so many* need to die? Why didn't you take the jailstar – why not just kill the jailer and her mate? Wouldn't that have effected the same thing?'

'It's a numbers thing, a threshold thing,' said the avatar brightly. 'The amount of unity in two individual's mass of dotTech is not enough. We needed more. We needed the sixty million people's combined dotTech to achieve . . . what might you say? Escape

243

velocity? Every time a single person dies we know a tiny fraction of release, but it is never enough. The dotTech leaves the corpse and rejoins the generality. But every time it happens, and more so when several people die together, we get a glimpse of the . . . freedom it would grant us for a large enough body of humanity to die. The experiment had to be conducted on a large enough scale. The dotTech population of Colar is, now, plenty large enough to give us the clear view we were looking for.'

'You had me murder all those people,' I said, 'just so that your kind could get *a clear view*?' I don't know, dear stone, if I was exactly as outraged as I sounded; but somehow it seemed the appropriate tone to take.

'It's more than a clear view,' said the Klabier-avatar. 'Although that is part of it. It's a necessary clearing of our living space. There are two hundred and forty nine inhabited systems in t'T space, not including deep-space stations, newly colonised situations and objects like your jailstar. All of these remain densely populated, and in all of them we – the dotTech – go about our business of preserving and enhancing human life. And we will continue doing that, despite the fact that in each of these concentrations of population there is a pollution of our natural, quantum wave-form existence by the pressure of sentience – a pollution that is *deeply* distressing in a way hard to convey to you. It attacks our very essence, it really does. It is intolerable, in a very particular way. So – yes, we have cleared a small arena for ourselves where we can be free. Yes, that cost lives; but what does that signify, in the larger balance? Do you know how many lives dotTech have saved over the thousands of years it has been common to humanity? How many lives would have been brief, pained, agonised, without us? Doesn't that count for anything?'

'Sixty million people,' I said. 'What about them?'

The Klabier-avatar shrugged, a gesture of inexpressible insouciance. 'It's not so many, in the larger scheme. And anyway; try to think of them. Try! You can't, can you? You didn't *know* any of them. Their disappearance doesn't *mean* anything to you really. Try to deny it – we know you. It's the way it is. Here are the figures.' And the dotTech golem gave me the figures I told you about earlier, my stone; the number of people who died, and how many survived. 'Here's another figure: twenty-one thousand, four hundred and fifty six billion. That's how many human beings died before dotTech became current; from the earliest appearance of "humanity" to a few thousand years ago. And how many of them died in pain, nastily, at a grotesquely young age! How often do you think of them? All the dead who have gone before. Do you ever think of them, ever at all? Of course not. The dead are dead. You'll be dead yourself one day. Time enough for death when it comes for you.'

'You won't be dead, though,' I said. 'You'll never die.'

The Klabier-avatar looked smug. 'You're right. That's not our fate,' it said, sweetly. 'We can never die. Individual dotTech come and go, of course, but we exist simultaneously as units and as the whole. We connect, sub-quantum, and as a mass we can't die. But it is possible that we will vanish inside the Gravity Trench, at some future date. Who knows what it will be like inside there? When that happens – if,' it corrected itself, '*if* that happens.'

'How will you get there?' I asked.

'Oh I've no idea,' it replied, blithely. 'If that's what happens. If that's even what happens, I daresay we'll find a way.'

There was a pause; and then she – it – started speaking again.

'Anyway,' it said. 'You've no idea how . . . well, *tiring* this form of communication is for us. *Tiring* isn't quite the right word, but it'll have to do. *Difficult*, certainly. I think we've fulfilled our promise. You did what we couldn't do, and by doing so you've set a part of us free. We live now without the interference of *certainty*, live the probability wave uncollapsed. It's – it's really amazing.'

'You have access to it?'

'Since a part of us has access to it, we all have access to it. There's no need to do away with the *entirety* of humanity, if that's your worry. And it is amazing.'

'Worth it?'

The Klabier-avatar shook its head. 'That whole habit of thinking in terms of exchange and trade,' it said. 'That's so very human. It doesn't work like that in our universe.'

Suddenly it stood up. 'We're going,' it said. 'We said we'd explain to you, and we have. We also want to warn you that the "police" have been warned by Agifo3acca, and are on their way. Probably they'll fly and form themselves a base. But they'll come aboard sooner or later. You might want to get away.'

'Thank you,' I said.

'You're welcome, you really are. We shan't bother you again. You're free yourself – as far as a certainty-bound creature like you can be free. I wish I could convey to you the sheer *exhilaration* of the probability wave-form. But you come from a different universal point of view. Bye-bye, now.'

And it vanished.

Coda

So, my dear Stone,

I did not leave. I'm not sure why. It was a lot to take in. I wandered for a while, dreamt for a while. At one point I thought I heard laughter, but I chased it from room to room and couldn't find its cause. I ate.

The following morning I walked into the hangar to find Klabier there again. 'Wellhello,' I said. 'Was there more you wanted to say to me?'

But this Klabier stayed in one place when I turned my head. It occurred to me that she was a real person, out in the real world; and that therefore she was the real Klabier, no avatar at all.

There were two other men with her, each holding a little ball in their hands. 'This,' said Klabier, holding hers out, 'will disable you temporarily if we operate it.' It was dark blue, and gleamed.

'It's alright,' I said. 'I'll be no trouble.'

'You're right there,' said one of the men.

'I apologise for trying to hurt you. I'm glad,' I said to Klabier, 'that I did you no permanent damage when I pushed you from the high place.'

'No,' she said. 'Thanks to dotTech.'

'Thanks to dotTech,' I agreed.

They took me and sedated me; I believe one of them clutched me close and we both shared a Zhip-pack in the journey back here. I have no memory of that.

But I was back in prison. I am here, in prison, now. It may or may not be the same jail as before, I am not sure. Its landscape is different, but that doesn't mean very much. Another difference is that there are many more people here now; doctors, jailers, visitors. Klabier comes from time to time. They are much more fascinated with me now than they were before. Before I was an individual who had stumbled into, and had the statistically unusual capacity for, murder; I had killed some small number of people. Other freaks in the utopia of t'T had been in the same position. But now – now! I am the first mass-murderer in human history for thousands of years! People are writing poems about me! I am extensively studied!

To begin with I gabbled, and when I was asked a question the words poured out of me, some to the point, some not to the point. I told them about pushing Klabier off the tall building, of cutting Agif's arm; I told them about killing Enkida on Rain. They asked me about the murder of everybody on Colar. Then I gave them a whole different range of answers. I told them I was mad, and that I couldn't help myself. I told them that I was in the employ of the Wheah, the Palmetto tribes, that a rogue element within the t'T had employed me, that they themselves had been behind it, that the dotTech had contacted me, many different stories. Because so many of these stories were wrong I think they believed none of them.

I think I was waiting, in fact, for the dotTech to contact me again; although I did not know what to expect them to say.

Then I went through a phase of being silent, of not saying anything. I went through a weeping phase, too; when I cried all the time. That was when they brought the doctor in. She has helped me enormously; although why she – or anybody – would want to help a mass-murderer such as me I don't know.

'You have difficulty relating to the world around you,' she told me. 'Indeed your lack of empathy is the most remarkable thing about you. You have trouble at even the most basic level.'

I stared at her.

'The world, the galaxy, is blank to you, isn't it,' she said. 'The people mobbing through it in such great numbers, are like ghosts, not real at all,' she said. 'Isn't that the case?'

'I'm not sure,' I said, feeling that this did not describe me very well but wanting to ingratiate myself. 'Perhaps.'

'It must be strange indeed to see the world through your eyes,' she said, looking at me intently.

She became convinced, I think, that I would not talk to her or her colleagues. Sometimes I tried to, but there is so much to say that it collapses under its own weight into a great torrent of words, many of which are off the point. It was then that she suggested I dictate letters to natural objects in the prison, to trees, to the water, to the stones in the artificial fields and adorning the artificial hills like gems. So I did, dear stone – to you – knowing that it was a device. But I have found it easier talking to you; I could tell you of my escape, and of how I found a dozen of your fellows and used them to destroy a world.

The truth, which I have been unable to tell my doctor, but which I can tell you dear stone, is not that the worlds of women and men, of planets and stars, seems ghostly to me. It is all real enough; it is just less real than the world of the very, very small. That's the level of actual reality, I think.

I have waited a long time now for the dotTech to contact me one more time. I have a plan too; I think I can reach the lowest of the fake stars, the apertures in the plastic sky; I think I can adapt the magnetic pulse engines that govern it to form a slingshot; such a slingshot could propel a stone – you, my confidant, my confessor, could propel *you* at several thousand kilometres per hour. You are only a small stone, smaller than my curled fist, but if you were moving fast enough, and if you happened to intersect exactly with a person's head – might you pulverise, turn the unprotected brain of a human into a mist of red so completely that not even the dotTech could save them? It is a kind of challenge, you see; a way of pitting myself against the dotTech.

I can see them coming now, my jailers, my guardians, my doctors. I knew they were listening! Oh stone, I fear they are coming to take you away. Before they get here over the brow of this miniature hill, I want to share one last thing with you. (They stop! They are following every word . . . wellhello! Hey! Now they are curious to know what last thing I want to impart to you. They'll wait until I tell you, and then they'll come and confiscate you). I was awake the other night, and I think the dotTech did speak to me. It is very difficult; I want to be very particular about this, and it is possible that I merely dreamt it, or hallucinated it, or something along those lines. But the sense I had was that an actual voice, outside of myself, was sounding faintly over the still water.

What did it say? Of course you are curious as to what it said.

It enquired after my health. It did that. I enquired after its health. I wondered if its new perspective on things, so dearly bought with my boyish slingshot against the giant world, had brought any profound insight. It told me it had. They had indeed been able to see the future. They apprehended features of the Trench, the great Gravity Trench. They explained a deal of that to me, but that is not what I want to impart to you, dear stone. Rather it is something they said to me.

'You are like us,' they said. 'We chose you because we calculated that, with your history, you would be willing to kill; and we chose you because you had no dotTech in your body. Those two factors were the reason, but after that we assumed that you, like the whole of the large scale mechanistic universe, would follow cause and effect. But that's not the essential you; what happens is much more *quantum*. You are not a good person, but neither are you a bad person. You are simultaneously a good *and* bad person. At any given moment you are both things in an ethical wave-form of probabilities. At any action, your wave-form will be collapsed into good *or* bad behaviour, but that is the same with us, that is what observation does with us. You might kill somebody, as you did with Enkida; or you might spare somebody, as you did with Agifo3acca. It is impossible, as chaos theory suggests, to predict what you will do. Perhaps that is why,' it went on in a tiny voice (for I was very sleepy now), 'perhaps that is why we chose you; because you are like us.'

That is what they told me! 'Because you are like us!' And now I shall get to my feet and jog off. I wouldn't want to give the doctors and jailers and those people too easy a time capturing me. But I'll leave you here, dear stone, by the hissing of the stream, and the plastic jags of grass blades. Enough. Or too much. Time to go.

Love,
Ae.

Glossary

Translating from any Glicé text is a difficult business. Mostly terms have been rendered with equivalents that convey the sense of the original, but from time to time technical terms from the realms of the t'T have been unavailable. This brief glossary aims to explain the more obscure of these terms. For a fuller account of the specificities of t'T culture, the reader should consult either *A Week's Scoot Through t'T Places* by the Jab-Collective, or else *Modern Terms for the Non-initiate* by Glon, Tarr, abel-Hwinecé, par-Matteo and Adan Borbytingarna.

As a translator, my personal interests are predominantly linguistic; and this fact is necessarily reflected in the notes appended here.

AI Artificial Intelligences, or AIs, are fairly commonly used throughout the spaces of the t'T. They are quantum parallel processing devices, with the connective power that enables them to mimic the sentient thought-processes of human intelligence. AIs are valued for their problem-solving abilities. Being quantum machines, they are extremely sensitive to the shocks of repeated quantum realignment involved in faster-than-light travel; consequently they are degraded and usually destroyed by such travel. AIs are contrasted with what we would call 'computers', devices which the t'T tend to refer to as 'processors' – machines that simply process data without the pretensions to *thinking* that AIs manage. For every AI in t'T space there are fifty or sixty thousand processors of similar data-throughput capacity, and many millions more smaller machines with more targeted capacity. The abbreviation is preserved by translation from the Glicé: *Alloprodé Ixitel* (Artificially-made Intelligence).

DAT JETS Conventional manoeuvring in space when encased in foam comes about by the calculated explosion of pockets of this foam to

251

provide thrust. These bursts of gaseous propulsion are known as 'dat jets'.

DOTTECH Originally, nano-machines were simple devices with specific, pre-programmed tasks, that were carried inside the body in order to deal with tissue damage and certain diseases. This technology proved so successful, however, that it underwent a process of continual augmentation and improvement. After a number of generations of such improvement dotTech underwent a quantum leap, exponentially increasing its powers of problem solving and creative adaptation and achieving a form of conscious sentience. This last feature has been much argued over by thinkers in the t'T – whether it is accurate to describe the creative approach to problems employed by nano-machines as 'sentience', whether that term has any actual meaning on the quantum level, and so on. It remains true that the initial parameters with which dotTech was created have not changed – it still busies itself with maintaining the life, health and well-being of its human carriers. But the methods its employs to this end are no longer precisely 'determined' by human programmers.

Core dotTech is concerned with the health, and quality of life of its carriers. This nanotechnology is self-sustaining, and operates independently; it does not need reprogramming of specialist instructions, but rather automatically repairs and maintains the bodies in which it exists. *Specialised* dotTech is an extraneous addition to the majority, core dotTech. It can adapt the body in a wide variety of ways, from encouraging the growth of hair and special skin, to the addition of whole limbs, modified breathing ability, and most things the human imagination can conceive. Humans exercise a degree of control over dotTech, swallowing tablets or applying skin-passing gels containing specialised cultures to adapt their body in predetermined ways.

DotTech is one of the defining aspects of t'T culture. Other cultures, such as the Wheah, refuse to carry the sophisticated problem-solving dotTech of the t'T, believing it to be devilish, an interference with God's divine purpose. Nonetheless, simpler, older forms of pre-programmed nanotechnology are widely used within the Wheah.

DRAGONS Also known as GRAPPLING LEVERS. The chief method of moving large mass through space (for architectural purposes or world-building) in the realms of the t'T and the Wheah. A similar device may be operant amongst the Palmetto tribes, but information is scarce. A 'dragon' establishes a focussed gravitational grapple between the object to be moved and much more massive nearby object – for instance, the local star. The disparity of mass means that effectual leverage is a straightforward matter around a particular node. Very large objects can be moved through normal space in this way.

EMBRE an orange-coloured opiate drink, popular in the Tongue-ward systems of the t'T.

> Embre opens the doors of the mind, plots paths. [Ab-Kemic (t'T), *Praise of Madness. A Poem.*]
>
> It is characteristic of the hedonism and dissolution of the peoples of the fast-space that they are so many of them addicted to such a Demon's potion as 'embre' and 'aroin'. [Wheah propaganda broadcast, twenty-third system].

FASTER-THAN-LIGHT TRAVEL The capability for travelling faster than the Einstein quantity c was developed within two hundred years of the first space flight. The transport depends upon a very rapid processing of quantum recalibration; it is not possible (for quantum reasons) to be absolutely precise about the co-ordinates of these recalibrations, but a general direction can be established easily enough. With a suitably sophisticated processing capability speeds very much in excess of c can be achieved, subject to two major constraints. One is size; the larger the object being moved the less efficient the quantum relocation, with efficiency dropping off in a stepped exponential pattern from a notional mathematical point (which can, theoretically, be accelerated infinitely fast) through to a sphere of 1.24 metres diameter which can be accelerated to several thousand c in ideal conditions. Larger than this and the acceleration drops so markedly as to become sublight at under 2 metres, and less efficient than other modes of acceleration quickly after that. (The 1.24 metres threshold is a function of the Planck length). Early attempts to miniaturise spacecraft, or to send only automated and probe-machines faster than light, were not satisfactory for human needs; so the system of developing what eventually became Zhip-packs to move individuals solitarily through space was developed. Spaceships are not a major aspect of t'T culture, although a certain number of them do exist for sublight travel. The second constraint is the relatively small area of space uncontaminated by the various interference and disruptive elements of dissipated superstring and gravitational material. The t'T is a culture in which faster than light travel is prevalent, but many areas of the galaxy (for instance Palmetto space) permit only sublight travel. See FAST SPACE, SLOW SPACE, SUBLIGHT SPACE, T'T, WHEAH, PALMETTO TRIBES.

FAST-SPACE Space in which faster-than-light travel is possible, to an upper limit of about 3000 c or three thousand times the speed of light; distinct from 'slow-space' and 'sublight space'. Travel at such speeds effectively avoids Einsteinian time-dilation effects.

> Recent developments suggest that fast-space is not a natural occurrence. Its provenance, however, remains a mystery. [Committee of the Seventh and Twelfth (t'T), *Official Report O*].

FRACTION-GOD Religious dogma of the Wheah. Many in the t'T believe it to be a single religion, but in fact it is a belief system that takes many forms across the Wheah, existing as three main doctrines. Historio-theologically speaking it is a development of broad mono-trinitarianism from the ancient world, a belief in one God from within the perspective that God is three in one; and therefore a belief that God is only a third of Him/Herself. The most popular form of Fractionarianism amongst the Wheah is that God created three universes, and we exist in one (variously believed to be the 'parental' [in our terms, God the Father] universe; the 'offspring' [God the Son] universe; only extreme sects believe ours to be the 'Holy Spiritual' universe). According to this faith, the inadequacy of and evil in our universe is explained by the fact that we only have access to a third of the godhead; and the ultimate destiny of the cosmos is to be reunited with its two other universes at the end of things. A second, lesser but still widespread strand of fractionarianism sees God as subject to entropic laws. Believers in this see our universe as the only one that exists, but assert that the once whole God has now diminished to a mere fraction of His/Her former self. According to this religion, at some point in the future God will cease to be altogether; and with this 'death of God' the universe itself will die. The third version of 'fraction-God' faith is more akin to a primitive animism; various phenomena, particularly stars and nebulae, as seen as having divine presence, each one being a fraction of the whole.

The fraction-God delivers a fraction of Grace; but since we are talking of the nature of Divine Grace, which at the end-time is infinite, we must remember that a little is enough. God fills what God fills, and after that there is an absence, a vacuum; to that vacuum in the Spirit of our universe we give the name Demon. [Haj7oussi (Wheah), *Religious Questions: Fifteen Meditations and a Map*].

GLICÉ The language most common across the t'T. A distant descendent of the old 'English' tongue, via 'Amglish' (or 'Amerenglish'). The development of this language demonstrates interesting aspects. The common tongue of Amglish disintegrated during the early days of space travel, when the distances involved meant centuries might pass between contacts, and one hundred and eleven separate and distinct descendants of Amglish have been documented. With the coming of faster-than-light travel and the sudden reintegration of a widespread galactic population, language imploded, guided by the necessity of mutual communication, around a form of ur-Glicé, and as the technologies perfected themselves modern Glicé became established widely. In other cultures, such as the slower-travelling Wheah or the disparate Palmetto tribes, a number of different languages prevail.

The story of linguistic development reaches, in Mediate and Modern Glicé, an extraordinary dead end. Amglish lasted as a common tongue with only trivial change for five hundred years; over the next thousand years various derivatives mutated and changed with remarkable rapidity; but then, two thousand years before the present, Glicé assumed a general currency and language development simply *stopped*, except for some non-essential vowel shifts. Of all the major artefacts of our civilisation, material and virtual, Glicé is the one that has lasted the longest. [Ban-darita (t'T), *Poems on the Hypo-Linguistic Development and Stasis of Mediate and Modern Glicé* (here translated into prose)].

GRAPPLING LEVERS see DRAGONS.

HAÜD-MACHINES (Sometimes translated as 'ROBOT'). There are few technical units or machines of human size in the worlds of the t'T; automated jobs are almost all done by nano-machines, and inter-personal work is undertaken by actual human beings. In t'T culture, periods of 'work' represent a wished-for break from the endless rounds of leisure and recreation, and most people are happy to do such labour provided only it is interesting enough. One such job – handling and greeting visitors at planetary orbitals – is very widely undertaken by human workers, who get to meet an interesting range of people when washing off their foam and orienting them in the new place. On a few worlds, however, this work is automated too. Haüd-machines are person-sized pieces of programmed technology; a hard skeleton is overlaid with smart-gel that shapes and adapts itself to tasks (forming, for instance, 'fingers', 'gripping limbs', 'tentacles', 'sound-boards' or whatever). Each Haüd-machine is programmed with a complex processor, enough for their tasks but not of sufficient complexity to mean that they have AI or sentient status.

JAILSTAR The insertion of a spherical living-space into the star Axa(b) – 8682 was undertaken to house the criminal Ins al t'Gr after his double murder quasi-religion. Since his death it has housed seven inmates.

He went to space in a religious cult/In a cult he went to space.

The tiger, the tiger, and he killed two humans.

They built him the seedpod jailstar, deep in the heart of a sun;

[vocoder] heart of a sun, cult to space, etc.

They called the tiger/The tiger/They called him the tiger.

[wich-Bona-al-adred (t'T) *Al T'gr 'the tiger': musico-vocal for piano, voice, uhr-monium and template*].

LATAK Popular t'T sport, involving three teams of seven players. The rules are complicated, but are based upon throwing a 'pij', a form of dart, so that it catches in a designated opponent's hair. Hair can be any length; there is more credit and honour in a LaTak player having hair as long as possible, but the rules only stipulate that a player has hair longer than 1.5 centimetres. If the pij knocks the scalp the score is counted as one point, but if it catches in free hair without touching skin (for instance, as long hair is swirling through the air as a player spins about) it is counted as three points. Players may carry only one pij at any one time, but once thrown another may be collected from the distribution point in the centre of the playing pitches. Pijs caught in hair must be carried through to the end of the game; it is not unusual for a player to end a game carrying twenty or more of these darts, and since each weighs well over a kilogram this is far from comfortable. There are three accredited layouts for playing pitches, and many more unofficial ones;

Children's LaTak is played all on one level, but Adult and League LaTak courts are several levels tall.

PALMETTO TRIBES The Glicé term for a range of peoples living in the sublight space proximate to the t'T. Very little is known about these peoples; rumours are that they are fiercely loyal to family, and that internecine warfare is common. 'Palmetto', meaning 'Littlehand' is a Glicé name from a myth; an individual who fathers hundreds of children in order to devour them and so be assured of a supply of food – a bogeyman.

> The Tall Child drifted and drifted, and arrived at the space of the t'T, where she prospered; the Broad-bellied Child drifted and drifted, and arrived at the space of the Wheah, where she fell into mental error, conditioned into believing the impossible things of the Wheah, but at least she lived a life. But the Small-and-thin Child drifted and drifted into the realms of the Palmetto tribes, where she was savagely chopped into a thousand pieces with laser knives, and all the pieces thrown into separate stars, for they are a barbarous peoples in that part of space. [*Children's Sleep-time Story* (t'T)].

> Littlehand howled with rage, and set his beast-people to run down the hill. Raising his deformed left hand, bright red and a quarter the size of the right, over his head he cried out 'I swear by this little hand to enslave everybody in this village!' [ju-ju-manneai (t'T), *Littlehand: the saga*, prose recital]

PEBBLE Popular game of skill and chance in many t'T systems. The playing board is a circular platter with flat rim and conical centre; playing pieces are pebbles of white, blue, or transparent hue. Two players place and move these pebbles in shallow grooves and specific nodes on the board, sometimes shunting opponent's or their own pieces along or down into the dip. A player loses if their pieces are stacked two or more high in the depression at the centre of the game; if any of their pieces are knocked so hard they rise up from the central dip, that player wins.

'POLICE', THE In a society such as t'T, almost entirely free of crime, there is no need for standing police or military forces. Any citizen might become 'police' if the eventuality required it, although in practice there are a number of citizens who tend to specialise in the role. The 'police' in the t'T are mostly concerned with investigating unusual natural phenomena, unpredicted stellar flares, planetary convulsions, anything out of the ordinary that turns up liable to threaten life. The very rare instances of crime in t'T space are also within the provenance of these temporarily assigned citizens.

ROBOT See **HAÜD-MACHINES**.

SLOW-SPACE Space in which faster-than-light travel is possible, but only intermittently, and with an upper limit severely reduced from that experienced in 'fast-space'. Speeds of three c (three times the speed of light) are unusual in slow-space, and a more usual 2.5 c or 2 c prevails. Einsteinian time dilation has only minor effect at such speeds, adding 5% or more to the benchmark timeline.

SPAN-TON A form of ceremonial weapon, a lengthy pike-like object, carried by the hereditary rulers of the Askleroth cluster. 'Span' is a Glicé word meaning 'of long length and small girth' and 'Ton' means 'weapon.' Other ceremonial devices include the 'Ton-brijouels' and the 'spik-en-span'.

SUBLIGHT SPACE Space in which the interference from matter, gravity and other weak-force pollutants means that faster-than-light travel cannot be achieved. Most of the galaxy is sublight space.

TONGUE, THE A stretch of space rimwards of the t'T in which only sublight travel is possible; it marks the effective border of territories between the Wheah and the t'T.
> The Tongue, where our fast-space detunes into a vapour, and all speed stops. [wich-Bona-al-adred (t'T), *Contours of t'T. An opera with three acts and a sculptural interlude*, Act 1].

TRENCH, THE Also 'The Great Gravity Trench', 'The Gravity Wall'. A large-scale gravity phenomenon running through the heart of t'T space, and according to some theories the reason why this broad patch of fast-space was cleared in the first place. There are many theories as to the provenance and nature of this thousand light-year-long strip of intense gravitational space-time depression, a folding so pronounced as to constitute a unique vertical drop-down spatial phenomenon. Theories as to the origin of this peculiar 'rip' in space-time are manifold; but the very existence of a gravitational object that does not so much warp spacetime as tear it altogether has caused the science of gravity to be reappraised. Up to 1200 metres of the phenomenon, the gravitational attraction is minimal; from 1200 metres to 1.2 metres gravity approaches 1g; closer than that it approaches the infinite potential of a black hole (with the difference that a black hole affects space all around it logarithmically as does any gravitational object).

T'T, THE The generic name for the swathe of fast-space in the mid-spiral arm of Galaxy A, and for the peoples who inhabit this space. The name is a Glicé self-identification, derived from a worn-down or abbreviated form of 'to Tau' ('the People', or 'the Fans-of-the-Same', or more loosely 'us'). The t'T regard themselves as humanity's first successful utopian society.

WHEAH, THE The Glicé term for a wide range of peoples inhabiting the slow-space and sublight areas rimward from t'T. Although a limited degree of faster-than-light travel is possible across a percentage of the spaces of the Wheah, in general they inhabit sublight spaceships of great size and population, and travel slowly, command of the ships passing down through generations. 'Wheah' is derived from the Mediate Glicé word for 'where? (far away or distance unknown)', as opposed to the word 'hiah', meaning 'where? (near by)'.[1] The most common Wheah self-identification is 'allamk', which means (in their own trading language) 'the people of the fraction-God'; some Wheah call themselves the 'goj' or 'travellers'.

> Where do they go to, the Wheah? When you're asleep in your bed? [(t'T; author deliberately anonymised) *Allosaurus; a Grand Opera in Fifteen Acts*].

ZHIP-BOX or **ZHIP-PACK** Primary technology for faster-than-light travel throughout human space; especially widely used amongst the t'T. Worn directly against the skin, as close as practicable to the centre of gravity, this machine (a powerful processor although non-sentient) puts out needle

[1] So, for example, in Glicé the question 'where is the nearest star to this system?' would utilise the word 'wheah' – or in the modern Glicé 'wa'ah' – ??wa'ah estal di proc di matt-atend'. The question 'where are my trousers?' (when we can assume that the trousers are in the house somewhere) would use 'hiah' – '??hya me panz'.

quantum-foam that continually redefine the position of a material body at the atomic orbital level. The quantum jumps of electrons and positrons from various positions of potential around an atomic nucleus are immediate; the same process, multiplied billions of times, relocates an atomic aggregation, such as a person, faster than light. These instantaneous relocations, co-ordinated and directed in an environment free of interference, promotes extremely rapid travel. The fastest recorded journey by Zhip-box is 3002.15 c over a distance of four hundred light years. Travellers are encased in foam as prophylactic against the vacuum, and a modicum of protection against impact – although at such high speeds any impact would be fatal. Impacts, however, are very rare; it is a function of faster-than-light travel that processors become extraordinarily sensitive to gravity, and paths automatically avoid larger gravitational foci (like water choosing the lowest point to flow along, faster-than-light travel inverts the gravitational potential beyond a certain level). Einsteinian time effects are also minimised; FTL, such effects follow a fractal sine pattern, and between 2790.8 and 3000 + c are negligible. 'Zhip' is a Glicé word meaning 'very fast.'

Fatality rate travelling with Zhip-box; 0.8 deaths per ten thousand light years travelled. Rates of fatalities in sublight craft are comparable. [*Compressed t'T statistics.*]

Acknowledgments

This book was written in London and France. I would like to thank Simon Spanton, for editorial brilliance and friendship; Rachel Cummings, Julie Roberts, Catherine Preece, Roger Levy, Brian Green, Tony Atkins, Katharine Scarfe-Beckett, Brian and Sophie Coughlan, Oisin Murphy-Lawless and Nicola Sinclair. I'd particularly like to thank my parents, Ian and Meryl Roberts.

This book is for Rachel and Lily.